# The English Problem

# The English Problem

*A Novel*

# Beena Kamlani

CROWN
NEW YORK

Published in the United States by Crown, an imprint of the Crown Publishing Group, a division of Penguin Random House LLC, New York.
crownpublishing.com

Library of Congress Cataloging-in-Publication Data
Names: Kamlani, Beena, author. Title: The English problem : a novel / Beena Kamlani. Description: First edition. | New York, NY : Crown, 2025. | Identifiers: LCCN 2023058154 | ISBN 9780593798461 (hardcover ; acid-free paper) | ISBN 9780593798478 (ebook) Subjects: LCGFT: Novels.
Classification: LCC PS3611.A4677 E54 2025 | DDC 813/.6—dc23/eng/20240415
LC record available at https://lccn.loc.gov/2023058154

Hardcover ISBN 978-0-593-79846-1
Ebook ISBN 978-0-593-79847-8

Printed in the United States of America on acid-free paper

Editor: Amy Einhorn
Editorial assistant: Lori Kusatzky
Production editor: Patricia Shaw
Text designer: Andrea Lau
Production manager: Heather Williamson
Managing editor: Chris Tanigawa
Copy editor: Trent Duffy
Proofreaders: Robin Slutzky, JoAnna Kremer, and Rob Sternitzky
Publicist: Gwyneth Stansfield
Marketer: Chantelle Walker

9  8  7  6  5  4  3  2  1

First Edition

*For Atma S. Kamlani, who inspired this story*

*For Yaddo, with deepest thanks*

∽

*In memory of Saul Bellow, and all the fabulous laughs*

How can I live without thee, how forgo
Thy sweet converse and Love so clearly join'd
To live again in these wild woods forlorn?
[. . .] Flesh of flesh,
Bone of my bone thou art, and from thy state
Mine never shall be parted, bliss or woe.

—Milton, *Paradise Lost*

Memory is a river that leaves traces of its history on its banks. At low tide, it invites you in and tells you its story. Embedded in its moist surfaces of clay and mud are a multitude of objects—trinkets and bits of armour, shards of pottery, and glimmering gold. Truth and reality are two different things. Truth depends on reason and calls forth the battlers of the mind—objectivity and logic—for discernment. But reality needs only the ring of truth, not veracity. It needs shards, glimmers. It needs the firebird's feather. Realness has but one judge—the listener's heart.

# Prologue

## London, January 1931

It was raining, English rain, that first night when he came to England. Thin, fine icicles that fell at a slant and made incisions. Standing outside Victoria Station, waiting for a cab, he felt its needle pricks pierce his skin like markings. This is how England claimed you—through its rain. His hands and face burned and tingled. He felt alive, his senses acutely picking up every impression, from the stone in his shoe to the gaslights rippling through puddles, their slight hiss. Exhausted yet exhilarated at having finally arrived at his destination, he noted how unsuitable for this alien cold and damp his thin tropical trousers and shoes were. The rain had already seeped through them, and the woolen coat he was wearing, which would have weathered a cool wave in the hill stations of India, was as useless as a rag here. Ah, how it reached for his bones, the chill damp. A low, whistling wind funneled through his clothes and up his neck; warmed by body heat, it seeped out of him like smoke coming out of the chimneys of London's homes. He scanned the traffic on Victoria Street for a cab. When one drew up, the cabbie rolled down his window and said, "If it's East London you're wanting to get to, I can't take you."

"No," he replied, his teeth chattering, his lips swollen with cold. "It's 24 Gloucester Square."

"Hop in, then."

Shiv lugged his suitcases into the cab and sank back into the seat. Fatigue held him now in a vise. From Karachi to Bombay, a two-day train journey; from Bombay to Marseille by ship—seventeen days that covered nearly seven thousand miles on the SS *Rajputana*. Then waiting to board the ferry at Marseille for Dover, and finally, the train from Dover to London. He sighed, drawing cold air into his lungs. Everything he touched was freezing. He hugged himself for warmth. The dampness of his clothes and the lack of heat in the cab made him certain he would catch some terrible disease.

"Raining nonstop since last night. Hardly anyone out this evening. Reckon they've all taken the tram or the underground home." Chatty and jocular, occasionally whistling during silent pauses, the driver was beginning to get on Shiv's nerves. He finally screeched to a halt outside a house on a quiet street. "Here you go, mate," he said, doffing his cap and smiling broadly at Shiv when he received an overly generous tip. The cab suddenly seemed like a place of warmth to Shiv, though his teeth had been chattering from the cold all the way and his nerves were at knife-edge. Even before the tip, the cabbie seemed not to know that Shiv was one of the colonized, the people his people lorded it over every day back home in India. Shiv had been treated with deference and courtesy in a normal world where everyone who got into his cab was an equal. "Cheerio, sir," the man said as he left the cab.

Standing outside the door of the house, with his suitcases on either side of him, Shiv felt his heart beating. He felt fear and impatience both. As he had walked out of his father's home with the family to board the ship for England, sobs threatened to break his cool exterior, a façade both he and his family needed so they could do the unthinkable—bid goodbye to one another. Now that he was here, the other side of parting—desolation and uncontrollable anxiety—bared its teeth. Had he felt this back home, he wouldn't have come, he told himself. He badly needed a pee and thought about his hosts, an English family who had offered to take him into their home, with growing nervousness. His father had met Mr. Polak on a trip to South Africa to see Mr. Mohandas K. Gandhi, who was then living in Johannesburg. The two men had become close friends, and when Mr. Polak visited them in Karachi, years later, Shiv had been a nine-year-old boy. "I want to be a lawyer like you so I can save the world," he told a bemused Mr. Polak. His moment had come. He stood outside the Polaks' door shivering uncontrollably. His teeth chattered. More than likely, his host wouldn't recognize him.

There was no going back now.

As his finger went to the doorbell, the door opened. A young couple, arm in arm, stopped at the door and looked him over, their smiles fading. "Yes, can we help you?" the woman asked in a formal tone of voice.

"I'm looking for Mr. Polak. I'm Shiv Advani and I believe he's expecting me?" He hadn't meant it to sound like a question. His voice sounded weak, unsure.

The young man by the woman's side gave her a quizzical look. She frowned at Shiv. But then, just as quickly, recognition seemed to run through her. "Oh my goodness," she said, clutching her companion's arm. "Of course, it's the Indian who will be staying with them while he's at the Inns of Court." She turned to him. "They were talking about you earlier. You're a day early," she said. Shiv stood in the doorway, his mind calculating the distance he had come, to be told he was too early. "I'm sorry," he said, deeply uncomfortable. "I'm sure the telegram . . ." She glanced at his luggage, noting, no doubt, the wet edges of his thin trousers, the skimpy orange silk scarf around his neck. "You'd better come in," she said. "No use standing there, getting wetter than you already are."

"Here, let me give you a hand," the young man said, reaching for the larger of the two suitcases. Shiv picked up the smaller one and followed him into the house. From inside came the sounds of laughter, and music. "It's their anniversary, Mr. and Mrs. Polak's," the young man explained. "Their twenty-fifth, and everyone's celebrating. There's lots of food, and champagne. It's very jolly." The woman by his side held out her hand. "Violet," she said. "I'm Millie Polak's niece." He wasn't sure what he was supposed to do with his hand—put it out to shake her proffered one or just nod. He nodded. She stared at him, perplexed. Finding his voice, Shiv said, "I'm sorry I arrived early."

"Early?" The man laughed. "You've only come from the other end of the world to us. Joseph Rowland, Joe to everyone." He held out his hand. On firmer ground with a man's hand, Shiv took it and released it almost immediately, aware of the English aversion to touch. "Less than a second," a friend back home had told him. "Touch it, then let it go." But Joe's grip was firm, friendly.

Shiv focused on him, his easy, smiling ways, his affluent charm. He sensed how much separated them—his dark skin, an almond brown, seemed to have turned several shades darker just standing there, and his clothes, wet and puckered around his ankles, would mark him for life in this man's eyes. He had picked an orange scarf to wear around his neck. "You'll need colour there," his mother said. "It is a cold, dark, rainy country." Now the bright orange scarf felt like a glossy python around his neck. He couldn't wait to throw it off.

Joe gave him a quick, curious glance. His discomfort grew. A wet, bedraggled brown man walking into a celebratory party—so far from the first impression he wanted to make. He threw a quick look at the hallway mirror as he entered and saw, to his dismay, a wary, uneasy face. He seemed as he felt, defenceless and vulnerable.

Joe left the suitcase by the stairs. "There's the lav, if you need it," he said, pointing to a door by the stairs.

Shiv nodded and went towards it with relief.

———

THE HEAT FROM the blazing fire in the grate hit his face, drying and warming him at the same time. He saw flushed red faces, glasses filled with wine, trays of cheese and smoked salmon, brown bread and butter. He recalled the pictures his English tutor back in Hyderabad Sind had showed him in anticipation of a time when he would leave India for England. "Beer." "Wine." "Smoked salmon." "Mince pies." "Spotted dick." Now here they were, those trays of smoked salmon and deviled eggs, wine and beer. The women were in pearls, the men in suits, and everyone was very jolly. Mr. and Mrs. Polak received him warmly, she with an embrace, he with a hearty handshake. "You're here, my boy," he said. "Just in time. We're celebrating our twenty-fifth, Millie and I and our friends. Feast today, we go back to gruel tomorrow!" Everyone laughed as they turned to look at him. Mr. Polak handed him a fluted glass and poured a hissing liquid into it. *Champagne?* Shiv wondered. "Cheers! Welcome to London!" Mr. Polak said.

Shiv squirmed as his guests examined his thin wet trousers, the bright silk scarf wrapped around his neck, marked his uneasiness. One elderly woman fixed her lorgnettes on him as she ran them up his body from head to toe. Her jowly face and bejeweled fingers glinted; her inquisitive eyes were like lice combs as they teased out his discomfort. He felt like an animal in a zoo.

"I've never seen one of them in the flesh before, Henry," she said, turning to her host.

"He won't be a stranger to you for long, Lady Sophia," Mr. Polak said. "You'll be seeing a lot of him, I promise you that!"

He came over to Shiv with the bottle of champagne in his hand. Shiv placed his hand over the glass. "I'd better not, sir. Still feeling a little sea-whipped from the journey here." He observed Mr. Polak's large, slightly red ears, like abalone shells. With ears like that, you'd miss nothing in a court of law.

"Nonsense!" Mr. Polak said. "You'll be the British in India when we leave." He refilled the glass. "You're here to learn, to work and think like us. Some would say that there's an even more important requirement—that you play and drink like us." When Shiv raised his glass to his host, Polak's genial face broke into a proud smile. "Good stock, this one," he said, turning to Lady Sophia.

Shiv watched Joe with a group of young men who resembled him, men whose strong, confident jodhpur-clad thighs pressed into the flanks of horses as they played polo back in India. Shiv considered Joe's smoothness, an assured quality that came from a natural assumption of one's place in the world. What was it called, that? He recalled the prized falcons of Hyderabad Sind and the balletic precision with which they landed on their prey from on high. To be so highly trained that your responses were ingrained, bred in the bone, was to assume a privileged place in the world. He had not been trained to hunt, to discern weakness in others, to conquer. He felt incapacitated. His thin frame felt weak and puny to him. He didn't have it, what these men had.

But with a glass of champagne in one hand, which he had disliked at first sip, and a smoked salmon canapé in the other, he laughed at everything they said, and tried to suppress the intense loneliness that gripped him as he looked around the room. These were his country's oppressors and here he was, one of the chosen, sent to live among them, become like them. His father's parting words came to him now, the bewildered look on his face, as if he was reconsidering his decision to pack his son off to the land of their oppressors: "It's too late to wonder if this is the right thing. There's no avoiding it. You will come back an Englishman, for that is the only way to succeed in their world."

A wave of sound rose and fell around Shiv. He heard the polite laughs and ironical accents of the men and women around him now—the women, their jewelry tinkling as they reached for their glasses, a little tipsy and gay; the men, so well trained in social mores that even when their voices, emboldened by drink, grew louder, their laughs broader, they were still, always, within timbre, within the wave. Nothing cracked the air around them—a smooth social atmosphere hid all tensions, blanketed all desires.

He glanced around as the crowd became merrier. They soon lost interest, the novelty of a brown-skinned man who had landed so un-expectedly among them beginning to wear off. As the observer now rather than the observed, he viewed them as members of a tribe at war with his own, and himself as an interloper in their midst. The steamy damp from the cuffs of his trousers travelled up his legs like a tropical breeze. Never, he told himself, as he took in the flushed faces of the guests and heard their champagne-fuelled laughter. I will never become an Englishman.

# Glasgow, 1941

On 31 May, 1941, *The Empress of Scotland* slips out of Glasgow harbour like the moon out of a cloud. Its gleaming hull cuts through midnight black waters as it sails up the Clyde estuary heading towards the Firth of Clyde. A young woman, just turned twenty-three, pins her eyes on the scene by the quay even as it slides out of sight. Though it was a foggy night, the top of the tower of St. Mungo's Cathedral could be seen, and once she's placed it, she knows exactly where her mother would be—there by the docks, still peering at the vanishing ship. She imagines her standing there, elderly before her time, a bent figure in her old tweed skirt and faded mackintosh, worn green wellies, grey hair sticking out from a scarf tied tightly around her head, and recalls her parting shot. "You take that ship right back, Mairi, my girl. India's no place for a young Scottish lass. Yer home's Glasgow, and don't yer ever forget it."

She takes a long, lingering look at the shoreline. The ship would sail past the Mull of Kintyre, then begin its long voyage through the Atlantic Ocean and across five seas—the Norwegian Sea, the North Atlantic Ocean, the South Atlantic Ocean, the Indian Ocean, the Arabian Sea. Her head spins just thinking of it. Water would be her element for the next two months. She follows the crew members indoors.

Mairi watches them wheel the gurney down a long, carpeted hallway. One of them stops by a door, turns the key in the lock. He opens it and stands back, "This is the room, miss." She examines it critically. Larger than her room at home, it has a bed against one wall; a desk and a chair; an armchair; a floor lamp for reading. The lamp has a red-fringed shade with glass beads hanging off the fringes, a decadent touch in an otherwise plain room. She turns the handle on the bathroom door. A tub, a sink, a toilet. Functional, spare, and adequate.

"We were told there would be a nurse tending to the patient. We removed the second bed so there would be more space for you to move around," he says. She nods, turns to look at her patient. He is unaware, still in a coma. Eyes closed, face impassive, body still and swathed in sheets, he looks incongruous—a young man who has seen the face of death and is still in shock from the encounter. The anxious pucker around his lips has gone. Maybe he's sensed that he's away from danger now, he's in safe hands. She reaches for his pulse. It beats as steadily as a metronome.

The other crew member says, "You all right, sir?"

"Sure, you go on upstairs."

"I hope my room is close. I will need to be with him all day," Mairi says.

"Yes, miss, this one's yours." He slides an interconnecting door open. A smaller version of the patient's room, just as adequate and functional. He shuts it. She watches his hands as they move back and forth, strong, muscular hands, hands she could use, if the need arose.

As if reading her thoughts, he holds out his hand. "I'm Will Sinclair, miss. Head purser. At your service." She takes it. "Thanks, I'm Mairi McNulty." He looks at the sleeping man on the gurney. His eyes take in the purple-black bruises covering the entire right side of his face. "What happened to him?"

"He was at a workers' meeting in Glasgow, giving a speech on British rule in India. He was shot, and fell. Fractured his skull and broke his leg. He's been in a coma." She looks at the stretcher. "Shouldn't be travelling in this condition but his father wants him back in India as soon as possible."

"Shot?" Will says. "By whom?"

"No one knows."

He gives the patient another look. "Poor bloke. Best to get him home quickly, ain't it? India, eh? Almost all the way to the end of the line then. Karachi's just before Bombay, our last stop."

"Yes, that's right."

He whistles softly. "It's long—especially the way we have to go now. U-boats and Krauts everywhere. The route used to be via Ireland, but they're neutral. The Krauts hide their ships there. Now we go up to Greenland, then down through the Atlantic to the Cape of Good Hope, past Mozambique and Madagascar, then across the Indian Ocean and the Arabian Sea to Bombay. Twice as long, but safer."

"And we'll get there when?"

"About seven weeks. May go faster, depending on headwinds." It oppresses her just to think of it.

"Goes by quickly, miss. Don't worry. Lots of entertaining characters on board. British soldiers who sing and play their harmonicas, Hindu strolling players, Arabs . . . and there's children who don't really know it's wartime so they play, like kids do, everywhere. You won't be bored." Then, looking at the gurney, "Do you want to move him, then?"

"Let's do it together," she says, putting her hands under the patient's feet. Carefully, delicately, the purser places his hands under the patient's shoulder blades and shifts the top part of his body sideways onto the bed; she lifts his legs and in one swift move, slides them to the bed. Will tucks the sheets tightly around the patient's body. "There! He's securely in now for the night."

"Are there any regulations we should know about?"

"A few. Lifeboat drills every day—when the klaxons start blaring, drop everything and follow the rest of the passengers."

She looks at the sleeping man. "He won't make it."

"Leave him here. I'll come down and help if there's a real problem."

"I'll be exercising him on the deck when he's strong enough. He's got to use his muscles."

"Aye, the sea air'll do him good. And there's one other thing—please leave those portholes blacked out. Can't even smoke up there on the deck. We travel in darkness."

"I'll be careful."

"Get a good night's sleep, miss." He rolls the gurney to the door.

"You from Glasgow, Mr. Sinclair?"

"That I am, miss. Born and bred."

Like me, she thinks, but doesn't say it out loud.

"Well, good night."

"Good night. Thanks." He shuts the door quietly behind him and the soft click makes her turn to the prostrate body on the bed. "It's you and me now," she says aloud. "I'm counting on yer."

She shivers, feeling the sudden slight chill in the cabin. "No lights soon," she says to herself, a reminder to unpack as quickly as possible. Forty-five minutes after departure, the lights will be turned off completely. She unzips her patient's bag, starts hanging up his clothes in the closet. Shirts, trousers, two pairs of shoes, a pair of sandals, socks, underwear, pajamas. Everything feels cared for, well worn to softness. The colours are muted, the bright yellows and reds of his homeland caught in skeins of wool in a scarf, or in a pair of woolen socks. There are two small oval silver frames. She picks them up, stares intently at the photos. Mother and father, she assumes, a petite, determined-looking woman in a sari, its drape covering her head; she has a heart-shaped face, full lips, and beautiful eyes, Mairi notes, the way they catch the light even in the dulled photograph; the father in a suit and waistcoat, his polished shoes shining out of the dull glass frame. The other photo is of a young woman in a tennis skirt and shirt, soft curls framing her face, holding up a tennis racket with a winning smile. *A white girl, girlfriend, maybe. A beauty, a tennis player—but a star, more like.* She puts the photos in a drawer; they'll come in handy later, to test his memory.

There are three books at the bottom of the case, along with a piece of fabric folded into a tight knot. It's flowery and silky. She takes it out and unties the knot. The garment cascades out of its folds, releasing a scent of faded lilacs, perhaps, she thinks, sniffing it. It is a kimono, black and painted all over with gay yellow, blue, and red butterflies. It is a vision of joy, and she shakes it this way and that. The butterflies flit about her as she swishes the fabric around. *His?*

She gives him a quick glance. Is it her imagination or is his mouth slightly open now? She takes his pulse again, checks his breathing. Everything is normal. She returns to the books. One is *A Passage to India*, which she remembers nearly buying in a jumble sale at St. Mary's Cathedral last year, until a pair of used wellies in good nick got her spare coppers. She flicks it open and sees an inscription on the title page.

> To Shiv, a great friend, a passionate orator, and a Londoner of the first order: The fugitive years do hasten by, dear friend, and it falls on the torchbearer to tell his tale. We await your story. —Morgan

*"Passionate orator."* She puts the book down. Her first glimpse of the man who was now her patient had been at a workers' rally three weeks earlier. Jamie Doncaster, a friend she sometimes met up with for a pint after church, had insisted she come. "There's an Indian bloke speaking at the library. About oppression in his country. Reckon it can't hurt to hear another side of the story, can it? We Scots have ours, too. And we like to tell it whenever we can." That's what decided it. She hadn't met an Indian personally before but you saw them down by the docks, the dark-skinned Lascars with their sunken cheeks and dull eyes, huddling together, shivering under blankets,

waiting for passage back to India. "First-class sailing guides, they are," a captain whose small ship did crossings to the Caribbean and back told them at the local pub. "Steady seamen in the worst storms at sea. But they've been used and chewed up. Now they're a liability." She'd felt the injustice of that, "used and chewed up," and thought no amount of churchgoing could bring decency to those who had none and had no desire to learn it. So she went with Jamie, expecting nothing.

She'd never seen the library hall so crowded before. It was the first evening event at the library since the bombings in March and it was probably because folks just needed an outing. It had been a frosty May; as the heaters sputtered on and off, people sat shoulder to shoulder for heat. Steaming breaths warmed the air. In the front row next to the lectern were fashionable men and women, dressed in suits and fine dresses and coats, looking as though they had come to a charity event. Behind them sat dozens of workers from the docks and shipyards, from the nearby woolen mills in Paisley and Bishopbriggs, some with their entire families in tow. Young and old packed the main floor of the library; the aisles, too, were filled with people, pressed against one another to make room for everyone. Her townsmen and -women, not one coloured face in sight, had come to hear what was going on in a country thousands of miles away from home. She felt proud that so many had shown up that evening. We Glaswegians may be a stoical, impassive lot, but we care about what's going on in the rest of the world, she thought, as her eyes turned from the crowd to the front of the room. The placard by the side of the dais bore the speaker's name: SHIV ADVANI, Barrister-at-Law. Beneath it, in red lettering, were the words *"No free nation can afford to be indifferent to the fate of freedom anywhere on earth."*

A tall middle-aged woman wearing a fur-collared coat and a Russian fur hat got up to speak. Her necklace of soft pearls gleamed softly in the fluorescent light. "I'm Grace Blackwell and I thank you all for coming to listen to our guest this evening. We all have worries on our minds. Some of us have lost our husbands, wives, and children in the bombings in March. We have still not recovered from our Italian neighbours and friends being rounded up as enemies by the British. The horrors of our time have sealed us off from the rest of the world. This young man is here to tell us about the true state of his country under British rule. We have been fed stories about how Britain has done marvellous things for India. But our guest comes to tell us that the British have hurt his country in ways large and small—damages that may never be reversed. It is a grim message, but we must hear it."

There was pin-drop silence as the thin young man walked to the lectern and began speaking. "Dear friends," he said. "I know this time was snatched from other important things in your lives—from domestic chores, from your children, from your families, from your shops and your farms. For making the effort to be here, I thank you from my heart." There were a few appreciative murmurs from members of the audience. She could see his humility had impressed them.

"We live in a time of great fluidity and great repression," he said. "The tension created by that condition is causing fundamental changes in the way we think and act out our thoughts. The energy generated within each one of us can be harnessed towards bad or good. In Germany, Hitler has found a way to tap into the fury of the country's population against onerous reparations placed on them by the Allies after World War One. He is directing it towards evil and the desire for extermination of the Jewish people and others he considers undesirable. Gandhi, on the other hand, has channelled the fury of his subjugated people towards a nonviolent march for freedom. Not with the guns, cannons, and muskets that have been aimed at us. But with the most powerful weapons in the world: the hearts, minds, and actions of a united people."

As his voice gathered strength, he spoke of his country, of how its natural resources—from cotton and silk, timber and steel, gold, silver, and diamonds, sugar and salt—had been seized and controlled to finance Britain's ventures in other parts of the world. He spoke of how villages, once self-sufficient, now relied on the British government for essentials like food, water, oil, and salt. He told them one million of his people had fought alongside the British in World War One, losing seventy-five thousand men in combat. They were out there now, in the fields of war, he said, along with the Allied troops. A volunteer army, over two million of them, fighting loyally to defend the British crown. But they were also fighting for their own independence, for that is what they had been promised in exchange.

When he mentioned the numbers of his people who had fought for the British, there were gasps from some in the audience. Few, if any, assembled there would have read or heard that the Indians were fighting alongside the British and their own Scotsmen in the trenches—they had only been told the Indians were an inferior godless race, and the white man's burden of civilizing these heathen races came at a heavy price.

Mairi listened as if to a new language. The speaker had a commanding voice. He believed his words—that was the thing about politicians, wasn't it? Half of them were hollow men, mouthing off without thinking about what they were saying. This man's voice was the voice of passion, of the future, of destiny.

"Our history has been one of reneged promises and lives lost as Britain extended control across the length and breadth of India. They came initially to trade with us, which turned to dominance, then to plunder, then to subjugation, rulership, government and administration, and finally to the grandest notion of all—to civilize us by making us give up our culture, our religious and spiritual beliefs. We didn't need civilization. Our civilization is far more ancient, sophisticated, and advanced than theirs. We didn't need the unbearable taxes that Britain levied on us for expansion in its colonies." He spoke of how divide and rule, the time-honoured tactic at the heart of Imperialist strategy, had created rifts within villages where Muslims and Hindus had once coexisted without strife and rancor. His strong, confident voice held the crowds and they all listened as his voice rose. "I am here to speak for India, and to carry its message to you. We bear you no ill will, for you are like us. Your hopes and fears—for your children, your families, your communities—are our hopes and fears, too. We all wish to live in peace and prosperity. We all want the same things—the betterment of our lot in life."

One man raised his hand. "Yes?" Shiv said.

"The reasons for the war in Europe are honourable—to defeat a madman, a man who seeks to destroy the world. How can you plead nonviolence at a time like this?"

"It is not well known in England that Indians are not permitted to bear weapons. The right to defend yourself from attack is a basic, inalienable, human right. Yet we have been deprived of that right. Nonviolence has become our creed perhaps because we have no choice. The other weapon we have is the truth. And we are using it. Our journalists have been jailed for speaking the truth, yet they continue to brave incarceration every day so that people at home and abroad may know what is really going on in our country. Prominent lawyers, my father among them, are defending these journalists and paying their bail to set them free." He looked around the room. "Have you any idea how dangerous it is to speak the truth in India today?" Some nodding heads showed that they knew. "We have perforce had to plant our struggle in nonviolence. Gandhi has shown us how to fight back with our conduct, our beliefs, our hearts. It will take longer, but we will win."

Mairi looked around the room as it went silent. Babies sank into their mothers' chests and slept, their snores the only sounds between pauses in his talk. Old men leaned forward on their canes and inspected him; women listened with knowing looks on their faces, as if they had heard it before, knew what he was saying. There was electricity in that room, for no cause speaks louder than the struggle for freedom.

Another man raised his hand. "What are Indians actually doing to expel the British from their shores?"

"We were slow, no doubt about that. We didn't know the extent of their ambition in India. But now, local people are coming together to protest and to collect funds for the families of farmers who have committed suicide. Factory workers, teachers, laborers, pillars of the community—all are willing to do their parts. At a recent town hall meeting, a disabled boy of ten gave his walking stick to the fund. A factory worker gave his watch. A cobbler donated a fine pair of shoes. A young girl put in her engagement ring. Another took off her gold earrings and placed them in the collection plate."

A young woman in the audience raised her hand. "Yes?" he said.

"Are these things enough to hold the British back?" she asked.

Some in the audience laughed—a walking stick versus cannons and gunpowder!

He nodded. "It's true, these are small gestures. But when what you give is all you own, it means the struggle has now captured the hearts and the will of ordinary people—the poor, the maimed, the workers, the street sweepers. Our struggle is no longer between the Houses of Parliament in London and the government stronghold in Delhi. It is between the people of India and the British government. It has now become that undreamt-of thing: a universal struggle, where each individual feels directly affected by subjugation. After decades of broken promises, India is limping towards its independence, and she will be free, without hatred, without violence. There is no doubt about it: India will be free!" Thumping the floor with their boots, whistling, and shouting out "Aye," the men in the audience, young and old, showed that they had heard him and believed him. The women stood with sleeping babies on their shoulders and clapped. Mairi was so moved, she climbed up on a chair just vacated by someone, and clapped with all her might.

She was still taking in his words when she heard scuffling noises towards the back of the hall, then the startling sound of shots being fired in the room, a quick succession of thunderclaps. There was a commotion by the lectern. The hubbub grew. Waves of confusion reached her as people asked in panic, "He's been shot? No, no, no." She jumped off the chair and hurried to the front, making her way through the crowds. She put her hands out as she reached the circle immediately around him. "I'm a nurse," she said. "Please let me through."

He had collapsed in a faint, and his forehead had hit the edge of the brass lectern. His head was bleeding, probably from the hit to his head as he fell to the floor. A stream of blood ran down his face. A man was pointing to where he had been shot—to the four bleeding wounds where bullets had entered his body: one narrowly escaping his heart, one in his stomach, one in his leg, and one in his right shoulder. Someone handed her a first-aid kit. One man handed her his handkerchief. Others followed and soon she had more than enough cloth to handle the wounds. She ripped the corner of a handkerchief with her teeth and then tore off strips, which she pressed down on the wounds to staunch the flow. She could hear his painful breathing, a jerky suspiration. When she touched his arm, the skin under her finger contracted, jittery with shock. As the men from St. Andrew's Ambulance Association pushed through the crowds bearing a stretcher, she cried out, "Wait, I'm coming with you. I'm a nurse." They allowed her through.

Grace Blackwell was immediately by her side. She took her arm. "A nurse?" Mairi nodded. "I'm not medical personnel, so they won't let me go with him. Please tend to him." She pulled out a pencil from her bag and scrawled something on a piece of paper. "Here's my address and telephone number," she said, putting the paper in Mairi's hand. "Let me know his condition as soon as you can." Mairi nodded and shoved the piece of paper in her pocket and followed the ambulance men outside. On her way out, she noted the turmoil in the hall, the ashen faces of the children, the stoic, grim-faced mothers, the old men shuffling out. "Violence, ain't it? Just what that Indian lad was saying. Shoot what you don't like, that's what the young ones are learning," one man said to his companion.

IN THE WEEK that they spent at the Royal Infirmary, he regained consciousness twice, his eyes fluttering open to ask "Where am I?" only to close them again, and the second was an urgent effort to say the name "Lucy." Mairi asked Grace Blackwell if she knew who Lucy was, and when Grace shook her head, Mairi said, "It doesn't matter. He must get well now."

Things began happening very quickly. Shiv's family asked that he be sent home as soon as possible, accompanied by a qualified nurse who would be paid well for her services. *The Empress of Scotland* was to set sail for Bombay two weeks hence and in that time, Grace Blackwell booked passage, and informed all of Shiv's friends back in London of his situation. Hospital beds were needed for wounded soldiers; Shiv was moved to Grace Blackwell's after the hospital discharged him, with Mairi in charge as nurse. A friend came up to Glasgow with a suitcase containing Shiv's things; and when Grace Blackwell gave Mairi an appraising look with her searching pale blue eyes and asked, "Would you be willing to travel to India with him?" she answered without hesitation, "Yes." No references were required. Overcome with emotion, Grace Blackwell took Mairi's hand, raised it to her lips, and kissed it. "Bless you, m'dear," she said. And that was that.

Mairi's mother said, "India? Can't go farther than that if it's forgetting yer after."

"You'll be all right, Ma, yeah?"

"Aye. Church folks come round all the time, you seen it. I'll be all right."

Mairi looked away. She handed in her resignation at St. Thomas's School down the road, where she had been filling in as a substitute teacher and part-time nurse, with relief. She'd been praying for a new life. Here it was. She couldn't believe her luck.

India: what did she know about this country that had enthralled her countrymen? Father John at St. Mary's hardly let a sermon go by without referring to the civilizing mission of the Christians in the East. "Twelve hundred new Christians in one month alone," he proclaimed. "And we're counting." She had disliked the victorious ring in his voice. The pastor spoke lovingly of this country he had never seen. "A man could go there with nothing and come back richer than he had ever imagined. For there is untold wealth in that land: the timber, the teas, the spices, the cotton, the rice, the grains, the gold, the diamonds, the pearls, the fabrics, the valuable minerals and metals, the wildlife." And there were its dark-skinned peoples waiting to be converted to Christianity. "There's work in India for those who want it—bridges to be built! Rivers to be navigated! Rail lines waiting to be carved into the steep slopes of hills and mountains!" Their minister could not have been a better emissary for the British government. But the Scots had their own problems with the British and they did not believe every word that came out of their overly enthusiastic minister's mouth. One of them, ain't he, her friend Jamie Doncaster said.

She feels the tug of the sea moving under her body as she lies flat in her bed. Her eyes close immediately, her body craves sleep.


HE WAKES IN the middle of the night. His head is swimming. He thinks he's drowning. He thinks he hears an owl hooting; there is the smell of disinfectant, and in the darkness, he sees shadows forming on the wall. There is the sensation of damp, of a persistent wet on his face. He remembers that wet. It is English. The river nearby, the jingle of keys on a chain, the half-light of passing faces, the long row of lamps casting planes of wavy light on the water as it crimped and eased in the wind. He lies there in the darkness, listening to his own breathing. It gathers pace, becomes measured, ticks in his ear. The feeling of not being grounded, of a rhythmic rocky motion beneath him, of pain shooting through him—all come at him at the same time.

A WIZENED SLIGHT figure, stick in hand, walks towards him. His bright eyes and round glasses, his thin, lithe fingers that pinch cheeks and begin fires. The magician. The half-naked fakir. Chocolate Jesus.

# Sind, 1922–1930

Gandhi it was, the man himself, who had picked him. His people had reached out to Ramdas, Shiv's father, in Sind. Ramdas's verandah was the community gathering place. Once a week, it filled with leading thinkers, local politicians, journalists, religious leaders of mosques, temples, churches, and principals of local schools and colleges. Debates raged, tempers flared, but in the end, everyone reached agreement on a concerted plan of action to protest, or to appeal, and funds were donated to the cause of liberation. His mother, watching their cook's assistants run from kitchen to porch with food and drink, once said, "He always offers our home for these meetings. Now everyone wants to come, and we can't cope." But Ramdas was one of the leading lawyers in their community, a man loved and respected by all. "I have to do it," he told his wife. "It is my duty."

Ramdas read the letter from Gandhi's aide to his wife and son, delighted that his house had been picked for the honour. "Bapu wishes to stay with you. He knows you know everyone and you host gatherings in your house for the independence movement. He asks, 'Will you have me?'" The entire household went immediately into overdrive as Ramdas wrote back to say it was an honour, that Bapu would be welcomed by the entire community—Muslims, Hindus, Christians, Parsees, tribal chiefs from the farthest reaches of Sind. Invitations would be sent to community leaders as soon as Gandhi confirmed his dates.

When he learnt it would be in two weeks' time, Ramdas set the machinery into motion. Floors were scrubbed till you could eat off them; carpets beaten free of dust until their colours glowed; orders were placed immediately for the freshest vegetables from family-owned farms in the area. People started sending gifts—dried figs, plums, apricots, and nuts came on merchant ships from Bahrein and Dubai, fresh fruits on camel caravans from Kashmir, Kabul, and Kandahar. Even Uzbek and Tajik traders magically produced fragrant apricots and golden peaches for the occasion.

"What about our worthy rulers?" Shiv's mother said. "Don't you think they'll assume it's a political gathering with Gandhi and his people there? What makes you think they won't start shooting us?"

"There you go, assuming the worst," Ramdas said. "The British will not risk alienating the tribal chiefs, who are showing up with their people in vast numbers. It's the tribals they fear most of all for those fellows can make arms out of anything. If a tribal wants to kill you, he will. They know that."

THE DAY OF Gandhi's arrival, the crowds started gathering at dawn. At the entrance to the driveway, Gandhi asked the driver to stop. A hush descended on the boisterous crowd as Gandhi got out of the car and began walking towards the house, smiling at people, placing his hands on their heads or on their cheeks, patting children's heads. The crowds parted to make way for him and as he reached the front door of the house, Ramdas embraced him. The people whistled, roared, clapped. Shiv, then ten, watched as Gandhi walked into their house, instantly drawn to him. When he opened his mouth to speak, everyone stopped whatever they were doing and turned towards him. He had lit them. They longed to serve him. Shiv lingered in his shadow, yearning to speak to him.

For two days, Gandhi was surrounded by community leaders. Parsee industrialists, Muslim mullahs, Hindu priests, Christian vicars, judges, farmers, advocates, artisans, all jostled with one another to hear from his lips that one day, India would be free of British rule. Everyone seemed to glow in his presence—even Shiv's father.

Shiv's moment to shine came much later, on Gandhi's day of departure. "Go, Shiv," his mother said to him. "Run upstairs. Bapu's forgotten his shawl." Shiv ran up to Gandhi's room. There it was, on the bed. He picked it up and turned to go when he saw the shawl reflected in a mirror. A large black stain, about six inches in diameter, covered one side of the shawl. That was why Gandhi had left his shawl behind. Someone had somehow spilled ink in its folds. He flung the shawl down and went to his father's room. He pulled out Ramdas's favourite shawl—a finely woven cream cashmere—from his cupboard and ran down the stairs. "What took you so long?" his mother said, frowning. Shiv went to Gandhi and handed him the shawl. "Here, sir," he said. One of Gandhi's aides rushed forward. "But that isn't the Mahatma's shawl," he cried, bounding up the stairs to Gandhi's room. He came back down with the shawl and handed it to Gandhi. Gandhi immediately saw the stain. He turned to Shiv and said, "You are a thoughtful boy."

"Our son has chosen the perfect gift," Ramdas said. "Please accept the shawl he chose—one of my own—from us." Gandhi smiled and nodded assent.

He turned to Shiv. "We have not met properly. But I know you are Ramdas's son. Mr. Polak is very impressed with you. Come," he said, patting the seat next to him. "Sit down and tell me about you."

As he spoke, Shiv felt the man's magic instantly. Gandhi radiated warmth and understanding. It was as if no one else was present. His

eyes were set attentively on Shiv, and the boy felt he could say anything to him and never be misunderstood. "What do you want to
be?" Gandhi asked.

"Like you," he replied. "Just like you."

Gandhi laughed, a tickled, playful chuckle. "It is very hard work."

"I'm not afraid of hard work."

"You will have to give up desire."

Imagining desire to be something like greed, Shiv said, "You
mean like ice cream?"

Gandhi laughed again—a deep, hearty chuckling laugh—and
nodded his head up and down. Again that sound of glee in his
laugh—as if he was savouring something in what you said that only
he could hear. "Yes," he said. "Like ice cream."

Shiv considered it and said, "Can you never have it?"

"No, never. Because a little bit makes you want more."

That was true, Shiv reflected. He could never stop with ice cream.
"I think I can give it up."

"Good," Gandhi said. Then an aide was by his side. "Goodbye,
son. We shall meet again," he said, putting his hand on Shiv's head.
He took the ink-stained shawl from his aide and said, "Here is my
shawl. Keep it. Your mother will know how to get the stain out."
Then another pat on the head and he was gone.

GANDHI HAD SHOWN him what true power was. But it was his father who had shown him what Indians were really up against. In
1923, the year Shiv turned eleven, his father invited Chief Justice
Williams over for tea. When the invitation was accepted, his mother
brought out the formal tea service—Royal Doulton, the Old Country Roses pattern beloved by the British in India—and the sterling
silver teapot, milk pitcher, sugar bowl, and tongs. Slender crust-less
tea sandwiches of cucumber and watercress lined a platter in neat

layers, and a glistening chocolate cake on a glass stand was brought in by a bearer as the judge and his wife entered the drawing room.

The meeting was social but the judge would have known, just as Shiv's father did, that the occasion was far from social. There had been rioting in the streets a few days earlier while Hindus moved peacefully in throngs towards the river in celebration of Lord Ganesh's festival day. Locals confirmed that Muslims not from the area had been bused in to create havoc and riots erupted as Hindu turned against Muslim. A local festival, normally a joyful celebration attended by both Hindus and their Muslim neighbours and friends, became a bloody battlefield. Seven young men were killed—four Muslims, three Hindus. The entire community grieved together for the men, local boys whose families had lost a father, a son, a brother. Hindus went to mosques to mourn with Muslim families for their loss; Muslims came to temples to pray along with their Hindu brethren for their dead. Through its leaders, the community placed a ban on violence. Where was the might of the British army then? his mother asked. Why were they not present to put out the violence? Ramdas had invited the judge and his wife to get to the truth of the matter. Why had the British not intervened?

As SOON AS the judge and his wife had been served their tea, sandwiches, and cake, Ramdas, determined to keep the occasion short and memorable, said, "I know what a busy man you are, Judge Williams. So let us get to the point immediately." He gave the judge a stern look. "My people, of all religious denominations, respect one another. I have personally given them my word that they will be safe, that no infighting will be tolerated, that all will be left in peace to worship at the altars of their choice. Last week, our community was racked by violence on a holy day of great importance to Hindus. Seven young men lost their lives as a result. Where were the British soldiers? They're ever present at all our functions. They know instantly when there is violence of any sort on our streets. Why were they not there? This cannot ever happen again," his father warned.

Judge Williams put on a placating smile. "But it is hard to know what happens between local groups. We can't keep tabs on everything."

Shiv watched his mother press her lips together. She frowned at Judge Williams. She was going to say something, he realized. Women were meant to be silent witnesses, civil, polite, capable of discussing the foliage in their gardens, and the trouble with servants these days. But no one dared to say anything more. "Your father is a key pillar of our community here in Sind. The British will never risk alienating him," his mother often said to Shiv. Perhaps it was this knowledge that gave her the courage to speak.

Her sharp, clear, high-pitched voice suddenly cut into the conversation. "Forgive me, Judge Williams, as a woman I know I must not express my views. But you cannot sit here, in my house, and not face facts. The fact is, you do keep tabs on everything. And it was well within your rights to control the rioting even if you had not been responsible for creating it in the first place. Not one member of the British army was present. Not one! Seven young men with bright futures before them died as a result. You treat us like human fodder. *That* is an affront to us Indians!"

The judge gave her an astonished look as he heard her address him directly. He instantly dropped all attempts at obfuscation. "I assure you it will never happen again," he said, shaking hands fervently with Ramdas. "You know how much respect we have for you. You're a highly regarded pleader in Hyderabad Sind and have the community's support and loyalty behind you. I give you my word of honour that nothing like this will happen again."

As soon as his car drove out of their driveway, Ramdas turned to his wife. "Bull's-eye! Leela, you hit the nail on the head. I hope you're not going to make a habit of surprising us like this in public with your opinions, but this once, you gauged the mood perfectly. He was guilty, and needed to make promises, whether they are kept in the future or not."

Leela gave him a pleased smile. "I know when to speak and when to stay silent," she said.

"So they *were* behind it all?" Shiv asked.

"You don't promise to not do something in the future if you hadn't done it in the first place. Note his words. 'It will never happen again,' he assured me. Of course they were behind it."

Everyone knew what the British were up to in Sind, but the pretence of not knowing, of having to act cordially towards people who were depriving you of self-rule, and therefore of sovereignty, was intolerable to Shiv. That one party had to pretend they didn't realize they were being made fools of and that the other pretended that they were behaving with goodwill and were fully in accord with justice and fair play, cherished notions of British social behaviour, represented a new low in human relations. "So they can do whatever they want here in India, with no one to stop them?" Shiv said.

"In the colonies, they are autocrats. They are rulers. Some British historian said, 'The playing fields of Eton lead to the frontier, not to the conference table.' Here is where elite British males come to harness their warmongering skills. To us." Ramdas put his arm around Shiv's shoulders. "Son, this is why we must fight them. Not with rage and violence but with their own laws, their rules. We who have come to know them, how high-minded they can be, how low they can go, we are the ones who will fight them. Not by the sword, but in the courts of law, by jurisdiction. Now you see why it is so important."

"Sir, you have my word I will do everything possible to make sure India is one day free." Shiv saw India's conquest through his father's eyes—a long history of betrayal, condescension, arrogance, and brutal suppression. They must go, he vowed. They must leave our country.

The year of his departure, 1930, was when Gandhi performed his first act of *satyagraha*—passive resistance, civil disobedience, or soul-force—when he organized a march to the salt flats on the Rann of Kutch. This salt was of such high quality that British salt could not compete with it. Ships from England came filled with Cheshire salt as ballast and went home loaded with salt from the Rann of Kutch, among many other things. Taxes from salt made up eight to ten percent of British revenue from India. Gandhi's march began with a ragtag group of a few thousand that swelled to over sixty thousand. When he bent down by the seashore and held a palm full of Indian salt up to the crowds, he initiated the first act towards Indian independence. Ours, he declared boldly to the world. And we're not paying for it. Ramdas told his son, "There's no turning back now. Civil disobedience as a form of protest is born." Gandhi and his followers were arrested. But he walked towards captivity joyfully. He knew the march towards independence had begun.

It was only a few months before Shiv's ship set sail. He felt the soft sure lick of fire within—he would come back and join that movement, he would stand in the front line with Gandhi, and the country would be liberated.

"You'll lead your country when we leave," Mr. Polak had told Shiv.

It was Polak who, after his initial meeting with his hosts' nine-year-old son, had nudged Gandhi to consider young Shiv's potential as one of the leaders of independent India. After Gandhi, too, visited the Advani home and agreed with Polak's assessment, Mr. Polak continued to feed Gandhi with reports on the boy's progress through school, his character and intelligence, as gleaned from his father's letters to Mr. Polak. "He has a natural disposition for leadership,"

Polak told Gandhi. "He listens to tribal chiefs carefully—he knows that's where the killer weapons are; he attends all community meetings and has impressed local organizations with his enthusiasm and passion for justice, for human rights. He brings the problems of the underserved to the table. People have already begun respecting him. He's still in his teens!" Gandhi began writing to Shiv's father, taking a keen interest in the boy's progress. When the time came, Gandhi paved the way—both for Shiv's admission to the Inns of Court, the Mahatma's own alma mater, and his room and board at the home of his dear friends, the Polaks.

But it was Shiv's mother who now raised objections, going on a hunger fast to make his father bend to her will. Hindu scriptures advocated fasting both as personal sacrifices to the gods and as powerful weaponry to make a point. They were in the jhula room, his mother on the day-bed swing that moved gently back and forth, his father in his leather armchair. Shiv was sitting on an ottoman beside his father. Govind, their houseboy, brought in a tray containing cups of steaming cardamom tea.

"He will never come back," she said, unreasonably offering no explanations for her dire prediction.

"Nonsense!" Ramdas said, reaching for a cup of tea. "England will toughen him up. Our boys turn into namby-pambies under their mothers' watches. Mollycoddled little sahibs. We'll need warriors in the new India. Old Blighty will make a man out of him."

His mother then raised the possibility of Shiv's marriage before his departure. "The Hiras are ready whenever we are. Seher has now turned sixteen. Such a beauty, she's not going to sit around waiting for Shiv to return. She wants to get on with her life. Now is the time, Ramdas."

He frowned at her. "Suddenly you tell me this?"

"It only just now came to me. We can have a small one, private, just between the two families and the priest. Big weddings are unfashionable in these times."

"Yes, but I was one step ahead of you. I already discussed the issue with Gandhi himself. Should my son get married now, before he leaves for London? Gandhi was vehemently opposed to it. He said, a man does not know what he wants in life when he is eighteen. We imprison our children in their marriages when they are so young. Wait until his return. Not now." He turned to his son. "What do you say, son? Would you like to get married before you leave?"

They expected him to know, for his desires were meant to mirror their intentions. "No, sir," he said. "It is better I wait so I can make the right decision for me and my family."

"I don't know why Gandhi decides everything in our family," his mother said, looking aggrieved. "What about me, the mother?" Ramdas gave her a sharp look. His wife continued: "His marriage is sure to bring him back home—and a child. There's ample time for him to make a woman pregnant before he leaves."

Her husband thought long and hard. "You have a point," he finally said. "A man comes back for his wife and his child, if for nothing else."

It was Shiv's life they were talking about. But he observed it dispassionately. It stretched before him, a long, dark road that would be shaped and paved by others and always lead back here, to where he was now, and to this moment in time. This is why he had survived his mother's womb—to fulfill his parents' hopes, their aspirations and desires. As for his own dreams: strangle them, he said to himself. His mission was to make his family's wishes come true. He wanted the British to leave India as much as they did. But his commitment to the cause did not give them the further right to determine his personal fate—his wife, his marriage, his home, his children. But nothing would come from starting an argument with them—Indian parents had full power over their children.

When his mother turned to him and said, "Son, your future will be secured. Aren't you happy?" he wanted to scream. She expected him, somehow, to be relieved. He silently seethed, yet said nothing.

And so plans were made, quickly, efficiently.

The next morning, he saw a bright painting made with coloured rice powder on the driveway. A large OM sign in fuchsia and purple that announced to everyone in the neighbourhood that the young man of the house was now engaged.

# Sind, September 1930

He hears the drums getting closer. *Rat-a-tat-tat, rat-a-tat-tat.* A procession of turbaned men in embroidered waistcoats and pantaloons marching down the road to their house. *Rat-a-tat.* A bugle sounds, splitting the air, and then a single flute, playing a local Sindhi melody, rises above all the other sounds, a thrilling joyous arc of sound that reaches him as he stands there in all his finery, awaiting his bride and her entourage. He sits down on a sofa to listen. His mother gives him an anxious look. "Tired already, son?"

He doesn't respond. His heart is racing. He looks away into the distance, at the shimmering Indus. She is coming to him via the mouth of the river, as all conquerors of Sind had come. *Sindh-ka-bab*—the Lion's Mouth, as it was named by the ancient Hindus who lived in the valley. Like all great rivers, it had been named and re-named by every conquering group that had crossed its shores. The ancient Aryans saw it as Sindhu. For the Greeks the river was Sinthus. The Chinese referred to it as Sintow. For the Persians, it was Abissindh. The Roman Pliny saw it as the mighty river that belonged to the land through which it flowed. Indus, he called it—from its cradle, India. Indus it became. "When it soars with rich mountain waters, it gives health; when its riverbeds run dry, it brings disease.

It laughs with joy, but its farts are toxic," their gardener, Krishan, had told Shiv.

His fiancée's home is downriver, towards the delta in Thatta. The two families had agreed that in a time of political upheaval and austerity, a small, private wedding would show more sensitivity to the public mood. When asked what he wanted, a big celebration or a small one, he said, "For it all to be over."

His mother says, "She is a lovely girl. And her mother and grandmother are old friends of the family. Her father is a merchant, it's true, a goldsmith. But one of the finest in Sind. No small achievement."

He doesn't answer. How can she expect him to care about people he does not know, has never met? She doesn't take her eyes off his face. He says, "It is all as you wish, Mother."

She gives him an appraising look; her eyes run over his dress, his shoes, his hair. He is wearing a white silk long jacket, an achkan, and slim silk pants. His feet are encased in leather slippers worked in fine gold embroidery; his grandfather's emerald necklace has been taken out of the family safe and is around his neck; in his ears are small diamonds. His thick black hair is brushed back showing off his long face, deep-set eyes, and high cheekbones. He is lean, and tall. She says, "You look like a prince today."

He doesn't respond.

"You are a dutiful son," she says. "This is why your father has placed his trust in you and is sending you all the way there, to No-Man's-Land. Just look at all the damage they have caused here. Don't be tempted by their ways. Come back to your own country with your law degree in hand."

He says what he always says to her. "I will do my best."

"We know." She looks at him closely. "Gandhiji himself told your father last year that he has high hopes for you. Everyone is expecting great things from you, son."

He bows his head and bends forward; his palms rest on the

arches of her feet for a moment in a show of respect. "It will be as you wish, Mother."

She smiles. "I have never had reason to doubt you." It is her day. She sees hardship ahead of her: he is the apple of her eye. Her only son. She will miss him. They will all make sacrifices to support him financially while he is in London. But he will return and make them proud.

HER NAME IS Seher. She is tiny in proportion, so slender he feels he could encircle her waist with one hand. She is wearing an unusual wedding colour sari—a spring sky blue, with small bees embroidered in gold on the silk fabric. Red is the colour of weddings. The sky blue is a surprise. And why bees? He wonders. Bees are not a wedding symbol. But according to local folklore, she explains to him later, bees are symbols of fertility—"they make honey"—and wealth—"they have everything they need in their hive"—and loyalty—"they have a queen, and their mission is to protect her." He likes the way she speaks, with understanding and intelligence. She says, "Bees always return to their hive because they are happiest there." He looks at her. "We will have to build you a hive, then," he says. In the sunlight, her eyes are brown-green, her eyelids hooded, her cheeks a heightened blush. She is like a downy peach, soft and delectable.

"But I already have one," she says. "And I am Queen Bee." Her smile is flirtatious. Is she the theatrical sort, acting a part? Something about her behaviour seems staged to him. Suspicious yet beguiled, he goes towards her.

When he lifts the veil of her sari to kiss her, she purses her lips and tilts her head back. She looks like a young girl—not sixteen, twelve, perhaps. He's only eighteen himself. They are children. His hands are sweating. His pulse is racing. His face feels like it's trembling. He can't still it for even a few moments. But he knows he

must be manly. He bends forward primly, like an old gent, and allows his lips to graze hers for a second before drawing away. He
knows it is cold and bloodless, but this is a performance. He doesn't
expect to play his part with flair; he's no star. Faultless is all he can
hope for.

When she gives him a surprised look, as though she were expecting something else, he realizes she doesn't know how to kiss either.
They do not yet know the urgency of passion. Their movements are
awkward, they speak at the same time, they fall silent together. Their
hands miss their mark, they don't touch the way they should. They
have no rhythm, and in the little time he has left before his departure, he doubts they will find it. He had assumed these things happened naturally—as if some external guiding force would smooth
the way. She turns away from him; he shakes his head, aware that he
has disappointed her.

In the other room, the priest is waiting. The sandalwood chips on
the lit brazier give off a wild, intoxicating scent. The priest starts
chanting as soon as they enter the room and take their places in
front of him. Shiv's parents are on the right, hers on the left. The ceremony involves repeating binding sections after the priest, joining
hands, then joining their bodies symbolically with a scarf tied on
either end to both their clothes. They walk around the fire seven
times, each time repeating a different vow. The vows commit them
to loyalty, to respect, to kindness, to prayer, to cleanliness of heart,
mind, and body, to truth, to the ways of God, to devotion to one's
parents and children. The priest pronounces them husband and
wife. They kiss again, chastely. Then it is over.

The celebration is small. There are eight of them altogether, including the priest. It's the smallest wedding celebration Shiv's been
to. Without the boisterous wedding crowds, the colour, and joyous-
ness, it feels more like a funeral. There is tea, sherbet, rose cardamom lassi, and a Sindhi specialty, thandai—almond milk with
cardamom, rose petals, and crushed peaches. There are sweets made

with milk and there is kheer. Her grandmother nibbles a piece of varo, a nut brittle with saffron and white poppy seeds. She has underestimated its hardness, and makes a sour face as it cracks against her teeth. His in-laws speak about the price of gold; his parents voice their concerns about Sind's fate if partition should become a possibility. There is no common ground. Her parents and grandmother leave, having refused his father's plea that they spend the night under his roof; his parents go to bed early, leaving them the gardens and verandah to roam in. He wants to sleep; she says, "It has been a very long day." He says immediately, "Shall I take you to our bedroom upstairs?"

"Yes." He leads her up the stairs to their room, then leaves her to unpack and settle in. When he returns, she is fast asleep. She looks so young. A child's face, open and trusting. She has no worries, having accepted her fate. She sleeps the sleep of angels.

He lies down next to her and exhales deeply. Sleepless and anxious, he listens enviously to her rhythmic breathing and thinks, *It has only just begun.*

THE NEXT DAY, he asks his mother if they can have separate rooms. She laughs. "Silly boy! That's not how it's done."

She says, "Take her to the gardens, to the river. You will find a lot to talk about."

BY THE BANKS of the Indus River, he asks her about her hometown of Thatta. She tells him that her best friend died of diphtheria when she was six, that she's never had a best friend since then. She loves astronomy, it was her favourite subject at school. She knows all the constellations now and recognizes them by their shapes. "I would train as an astronomer if I were a man. I know there is life out there, far far away. If only we could speak to them."

He knows it's just a dream. Men aren't allowed to fantasize about their futures, so how can a woman dare it? She's as bound to her role in life as he is to his—their destinies have been charted from the day they were born. But he admires her for having dreams, and for not keeping quiet about it.

Seher says, "When will you come back?"

"I don't know."

"Will it be many years?

"No, not many years. But some years, till I am fully trained and called to the bar."

She is silent. They have walked to Rani Bagh, where summer's profusion is everywhere. Flowering hydrangeas and hibiscus, jasmine bushes perfume the air. The extreme heat has kept crowds away and the beautiful public gardens are practically empty. She says, "When you come back, will we have children?"

"Yes," he says. "I expect so. Everyone does."

He wonders whether she's asking him obliquely about sex, about when they'll have sex. His father had taken him to his study one afternoon and showed him two drawings. One was of a penis. The other was "a vageena," his father said. "It's the woman's part." It was only in later years that he remembered how his father said "vageena," and the fact that he hadn't known now to pronounce it correctly, when everything else he did and said was so correct, told Shiv that his father had probably looked it up in a dictionary.

Disembodied and without context, the large drawings seemed grotesque. His father said, "One goes into the other. There is fertilization, and an embryo is formed. That embryo is contained within a woman's womb and in time matures into a baby. This is how babies are made." But how did the one thing go into the other? He had wanted to ask his father, but his father's cheeks had reddened, and he thought it best to make whatever sense he could of it on his own.

He stares at her now, in the Rani Bagh gardens, wondering where exactly, how deep down her thing was, and how on earth was he supposed to put his thing inside her. She says, sharply, "What are you looking at?"

"Oh, nothing, nothing."

Despite the awkwardness, two nights later, he tries it, frustrated and annoyed that he knows so little and is expected to know so much. He asks her to strip. She does as he says, pulling off her sari, then the blouse, then the petticoat, finally, her panties, then her bra. He's so intent on finding it, he barely notices her tight beautiful breasts, her slender body, its rosy flush, youth just before its prime. He says, "Where is it?"

"What?"

He strips, too. "Where I'm supposed to put this into." He holds up his penis.

He fears she'll walk out on him. He's already come across as a buffoon to her, a man who knows nothing. But she laughs and laughs, holding her stomach.

He says, "What are you laughing at? Shhh, you'll wake up the family."

She laughs again. "I don't know much. But you know nothing!" She can't stop laughing. Then she says, "Why don't we just try it?"

She comes towards him and takes his penis in her hands. She's puzzled. It has grown larger as she holds it. She looks at it a little fearfully. "If it becomes any bigger . . . will it fit?" It grows and grows. "Oh my goodness," she says.

"I can't control it." He's so embarrassed, he wishes he could just lop it off.

"Well, we have to try it." She frowns. Then she noses it towards the opening of her vagina. "Push it in," she says. He does. "Deeper," she says. "Deeper," and "Deeper." And then he's in. He starts moving against her and it is as if their bodies, first his and then hers, fall into some kind of rhythm. He's very excited and is aware of something wanting to explode within him. "Am I hurting you?"

"Yes," she says, biting her lip. "But it's meant to hurt."

"What?"

"Yes, everyone told me it would hurt." He's panting; he pushes deeper as she cries out with every thrust, small, mewling cries like those of a wounded animal. Then he comes inside her, and sees tears trickle out of her eyes. "I'm so sorry," he says. "I am so very sorry."

The next morning, he sees blood on the sheets. Small droplets on the edges, one large stain in the centre. He turns away, repelled. He never tries to have sex with her again. The hurt in her eyes deepens as he turns away from her every night and feigns sleep.

HIS FATHER, PROUD to show him off, invites the newly wedded district commissioner over for drinks with his wife. They were married six months earlier and his wife is trying to put together "at home" teas for the wives of well-placed Indians in Hyderabad Sind. She is a snob and has made it quite plain to everyone that she hates being in India. Aggrieved about missing the London season of balls and garden-parties, which was just about to kick off, she says India is not quite what she expected and it was taking a lot of getting used to. Ramdas talks with the district commissioner while Leela converses with the commissioner's wife, and Seher, looking bored, stares with downcast eyes at the carpet. An awkward silence descends between the two women, so Ramdas's request is heard by everyone in the room. "Our townspeople must be allowed to meet regularly at Homestead Hall. The library is little used these days and this would be a fine way to get locals to use it more."

"Why would you want to meet?" the commissioner asks. "What would be the goal?"

"The people have a right to meet to discuss social and cultural issues as they arise. We are capable of making our own decisions—we do not need to run up to the district commissioner for every little thing," Ramdas says.

"Our office is used to handling everything, from problems big and small. That will not be necessary, Ramdas. You have celebrations enough."

"Meetings are not celebrations, sir."

"Our office is quite capable," the commissioner says, rising to his feet. "Tell your people our doors are open." He holds out his hand. Ramdas shakes it with an enthusiasm he does not feel. But the British judge you by your handshake. You couldn't use it to convey revulsion.

As soon as the couple leave—the wife nodding curtly at his mother as if she were the maid being asked to leave the room—Shiv turns to his father. "They teach us to say thank you for everything, from acknowledging you with a raised eyebrow to your right to exist. But neither of them said thank you to you or to Mother when they left—as if it is their right, not a courtesy, to have them over. They have to go, Father. They have to leave. We don't want them here and they don't want to be here. They have to go." Shiv's hands have balled into fists, as if preparing to punch the man's face. His mother says, "Calm down. These people can't be got rid of so easily. We will have to fight them, as your father says, diligently and with brilliance. We will match them at their own game."

"So how do we fight them? What do we have that they don't?"

"A good question," his father says, taking him to his study, where he pulls out a book on the shelves. "Understand, Shiv, what has happened to us. The British condemned Arabic and Sanskrit as valueless languages. Their representative for education in India, Thomas Babington Macaulay, said, 'a single shelf of a good European library was worth the whole native literature of India and Arabia.' Our dialects, he claimed, 'were fruitful of monstrous superstitions.' What he went on to advocate was the training of a class of interpreters 'between us and the millions whom we govern—a class of persons Indian in blood and colour, but English in tastes, in opinions, in morals, and in intellect.' This class, now the superior class, just like theirs back home, would, in time, become 'the vehicles for conveying knowledge to the great mass of the population.' These declarations were made in his Minute to Parliament on 2 February 1835. Nearly a century later, they have achieved it. We are now divided not only by caste, which the British had little to do with, but also by education, and critically, by the language, their language, they have imposed on us. They want us to vie with each other to be as English as the English, to judge ourselves by that standard. Yet, for them, we will always be an inferior subspecies, trained to be like them, but unequal by colour, race, and religion."

"This is what you want me to be, Father? A member of an inferior subspecies?"

"I'm sorry, there is no other way," his father says. "We must learn their ways in order to get rid of them."

Shiv lets out a long sigh. It was so premeditated. "A hundred years later, they have done it, they have taken ownership and autonomy from us," his father says. "This is what Bapu is showing us— how we have been degraded, how self-respecting people have become servile, and why we must regain what we once were."

The atmosphere in their house is heavy that evening. "The meetings are necessary. People are getting restless," Ramdas says. "We must urge them to be restrained. We must not use force. There will be countless deaths if the British turn their arms against us. Nonviolence is the only way."

"That I don't believe," his mother says. "I know Gandhi has convinced everyone that is the only way—but just look at them, look at how they treat us in our own homes. He thinks we can get rid of them and their armies through nonviolence. It is rubbish, I tell you, Ramdas, rubbish. Talk to the tribal chiefs. They will organize a first-class militia and arm our men to the teeth with the kind of weapons the British can only dream about. We must arm our people—"

"Leela, you belie your name this evening. Lighthearted, playful, sweet. You are hardly that. You are a raging Durga—rage leads nowhere. Fight their cannons, their guns, and their muskets with arrows and catapults? We can be executed for owning weapons. No, Gandhi is right. Nonviolence will rule the day."

"When? A hundred years from now? Two hundred? When our people are so beaten down, they will forget all dreams of independence? No one hated these people when they came. But they turned us against one another. Divide and rule. Now we hate them. Wait, you say. Wait for what? More violence against us?" She starts walking up the stairs, her sari drawn tautly around her shoulders, her back ramrod straight.

His mother is right, Shiv thinks. It was time to throw them out, to take it back. That they had convinced a civilization much older and far more refined than theirs that they were the heathens, and the invaders the civilizers, was evidence enough that something was terribly wrong. Macaulay's hand was everywhere. They had taken away the fundamental right of self-defence by prohibiting Indians from bearing arms so that if another nation attacked, decisions would first have to be made in the halls of Westminster before the country could be defended. Yes, Indians were complicit—in allowing a patriarchal system to flourish without any checks; in forcing women to suppress their ambitions in service of the family; the greedy moneylenders who loaned the British traders money to stay on in India at a hefty interest should have known better; there was a caste system, which was convenient to keep everyone in their place, but was a powder keg. "The British love the caste system and will do nothing to get rid of it. It reminds them of their own class system back home where everyone has a place and you don't dare aspire to the level above you." His father's words.

Like others of his class, Shiv knows Keats but not the Indian poet Kabir, he knows Tennyson but not the Indian Nobelist Tagore, he knows the Psalms from Bible class at school but not the Vedas, the principal holy books of the Hindus. His knowledge of the forests in India and the animals that lived there comes from Rudyard Kipling. He can recite Shakespeare but not Valmiki and knows not a word of the *Bhagavadgītā*. His mother had told him stories from the *Mahābhārata* while he was growing up because her father had been a translator of ancient Hindu texts from the original Sanskrit to Gurmukhi, the language of Sind. But the everyday context in which they had once been used and referred to was gone, obliterated by the Empire's footprint. They had become fairy tales to him, not the myths his ancestors had lived by. The whole effort in education was to deny Indianness, to accentuate Britishness. Indian literature was not taught at school. Greek and Latin were obligatory, and Sanskrit was an extra-curricular offering that few actually registered to learn. He is fluent in English, stumbles in Hindi. He is a product of colonial England, not of India, he realizes, and he knows he lacks indigenous fibre, the self-preservation that comes with knowing your native soil.

Shiv sees what he has to do then. For years he along with other students had recited Shakespeare's monologues in school drama competitions, acted the parts of his villains and fools, been the young swains that made the tender hearts of young girls bleed, experienced life as children of people with a conscience and a cause. Now Shakespeare and his sense of justice in an unfair world would make a true freedom fighter out of him. He would learn the art of persuasion as a barrister and wage war from the pages of Shakespeare's immortal plays.

EVERY FRIDAY AFTERNOON, he and his father visit Thacker & Co., a local branch of the large booksellers in Bombay. Here he is allowed to roam the stacks and pick whatever he likes. Shiv, helped by the knowledgeable bookseller, picks books by the writers he wanted to read: Tolstoy, Balzac and Daniel Defoe, Thomas Hardy, Dickens, the Brontë sisters in fiction; Gerard Manley Hopkins, Byron, Wordsworth, and Shelley in poetry; Oscar Wilde's writings. Apart from Rabindranath Tagore, who wrote in English, and who was the first non-European writer to win the Nobel Prize in Literature, there are

no other representatives of Indian literature. The bookshop's offerings of more contemporary literature are just as meagre—"It takes so
long to get current titles" is the bookseller's complaint. Armed with
his treasures, Shiv takes off for his bedroom as soon as he gets home
to read and think, for these are the times that he can call his own. He
opens the books one by one, sniffing along the gutters, the spines,
the headbands. Glue, starched cloth, the metallic smell of printing
dyes, the smoky wood-almond-vanilla smell of new paper. The most
expensive commodity in his world, books are considered the real
teachers. Even the British can't censor Tolstoy and Hardy the way
they did the history books they studied at school. Natives weren't up
to snuff, the British reasoned, letting novels crowd the shelves at
Thacker & Co. The silence of his room embraces him as he lies back
on his bed and begins reading.


THE NIGHT BEFORE his departure, his father leads him into his
study. There, over a cup of cardamom chai, he explains how the one
book that had affected him deeply was Homer's *Odyssey*. "It is the
story of a homecoming—a very long homecoming. Ten years of war,
and then ten years of travels—ten years it took him!—to reach his
home again. The diversions were so many, from bad weather to beautiful women who offered him everything to stay and make their
home his home. But he knew where his home was. And he used
everything—everything!—he had, cunning, resourcefulness, his talent as a storyteller, his skills as a sailor, his great gift as a leader of
men, to meet all the challenges. And there were many, as you can
imagine. On the voyage home, he was like a slippery eel, fighting for
survival with ingenuity and cunning, refusing to be pinned down,
but when he got home, he clasped his weapons and roared like a lion.

"His real moment of triumph was not in the destruction of Troy.
It was when, beaten and flattened like a leaf, he came back to Ithaca
and regained his home. Fought off the suitors who had tried to claim

his wife and his house and lands in his absence. He took his rightful place as husband, father, leader of his men. Home shows exiles its teeth. *Nostos*, a hero's return home, is also winning it back, fighting for it to become yours again. Here, son." Ramdas hands him a beautifully bound leather book. "Everything is in it—answers to who we are, what we want without even knowing we want it, how we live with what we don't want because we don't know what we do want, and where we're all going. And it's a cracking good story." Shiv understands what his father is trying to tell him. His ship was about to sail for new adventures, trials, and triumphs. But it would turn around eventually and bring him back home, where he belonged.

THEY ARE ALL gathered at Karachi docks. The SS *Rajputana*, its two funnels whooshing steam, is ready for departure. Shiv feels the urgency to be gone. He embraces his mother, who bursts into tears; his father gives him a quick, manly hug, but the tics in his face speak of his emotional distress. His son, his only child. "Godspeed," he mutters, holding up his hand, and then turns away. His wife stares at him. They have known each other for twelve weeks but have remained strangers. She bends down to touch his feet. He rushes to pick her up. "No," he says.

"You are my husband," she says. "The father of my unborn child."

He gives her a puzzled look. "What are you telling me?" In response, she puts one hand over her stomach. He understands.

They look into each other's eyes. Expectant pride shines out of hers. She's done it, despite the odds. His heart is racing. "I will write."

She nods. Then he turns his back to them and starts walking up the gangplank. Some part of him, he knows, is going to stay behind with them, with the child forming in his wife's womb. It won't board that ship. It refuses to leave these shores. Even as his body forges ahead, his feet yearn to reverse their steps and go back, towards the familiar light of home.

## The Empress of Scotland, June 1941

He turns his eyes to the porthole. It is daylight; a small portion of it has not been covered up with black paper and through the small hole fall golden-coloured eggs of sunlight, tumbling across the mouse-grey carpeted floor. His eyes follow the path of light, and he longs to put his lips around one of those eggs, feel its warmth and pressure on his lips. He becomes aware of voices—a man's, a woman's. She says, "You're kind to offer to take me up to the deck. It can get a little suffocating in here, with a sleeping man for company."

"Any time, miss. I'll look in on you often. You let me know when you're ready to go up there." His voice sharpens as he calls out, "Miss Mairi, look! Turn around!"

"What?" He points with his chin. She leaves the washing in the sink and turns to face the bed. "He's awake. Oh, thank god." She rushes over. His eyes are open, his lips apart, as if he's thirsty. She fills a glass with water, and places a napkin below his chin as she holds it to his lips. She's holding the glass at a tilt—drops reach his lips and fall into his open mouth. He's conscious of every drop, of how it moistens his lips, his mouth, calms his parched throat. "They told me he'd come out of the coma, that he was just very tired. But looking at him, in such a deep slumber, I wondered if they were right. Most people come out of it in two to four weeks. He was right on the nose. But then he went back into a slump and the doctors said, He's processing. Give him time. A body can survive for three days without water, they said. They're good at giving hope."

"If they hadn't been right?" Will asks.

"And if purple dolphins came sailing out of the sky?"

Will laughs. "That'd be a sight all right!"

It's a jumble of noise to him. His body is grateful for the slow trickle of cool water the nurse is guiding into his lips. From the timbre of their voices, he can judge that they mean him no harm. He senses that his welfare matters to them, and they are looking after him. He shuts his eyes again.

She is by his bed when he wakes. She tells him that her name is Mairi McNulty and that she is his nurse, accompanying him back to his family home on this ship, *The Empress of Scotland*. He has no recollection of ever meeting her; she is a stranger to him. Yet her hands reach for his bedpan, as they do now, with a sure knowledge. She is intimate with his body and its weakness; she knows it at this point probably better than him. He senses her familiarity and is puzzled, even a little dismayed by it.

He is suspicious. Who managed all of this, got him onto a ship, packed him off home? His memories are spotty, they begin and stop. He tries to reach beyond but there is a still point, around which he lingers like a dog with a bone, wanting to suck it dry. He knows only what she has told him: he was at the library in Glasgow, where he had given a talk—"very powerful," she said, "everyone came to hear you"—and then he was shot and fell. "Two men entered the library as you were finishing your talk. They came within firing distance and began shooting. They were gunning for you." He sees them now, moving with menace towards him. It's the still point around which memory buckles. The exhilaration of resounding applause, the despair as his eyes met a gun's barrel. In his head, he hears chanting policemen surrounding a small black boy by the Thames. "Blackie Blackie Eagle, Stick 'im wiv a needle, Pull 'is cock, Make 'im 'op . . ." He knew that boy would die. He stepped in, showed his credentials as a barrister, and while the bobbies sparred with him, the little boy got away.

He turns to look at Mairi. "Who . . . shot . . . me?" One at a time, the words come out in a low whisper from his mouth.

"They don't know." It was a bad fall. "Your ribs are very tender, your bullet wounds are beginning to heal." He raises one hand to his face, which feels rocky, cratered. She tells him they had kept him in hospital, unconscious all the while, for a week. But the beds were needed for soldiers coming in from the battlefields, and the doctors had argued that he was on his way to recovery. He was moved to Grace Blackwell's to get stronger before the ship's departure. "You would still have been there but your father wanted you back home with the family as soon as possible."

HE BECOMES AWARE of time passing, of liquids and food being coaxed into his mouth, of the burn on his cracked lips. He knows it is day when the sun begins to searchlight the mouse-grey carpet in lemon-yellow egg shapes, nightfall when his nurse, exhausted by being on her feet all day, lets the day out with a long sigh and slides the cabin door open to go to her own room. Days pass.

SHE IS AS neat as a pin, and her chestnut locks, tied back into a ponytail, remind him of someone. He says little to her, working her out, her intentions towards him, whether she was a benevolent or intrusive influence, or if she had a plan. He observes her in silence. The golden sun eggs have crossed the floor and now lie at a slant across her dress. He watches them scatter as she moves. Cheap fabric, that cotton; thin, the sun seeps through it. There is a patch of sunlight as large as a dinner plate on her skirt, and he can see the outline of her stockinged legs through it. There are tinkling noises coming from the direction of the sink. He is aware of what she's doing. She's mixing his painkillers with water and will soon hold the steel glass against his lips, lowering it so each drop slides securely into his mouth and won't stain the sheets. Her fingers, touching his lips, smell faintly of a scent he knows. Then it flies into his vision like a butterfly from a bush.

He says, "I smell roses."

"Oh." She turns and gives him a wide-eyed look. "You scared me. I never know when you're awake or asleep."

"Is it roses?"

"Yes. From my mother's backyard in Glasgow. She sprinkles the dried petals in our clothes. I'm sorry if it offends you."

"No," he practically shouts. "I love roses." The effort makes him cough.

"Your voice is quite bright and lively today." She brings him some water. "You'll be delivering speeches soon!" He tries to laugh back but the sound is like a cracking pottery plate.

Roses, a scent from so far back he feels it was with him in his mother's womb. He would watch her as a boy pluck the trembling roses while they still had dew on them. "Watch, Shiv," she told him once. "You might need to make this someday." Dutiful boy that he was, he reached for paper and pen, and wrote her instructions down. "Fill one side of the alembic with water, not all the way to the top, and put in rose petals. Attach it to its counterpart, which should be clean and empty, and seal the top with a paste of flour and water. Set the alembic over a coal- or wood-burning brazier. Drop by drop the water will drip into the attached empty receptacle. Remove the flour paste only when all the water has steamed and condensed, and fill sterilized glass bottles with the cooled rose water." This intensely fragrant rose water she sprayed onto their sheets and, like Mairi's mother, on their clothes and socks, so he always walked around in a cloud of rose scent and smelled like a girl. You, too, suffered this as a child, he wanted to tell Mairi, but he couldn't say it, couldn't establish that kind of intimacy with her. He needed silence, and he needed his memories; this spirited nurse had no place in his world.

He asks, "Why did you undertake this voyage?"

She's startled, jerks her head around to look at him.

He says, "It's a long way."

"There's only so much learning in a place you've known since you were born."

"What about your family?"

"I've got me old mum, that's all. She'll be all right, with the neighbours and the church. There's no one else." A pained expression crosses her face for a moment, but he's not sure if he imagines it.

He stares at her. He knows better than to ask for more but her answer comforts him.

She says, "I was to tell you that your suits came up from London. Your friend, Miss Grace Blackwell, was anxious for you to know so you would not be disturbed on any account."

"Suits?" He tries to crack a smile. "I see I'll be using them a lot on board."

"I'll see what I can arrange with the purser," she says, giving him a playful smile.

BESPOKE SUITS MADE for London winters, and London gents. That first one. How could one forget it? From the start it was seen by his hosts that he lacked what the English called "proper clothing."

"You can't go around London in that," Millie Polak said, giving his tropical trousers a critical once-over.

Mr. Polak insisted he accompany the young lad to his tailors in Jermyn Street. "They'll get you kitted out soon enough," he said.

"No one goes to Jermyn Street anymore," Millie said. "It's too dear. It's the East End, that's where the good Jewish tailors are."

"Mrs. P, when I need your opinion on bespoke tailoring in London, I'll ask for it. In the meantime, Shiv's going to my tailor, and we're not discussing that further."

Jermyn Street. A brick and wood exterior with barrel-shaped windows supported a gleaming black wooden sign with lettering in gold that read "Bulstrode and Sons." A uniformed doorkeeper on the inside pushed the door open and ushered them in. Almost instantly, they were greeted by Mr. James Bulstrode himself, whose father had opened the original tailoring shop. Mr. Bulstrode exchanged some pleasantries with Mr. Polak, who turned to Shiv and introduced him. "He's going to be representing the best of Britain as a barrister, so nothing Continental, please."

Mr. Bulstrode led them both to the cutter's room at the back of the shop. The walls were lined with newspaper clippings of strapping young English lads in their bespoke suits, made in these very back rooms no doubt. "Mr. Rayner is the envy of every suit maker in London. You're in the best hands." He left them to it.

Mr. Rayner held out his hand and greeted them both. Shiv felt like a mannequin when Mr. Rayner turned to look at him. His critical eyes scrutinized his frame; his hands pushing his shoulders back a bit as if judging how a certain tuck would fix the look. Shiv saw his body through the suit cutter's eyes: slight frame, lean body. A slight stoop.

"A suit for important social occasions, I take it?"

"Yes, exactly. But classically British, as you make them," Mr. Polak said.

So began Shiv's education in the art of the English suit and how to wear it. Mr. Rayner said, "There's three things to our suits—the cut, the fit, and the drape. And for this, we'll do three fittings—the first, a rough one made of scrap bits of cloth for the cut; the second, to ascertain the fit; and the third, for a clean, elegant drape. The look in fashion now is militaristic—broad shoulders, narrowing to a tapered waist. Think of Edward VII. Unpadded wide shoulders, higher armholes. We're as different from the Italians as can be."

His heart raced with excitement as Mr. Rayner measured him, turning him around, jotting down numbers on a pad, talking all the while of the "new look" and what "the most fashionable men in Piccadilly" were wearing. "For a suit to fit perfectly, the measurements must be precise," Mr. Rayner said, holding a device to Shiv's shoulder. "This is for the slope, so we know how much padding is needed. And this"—holding a tape measure down his back—"is to know the tilt of your back, which gives us the length of the jacket." He wrote things down and proceeded to what he called the "back rise," and then the inside leg for trouser length. "A poorly cuffed trouser can instantly destroy your look. And now the button. Where should it be placed ideally to allow your jacket some give for movement and yet look perfect on you at all times? Too high, and it will look ludicrous. Too low, and it will seem cumbersome, and gap at the chest. You want a clean, seamless look, a well-tailored jacket."

Soon difficulties emerged. "Had a colonial here the other day, a rajah, I believe. The thing with you lot—orientals, I mean—is you're too thin, your frames are as slight as women's. Not really made for suits, to be honest. It's hard to get the drape right." Shiv considered Mr. Rayner's words—were they thinly veiled criticism or did they represent an honest assessment? It was impossible to tell. Besides, this was the body he had. All right, World's Number One Suit Cutter, show me what you've got, he wanted to say. Anyone can clothe perfection. Let's see how you do with the imperfect ones.

"See this?" Mr. Rayner pointed with a ruler at the slight stoop in Shiv's back and turned to Mr. Polak. "When you're cutting a suit, that's trouble."

"Mr. Rayner, what they lack in physique they make up for in

brain power," Mr. Polak said. "I'll have you know this is one of the smartest young men you'll have the privilege of meeting. In any case, you've sized everyone, haven't you? You shouldn't have any difficulty with this one." That shut him up.

Shiv left Bulstrode's establishment feeling confident he'd have the suit of his dreams before long. By the second fitting, a week later, the fit was gauged near perfect. And by the time of his third fitting, Mr. Rayner's keen eye and intimate knowledge of his body's geography had made all the necessary alterations. That slight protrusion below the upper left shoulder that caused his stoop—a deformity from birth—had been noted; the extra material was worked in so the drape was secured. Long stitches with a bit of give, Mr. Rayner explained. "That's what makes it possible for the suit to move with you so you're always comfortable. The key to elegance is comfort. If you're uncomfortable, it'll show in your walk and gait." The jacket was single-breasted and two-buttoned, with a peak lapel. The legs of the high-waisted, wide-cuffed trousers had a sharp pressed pleat running down the front, and another, smaller pleat closer to the navel. The navy suit fitted him like a glove. When Shiv looked in the long mirror, he stared at himself, disbelieving and enchanted. Mr. Polak applauded both Mr. Rayner and him. "Well done, Mr. Rayner! You've done it again!" He turned to Shiv. "You're already a Mayfair dandy, my boy. Can hardly recognize you."

Payment was due in full after the third fitting. Savile Row and Jermyn Street usually worked on credit. That tradition had clearly been waived in his case. Cash only, please, Mr. Bulstrode explained. "I'm terribly sorry, sir. Overseas gentlemen aren't offered credit until we get to know them. We're not the only ones." He lowered his voice as he put his hand up theatrically to his mouth, and spoke to Mr. Polak. "There have been defaults, sir, you understand. Some of them aren't the gentlemen they appear to be." He removed his hand and addressed Shiv, who had heard every word, as intended. "It's standard on the street, sir." Shiv forked over fifty pounds—"the finest wool herringbone on the market"—and was promised delivery the next day.

That evening, conscious of the vast sums of money that would be required to keep him in England, he asked Mr. Polak to give him a sense of what the next few years involved. "My father gave me a general idea, but I would be much obliged to you, sir, if you could give me an outline of the years until I am called to the bar. And potential expenses."

Mr. Polak gave him a surprised look. "Ah, I see you haven't been properly initiated. Well, sit down, son, and let me put it all in context. First, a bit of history you may not know. It's a glorious one, beginning with the constant battle between the Crown and the Knights Templar, who had occupancy rights of the Temple precincts. They built that magnificent church—the Temple Church, as it's known. The Inns of Court began in 1215, when a tyrannical king, King John, agreed to the central condition of the Magna Carta—to obey the law. All free men were guaranteed basic rights, and liberty. No one was above the law—not even kings and queens. After several revisions, and a papal annulment, it was finally adopted as the principal charter of rights in England. In 1292, Edward I commanded the Chief Justice of the Court to select apprentices from every county to form a court. The Inns of Court began housing learners, who were trained to become advocates of the law."

"It's quite a history, sir."

"Yes. It is the stuff of legend. Many of England's greatest figures—in science, in history, in literature, in theology—have been guests of the Inns. Shakespeare presented his *Twelfth Night* in the hall at Middle Temple in 1602. Henry Fielding, Wilkie Collins, John Donne, to name but a few, studied there. By 1846, after some amendments and changes, we got the King's Counsel. These are very senior barristers who have applied to take the silk—from the silk gowns they wear after they have been appointed to the king's bench. It isn't just about fabrics—it indicates that they are the highest authorities in the land where the law is concerned. Today, we have the advocate and the counsel, barristers, solicitors. Barristers, qualified students who are called to the bar, hence barrister, know the law and how it is practiced in the courts. They are advocates—pleaders, like your father—and are hired by solicitors to guide their clients' cases in court. That's the background, in a nutshell."

Mr. Polak told him that his call night—when he would be called to the bar—would be the most thrilling night of his life. It would come at the end of three years, after successfully passing the end-of-term exams. "There are three terms in a year—during which, in addition to your studies, you will attend court sessions in the High Courts of Justice just across from the Inns in the Strand to see how your learning works in practice. You will study a range of subjects, such as Roman law, constitutional law (English and colonial), criminal law and procedure, legal history, real property and conveyancing, common law, equity civil procedure. And remember, you must always be seen as a barrister, even before you are called to the bar."

Shiv nodded. "I understand, sir." But he didn't. To be seen as a barrister. How would he do that? His brown skin would announce him before he could. Even as he said the words, he saw the hurdles piling up. To be seen: what did that look like?

Mr. Polak said that the smart would-be barrister started picking things up from day one—the undercurrents were as important as what was on the surface. "It's grooming, cultivating know-how," he said. "Learn to interpret signs, impressions, the looks on people's faces. Know what can be useful to you as a barrister." And then "there are the fees, which have to be paid at the beginning, with provision made for 'commons' and term fees, admission fees, and caution money—all in all, about a hundred and fifty pounds sterling."

Caution money? His heart sank as he heard the sums involved.

His entire family could live off half that money for a year. "One of
the most important requirements is that you fulfill your quota of a
hundred dinners in the dining hall—at least, and at the very minimum, seventy-two in total. You'd have to be a hermit to shirk that
obligation. It is expected that every student will look forward eagerly
to every dinner he eats in the dining hall. This is what makes the
British system so different from anywhere else. While you drink
wine and break bread with others in that hall, lifelong friendships
are formed and cemented, and these friendships are what you come
to rely on for the rest of your working life. You will be like light-
houses to one another in the stormy seas of life."

"And then, after three years of exams, and a hundred dinners,
and frequent trips to the Courts, and attending lectures, and passing
the exams, I will be deemed fit to be called to the bar?"

"Yes. You will be allowed to purchase your wig, your gown—
these are not cheap, but we will face that later. You will be a gentleman of the King's Court. You will be an advocate, fit to present cases
to a judge. You will then begin pupillage at the chambers of a member of the bar. Pupillage lasts twelve to eighteen months. There is a
fee involved there, too—it's a hundred guineas. But we can discuss
all that a bit later. Call night is what you're working towards now."

"And if, just supposing, of course, if I don't make it?" How low
would he have to go if that happened?

"You will not fail. It is a joyful thing to me even now to see a fine
young man inducted into our profession. I remember my call night
clearly. It would not be stretching it to say that wives and girlfriends
may leave, children will go their own way once they're grown, but
your fellow barristers are your companions for life."


THE SUIT WAS only the first step, he learnt, as they were back in
Jermyn Street soon after the suit was delivered, this time on an expedition to Turnbull and Asser for a shirt. "You should get three. Two

for regular circulation, one a spare for those times when a spanking new look is called for," Mr. Polak advised. Shiv was fitted by a Mr. James Poole, who said, "Blue's his colour, no question about it."

Mr. Polak agreed. "I'd do one of the royal and two of the sky blue. And cuffs. Three buttons."

Shiv's compliance wasn't even necessary. He handed over the guineas Mr. Poole asked for—seven in all. And he was nowhere near done yet.


Lock and Co., world-famous hatters from time immemorial. Even his father had a hat from Lock and Co., tucked away in its white box with black Victorian script on the top shelf of his closet. His father kept his for special occasions—when the British commissioner came calling, or when he was summoned to Karachi for meetings with fellow judges. Shiv's would have to be used regularly, perhaps daily. He hated hats, felt suffocated in them. But when he expressed this to Mr. Polak, his mentor simply said, "You'll have to grin and bear it, old chap. Hang on to your hat! Can't be without one."

There was a story to everything. Here was the one about the hat. "An ancestor of the Lock family was the inspiration for Lewis Carroll's Mad Hatter. The mercury used in hat-making drove some of the cutters and fitters literally mad—ah, here we are." Mr. Polak pushed open the door. A tinkling bell announced their arrival. Shiv followed him in. After some discussion about a possible silk hat, for which Shiv subjected his head to a conformateur, a machine used to measure head sizes, Mr. Polak decided that a regular man-about-town hat would be more suitable for Shiv's purposes. A classic Lock bowler in navy felt with a narrow matching band was chosen, and after some steaming and adjustments, it fitted his head perfectly.

"My gift to you, son. Wear it well, and hang on to it when the wind blows!"

Shiv adjusted his pace to Mr. Polak's as they stepped out again. His feet were longing to run, to take in everything. The rush of the streets, the diverse human crowds that filled them, their faces speaking of their ancestral origins—Teutonic, Slavic, Gallic, Sephardic, Arabic, Mediterranean, Catalonian, Mongolian, Moorish; the narrow byways, leafy lanes, and wide avenues; the sounds—from the foghorns on the Thames to the church bells that pealed day and night; the smells—engine oil, gas fumes, wood fires, bread baking, meats roasting; the sharp scents of dried mint, heather, and lavender sold by young girls carrying baskets; the street vendors, organ grinders, and banjo players. Here was the human spirit in all its forms. Thronging and moving around him in an overpowering wave, it resembled nothing he had ever seen. In Karachi, you saw large crowds and sensational specimens of humanity—fire-eaters, snake charmers, skinny little children balancing on thin poles held high by men—but it was the diversity of these London faces that enthralled him. They seemed to be from every corner of the globe.

"And now there's the scent—it tells people immediately what sort of man you are," Mr. Polak said. "We're going in here," he said, slowing down.

A scent? So much rode on a scent? Mr. Polak stopped before a quaint shop, its leaded glass windows showcasing antique perfume bottles from around the world. A ruby-coloured cut-glass one made him recall his mother's dressing table, where he had often played as a child, spreading her crimson lipstick on his lips and sprinkling her scent all over his clothes. The bevelled glass edges of the oval swing mirrors, which showed different sides of his painted little face, glittered in the sunny room. He pursed his red lips, then spread them wide as she did, loving the way the paint transformed him—not boy, not girl, maybe both.

Mr. Polak pushed the door open to a heavenly fragrant cloud. "Come on, my boy." Mr. Jeavons, the manager and part owner of the shop, began a long discussion about scent, and why what you wore said so much about you. He spread his hands elegantly as he spoke, long speaking hands like a ballerina's. "Scents are naughty and nice; clean and dirty; austere, astringent, calming, exciting, sultry, exotic—as pure as lily of the valley or as heady and musky as peony in full bloom. A scent can be as sharp and piercing as an orange or as creamy as rose; as brisk and bracing as fern, as smoky and sweet as tonka bean, or as mystical as sandalwood and oud. What do you prefer, young man?" he said, turning to Shiv.

Mr. Polak cut in. "He is on his way to becoming a barrister, a responsible member of the judiciary in England, a member of the Commonwealth, and a representative of our sovereign laws and government. He must always come across as reliable, sincere . . . stable, and show indubitable integrity. Now, Mr. Jeavons, what do you have that represents the best of British?"

Mr. Jeavons laughed. "That's a tall order, sir. But our English Fern fits the description perfectly. It is dependable, conveys sincerity, and has that clean quality of assurance, while bringing home the scent of the English countryside." He picked up a glass dropper and put some drops on a cotton-wool ball. "Would you care to have a sniff, sir?" he asked Shiv.

Shiv held the ball to his nostrils. It was a nice understated scent—woodsy and clean. Mr. Polak smelt it and said, "I prefer Blenheim Bouquet myself, but it's the scent of an older, established man."

Shiv saw a bottle labelled Douro. "Might I have a sniff of that, Mr. Jeavons?" he asked.

"Certainly, sir. One of our finest. But that"—he picked up the bottle and pulled out the glass stopper—"is not what I would call a"— he turned to Mr. Polak—"a 'stable' scent you said, sir?" A couple of quick sniffs later, Mr. Jeavons said, "Hmmm. No use describing it, you should smell it yourself." He held the stopper under Shiv's nose.

Nagpur oranges and blossoms, Quetta lemons, sandalwood from Mysore burning in incense jars throughout the house in Hyderabad Sind—the familiar smells of home shot out from the bottle. He couldn't stop sniffing the scent, each inhale more seductive than the last. Who cared about rock-solid stability when you had this, this teasing fragrance of wet earth and orange flower, of refreshing citrus and lemon peel, of heady musk and sandalwood. Why would he settle for tart limes and moody ferns that needed coaxing to reveal their scent when his heart cried, Be bold, declare yourself, embrace desire. He said, "This."

"What is it?" Mr. Polak said, drawing closer to take a sniff. He spritzed a bit on the back of his hand and held it to his nose. "Oh, this won't do at all," he said. "This is a woman's scent."

"Oh no, begging your pardon, sir, not at all," Mr. Jeavons said. "It is most certainly male. It is for the male who wants to embrace the feminine within. It takes its inspiration from Portugal—where the scents of the East are appreciated more than they are here. It's a growing trend here in Britain, too, now. We have tried to serve it."

"Mr. Jeavons, if you were looking for a barrister to represent your best interests, would you pick one, however brilliant he might be, who smelt like this?" Mr. Polak was frowning and rubbing the back of his hand with a large white handkerchief he pulled out of his waistcoat.

As Mr. Jeavons considered the question, his face fell. "Well, not exactly, sir, but this scent was not created to—"

"Well, that's my point. A barrister in court is all spit and polish, and is expected to exude a robust confidence." Mr. Polak gave Mr. Jeavons a stern look, expecting him to play along with him.

"I want this," Shiv said. "This is the scent I will wear." Mr. Polak turned to look at him, as if expecting him to retreat from a foolhardy position. "No, this is the one." He pulled in the muscles in his face, tightening it to confirm his decision.

"Wrong choice," Mr. Polak finally said. "Ill advised. But so be it." For the first time in the entire shopping spree, Shiv felt content.

———

THEN THE SHOES—brogue with a classic Oxford toe—from John Lobb. The silk socks and kid gloves came from Harrods. And last but not least, Mr. Polak found an ebony-handled umbrella made by Fox and Sons, a custom order placed by a no-show and therefore a bargain waiting to be had. When Mr. Polak handed the umbrella over, he said, "This is a gift from Millie. She noticed your flimsy one. Here it is, my boy. On Friday, we dine in the Middle Temple Hall, your first!"

THE FOLLOWING DAY brought his first experience of Sundays at the Polaks', a day that became a marker for them every week, resetting their clocks with its regularity, its predictable pleasures. These Sundays came to define Shiv's entire experience of living with them. Mr. Polak, eager to show him London on its day of rest, insisted on taking him to Hyde Park, where they walked briskly for an hour and a half, stopping only to look at the ducks swimming in the water in spring, and the frost crimping the water's edges in winter. Come rain or shine, blustery winds or chilling rain, the ritual of walking through the park held.

As soon as Mr. Polak turned the key in the lock and pushed the front door open, they were greeted with the scents of garlic and rosemary in the lamb or chicken and potatoes roasting in the oven. Steam rushed to their faces as cold met warmth and they unlaced their walking shoes. Millie made her grandmother's ginger shortbread and laid the table with her finest cutlery and crockery. The old silver sat on a crocheted tablecloth and gleamed softly beside their plates. Glasses sparkled and candles dripped wax from silver candlesticks. A silver tray containing prettily arranged triangles of ginger shortbread on lace doilies breathed spice scents into the air. "My trousseau when I married him—we may as well use it!" she said. There in the soft shine of a late Sunday afternoon, they shared the week's woes and lighter moments.

Gandhi's presence lingered over their table; and sometimes, Mr. Polak let down his guard a little about his friend and mentor, expressing fears for Gandhi's life. "It's not far-fetched—Hindu extremists are already talking assassination. Gandhi lacks that crucial ability in a leader—the talent for reading a room correctly. If you're speaking to a group of Hindu extremists, and you're trying to convince them that the only way forward is for them to join your movement, you don't do it by insisting on the one thing that is anathema to them—caste equality. You know that's a red rag to a bull. He flashes it constantly and the bulls react. Many Indians think that is what is so charming about Gandhi—his lack of political know-how—and they say that is precisely what makes him such an effective politician. They may be right. We are redefining the essential qualities of leadership in our time." And on Ramsay MacDonald, then prime minister: "Speaks from both sides of his mouth. Funny how I thought he was the perfect man to lead Britain at this time. I was so wrong." *Wrong*! Mr. Polak! Shiv's own father would never have voiced such an admission. It took humility to say it, and the willingness to risk being taken down a notch or two. His father, as a key leader of his community, could never risk it.

*Read a room correctly*. The phrase stayed with Shiv.

Once Millie happened to mention that she had just finished reading a book Virginia Woolf had sent her—a book by Sigmund Freud. "Why on earth did she send you that? Isn't he some sort of psychologist, doctor crank?" Mr. Polak asked.

"I had mentioned to her that Gandhi's insistence on self-denial was a little disturbing. . . . He spoke of it often, and it always seemed a little unnatural to me."

Polak shook his head. "And?"—Mr. Polak quizzed Millie. "What did you think of this Dr. Freud?"

"He is a very brave man, for the things he says would constitute blasphemy in some circles. But he says we must face our unnatural impulses, however distasteful they may seem, and try to understand

them. He says Oedipus put out his eyes when he realized his children were the offspring of his marriage to his own mother. But that
act, Dr. Freud claims, is a manifestation of his belief that boys are
attracted to their mothers, daughters to their fathers, and that stamping out that desire for the forbidden from ourselves as we grow takes
its toll. We must, of course, but it isn't easy." She heaved a sigh. "This
isn't bathtub reading. But I was curious and I fear this Dr. Freud is
right—that we must look at things that disturb us. Gandhi deludes
himself into thinking desire can be overcome so easily."

Shiv stared at Millie, astonished by her understanding of his
main conflict with Gandhi and his mission. "We have to understand
what we're fighting," she said. "Whether it's in us or around us."

After dinner, the Polaks listened to Verdi or Mozart, and often to
Mr. Polak's favourite composer, Beethoven. In the mellow lamplight
of the room, faded carpets showed their colours, and Shiv felt the
comforts of a family life he had never had back home. Whatever ir-
ritations life might have had earlier in the week, it rounded itself in
these late Sunday afternoons to please. He felt he could say anything
to them, and not be misunderstood. As time went on, Shiv began to
rely on their Sunday dinners as much as his hosts did.

Mr. Polak led the way in to the Middle Temple Hall like a king's vi-
zier with the keys to the kingdom. His domain, and he took great
pride in showing it off to a young hopeful law student from the colonies. His mentor was still in awe of it all himself, Shiv realized, still
so impressed. The presence of the English court was everywhere—in
the pomp and table dressings, in the presentation of silverware and
crystal and the tailored finery. The long, white-clothed tables were
set with cut crystal goblets and ornate cutlery; table lamps and candles in tall silver holders cast a soft gleam, lighting up the dourest
features. Sunken cheeks shone and became shapely; dulled eyes ac-

quired brilliance when caught in the fire between glass and glowing candle. Large silver bowls containing apples, pears, and grapes were placed at even distances, four to a table, and discreet waiters bent over glasses pouring wine. Rose-coloured electric lights gleamed from the walls on either side. The intricately carved oak double hammer-beam roof extended inwards from the side walls and through its carved arms could be seen the majestic armorial window. The evening light broke into diamond shapes as it flashed through the vivid panes of glass. Beauty glittered here as he had never seen it before. Ritual, deeply allied to royalty, to court protocol, to the pageantry of the English church, was in full display here. India had lost its aristocracy—most of them had turned to the British for protection, losing their sovereignty and their fortunes in the process. The formal aspect of ritual, as rooted in pomp and circumstance, had gone, had left public life in India.

The benchers, leading barristers, proceeded to the high table. Everyone stood and fell silent as the head bencher began the grace:

*Benedic, Domine, nos et dona tua*
*Quae de largitate tua sumus sumpturi*
*Et concede, ut illis salubriter nutriti*
*Tibi debitum obsequium praestare valeamus*
*Per Christum Dominum nostrum.*

*Bless, O Lord, us and your gifts, which from your*
*largesse we are about to receive, and grant that,*
*nourished by them, we may obey you through*
*Christ our Lord.*

The collective noise of chairs being pushed back, the chorus of rising voices that rose from tables as everyone sat down. "You're looking splendid, young man," Mr. Polak said. Shiv was wearing Mr. Rayner's blue suit with its perfect drape and cut. "But I see that you did put on some of that Portuguese stuff! It's really not the right scent, you know. Continental. Puts you in a different category."

"I will remember not to use it at Temple dinners the next time," Shiv assured him. Around him, he heard English laughter—mild titters and half-suppressed guffaws. Animated voices engaged in witty banter mingled with the aromas of wine—a partnership he would meet over and over again across English tables, perhaps less grand than this one, but no less well endowed. As Shiv watched the waiters coming in with trays of food and placing them in front of the diners, he noticed some men dressed far more formally than others. No one was talking to them. "Why are people in black tie?"

"Probably ignorance. This is not a black-tie dinner."

Black tie. Another costume for preening purposes, another fifty or a hundred pounds down a snooty tailor's throat. He practically retched as a bowl of soup was set in front of him.

Without much fanfare, he had made peace with his vegetables-fish-fruit upbringing, and starting that first morning at the Polaks', he had eaten whatever they put before him for breakfast—kippers, eggs, toast, bacon, and jam. The alien tastes and textures nauseated him in the beginning, but the lion roars of his stomach were louder than his qualms. Even so, the spring-green watercress soup steaming in front of him was still the most inviting thing in the world. While the waiters went round the long table to serve everyone, Shiv watched his bowl of soup lose steam. After everyone had been served, he finally raised a spoonful to his lips—the soup was lukewarm and thick, unappetizing. Shiv turned to look at the man sitting next to him, who immediately held out his hand. "I'm Michael Butler, new here."

"I am as well," he answered, shaking it. "Shiv Advani. Pleased to meet you."

In observance of fish on Fridays, there was a fillet of Dover sole with lemon butter for the next course, followed by rhubarb tart, and bread and cheese, and accompanied all the while by chatter and endless glasses of wine. "Go on, my boy," Mr. Polak said when the butler came round with the wine, "top up. Everyone lets go a little at these dinners!" Obligingly, Shiv gave the butler a nod, and the glass was elegantly refilled.

The fish was dry. "Unless it's breaded or fried in deep batter, the British aren't very good with fish," Michael said, looking at the hardened interior of the fillet. "They overcook it. The Italians, Portuguese, French revere fish—lightly seasoned, moist."

"We revere it in India, too. Melts in the mouth the way we cook it. And it's fragrant."

Michael, the son of a Middle Templar, was from New York, and had just graduated from Harvard. They talked about New York and its winters—"They'll freeze your nose off, it's that bitter"—his horse Charlie and his rides through Central Park every morning; his brother, Tim, who was a sculptor. "So where's your home?" he asked. Shiv told Michael—"call me Mike"—about summers in Hyderabad Sind, and his best friend, Morty Saxena, who was now at Oxford; he also, shyly, told him he was married and was to become a father fairly soon. "You don't say!" Mike said. "You must miss your wife terribly." Shiv smiled at him. He had been so preoccupied with preparing for his entrance that evening he hadn't thought of her even once in the past week. He liked Mike immediately—his easy ways, his unaffected smile, his lack of formality. They had no history and no freight between them. They were free to take each other as they were.

They all rose to their feet as the senior bencher said the second grace. "*Benedicto Benedicatur.*" *Let praise be given to the blessed one.* People began rising from the tables and saying their goodbyes.

"Ninety-nine left to go," Mike said, looking around the hall with an ironic smile. "One's enough, don't you think?"

"It seems you can get away with seventy-two," he said.

"Ah, but that would not win you any favours. A hundred is the silent rule, it seems."

"We'll survive it," Shiv said.

"We will!" Mike laughed. "We'll have to. I've got to get going. See you soon!"


RELEASED FROM THEIR designated seats at the table, people got up and mingled with one another over port or wine. Endless introductions followed. Mr. Polak, who knew everyone, took him around and introduced him to his fellow barristers. "Not going to follow in his countryman's footsteps, I hope!" a jowly senior barrister said. Shiv supposed the man meant Gandhi. Conversation and inquiries about India came thick and fast. Gandhi was clearly on everyone's minds. "What's that Gandhi chappie doing these days? They haven't let him out of prison, have they?" He smiled and said, "I haven't heard." Someone else said, "Shame, really. What happened to the man? To think he was trained right here, in these precincts, and attended dinner here, in this hall, like us." Another person said, "A wrecking ball, if I ever saw one." Expecting Mr. Polak to field that one, Shiv stayed silent. To his surprise, Mr. Polak spoke only to announce their departure. He had said scarcely anything else, other than to state that his protégé was most certainly going to surprise them all.


MILLIE WAS WAITING for them when they got home. "Thought you'd be in bed by now, Mrs. P!" Mr. Polak called down the hall corridor as he took off his coat.

"I couldn't. How did it go?"

"Splendidly. He's one of us already!"

"Congratulations on your first Temple dinner, Shiv," Millie said, as they went into the drawing room. "You're following nicely in the steps of a former Templar, Gandhi himself." So much was riding on that first dinner, Shiv realized, looking at Millie's flushed face. He had been vetted.

Mr. Polak was in a reflective mood. "Your father came to see us in Johannesburg in 1912, the year you were born. We became very fond of him. Incidentally, Bapu's middle son was also called Ramdas. I never asked him whether he was named after your father. Bapu used to say, 'Ramdas is the salt of the earth. Fearless, bold, principled—he is a defender of the truth. Among my close circle of friends, it is Ramdas I turn to for good counsel.' He knew how your father defended journalists jailed for speaking the truth despite pressure from the British government, that he worked pro bono. 'That is the kind of man he is,' he told us. I have said it often enough, you come from good stock. Your father is highly esteemed by both Gandhi and me."

"I remember the affection with which my father regarded you, sir. Your trip to see us in Hyderabad was one of the highlights of my childhood."

"'I want to do everything I can for my country,' you told me. 'I want to become a lawyer like you and Papa.' You were nine then. And here we are!"

"Why were you in South Africa, sir?"

"Gandhi decided to try his luck in Johannesburg after being called to the bar in England, and I was articled to him. He asked me to join him. We set up shop together to protect the Asian community there from persecution under apartheid. We lived together, the Gandhis and us, and became one large family."

"How, under apartheid, did you all live together like that?"

"It's strange, isn't it? I, a Polish-English Jew; my wife, a Scottish Christian woman; the Gandhis, a young Gujarati family. Such different backgrounds, but we got on well. He was best man at our wedding. We were defiant, Millie and I, and the Gandhis became attached to us. He picked me, you know. 'You're my man,' he would say to me."

"He adored our firstborn, Waldo, and often held him in his arms, crooning and singing softly to him," Millie said.

"Waldo?"

"Yes, he died soon after we moved back to England in 1917."

"I am so sorry. How did he die?"

Millie sighed. "Not now, dear. I am in Johannesburg tonight, watching the fireflies flickering in the trees. The Gandhis, our friends, our life there."

"Why did you leave?" Shiv asked.

"We had always planned to come back to England. We decided on 1914 but by then, Gandhi had decided to return to India because he felt the war for Indian independence was waiting to be fought. He asked us to stay a little longer so Henry could look after the Indian community in Johannesburg. So many had been imprisoned under apartheid's worst excesses. We left for England three years later," Millie said.

"Gandhi is a complicated being," Mr. Polak said. "It took a while to convince him that the struggle for equality being fought by the blacks and the Indians was the same struggle—both groups were battling oppression. And when Hindu scriptures became part of his political message—well, you can see how that sat with me. But I have always had the greatest respect for him. He is a genius—no one should doubt that or underestimate its implications. The British in India fear him. Rightly so."

"Henry has never stopped working for Indian independence, you know," Millie said. "He edited a journal called *Indian Opinion* that came out of Durban with Gandhi. When the legal work intensified, a different editor was hired. Now Henry fights for India through his engagement with Parliament. It's his dream—our dream—too."

"Have you heard of Leonard Woolf, of the Hogarth Press?" Mr. Polak asked. When Shiv answered that he knew the press published some of the finest literature in the world, Mr. Polak said, "That they do. They are decidedly anti-colonialist. We—myself, Leonard Woolf, Major Graham Pole, George Garratt, and Sir John Maynard, as members of the Joint Parliamentary Committee on Indian Reforms—continue to send, as we have since 1923, our reports and recommendations on India to our government. Which, thankfully, is Labour now. Woolf's a good friend of mine. You must meet him."

"Do they even read your reports?" Millie asked.

"They do, surprisingly. The P.M. himself often asks us for clarification."

Mr. Polak turned to Shiv. "That senior bencher tonight, who called Gandhi a wrecking ball?"

"Yes?"

"Your first lesson in English diplomacy. Never court controversy. No one could have won against that sort of intractability. He wasn't inviting discussion, simply making a statement he wholly believed in. Only a fool would try to counteract it. I let it go, which was the right thing to do."

He nodded. "Understood, sir."

Millie, with a tender look on her face, said, "We have lost one son, but we have gained another. I was just telling Henry that the other day, wasn't I, dear?"

"Yes, God-sent, you said."

"No, it's the other way round," Shiv said. "The God-sent part is the two of you, opening up your doors to a relative stranger. I'm the lucky one!"


LATER, HE SAT down at the small desk in his room and pulled out the pad of airmail paper from the drawer. His mind went back to that moment at the docks when Seher placed her hand over her stomach and conveyed that she was pregnant to him. How his heart had lurched. He was going to be a father but he would not be there for his child's birth.

The glow of pregnancy was in her face; her eyes sparkled. How beautiful she had seemed to him then. She knew now that he would come back. His mother was right. Men come back for their children and their wives if not for their elderly parents. He hadn't wanted to leave. He wanted to see their baby being born, to be always by her side.

My dear Seher,

It has been over two months since I have written to you. I am very sorry for my silence. How are you? How is our baby? I hope you aren't experiencing too much discomfort. You are now in your fourth month. I am told it gets easier as time goes on. I'm sure my mother is taking good care of you.

I have settled in with the Polaks, who couldn't be nicer— they have already claimed me as their own. If it were not for them, I would languish in this cold, hard city. Their home is a sanctuary. They lived with the Gandhis in Johannesburg. Though thoroughly English in their ways, I feel that in their sympathies and in their hospitality, they are Indian, too.

I miss you all very much. I will write again as soon as there is more to report. I am well and happy. There is no need to concern yourself about anything. Please write and let me know how you all are. I worry about you all the time and my thoughts are with you all.

Your loving husband,
Shiv

He sealed the letter, brushed his teeth, and got into bed. Stretching his feet to find warmth against a hot water bottle at the end of the bed, Shiv thought a bright star had shone on him when the Polaks had taken him in. He would do everything in his power to honour their trust.

———

IT TOOK A few months to hear from them back in Hyderabad Sind but when the letter came, it brought good news. His son had been born on 10 August, 1931. "He is a bonny boy," his mother wrote. "Seher had already decided to name him Sher. She said he looks like he's going to be a king, a lion, a leader of men. I am convinced he knows something none of us do because when he hears music, he stops crying and screws up his face, listening, listening. He is a dear boy. We are all in love with him. Seher says she cannot write as she is so busy with Sher, but she asked me to send her love." His heart swelled with pride. Sher: she had chosen well, his intelligent wife. Lion, after the mouth of the river Indus. Shiv. Sher. Seher. There was poetry and rhythm in the union of their names. He remembered the light in his wife's eyes when they said goodbye. She would be waiting for him and he would make it up to them both for all his years of absence by loving them both as deeply as they deserved. In the meantime, he would fight here to make sure his son inherited a better world, a world without fear and the threat of violence.

Someday, he thought, as his eyes closed. He smelt the almond cream Seher used on her face every night, a bitter, off-putting scent that he hated. It had the effect on him it had always had—of bringing on sleep.

## *The Empress of Scotland*, June 1941

At noon every day, she had warned him, the klaxons would sound off, loudly, for the lifeboat drill. "The captain says you can stay here, but I'll have to wear my life jacket and run up to the deck to stand ready with the others to board the life rafts." He waits every day to see her suddenly stop whatever she's doing and grab her life jacket. Her face goes suddenly alert, and she gives him a quick look, before rushing out of the cabin.

She's back, he realizes, her tinkling laugh outside the cabin door. He hears a male laugh. It's the man he has heard in his cabin before. His accent is odd—he can't quite place it. The man says, "Let me know when you want to escape again. Quiet seas for now and good for taking a turn up on the deck."

"I'd like to take him up there when he's a bit better," she tells him. "He must get some exercise." He notes her concerned tone. How badly wounded was he?

"When we're in warmer waters, we can take him up every day."

"You're a comfort to me, Will."

"At your service, Miss Mairi." Their voices are spirited, eager.

She enters the cabin and comes to his bedside; her face is flushed. "Hungry?"

"No. Just water."

She brings him a glass, puts it to his lips. He sips it slowly, feels the liquid dribble down his chin. Drop by drop he drains the glass. She wipes his chin with a cloth. "My family in India knows what has happened?"

She gives him a puzzled look. "I expect they do. Miss Blackwell said they wanted you back and you had no family in England. Your father made all the arrangements with Miss Blackwell. 'No place for a sick man far from home,' she said to me."

Ah, Grace. He could imagine her urgent trunk call to his parents. She had boosted his career as a political activist. "You're exactly what Gandhi needs in England now. A smart qualified barrister leading the cause, a young man with principles and charm. You've got a strong lead role to play, Shiv. Focus. Don't let the opportunity slip you by." Convinced he could play John to Gandhi's Jesus, she found opportunities for him to speak everywhere—at the Oxford Union, where his speech gave further validation to the students' pledge that they would in no circumstances fight for king and country, and in Edinburgh's exclusive clubs.

One grueling mission involved eighteen cities, Manchester, Canterbury, Leeds, Bath, Oxford, Cambridge, so many others—where he and his aide, Sam, collapsed in their lodgings as soon as they got home after speaking to crowds all day. Sam handed out leaflets, he spoke. In Dublin, the Irish showed particular empathy when he said, "We will not have our destiny controlled by England. India was a free country once—it has never in its history set sail to conquer other shores. In fact, it has welcomed persecuted people from across the globe. Its demands for freedom will be met." They cheered and clapped and many showed interest in joining Gandhi's cause.

Up north, in Birmingham and Manchester, and Lancaster and Newcastle upon Tyne, manufacturing towns where factory and mill owners felt particularly threatened by the growing workforce out in the cotton and grain fields of the Punjab—"They want our jobs!"—

and a whole generation had come of age believing that the Indians were responsible for their lack of employment, he told them how England was fully in charge, and the workforce in India was being cultivated to fulfil Imperial ambitions at the cost of workers everywhere. "Greed is the enemy," he told them. British entrepreneurial investment in India and the demands of the global marketplace were controlling India's fate. "Britain wants to compete in sugar and cotton manufacture, revenue sources that are being dominated by the Americans. And to serve those ends, they have taken over our resources and bent them to their own ambitions. Our cultivation of our land became their cultivation of our land. Indians have had no say in their destiny.

"Last month, six farmers from the fields near our home made a pact to lose their lives together. Crippled by high interest rates on their loans, and taxes they could not pay after an extended season of drought, they decided to abandon life and forgo imprisonment for nonpayment of debts. The children left behind are being taken care of by our community for now. But what will happen to them in the future? A generation of penniless orphans is coming into being. Young boys beg in the streets to support their mothers and sisters. We are facing tragedy." He said Indians had no quarrel with the British mill workers or with the production of cotton in Britain. "But Indians have always made the finest cotton in the world. In the nineteenth century in France cotton was known only as *l'indienne*. The Indian. Artisans spin and weave our cotton, dye it, embroider it. It is creative work that has been done for centuries." He looked around the room. The unspoken struggle—big profits to benefit companies and corporations versus individual prosperity—was known to them all; the mill workers, miners, farmers, and factory workers in the audience showed they understood by their intent expressions and frequent nods. "Industrialization of cotton manufacture is killing our homespun industries. Our markets are flooded by cotton now manufactured in England and sent back to the colonies for sale. We must make cotton in India. It is our survival. Our people rely on its production as much as you do here." It was a story they all recognized through personal experience, through collective communal memory, and when they applauded him it was as much to join him in his resounding call to the British to quit India as it was for his personal charm and persuasiveness. "We know each other now," a mill owner in Birmingham told him.

"You're authentic," Grace Blackwell said. "That's why they believe you."

WHILE GANDHI'S MISSION to drive the British out of India had always inspired Shiv, the stringent requirements to become a Gandhian, a devotee in service to its highest ideals, often felt impossible to fulfil. When Gandhi arrived in England for the Round Table Conference in September 1931, he stayed with Muriel Lester in Kingsley Hall. One of Gandhi's closest friends in England, supporter of the cause for Indian independence, and self-styled "Ambassadress of Reconciliation," she and her sister Doris had put their not inconsiderable inheritance in building Kingsley Hall, Millie told him, to support East Enders and to create a social environment that would take care of them and their children while their husbands worked in mills and mines and builders' workshops all across London. "It is a remarkable institution," Millie Polak said to Shiv. "To create a place like that and then to live in it with the people you're serving is unheard of, a one of a kind. The class barriers in our society are less evident there. Although, of course, even with a place like that . . . Muriel, with her posh upper-class accent and upbringing—everyone knows where she belongs. Still, and because of that, the intermingling is extraordinary. You can imagine no other place has quite the same appeal for Mr. Gandhi."

Mr. Polak was incensed by Gandhi's decision to stay at Kingsley Hall. "There's nothing happening in the East End. It's all here, in

Westminster. This is where he needs to be. Muriel Lester should not have twisted his arm to stay with her at this time." But when Gandhi got in touch with him, Mr. Polak put aside his differences and invited the Mahatma to dinner. "It will give Millie and me great pleasure. And your protégé, too. He's been chomping at the bit to see you."

Mr. Polak had been formal, restrained, still upset that Gandhi had refused to take his advice about living closer to the circles of power in Whitehall and St. James. But as the evening unfolded, they rediscovered their old ties and affections, spoke about their time in Johannesburg. "You looked after the Asian community there so well after I returned to India in 1914," Gandhi said. "Thank you for taking over the reins after my departure."

"I've often wondered about that," Mr. Polak said. "If you and Kasturba had stayed in Johannesburg and Millie and I returned to England with our sons then, as planned, perhaps South Africa would be on its way to emancipation, India at least half a century behind where it is now! But you were so keen to return to India. And now look where we are!"

Shiv said, "Gandhiji, I'm often asked how Indians expect to win, without weapons, without international support, without the world's journalists pleading India's cause. How can you win? they ask."

Gandhi chuckled. "We have the weapons, Shiv. That's what you must tell them. We have the goodwill and full dedication of our people, an enormous voluntary army, and we have devoted followers all over the world. Look at Muriel Lester, at the Polaks, at Mr. Woolf and his press, at journalists in our country and all over the world writing or watching our struggle with great interest. And we have the greatest weapon of all. Nonviolence is strong enough to paralyse the mightiest government on earth."

Shiv drew in a sharp breath. What a message. What conviction. Gandhi said, "My boy, do you remember the ink-stained shawl you tried to protect me from?"

He had remembered. "It is my prized possession."

Gandhi smiled. He caressed his shawl with his hands. "I knew, when I gave it to you, that you would treasure it. And here is the one you gave me." With a shock, Shiv realized that the shawl Gandhi was wearing was the one he had hastily pulled out from his father's closet. "Yes, it's the same one," Gandhi said. "You told me then you wanted to be like me. I told you then you would have to give up desire. Tell me, are you still willing to give up desire?"

Shiv looked down at the floor. That evening, from the way Gandhi kept examining his face, he sensed desire was something you had to know. No one should be expected to give up something they didn't know, he reasoned. He felt he was inside an aviary that contained the most exquisite birds and he was being asked to clap his hands over his ears, and shut his eyes in order to avoid hearing their songs and seeing their radiant beauty. Was there a being on earth who would agree to such a pact? He had not signed up for monkhood yet. Gandhi did not make it a deal breaker. "We are expecting great things from you." He had reached out to touch Shiv's cheek, as if he were still a small boy, and smiled at him. Whenever Shiv touched the spot, it burned, and he saw that toothy smile in a wrinkled face. He was mesmerized by Gandhi from the very beginning, but felt acutely the danger of being Icarus to his brilliant sun.

# The Empress of Scotland, June 1941

A young lad called Jim comes to the cabin three times a day with meals from the kitchen. Soup, porridge, eggs. Nothing too challenging. Mairi eats quickly in her room then comes to feed Shiv. She's been feeding him for a few days now. His back hurts when he tries to sit up and his hands are too unsteady to guide food to his mouth. His lips are chapped and rough around the edges. Food burns and disappoints. He's had watery porridge and scrambled eggs made with powdered egg more times than he cares to remember. Varying degrees of sponge is how he thinks of it as he swallows it down. When he tries to feed himself, he catches the raw painful skin around his lips with his fork, and most of it, specially the hard scrambled eggs, fall to the sheet and onto the floor. She scolds him. "Food's not for wasting around here." She guides spoonsful delicately into his mouth so it doesn't burn or hurt. She sits by his bed with a plate of orange crescents and pricks the thick outer skin of each one before she puts it into his mouth. When she puts a crescent on his lower lip, he presses it between his lips so there is an immediate pleasurable squirt in his mouth. The burst of orange juice is delicious and cool. He opens his mouth for more. Pain does its daily walkabout within his body—a wince here, a jab there, a burst of sharp pinpricks in his thigh or his lower abdomen. But the larger pain is in his head. His body cries for morphine.

"You're too stingy with this stuff," he complains.

"There isn't an endless supply. We've a long way to go yet."

She hands him a picture in a frame. "Who is that?"

He peers at it, pulls it closer, so close his nose is touching it. A girl in a tennis skirt, holding up a racket, a smiling face, shapely legs. He sighs deeply, the corners of his eyes crinkling. The frame slips from his fingers, falls on his chest. She notes his silence and takes it from him.

Julia. The girl at the party he couldn't reach, couldn't even get to. Forbidden fruit he had reached for anyway.

# London, April 1932

It was late one evening when, as he wrapped up his papers, he realized something had changed. He didn't want to go back home. The Polaks had gone on their annual visit to Millie's sister in Cornwall and he had been rattling around the large, empty house, where footfalls echoed on the wooden floors and mice skittered about emitting sharp, delirious shrieks. He was with William Grosvenor, Peter Gaylord, and Jeremy DuTour, three others who were often in the library with him. They usually parted ways by the Temple Bar, sometimes going in for a quick pint or two before walking home, but that evening everyone seemed to be in a different mood, lingering over their pints, reluctant to disperse quite so early. The soft breezes coming off the Thames, the balmy evening, the trilling sounds of nesting birds in the air made them impatient for something else, what it was he could not tell. They didn't want to send their brains scuttling down Britain's statutes and by-laws, poring over tort law or precedents or the burden of proof beyond reasonable doubt. They weren't going home to that. On an evening like this, their appetites surged for life experiences.

———

William Grosvenor was part of the inner circle, the people who made up the aristocratic social set at the Middle Temple. They didn't flaunt it, they didn't shout it in any way, but you knew who they were and you knew they wanted you to know though you were never to mention it directly to their faces. It was rare for anyone from that circle to announce their pedigree. But from time to time they let you know of their special privileges and that you were being considered as a worthy candidate to share some of them. "Come with us, won't you, Shiv?" William asked.

"Where?"

William said he had been invited to a party in Maida Vale. "Poets, writers, musicians, some bohemians and artists—a friend from Eton's come back to London from Lisbon. He's famous for his parties! We're all a bit worse for wear but let's have some fun this evening. Casual but smart dress. Come along!"

"All right, future lawmakers of Britain, we're crashing this one, like it or not," Jeremy DuTour said, to loud cries of approval.

After some hesitation, Shiv accepted, along with the others, and went back home to change. Just before leaving, he sprinkled a few drops of Douro on his neck and close to his armpits. As he stepped out of the house, he looked up and saw a sapphire sky streaked with red. He felt immediately the power of something new—of being alive and young in a world where everything lay before him: friendship, fame, even fortune. He was learning that behind the labyrinthine formulations of law, there lay one basic human principle—that all men are created equal, that the right to exist as a free person and the right to be innocent until proven guilty was extended to all. What a beautiful thing it was—that one word: EQUALITY. He was aware that in that moment he was choosing not to dwell on the numerous infractions of equality that he had already experienced, putting them down to ignorance, and embraced it now as the holy grail of life. He'd never felt like this before—this confident, this strong.

His steps quickened as he walked briskly up Westbourne Terrace to Maida Vale.

He wasn't going to stick out like a sore thumb, for his friends were dressed more or less like him: single-breasted suits with two buttons, peak lapel, and folded handkerchiefs in the breast pocket. Their trousers were full cut, with tapered wide legs and a single pleat in front. Shiv had on a French blue tie; the others, too, were wearing different shades of blue or red ties. He had decided to leave his hat and umbrella behind, more for fear of losing them than a considered sartorial choice, and he noted with relief that one or two of the others had done the same. The notable difference was that they smelt English, and he felt Mediterranean—warm scents of orange blossom rose in pungent whiffs from the collar of his shirt. "You're looking rather spiffy, old chap," William said, giving Shiv the quick once-over. William sniffed. He'd put on too much, he knew. William said, "Oranges?" He nodded. "Douro?" When Shiv nodded yes, he said, "It's right in line with the Lisbon pedigree, old chap. Well done!" A faux pas spun into a clever tribute. This, too, was a social grace he'd observed in the English—that thoughtful tendency to spare a friend embarrassment by turning a social misstep into a grace. Decency had no colour, no nationality. Perhaps this was the fraternity Mr. Polak was so fond of referring to. If so, he was now a member of the tribe. He felt some barriers slip away as he walked beside William, feeling every bit equal to him in manner, dress, education, and style.

THE HOUSE, WILLIAM said, was a "model of Regency architecture— look at that coloured pane fanlight over the door and those stunning glass windows overlooking the canal on the top floor." It was painted white and glowed moonlike as they approached. They walked into a room filled with pretty, fashionable young women in loose, long shifts, bold jewelry, pointy-toed shoes. The smoke-filled air, the laughter, the flowing drinks. Almost everyone there was either in their twenties or early thirties, apart from a few elderly ladies who held court. He watched as his friends disappeared into the crowd. Not knowing anyone else there, he stood by the door, watching, and planning his escape. Canapés carried in by white-uniformed footmen on silver trays were making their rounds. He picked up a smoked salmon triangle and began walking aimlessly towards the windows at the far end of the room.

At that moment, his eyes were drawn to a fresh-faced young woman in a simple dove grey dress with a white collar. A gold chain circled her neck and from it hung a single lovely white pearl. There was nothing flashy about her. He watched her laugh, pearly teeth shining in the evening light. She was by the windows, and from time to time, she put out a hand, as if to steady herself, and placed it lightly on top of the mahogany bureau next to her. The man standing by her side was leaning into her, his attitude aggressive, his posture overbearing. He needed some competition, Shiv decided, walking towards them.

He wanted to reach her side; his footsteps were propelling him towards her. He was nearly there, when a man cut across his path. "Where do you think you're going?" Shiv turned to face his interrogator. "Not there, no, you're not. She's spoken for, mate, so bugger off." The man put out his hand like a bar. Undeterred, Shiv continued walking towards her. "You don't get it, do you? You can't go after our women, do you understand, you silly *wog*?" his assailant said. Shiv reeled back, as though he'd been shot. *Wog?* The derogatory term for Western Oriented Gentleman, all educated men of colour. With a reference to golliwog. Wog. The acronym—who cared? The abbreviation—an insult, and meant to be understood as a humiliation. He sighed deeply, biting back his rage. He wanted to break the man's neck, he wanted to hit out and draw blood from his face. He felt his rage grow. What was the proper response to such humiliation? He stood his ground. He couldn't remove the bar before him, but he refused to back away from it. As he looked towards the windows, he saw the woman he'd been trying to reach look at him. She had seen the encounter and had started walking towards him when a man took her by the arm and briskly led her to another room. She looked back at him. "I'm sorry," she mouthed. He relaxed the muscles in his face, managed to smile. He gave her a nod. Then she was gone. Spying William, he went to him. "Who is she?" he asked, pointing at the woman's vanishing back.

"Ah, that's Julia Chesley. She works at the Hogarth Press—the Woolfs' concern, do you know it?" Shiv nodded. William continued, "She's quite a poet, too, I hear!" For now, he'd been stalled. But Shiv knew he would make his way to her, sooner or later. He could see her lips, upturned in a laugh. He wanted to hear that laugh. Then he heard a high-pitched voice say, "The trouble with parties these days is the coloured element . . ." Anger snaked within him. They had witnessed his humiliation, and thought *he* was at fault—not for not standing up for himself but for being there at all. When William said, "We're going to another party later; do come along," he immediately offered thanks but excused himself. "You're sure you want to leave, old chap? The evening's young."

"I'm just not in the mood."

"I understand." William was eager to go back to the party.

Shiv eased himself through the crowd towards the front door. Lady Sophia, the Polaks' friend, was there, too. She waved in recognition. "Ah, the Indian. Millie Polak's lodger." She was merry, large glass beads glittering, wrists encircled with strings of pearls, tomato-red face, her voice drunkenly warbled. *Lodddggger*. Several people turned to look at him with curiosity. It sounded like a taunt.

He waved back but continued doggedly towards the door. Lodger. What did it mean? He was back again in familiar territory, the writhing of humiliation within, resentment flaring up like hives across his arms. The minute he'd walked into the room earlier that evening, he saw it: people avidly scanning the room like searchlights, pausing on faces they thought were worth their attention. He saw himself being skipped over again and again. The Invisible Man, the one coloured man in the room. Self-loathing filled him. His colour marked him, made him stand out wherever he went. You couldn't walk towards a girl in this country without having your race thrown in your face. He felt like a prisoner being tortured for a crime he didn't commit. British justice played out in the courts. With such reverence, he pored over thick binders containing past cases in the Middle Temple library. The knights, the priests, the abbots, the bishops, the Domesday Book. Curia Regis. The Magna Carta. The Inns of Court. The King's Counsel. All the enshrined landmarks that had made British law the envy of the world. Backed by cases and precedent, guilt and innocence moved about like pieces on a chessboard and the outcome relied on the skills and knowledge of the players. In the houses of Londoners, at their dining tables, in their country homes, and in the streets of London, a tribal loyalty—often barely discernible and impossible to know—controlled a person's destiny. Despondently, he realized he would always have to be careful, even when he felt most like them. Especially when he felt most like them. Us. Not us. They. Demarcations that remained hidden but rose to the surface when required—when tribal loyalties emerged as snubs to put people in their places, violently surprising those who did not expect to encounter them in convivial circles. They were like thorns in bushes. You went towards the rose and cut your lip in the process. You didn't have to see the dividing line to know it was there.

Leaving the house behind him, he made his way to the canal. Water soothed him. From his room in the house in Hyderabad Sind he would watch the reflections of people and animals ripple on the water's surface. The Indus was a loud, clamorous river. Its full waters gushed and flowed. It called in trills and shouts, and it needed to speak in a way London's river did not. The canal was a waterway linking the Thames to Paddington. It was quieter than its grand, moody parent. But it spoke of its origins in its steamy odors, its atmosphere of peat and mud.

The Thames's surface brustled with deep and underground sounds. It was shrouded in veils, in smoky mists. From its sulfurous depths rose the smells of fermenting waste. A mighty, capacious river, awash with sewage, industrial waste, and rotting vegetation, it yet bore on its mighty currents the vast returning cargo ships filled with the jewels, spices, and natural resources of other lands. Its depths spoke of untold secrets and the weight of the past. England's destiny, some called it.

He watched the longboats out on the water, their gay strings of lights flickering in the slight breeze. A woman's bright laugh, straying from one of the boats, reached him and he turned his eyes to look in its direction. It disappeared behind a larger vessel, perhaps a barge, and could no longer be seen. There was life out here—flickers and flashes of lamps swinging in longboats as they slowly plied the water, and voices, gruff, high-pitched, came towards him as he walked.

The Indus, one of the world's mightiest rivers, survived despite all threats—it faced either being baked into the earth during drought, or becoming a raging monster when its tributaries, swollen by snow-melt, came rushing down the mountains. Filled with debris during the monsoons, it flowed swiftly to empty itself into the Arabian Sea. It ran its lonely course for hundreds of miles from the Lion's Mouth, its origin high up in the Karakoram Range in Tibet, winding down steep slopes through Kashmir, Ladakh, through the flatter plains of Pakistan and on to the sea. Its five main tributaries were enshrined in myth—the Beas, the Sutlej, the Ravi, the Chenab, the Jhelum— and also superstition. It, too, like the Thames, fed its people, offered calm and solace, and when natural disasters hit, the river became a transportation highway. It had its poets and its deities. Songs floated downstream from one village to the next when babies were born, when marriages took place, when people died. River gods, every-where, bringers of good harvests or bad, held the fate of humans in their hands.

An owl hooted nearby. Shiv heard it, the sound impressing itself like a seal on wax. An unlucky omen, some said. Or a lucky charm. He quickened his step.

The reviving scent of oranges reached his nose. He held his wrist up to his nose and breathed in deeply. It was his scent, he had already embraced it and made it his own.

He had strayed so far from his own kind. But what was his kind? There was one other Indian in the Middle Temple, and he barely acknowledged Shiv. Every time Shiv tried to break the ice, the man nodded quickly and fled as quickly as he could. He was clearly friendless and seemed to prefer it that way. His one close friend, Morty Saxena, was at Oxford, studying politics and history, and hardly came down to London.

He deserved what had happened earlier that evening. He was a married man. Repeat slowly: I am a married man. I have a son. I am a married man. I have a son. But the strangest thing began happening: the more he repeated the words, the less truth they seemed to have. A man. A married man. What was a married man?

He heard footsteps behind him, and quickened his pace. Now the canal on one side of him felt dangerous, its unknown mysteries threatening: a low hum of frogs calling, and the sucking, air-filled sounds of floating plankton; a foggy, nighttime damp he would always associate with the Thames. A moth, perhaps a China mark, fluttered past his nose. The smell of rusting iron and rotting fish assaulted his nostrils, increasing his sense of fear. "Don't run," a laughing girlish voice said. "I won't eat you, I promise. Slow down." Shiv stopped and turned around. He gave the man a closer look. What an interesting face it was—heart shaped, framed by curls, a deep dimple in the chin, and even in the dim pallor of a gaslight above, he could see the boy's eyes—like stars, or diamonds. "I wanted to give you back something you left at the party." That voice, like hammered silver.

"Who are you?"

"You can call me Lucy."

"That's a woman's name," Shiv said.

"Depends on how you look at it, doesn't it?"

"I didn't see you there."

"Ah, but I saw you. And I could claim that this"—he held out a bunch of keys—"is why I followed you. But I wasn't even sure they were yours."

Shiv fished in his trousers pockets and realized that the keys must have fallen out at some point during the party. "It's very kind of you," he said, holding out his hand for them. He closed his eyes for a moment, horrified by the thought of what it would have meant to lose them. He didn't know where the housekeeper lived and his only access to a phone was inside the Polaks' house. He would have had to spend the night on the steps of 24 Gloucester Square. "You can't imagine what it means to me to have them back."

"You don't have them back yet." The young man's smile was teasing, provocative. Shiv sensed his vitality instantly in his quicksilver laugh, the lively fingers.

"No," Shiv said, looking at him warily. "Are you trying to rob me? Because if you are, I might as well declare that I have nothing except this on me." He held out a guinea.

Lucy laughed. "Not much I can do with that." He gave Shiv a mischievous look. This was getting tiresome, Shiv thought, longing to be back in his cold room, warming his feet on the hot water bottle under the covers.

"What do you want?" he asked, wondering at the same time why this plummy-voiced, aristocratic man-boy had followed him. His voice was as posh as William Grosvenor's but its musicality made it much more interesting. Shiv felt fearful and anxious and his voice was beginning to break a little.

"Oh dear, I'm beginning to frighten you, aren't I? You caught my eye as soon as you came in, a gaggle of barrister types behind you. I was determined to get to know you. But you started saying goodbye so soon, I knew I had to come up with something quick. And then you dropped your keys."

Shiv held out his hand again for the keys. "Not so fast," Lucy said. "First you're coming with me to the Red Hart for a drink, and then, perhaps, I'll let you go home." His voice vibrated like water gliding languidly across the frets of a harp.

The night was young, the air like velvet. The scent of orange blossom was still strong on Shiv's inner wrist, on the beating pulse points in his neck. "I don't see I have a choice." Lucy laughed. That laugh—joyful, teasing. He wanted to hear it again and tried to think of something funny to say. But only earnest words, words betraying fear and excessive caution, rose to his lips. He walked silently beside him, uneasy and curious at the same time.

GERRARD STREET. No street in the world would come to mean more to him. Everything of consequence in his social life in London had a way of coming back to that street.

The Red Hart was a unique establishment. He learnt quickly that it was a social microcosm unto itself and its patrons wanted it that way. They did not want acceptance in London's larger social milieu. They wanted secrecy, gaiety, and discretion. They wanted to veto those who came in and throw out those who were seen as unacceptable. You had to read between the lines—catch an uplifted brow, or a sardonic comment hurled towards someone. You had to watch the attitude of the "girls" who ran the place and cajoled guests into buying bottles of champagne or ordering sausages, eggs, and toast at three a.m. at a king's ransom. There was a code of conduct, a form of politesse. This was not where loose women plied their wares. The outcome of an evening depended entirely on how the girls treated you, how you treated the girls. An unwritten code governed the place, and you had to know it to be considered thoroughly acceptable. It was that quintessentially British establishment—a gentleman's club, but with its own rules. Where the gentleman's club was cosy, a place where men could rely on comfort food, familiar ritual, and chatter, this place was delirious with energy and shot through with danger. One man, perhaps Chinese, or Thai, was glued to the front door, watching it anxiously every time it swung open to let a guest in. Perhaps he was expecting a police raid. And yet, the place beguiled with its lack of boundaries, its illicitness. Shiv was alert to danger yet also at ease here. Long after the tube had closed down and the last buses had left for the vast green reaches of Richmond, Roehampton, and Hampstead, London's night places filled with people hungry for the kind of company their everyday lives denied them. Lucy had led him to a secret place, and he'd gone through the invisible door. Now, bewitched, he would have to follow where it led.

THE LOVELY GLOWING servers in their shapely dresses and high-heeled shoes were known as "Merry Maids." Their clientele ranged from bored married men to homosexuals, cross-dressers, and those who liked it every way they could get it. On one table a group of men sat waiting to be approached by coaxing women, who were trained to appear nurturing and naughty. At another, a group of young men and women laughed and talked and smoked; only when you looked closer you saw that some of the men were women, and some of the women were men. The dance floor was full of couples—black men dancing with white women; white men dancing with black women; men dancing with men and women dancing with women. Jews, Italians, Russians mingled with one another, danced and got away, as they all did, from their confined spaces in the world outside those doors. A jazz band played swing as couples shimmied and gyrated across the dance floor. Shiv looked at the white moon globe that hung from the ceiling and cast a silky glow on the dancers—he gaped at them, realizing that outwardly at least, here there were no boundaries. All the no-go zones on the outside had vanished here.

You could go anywhere you wanted to, be anyone you wanted to be. Tremors of excitement filled him, as the pent-up frustrations of the past eighteen months began a slow, painful release from deep within. His mind flashed back to the party earlier that evening: "the coloured element." Here the coloureds made the place sizzle with their shimmering dresses, their wide smiles, their gleaming teeth. Their feet crackled across the dance floor. No one here was hiding. They were proudly, openly, themselves. Lucy was watching him. When Shiv turned his eyes away from the dance floor to Lucy, he felt shot through with sunlight, as if with a fresh understanding of the world.

Lucy said, "What is it?"

"What?"

"The way you're looking . . ."

"How?"

"Different, somehow—lit."

They were seated together at a table. Lucy'd seen it, the way Shiv was feeling. Lucy poured champagne into his flute. "Bollinger," he said. Shiv nodded, as if he knew the difference. He took a sip. "I have to say it, I hate this stuff."

Lucy burst out laughing. "I would never have known. You're guzzling it almost as much as me."

"I want to drink what you're drinking."

Lucy gave him a surprised look. "So, do you know why I noticed you at that party?"

"No, you tell me."

"You came in looking as if the world belonged to you. Like a prince, your eyes coolly sweeping the room, as Antony might have done with the hoi polloi in Alexandria before its queen enslaved him. You had a glow—your radiant skin, your shining eyes. I was drawn to you like the light."

Shiv felt uncomfortable by the man's praise. Here was something new and different. Men didn't speak to other men in that way, surely.

This was the kind of talk a man indulged in with a woman he was deeply attracted to.

"I'm sorry I've disappointed you, as I must have, now that you're up close and can see the object of your fascination quite clearly. I'm none of these things, I'm afraid. Just a foreign student in London, missing home terribly."

"India?"

"Yes, Sind."

"Ah yes, the last principality to fall to the British, wasn't it? Your people held out brilliantly. It was a shame that it was overrun in the end."

Shiv looked at him closely. "You're from London?" he asked.

"Born and bred, mate. Yes. The inner sanctum and all that. Father's in the House of Lords, mother's managing our estates. I'm their terribly inconvenient only child, their homosexual son."

Shiv stiffened. He'd never met a homosexual before—heard about them, of course, even back home, and wondered about bachelor uncles who routinely disappeared to places like Kabul, Zanzibar, Athens, and Cairo. They showed up at family parties bearing exotic presents, charming everyone, no wives or children in tow. But everyone referred to their "sad" lives, their lack of companionship, as a curse. Lucy exuded vitality.

The knowledge that the beautiful man Shiv was with was homosexual didn't change anything really. He felt drawn to him as a friend. And when, after a few more glasses of champagne, Lucy asked Shiv to dance, they lit up the dance floor, two young men with boundless energy ricocheting off each other like sparks, their movements making them draw closer, apart, even closer, apart, in perfect synchronicity. Fireflies at mating season flashed with the same kind of energy as they painted glowing circles around one another in the dark. At one point, their hands touched, lingered. Shiv, shocked, drew away. Lucy laughed. Tall, lithe, and beautiful, he shimmered under the moon glow of the hanging globe, enchanting Shiv with his laugh.

And much later, as others at neighbouring tables tucked into their breakfasts, and the smells of fried sausages and eggs and burnt toast filled the air, Lucy leant forward and gave him a long, lingering kiss. Shiv wanted to draw back, shriek in horror, something. But instead, he looked deep into those glacier green eyes, the irises as warm as honey, and felt their singe, and allowed himself to be kissed again.

IT WAS ONE in the morning. Lucy said, "I'm not that far. I live at Grosvenor Square. I'll walk you home."

"You're sure? It's a long walk."

"It's nothing. But fair warning: we can't be too close on the streets. There's our wonderful DORA, and the cops are zealots. Get those bum boys! They're out there now, scraping the streets for undesirables. We must be careful." Shiv moved closer to the edge of the pavement. "Now that's unnatural," Lucy said, laughing, pulling him a little closer.

"What's DORA?"

"The Defence of the Realm Act, a law from 1915 that lets the coppers handcuff perceived homosexuals—'nancy boys'—Jews, any threatening foreigners, and cart them off to jail."

"Oh my."

On the way, Shiv told him about his family back home, the expectations they had of him. "You're the jewel in their crown," Lucy said.

"Yes," Shiv laughed mirthlessly. "More like a pricked balloon at their party, the way I feel these days. It's never-ending, to be honest, this mission I'm on. I'm supposed to know how to carry forward Britain's legacy in India. I mean, after they've gone."

Lucy gave a snort. "Bugger that."

Shiv looked at him again, and laughed. "You know, I'm not sure you are an Englishman."

"As English as they come, darling, don't you worry. It's just that I see where we get our bloody money from a little more clearly and don't hold my tongue. And I may not show it, but I've done what everyone else expected of me as well."

"Really? You seem such a . . . free spirit," Shiv said.

"You have to meet my mother. Threatened suicide all her life to get me to do something—top marks at school, swotting my arse off to get into university, or affecting the fawning obsequiousness required to get into White's, her favoured gentleman's club—all she had to do was to come towards me waving packets of Veronal and a bottle of Johnnie Walker Black, and I was hostage."

Lucien ("Lucy") Calthorpe was the only son of Lord Henley and Lady Regina, and, per aristocratic protocol, sent to Eton at eight, and then on to Cambridge. It was there, in very difficult circumstances, that he found out he was homosexual. "I love women, but I'm not attracted to them. I'm drawn, especially, to men who look like you. Our dusky colonials in the Southern Hemisphere."

Shiv cringed. Dusky colonial was not how he wanted to see himself, and especially not in relation to Lucy. For a while there, at the Red Hart, it seemed they had crossed those barriers, levelled out their differences. But here they were again, observing the same demarcations, using the same language.

At the door of 24 Gloucester Square, Shiv said, "I've earned back the keys, I think."

"In spades," Lucy said, dangling them so he had to lean forward, and as he did so, Lucy brushed his lips quickly across Shiv's. Shiv put out his hand, felt the icy drop of cold metal in his palm, and then Lucy was gone, a graceful sprite disappearing down the street.

Shiv turned the key in the lock and went into the house. His lips burned with the illegality of their kisses.

Lucy had kindled something in him. He hadn't experienced anything like this before. He hadn't even kissed a girl, leave alone a boy, with desire. His head spun. Seher had become his wife. He had tried to serve her out of duty. What was this new thing, this deep want, this inexplicable yearning? It crackled like fire within him, arched like a cresting wave. Did this body, so expressive, so finely sensitive, even belong to him?

Lines from a strange poem he'd known by heart in his youth, "Romance" by W. J. Turner, came to him as he stood in the entrance hall of the Polaks' house. A class full of children reciting the verses, without knowing what they meant: "I walked home with a gold dark boy / And never a word I'd say. / Chimborazo, Cotopaxi, / Had taken my speech away; . . ." And then the magic hour ended as desire's dark side showed itself: "The houses, people, traffic seemed / Thin fading dreams by day, / Chimborazo, Cotopaxi, / They had stolen my soul away."

On the way up to his bedroom, he went into the bathroom on the landing and vomited, feeling fear for the first time in his life.

# The Empress of Scotland, June 1941

He wakes now, and runs his fingers across his lips. So chapped and rough, his fingers bristle under the touch. That kinetic body, the way he wrapped himself around you when you were sad, or homesick, or yearning. That thin stalk of a body, the drooping head the flower, the long neck and face, the cool moss of his eyes that hardened into emeralds when he felt the fire of desire. His body moved to an inner music; his mere touch made Shiv aware of deep longing. Lying in his watery cradle, Shiv remembers now how, unable to move his eyes away from Lucy, he wanted to be that body, that fine eggshell skin. It was how Lucy experienced things—his body was like water, it vibrated with every crimp, every inflection, every sound in the external world. He was so free, and his freedom allowed him to experience life at a very finely tuned register—like breath trembling on gold leaf. Lucy had shown him what freedom looked like but Shiv was under no delusion that that freedom could be his. Compared with him, Shiv felt like an imprisoned man making his way down a path patrolled by uniformed armed guards on either side. He suppressed the thrill of experience, fearful of what its true cost might be. One wrong step and he'd be nothing, no one. The thought of Lucy, that first time, that charged, electrifying experience, comes to him now, and his body, remembering, convulses, like milk membrane under heat. His spine tingles, his heart climbs up to a quicker beat, and he feels his blood at last, running through his veins.

"How do you feel about going up there, to the deck? The weather's been decent. We could take a chance." His neat nurse in her uniform is by his bed, asking.

"What's up there?"

She laughs. "The sea, acres and acres of it. You watch some dolphins bob up and down from time to time, there's English soldiers playing their harmonicas and singing of home. Quite a lot of entertainment up there, if you're in the mind for it." She's doing something by the sink. He hears the chop of a knife on a hard surface. She turns around and brings him something on a plate. It's cut and yellow and glistening. He says, "This is something I know."

"What is it? You have to remember."

He stares at it. A range of smells, some musky, some floral, come to him. He can taste it in his mouth. Juice running down his chin. "*Mango!*" he says. "It's mango." He hasn't seen a mango for ten years.

"The captain had a few he was handing out." She feeds it to him, piece by piece. "There's an Indian soldier aboard. I thought you might like to meet him." The soft squishy pieces jam against his lips, sending juice dribbling down his chin. She wipes his chin with a dish rag before she puts another piece in his mouth. "Open wide." He feels like a baby.

He says he's not sure he's ready to meet anyone yet. He has forgotten his social skills. "Just look at me."

"He's very easy to talk to," she says. "He's lost one arm. It's why he's being sent back home. He seems lonely. He's got the morbs, too, like you."

"Morbs?"

"Yeah. Down. He's really down. Try to cheer him up a bit, won't you?"

SHE BRINGS THE old soldier in, leading him by his good arm to his bed. "This is my patient. And this is the brave soldier who's fought in both our wars."

"Hello, sir." The man stands by his bed and holds out his left hand. Shiv takes it, notes its coarseness. The man looks weather-beaten. Thin and hollowed out, but his smile, revealing chipped brown teeth, is warm. "Amar Singh, from Garhwal."

"You're from the Gurkha regiment?" Shiv asked, noting the insignia on Singh's jacket lapel.

"Yes, sir. We served at Verdun in the first one, and now Tripoli, where this happened. I lost an arm to a sniper."

"Brave man. Sorry about the arm." He shook his head, felt pain wincing down his spine. "You chaps made us all proud, back in London, especially the Indian students. Brainy but weak, we're known as. But you Gurkhas have set a new standard. Tigers—the first to go over the hill and face what's on the other side."

Amar Singh nods. "We surprised the British with our courage. We outlasted them on the field, we never stopped. So many died in the First War. This time the casualties will be much higher."

Mairi gives the soldier a plate containing the rest of the mango, their sunflower yellow cheeriness an eccentric anomaly in their world. "Mango?" he turns to Mairi. "Where did you get a mango?" He can't stop looking at the plateful of sunshine. His eyes water.

"I have my ways, sir," she says. "And I'm not sharing them, in case you've got any ideas." She smiles at him and then turns to Shiv. "I'll take a turn on the deck while you're socializing, all right?" He nods. Amar Singh falls into a deep silence as she leaves the cabin. He stares at the fruit. "I did not think this would be the first thing I would see from my country."

"Eat!" Shiv commands.

The old soldier looks at the plate, then at Shiv. "It is a thing of beauty. Looking is enough." He gives him a shy smile and pushes the plate away.

"Did you lose many friends?" Shiv asks. Why won't the man eat?

The man's shoulders shake. "All," he finally says, wiping the tears away with the edge of his shirt. Shiv cringes at the sight of tears, then remembers it is now all right to cry if you feel like it. Indian men do not shy away from tears, a natural expression of sorrow.

Singh places the plate on Shiv's bedside table. He hasn't eaten a single piece. "The war has changed all of us. We do not go back as the same men we were when we left."

Shiv doesn't answer.

"We have seen terrible things." The old soldier moans to himself. "Men gunned down by machine guns on the other side fell on top of the ones below them like skittles. They crushed one another to death. The earth shook with their cries; their heartbeats boomed like church bells, each one a gong."

Shiv closes his eyes. But the voice goes on relentlessly. "Their cries are in my head every night—*khuda hafiz; bachao, Bhagwan; Shanti, Shanti, Shanti*. Who hears them? Only us mortals." He'd heard it said often enough—on the battlefield, believers lost their faith; agnostics turned to God in terror. Mortality makes equals out of us, for fate is indiscriminate. "The British went down in great numbers, too. *Bloody hell*, they cried, just before a landmine exploded in their faces or a gun began firing bullets at them. *FUCKing bollocks!*" The soldier's soft Indian accent makes the curses sound like endearments, as if the soldiers were reaching out to loved ones. Perhaps that is how we go—not with hate or fear, but in a state of adoration.

"You have been through hell," Shiv says. He feels a sharp stab of pain as the man speaks. A voice, a smile, a crumpled kimono—Lucy! Oh dear god, was Lucy alive? He listens now to the voices of the departed filling his cabin room. "Please for god's sake, stop, STOP!" Shiv cries. The man goes silent.

He hears Mairi coming in. She's hardly been gone a few minutes. "The sky is the most intense blue," she says. She stops by Shiv's bedside and silently wipes his face dry. He is shivering. Both men look ashen.

"When I saw you both together, I realized you'd probably bring each other down. It's what made me come back so quickly. You're a fine pair," she says. "You've both got the morbs now." She turns to Amar Singh, who nods, and leaves quietly.

She goes to her cabin and brings back *Orlando*, with its heartening inscription from the author herself. It must have been a high point. She knows the passage and finds it quickly. *"He loved, beneath all this summer transiency, to feel the earth's spine beneath him; for such he took the hard root of the oak tree to be; or, for image followed image, it was the back of a great horse that he was riding; or the deck of a tumbling ship—it was anything indeed, so long as it was hard, for he felt the need of something which he could attach his floating heart to; the heart that tugged at his side; the heart that seemed filled with spiced and amorous gales every evening when he walked out . . ."* He is asleep. She hears his gentle snoring. She knows by now that words, read softly, tether him, like the hard root of an oak or a horse's back.

Her patient's life, she sees clearly now, is only just beginning, for it is now that the events of his past will begin to exert a life of their own. He sees himself as a man derailed, hanging on for dear life, awaiting that final, releasing lash. She sees a phoenix rising.

Like me, she thinks.

⁓

Father Lawrence at St. Mary's responded quickly when she went by the church to say her mother had fallen down the stairs and it would be some time before she returned for services. Mairi asked, hesitantly, whether a priest could stop by from time to time for communion at home. "It would help her recovery," Mairi said. He replied, too eagerly, she observed later, and with a sudden gleam in his eye, that he would come himself. She thanked him and left the rectory immediately.

He came the following day. She received him at the door, took him up the stairs. She left him in her mother's room. Something told her she wasn't safe. She dragged the dresser in her room to the door, put a chair on top of it, locked the door, and waited for him to leave the house. She held her breath as she heard him shut her mother's bedroom door. It was always left open so she could hear her if she called. The priest had shut it. She knew then what he intended to do. He stood outside her door; she was on the other side listening for his every move. But then he must have had some qualms for he left quickly and went back down the stairs and out the front door. She was shaking with relief. If he had had improper thoughts about her, she forgave him. She was in the clear. He'd fought with his god, and his god had won.

He came again the following week. She heard him talk to her mother gently, offer her the wafer and the wine, pray with her. This time, she didn't take the precautions she had taken during his earlier visit. He had surely seen the error of his ways. She was in her room, sewing by the window, when he suddenly came in and lunged at her. She dropped her sewing, and hit out at him but he was much stronger than her. He pinned her down on the bed and forced himself on her. She could only think of the choir service at church, his regally garbed form leading the lay priests down the nave, his lips twisted in prayer. It was then that she began hating religion, for its unbearable hypocrisies. He was by the door when he turned around ominously and spoke for the first time since his entrance into her room. "You tell anyone about this, my girl, and you and your mother will suffer terribly for it. I swear to God!"

She found her voice then. "Your god does not scare me, Father," she said in a quiet, firm voice. "If he can tolerate the likes of you, he's not worthy of our prayers and our reverence."

He left quickly and she never set eyes on him again, even after her mother was better a few weeks later and they started going to church together again. Talk was he had been transferred to another parish somewhere in Scotland.

One day, she felt cramps in her stomach; her period was late, and she hadn't been overly anxious. It was often late. But the days went by, became weeks. Then she began fearing she was pregnant.

Her worst fears were confirmed when the vomiting began. By then it was too late to take pills or the potions the nuns used for their younger, more unruly charges. No potion was going to help her now.

The doctor who performed the abortion was a kind man, but it was clear he couldn't operate without drink. She watched him take swigs from a silver hip flask on a desk by the operating table, the flash of silver wire in his trembling hand, and knew she was doomed. She came out of there bleeding, fearing she would probably never be able to have another child. For weeks after, she felt her body wasn't the body she had once known. It twinged with deep wounds; nerve endings exploded with rage like knifings through her body. She touched her bruises and massaged them gently, willing the pain away. But her body didn't respond to her ministrations. It had seized up and refused to let her in. She sat alone in the evenings, while the sky darkened outside their home, feeling tortured, disembodied, wondering how long this feeling would last, how to get through another day. She had never known anything as disorienting as this severance from her body. It had always been hers to control.

If her mother suspected, she never said. But as the days went by, Mairi began planning her escape from her stifling hometown, where she saw her history in every woman's face. How many had suffered as she had? How many couldn't go on? How many did, by shutting the door on their pasts and simply, valiantly, carrying on? Was every woman abused like this?

She had to get out of there. In preparation, she began training as a nurse. A nurse could have performed her abortion far better than a drunk doctor, she reckoned. When she leapt off the chair she was standing on at the library and followed the ambulance men with a stretcher for the injured man who was now her patient, she knew her moment had come.

She remembers the horror of those days now. The church couldn't be trusted; her body was impossible to live with. Mairi saw her mother's narrowing eyes, as if homing in on her daughter's true ailment, and knew the distress it would cause her to know the truth.

All the while, *The Empress of Scotland* waited in the harbour, whooshing steam, waiting until she was ready to hear its clarion call.

ALREADY, SHE SENSES a new life beckoning. On every trip to the kitchen for supplies she sees Arabs praying, Indians playing their flutes, children jumping rope, British soldiers happy to be off the killing fields and in the company of their mates, drinking beer and singing folk songs. The ship, with its assortment of passengers and crew, is breathing new life into her despairing heart. And then there's Will, the purser. What a charmer he is, she thinks. He makes her laugh, tells her things she doesn't know, brings her little gifts from the kitchen, gifts she uses to tease her patient's memory and taste buds. He will be entertainment enough all the way to India.

She tells her patient she's going to shave him. "You look like a caveman," she says. He does, she thinks, looking at him. "You have a beard." He knows, he's put his fingers up to his chin and felt the growth. Every time his fingers move about his chin they linger, as if he's unsure that chin is his. He feels disembodied, again confused about what happened to him and why he is there on that ship. He doesn't know his body.

Mairi sees his confusion every time he touches his face. She knows how disembodiment can lead to a loss of self, a kind of madness. She's seen him feeling his chin, pulling at the growth, the puzzled, wondering look on his face—how did it get there? He gives her a sideways look, anxiety mounting in his clouded eyes.

She has a wooden bowl with shaving cream, a comb, scissors, and a razor. Has she ever shaved a man before? Is he her guinea pig? He braces himself for more pain. He doesn't feel the blade until she's cut off most of the growth with her scissors. Then he feels the blade's cold sharpness against his raw skin as she soaps and scrapes against the stubble. He's waiting for her to draw blood. She's frowning, shaking her head. "Your face looks as though it's in rigor mortis. Can you please relax?" He exhales slowly, and as he does so, his skin goes lax. She runs the razor across it and clears it of fresh growth. She's smiling. She hasn't drawn blood. He knows it's over. He sighs a huge sigh of relief. She says, "You're such a handsome man, you are! Can't wait to show you off to the hoi polloi! You're ready for your excursion upstairs now."

SHE FEEDS HER patient some broth, which he dribbles down his chin, deliberately this time, just to feel the rough cloth in her hand brush against his mouth. He craves touch. He longs to kiss someone, and be kissed in return. His desires are inappropriate, and cannot be quenched. "*I love you like certain dark things are to be loved, / in secret, between the shadow and the soul,*" he recites the lines of poetry to himself. Someone great had written those lines. Someone who knew touch and how it lit desire. He cannot recall who it was.

His mind, enraged and in pain, takes him back again and again to Lucy, to the spartan flat in Bayswater, where they had cupped each other, he and Lucy, inseparable, whole; where winter's soundless dawns were suspended in time and he had watched frost patterns forming on the windowpanes while his lover breathed softly down his back. Their shared world was a warm glow that encompassed them both. Outside lay the forbidding world of combat, the never-ending steps to climb, the relentless struggle to assert one's worth to oneself and one's peers.

# London, 1932–1934

Between making regular appearances for meals at the Polaks',
and sleeping in his own bed at their house—where he stretched
his frozen legs to let his feet curl around the old copper bedwarmer
Mrs. G, their housekeeper, unfailingly left there—Shiv would ab-
sent himself, pleading a long night at the Middle Temple library,
and rush to Bayswater to fall into Lucy's waiting arms. The flat, in
fact the entire building, belonged to a friend of Lucy's, who was
happy to let Lucy have the space. "Going down the scale a bit, aren't
we?" he'd said, as Lucy laughed and replied, "Useful for trysts."
"Ah," the man nodded sympathetically. "I should warn you, there's
an old biddy living next door, a Mrs. Parnell. Daddy's old nanny. So
keep the noise level low at night, won't you? I doubt she'll be
any trouble, but we know she never leaves her flat." Shiv often wondered about old Mrs. Parnell and what she made of the two of them,
men not throwing rowdy parties but very quietly being with each
other.

After a night of making love, he would linger by Lucy's side, trail
his fingers through his soft brown curls, trace the outline of his sen-
suous lips with his finger, let it travel down his sharp jawline, imagine the sleepy soft green fluorite eyes turn crystal sharp with the leap

of desire, ponder every feature of that loved face as he slept, plant a kiss on his delicately flushed cheek. How this man-boy moved him, enchanted him. He felt it in the pit of his stomach—a sharp, clenching pull. Lucy would murmur sleepily, "Don't go yet, darling. Stay." The same age, they both were, when you stopped to think about it. Twenty-one. Yet Lucy was touched by the wand of eternal youth as he himself was not and it showed in his lithe long limbs, his forward thrust, as if impatient to meet the world, his pent-up energy. He curved his body around Shiv's like a swan.

Shiv would turn away reluctantly and dress quickly in the ice-cold room, longing to get back into that bed and let Lucy's arms encircle him. But he'd always leave, guided by caution, and return to the Polaks'. He was there in England on the strength of the promises he had made, and by god, he would keep them.

Nearing the front door of 24 Gloucester Square, he'd feel great tenderness. His innocent, unsuspecting guardians asleep in their beds thinking he was burning the midnight oil in the Middle Temple library. Filled with guilt, he'd enter the house and climb softly up the stairs to his room. Every day the distance between their house and the Bayswater flat grew larger, more insurmountable, and yet, he wanted nothing more than to be back there, in Lucy's arms. Every time he told himself he would have to cut it off, his impatience to see Lucy grew even more. Reason knocked in vain against the doors of desire. He stopped fighting it.

When Mrs. Parnell started toeing her door open as he passed her flat, he told Lucy, "She's definitely keeping tabs on us. I saw her nudge the door open again today."

"You saw her or her velvet-slippered feet?"

Shiv laughed. "Her feet! I don't think we'll ever see her!"

Lucy sighed. "Look, she's only got that bloody cat that chases me down the stairs for company—of course we're her daily show. She's got nothing else going on."

Shiv said, "I expect you're right."

"Of course I'm right. She's a curtain twitcher! She can't believe her luck—these two handsome men living on the other side of her wall, clearly in love, and no noisy, drunken parties going on. She's beside herself with joy. She's not going to turn us in."

LUCY LIVED THE life of a young aristocrat about town during the day. He'd meet spinster aunts at the Ritz for tea, where he'd entertain them with juicy tidbits about the sons and daughters of their friends and acquaintances, his fingers flying like hummingbirds from tiny tea sandwiches and silver tongs for sugar cubes to small, ivory-handled knives for smearing clotted cream on scones. He would lunch at his club and gossip with friends over poached salmon and Meursault, or spend an entire rainy afternoon at Hatchards, presenting Shiv with a list of books "you absolutely must read." Sometimes Shiv would accept an invitation to attend a cocktail party somewhere in the smarter precincts of London—Mayfair, or Kensington, or Belgravia—and as they entered the room, he would feel the truth of what Lucy often said, "We look fabulous together, not just because we're beautiful, my love, but because we look like we belong." At first, he thought it was because he was a brown man; that, together, he and Lucy created an uneasy stir in others—perhaps they even inspired revulsion, and this was what made people stare. Then he began to see that it was their special aura, their beauty together, that drew people's eyes to them. They fell into lockstep with each other as they walked into a room or left it, their long, lean bodies knitted by desire striding across the floor. He wanted it over and over again—that special authority they seemed to have when they were in perfect sync, attracting the admiring stares of those who watched them go by.

⁂

One rainy afternoon, Lucy suggested they meet at the London Library after Shiv's court session. "If there's one place in London that deserves my devotion, no, I'll go further, my unqualified admiration, it's this place. I want to show it to you."

Lucy met him at Green Park Station and they walked down Duke of York Street to St. James's Square together. "I've been coming here since I was a child," Lucy said, as he gave him some history and background. "In the 1830s, Thomas Carlyle came up with the idea for a public library. He found benefactors and public support, and it became an institution in 1841. But as you know by now, nothing about English institutions is ever 'public,' in the true sense of the word." Lucy went on to list everyone who had belonged there, from George Eliot, to Dickens, Hardy, T. S. Eliot, E. M. Forster, H. G. Wells, all members, all loitering among the stacks and in these halls. "It's by membership only and some find the dues quite high. Virginia Woolf's a member, though she thinks the library quite clubbish, I've heard. You should belong! I'll propose you, if you like!"

"How much are the dues?" Shiv asked.

"Don't worry about it—early Christmas. Let's face it, there's nowhere like it in the world!" They walked up the stairs to the glass entrance door. In the issue hall, a few members sat on benches reading. Lucy introduced him to the librarian at the front desk. "You've been here before, I take it?" one of them asked.

"No," Shiv said. "It's my first visit."

The man laughed. "It's certain to not be your last! You'll be a fellow addict before long." The staff behind the front desk were checking out books for members, some engaged in lively conversation, others looking up as they walked past, lingering on Lucy's presence. They recognized Lucy, who was a colourful sight in his long raspberry red silk scarf wound loosely around his neck, its ends trailing down the front and back, his toffee-coloured wide trousers and close-fitting French blue jacket. *He gets away with it—in fact, people stare with admiration, not with censure. How does he do it?* Shiv examined his lover with their eyes, accustomed to English drabness in everyday attire, and saw what they saw—a splendid vision of independence and spontaneity.

The library didn't, at first, look anything like a place that would command anyone's, especially Lucy's, devotion, but things changed almost immediately as they walked up the red-carpeted stairs to the reading room. Portly men snoozing off their lunches filled the red leather chairs in the vast room, which looked out onto St. James's Square. Their snores broke the silence of the room. Shiv took it all in—the solemn yet cosy splendour of the red-carpeted room with stairs leading up to the rows of bookshelves on the tier above, the vast space, the long windows facing the square—it was midsummer and the trees were full and green—the square white pillars on wooden bases between the desks, the large fireplace with a clock ticking above it, the mouldings above, the frosted glass lighting globes suspended from the ceiling, and the concentration. Lucy picked up the day's issue of *The Times*, and Shiv followed with the *Illustrated London News*. They settled down for a few moments to read.

When Shiv got up to place the newspaper back in its holder, Lucy said, "It's time for the stacks!" The stacks?

As they went up the stairs to Literature, he said, "You can find anything in here if you know how to look. You have to think like the wonderfully eccentric librarians in here. So there's Demonology, and Domestic Servants, Military Medicine, Hops and Hopping, Hysteria, Science and Misc. There's Small Books, and Imaginary History, and the Hand. There's Suspended Animation." He laughed. "Science and Misc. is a world unto itself. You never know what you'll find there! And in order to find Pleasure, you have to go through Pain! I find it terribly amusing and quite wonderful. Some gnomic figure sitting in a back room with a wicked sense of humour and imagination is thinking up these labels, I'm sure."

Lucy revealed his absolute devotion to the place in full when they got to the stacks. "Look at the flooring—iron grillwork. It's a unique feature of the place. As you look down to the floor below through the grill you see someone else below you, doing the same thing you are—opening up a book and breathing it in." As if in confirmation, when Shiv looked below, he saw a young man so deep in the pages of his book, he didn't even look up at them but continued reading undisturbed. Lucy had turned on the lights in their section. "Women are warned not to wear skirts if they plan to visit the stacks!" he said with a laugh. "You can see why!" Strings suspended from the ceiling with little plastic inverted bells at the ends could be pulled to turn the lights on and off. Notes and reminders pasted onto the walls directed readers up the stairs to History or down to Topography, or to turn off the lights.

It was cold in the stacks, Shiv noted. He was shivering. "What's the smell?" he asked.

"It's the smell of ages packed between the pages of these books. Of hands reaching eagerly towards something they want to devour, of must, dust, old tobacco and bay leaf. Of isolation and companionship, of longing and expectation. And your orange grove scent. There's something quite fragrant, lusty, about it. I've actually always found it quite erotic."

Shiv suddenly saw a book he recognized. "This is in my father's library back home," he said, pulling it off the shelf, astonished that something so familiar should be here, in this quintessentially English establishment. It was a leather-bound volume of Byron's poetry, illustrated with steel engravings of all the female personalities versified. He stopped at the one of Don Juan and Haidee—how that particular engraving had once held him with its stylized tenderness. He held the book open and ran his nose down the gutter, breathing in deeply—a multitude of scents filled his nostrils. The smell of amber and old sandalwood, of musky potpourri—how had the book acquired those scents? He flipped through the pages, then looked at Lucy. "I feel I'm back home, holding this in my hands." Spying a few other books he'd known from his father's shelves, he went eagerly towards them. How unexpected, this leap into the past—after all this time in London, the one thing that took him back home to his father's house was the books he had grown up with in his library.

When Lucy reached for him, simultaneously pulling on the light switch so it went dark, Shiv, surprised, gasped. "Not here, Lucy," he said in an alarmed whisper. "Not now! Really!" Lucy chuckled as his arms went around Shiv's waist. "What takes place in these stacks stays in the stacks," he whispered back. "Another one of the library's delicious unofficial rules." Shiv heard the tiny tremors in Lucy's voice as it broke with desire. He felt the thrill of it though his heart was thudding.

"Thank you," Lucy said later, as they left the library. He was happy; it showed in his newly appraising look, in the playful way he pushed against Shiv's arm as they descended the steps into Green Park Station.

Shiv feels the *Empress of Scotland* lurching, as if in sympathy with his own longings. Conscious again of the ship's forward motion, its steadying, he closes his eyes, imagines Lucy there beside him, and feels the most intense joy and pain.

London spring evenings. His mind returns to a particular one. Cool, the air thin and pure, the skies eggshell blue, turning later to cerulean. Pigeons' marbled cooings coming from nearby bushes, the pathways by the Thames blocked with prams and gossiping nannies, suited men with newspapers under their arm, skipping children, dogs running after rubber balls. Old men dozed on iron benches or gazed at sparrows with dreamy looks in their eyes. Tall iron railings covered with flowering honeysuckle. Young lovers holding hands;

the lime light of the grass; the sulfuric stench of the river; the fevered glances of men looking for company.

Shiv had left the Middle Temple library to clear his head. It was getting dark. The lamplighters were already up on their ladders, the sun was setting behind dense foliage alive with birdsong as thrush and blackbird flitted through trees. A breeze so clean came off the water in that second, it hurt his nostrils to breathe. He felt prickly, desolate, as if his tongue had been ripped out of his mouth. In class he had dared to question precedent, a cornerstone of British law. *Stare decisis*. Let that which has been decided stand. He'd pondered it for days, finally raised his doubts about its infallibility. "People change, mores change. What was held true twenty years ago may not be true of us today. The world is getting larger, more global. Judgements made elsewhere surely must prevail on the system here. A decision based on current knowledge of the past should be revised to fit in with our contemporary concerns and beliefs."

"Rubbish, utter rubbish," shouted a senior bencher who happened to be in the classroom that day. "You go by what has been done before. That is our time-honoured way." Shiv had recoiled in horror as he realized the senior bencher had been present to hear him challenge the sacrosanct rule of precedent. "Sorry, sir, just for the purposes of debate." Senior benchers were like minor gods in the Inns of Court. They were members of the governing body, elected to serve by the council. They had served long as King's Counsel. No one took on senior benchers for the "purpose of debate."

"That's a spurious debate, based on a preposterous presumption! Your lot will never understand the basic tenets we operate by. You were selected to be here"—the senior bencher barked out the words, practically foaming at the mouth—"by the good graces of our administrators in the colonies. You're all heathens, novices at our table." The insults were meant to convey outrage, transgression. From the sudden silence and crestfallen faces of his fellow students, he knew he was alone. Unable to counter the judgement, Shiv packed up his things for the day and left for home, skirting the Thames as he took the Temple stairs down to the water. Peat smells wafted off the mudflats at low tide, filling his blood; coagulation, a sticky loam, ran thick and heavy within him, pulling him down, smothering him. Ambition's dark side—when anger and frustration came together— was beginning to paralyze him. The steps upwards, as intricately designed as the interior chambers of a nautilus, beckoned and induced immobility at the same time. Would this place accept him, his talents, allow him to succeed in his mission? Or would he be forever a brown man in a world that was not his own, destined to be one of the sheep, headed for failure? He was constantly being made aware of how fortunate and blessed he was to be one of the chosen few, for he had been let in, permitted to follow the gilded path to success. Every time he heard it, his mind translated it into words one used for an unruly dog. "Down, boy, down!" *Know your place.* Who were they, these rulers? How had they subjugated them? Why did every close encounter with them turn one's blood to fire? He longed to uncover them as thoroughly as they had uncovered him, but he knew the steps were covered with slime, likely to trip him and send him hurtling down again. What was the bloody point of it all?

On his right, Waterloo Bridge glimmered through veils that concealed ghosts of the past. How Claude Monet had seen it, a state of solidness in a fluid landscape, where cloud and mist and water came together to confound the senses. But the stone structure was solid, had weight. He would climb those shrouded slippery steps that led upwards, he would come to know these people as well as his own and he would, finally, win acceptance by this relentlessly hard city.

Mr. Polak, pacing the drawing room with rage in his step, was waiting for him when he got home. His large ears—his most expressive feature—were lobster red. He demanded an explanation. "What's this? What happened today?"

He had already heard about it. Shiv gave him a summary. "You took on a senior bencher?" Mr. Polak said with an incredulous look. "The arrogance of it! The sheer arrogance! It's what they say—give them an inch and they think they're going to rule the world!"

"Sir!"

"No, don't sir me! Do you realize what you've done? You've just added another hurdle to your struggle for success. You've shown your teeth—and he will fight you, mark my words! He's got you over a barrel now—a troublemaker, a firebrand, a detested species in the world of law. Foolish! Foolish! Foolish!"

"It was just for—"

"You're a learner, a pupil. What the devil did you think you were doing questioning a cornerstone of British law? It's an outrage!"

"Sir, I didn't know he was in the room."

"That's not the point. You saw fit to question British law and offer your unsolicited opinion—an uninformed one, at that. You flirted with arbitrariness—don't you know by now that this is a hated word in English law? Our practice is based on constancy, on reverence for older decisions. We remain objective that way."

Theatrical as always when he needed to make a point, Mr. Polak scowled at Shiv, his fury thick and genuine. Shiv saw his concern through the stage gestures. He looked down at the carpet, swallowing his own disappointment. "I'm sorry, sir, for having caused you grief. Rest assured it won't happen again."

Mr. Polak softened a little. "This is very thin ice you're skating on, my boy. Your duty, your obligation, is to follow the rules. Accept what you're told. Absorb everything. Learn. You don't question—at least not now."

"But one learns through discussion—what good is my intelligence to me if I can never use it?"

"No! Yours not to question why. Lie low. Fly under the radar. Never be caught with the short end of the stick. Ask me whatever you need to. And if you can't keep your own counsel, I'd rather see you pack up and go home."

As Shiv's heart slowly contracted, he made a vow: he would bite off his tongue; he would stamp out the fire within himself; he would reap the rewards of silence. He would be a silent sheep, a follower. He would never question their "cornerstones" again. He would not try to stand out with his intelligence. And he would, by god, earn his stripes. Ambition, freshly honed, filled him. He would wrest recognition from them as an athlete who had sharpened his skills with dedication and precision, and, in the end, he would win their admiration. His country would be led not by beggars with tin cups in their hands but by Olympians who had mastered the game.

"Good." Mr. Polak leaned forward, pressed the fingertips of both hands together, and looked intently at Shiv. His glasses had slid to the end of his nose, and as he peered over them at Shiv, he looked like God might have looked to Moses when he laid down the Commandments. In a grave voice he went to explain how important it was to have savoir faire. Recently, the Indian High Commissioner, a British appointee, had complained about how Indians lacked it. "Do you know what that is, Shiv?"

"It's polish, knowing how to be in civilized society."

"Yes. Here is a small piece from a venerable old publication called the *Rambler*. Read it. Memorize it. A bencher gave it to me when I was young and cocksure and it helped me enormously." Mr. Polak reached for it on his desk and handed it to Shiv.

He read it later, in his room.

> When not precocious, however, Savoir faire is undoubtedly a very valuable equipment for the battle of life, and frequently stands its proprietor in better stead than more sterling qualities because it is always in re-

quest. Courage, virtue, devotion, etc., are, of course, inestimable possessions, but they are not always wanted in a civilised community. I believe it looks pretentious to put them on and parade them for everyday wear, and is apt to make people envious who are not so fortunate in apparel, or make them doubt the genuineness of the articles. Besides, you are not required to fight dragons, fly the fascination of serpents, or die for your country, sweetheart, or friend. . . . With the inner performances, mankind are not particularly interested. But no day, no hour passes, without your being called upon to show that you "know your world" and your duties towards it; that you recognize the necessity of refraining from treading on your neighbour's corns and afflicting his ribs with your elbows, and of accommodating yourself pleasantly to the circumstances wherein you are placed, remembering that you will probably have to live among men and women for the term of your natural life.

It was a small requirement, wasn't it? Know your world so you don't step on anyone's toes, so you pass by unobserved. The "inner performances"? High drama, not life. Life was being a neutral shade of carpet, which neither delighted the senses nor stimulated passion. And if it felt like digging a little mound in the earth and lying in it for a short while, surely he could satisfy it? Anyone could do it. Lie low. Be a rug.

He turned down the Polaks' invitation to accompany them on their annual trip to Cornwall, offering an excuse he knew Mr. Polak would find no objection to. "Studies, sir," he said, noting Mr. Polak's instant approval. He stayed on in Gloucester Square, watching spring unfurl buds on trees and bring soft breezes into London's dusty streets. It was an enchanting spring/early summer season.

Lucy was in Chios, in Greece, with his mother, tied up with a family wedding there. "I'll get back as soon as I can, darling," he had said, tenderly, the night before his departure.

Pre-dusk. The latched gates of gardens in squares clanging shut as metal met metal. A wash of ginger-yellow light on the white façades of Georgian houses in mews and crescents and closes across London. Dusk—that in-between time, neither night nor day—filled him with a sense of mystery, of undiscovered potential. He tried not to think of Lucy.

From time to time, he would stir the fire in the grate in his room and peer into its depths. You could hear English houses speak only when they were emptied of people. That lonely house spoke to him now. A creaking floorboard; a scurrying mouse; tree branches heavy with spring buds, scratching and brushing windowpanes when it was windy; the spitting, crackling fire in his room. Occasionally a thin draft of air whistled in through the cracks and slammed doors shut. He walked through the rooms and saw and felt every emotion in them—from sadness and longing, to the soft joys of companionship. He entered Millie's room and smelt her lavender scent in there. Surprised, he backed out, as though he were an intruder. In his room at night, when the air was so cold you could cut it with a knife, he listened to all the sounds and felt lonelier than ever. He spent his days devouring cases, and eating fried cheese sandwiches, celery soup, and tinned peaches, things the Polaks' housekeeper, Mrs. G, knew he liked and prepared for him while her employers were away. The time apart from Lucy brought its own grounding strength. His hours at the Middle Temple library had solidified his mission, which had him deep in its hold again.

# Middle Temple, the Inns of Court, London, Call Night, 1934

"Mr. Shiv Advani, I call you to the bar and publish you barrister." Three years earlier, in this very place, the Middle Temple Hall, he had felt this night would never come. He had been just shy of nineteen then. He was twenty-two now. Where he had once been a stranger, now he felt this world had been fought for, and become his. He knew his world, what he stood for. He had authority. Clothed, for the first time, in the wig and the gown of a barrister, hearing the portentous tones of the senior barrister say his name, Shiv went forward to sign his name in the Call Register, which rested on an ancient table that had once been part of the *Golden Hind*, the ship that had taken Francis Drake around the world. He entered his signature with a steady hand in the book. History, desire, and the flame of ambition burned together as he noted his neat and precise hand. "That will remain there forever. It is done," he told himself. "I have fulfilled my mission."

A scene came to him suddenly: the Sind Club, Karachi. At the entrance a sign that read: "Women, Indians, and Dogs Not Allowed." Blistering shame on letting his eyes skim the words again, and rage. In the near distance, the aqua blue of a swimming pool for club members only, white bodies draped on lounge chairs, bathing in the tropical sun. An Indian gentleman in formal Edwardian dress, ivory-topped ebony stick in hand, top hat in the sweltering heat, and his only slightly less formally dressed sixteen-year-old son walk through the front doors to the astonished stares of the native staff. They are met in the grand entrance hall by a representative of His Majesty's Government. His father was considered a loyal subject of the Crown, one who could be counted on to adhere to, if not actively promote, British values among the natives of Sind—in other words, a necessary man in a province considered extremely important to British interests in India. "Bit of a loose cannon," they said of him. "A nationalist. But revered by his own people and therefore indispensable."

The official in charge of managing the quotas for Indian students in England examines Shiv carefully from head to toe. The man's blue eyes, a pale washed-out blue, are pinned on him, trying to gauge if the Indian was up to snuff—is he good enough to be among the chosen few? When it comes to the interview, they want his father to know he is deeply in their debt, so they keep the questions simple. They ask him whether he plays polo and what he thinks of King George V. He answers truthfully that he loves polo and he doesn't know King George V, but supposes him to be a wonderful man and excellent king, judging by all he has heard and read. He is deemed suitable and allowed to take the exams for entry to training for the bar. He passes them with flying colours, but it is still seen as a favour to his father that he had been allowed to take the exams in the first place.

Faustian pact or no, he and his father left that morning feeling deeply beholden to the British. Again and again his father said, you must make us proud of you. "Never let your family down. Family honour is personal honour." The look in his eyes had been of unswerving trust. Shiv, burning with pride, said, "Father, you can count on me."

News of his call to the bar had already reached home. His mother
had timed her letter to him perfectly. It was waiting for him when he
got back to the Polaks'. "Dear Son," his mother wrote:

> Mr. Polak told your father that he was confident you would
> make your call to the bar. You have worked so hard for this
> moment. I am writing to tell you that your father has invited
> all his friends over for the night of our success—the night of
> your graduation. It is your triumphant day. Father always
> says, you reap what you sow. Now it is time you returned
> home. Your duties and obligations here are awaiting you.
> Your wife has been restless for the last year. There are many
> young men here who, knowing her husband is away, have
> their eyes on Seher. She is even more beautiful now. You
> must come home, reclaim your position as her husband, and
> be the father your son misses. Sher is now nearly three. He is
> your father's delight. Bright, bristling with energy, he hurls
> his tiny body on our bed in the mornings, his eyes raining
> diamonds. The two chase each other around the house all
> day, having fun. I have never seen your father laugh so
> much. As for me, I try to insist on Sunday afternoons with
> him, but there is always serious competition! I tell him
> stories and make him laugh so he looks forward to time
> with me as much as he does with your father.
>
> Seher looks sad. She is always restless. She leaves things
> half done. She has become dreamy, says she wishes she were
> elsewhere. So, for the sake of your marriage, and us—for we
> are not getting any younger—you must start making plans to
> come home now.
>
> Your loving Mother

He put the letter back in the envelope and let out a deep sigh. He had a son, a son he had never seen, who didn't know he existed. A three-year-old son. His mother was right, it was time he returned home.

Henry and Millie Polak had arranged a champagne reception for him that evening, and as he downed a few sips of the dreaded drink (he never developed a taste for it no matter how hard he tried), he listened to a senior barrister friend of Polak's tell him that the time to don his armour had now arrived. "You have won permission to begin on the first step in the ladder of your journey. I wish you luck." With a sinking heart he muttered his thanks. Of course his call was only the first step—the "easier" one, for it had been up to him. The next steps would be up to others and to his ability to ingratiate himself within a system that would sooner he take the next boat home instead of fighting hard for a place within their social world. But his mother's letter had squared that away neatly, hadn't it? He wouldn't even have to try now.

When he mentioned his mother's plea to him to return home, Mr. Polak shook his head vehemently. "No, no, she doesn't understand. Your wife and son will have to wait a little longer. You can't rush back home now. You need to work and earn your stripes. I'll write and tell them." Shiv sighed with relief. Apprehension and anxiety filled him every time he thought of his wife and child, his aging parents. He should have been feeling elation—he had succeeded where so many had failed. But success itself brought new worries as his usefulness to his country and to his family continued to be re-defined. It was waiting for him, that life—a life destined to be con-trolled by others—but for now, he wanted only to love, and to be loved. For this brief moment in time, it was surely enough to crave it, hold it, and to experience it as fully as possible.

But as he walked to the Bayswater flat to meet his lover, his triumph burned within, mingling with desire, and excitement. He imagined Lucy waiting for him on the sofa, his eyes turning from his book to the door, his look pleased, curious, as he walked in. There was a fresh confidence in his steps as they hit the pavement, a sureness he had not felt before. He quickened his pace.

Lucy, in the flat in Bayswater, had been waiting impatiently for him to arrive. It was ten p.m., the earliest he could get away from the Polaks. He told them he had promised to meet some fellow barristers for a celebratory drink. "Ah yes, you must," Mr. Polak said. "Very important that." Muttering his thanks, he had rushed out of the house.

Lucy had dressed up in a beautiful gold-embroidered achkan and white silk pants. He wore slim black leather babouches, and had wrapped a fuchsia silk scarf with small gold paisleys on it around his neck. He looked stunning. He was tanned and radiant. He met his lover with shining eyes. With a deep curtsey that hugged the floor and him at the same time, Lucy said, "Eminent barrister, my humble hearth and heart do welcome you for an evening of feasting and celebration. We await your pleasure! Enter, esteemed sir, and let the festivities begin!"

The flat was a breathtaking sight. Lucy must have spent days planning the evening. The lighting was low but dramatic, the air was scented with the fragrance of bluebells and irises, a fire crackled in the grate; the cushions were plumped and welcoming. Lucy's gifts and charms were in full display: his quick wit, his beauty, his intelligence, his kindness, his irreverence, his laugh—that laugh. There were flowers and candles on the fireplace mantel, a bottle of "my father's cherished, signature fifty-year-old single malt"—a table laid with caviar and toast, spreads of all kinds from Fortnum & Mason's. The sultry tones of Duke Ellington's "Sophisticated Lady" playing in the background, the naughty welcome in his smile. There was a large wrapped box on the dining table.

Lucy took Shiv in his arms, and embraced him as fully as it is possible to be embraced with one's clothes on, his arms encircling him, his lips desirous and deliciously kissable, the touch of him like a precursor of the fiery single malt that awaited them on the table. I'm losing myself, Shiv thought, not caring in the least. And a minute later, Or, rather, I am lost. But the evening's festivities were just beginning.

Lucy spooned some caviar on a toast triangle, garnished it with a small dollop of cream, and slipped it into Shiv's mouth. He peeled grapes with a small pearl-handled knife. "You don't have to do that," Shiv said.

"I've always dreamed of doing this for my lover, sitting by his side, peeling grapes which I pop into his deliciously curved, waiting mouth. Open!" Shiv complied, letting the grape sit on his tongue as a love offering before pressing down on it to release its juice. The grapes and caviar kept coming, the malt lit his insides liquid gold. Lucy kissed his lips tenderly, then took his hand and led him to the table. He pointed to the big box. "Go on, open it!" His eyes sparkled.

Already sated, feeling indebted to this man for bringing him so many gifts, Shiv looked anxiously away. Lucy said, "I'm going to open it then!" He began unravelling the bows and taking apart the paper until it was there before him: a spanking new His Master's Voice gramophone. "Oh, Lucy," Shiv said, partly with dismay, partly with joy. "You're mad! I've always suspected it, but now it's confirmed!" The card read: "*To my adored one—Forward—let's dance to the stars and beyond! Your loving Lucy.*"

As his arms and lips reached for Lucy, he felt himself as totally in love with another human being as it was possible to be. So this is it, he said, this sense of longing, of unimagined desire, of not being moored any longer to anything you know. Desire toed no lines, had no geography. Touch, taste, sight, sound, and scent fed it until it bloomed and flowered. Then it became irresistible, as essential as oxygen. No regions, nations, loyalties existed in his mind at that moment. There was only the state of Now, and how best to embrace it, treasure it, prolong it. Dangerous, wasn't it, to think it could last, but how could one stop this? Who would have the strength to resist it? Lucy put a record on—Fats Waller's "Ain't Misbehavin' "—and as the tempo picked up and Waller's fingers flew across the keyboard, Shiv twirled and threw his arms up in the air and slipped in and out of Lucy's arms. He was exhilarated, nothing seemed to hold him back, not even the thought of Mrs. Parnell marching down to the police station to complain about noise in the flat next door.

"What would you have done had I not made it?" Shiv asked him.

"We would have celebrated anyway. It's the effort, my darling! You have worked so hard for this. And so have I. Do you know how many times I had to chain myself to the sofa to stop myself from coming to your library to pull you out and bring you back here? Countless! So this is as much my celebration as yours!"

We don't celebrate effort back home, he wanted to tell Lucy. Effort is taken for granted. We celebrate *success*. Everything that falls short of that is a failure. *A miss is as good as a mile*—one of his father's favoured adages.

There was a second gift: We're going to Glyndebourne next week.

What's Glyndebourne?

"It's a new music festival where people get dressed up and take the train to Lewes in Sussex and tramp through mud to listen to opera."

"What?"

"Yes, you'll see. It's the very first performance at the place. An opera house in the middle of the countryside. Mother's come down with a bad cold and can't use her tickets. She's upset—it is the event of the season—but was happy to let us have them."

"Us?"

"Yes, she knows. I mean, about us." Lucy gave him a quick look.

"But was that necessary?"

"What? To tell her, you mean?"

Shiv looked away. The thought of publicly embracing what had become a way of life filled him with horror.

"We're not pretending any longer, Shiv. We're going out there as a couple. English hypocrisy has no place in my life. You can do anything, absolutely anything, in private. Just don't offend the genuflecting churchgoers. If their public schools churned them out with the usual tar brush, you can bet that none of these men have entirely lost their homosexuality. So it's really a case of envy of those who aren't afraid."

His mother's face swam into Shiv's consciousness. Your wife, your child. Then *his.* Your life here. Us. He looked out of the window trying to quell his panic. How long before someone in Lucy's set met Millie Polak, told her what was going on between him and Lucy? Why could they not have kept it quiet, secret, as they had until now?

"She asked, all right? I would never have lied to her. We're not hiding, you and I. We have a right to be seen as a couple in love."

"I thought we didn't have that right, at least in public." There it was again, that deep, unsettling fear he felt in the pit of his stomach.

"We don't wait to be given the right. We take it. That's what should be happening in India as well. Don't wait for the British to leave. Fight them tooth and claw. Kick the buggers out." Lucy gave him a look. His eyes were sharp olivine. He was like a tiger before the pounce. Shiv picked up the glass of scotch by his side and gulped down its contents. He'd never felt fear like this before. "Is there more?" he asked, holding out his glass.

"You sure?"

Shiv nodded. He was cold, his stomach was in a knot.

Something had changed. The atmosphere was heavy, weighted. He downed the scotch in one shot.

When they went to bed, Lucy reached for him. Shiv murmured, "I'm sorry, I think I'm too drunk." His body gamely complied, send-

ing up a series of hiccups. Lucy gave him a deflated look, as if he'd
been punched in the gut. "Right, that's that for Daddy's Macallan.
We're sticking to the juice of the grape next time." He turned huffily
to face the wall and was soon asleep. Shiv stared into the darkness.
Some indefinable pain had taken hold of him, some deep agony, and
he had no name for it.

On 28 May, 1934, they boarded the 2:53 p.m. train from Victoria
Station to Lewes. Lucy looked stunning. His skin was glowing, the
pink and white suit he was wearing was meant to create a stir—only
someone like him could carry it off, Shiv thought. The sharp sculp-
tured planes of his face like one of Balthus's young girls, his expression cool and consciously indifferent, the shoes pointy toed and
white, the green of his eyes and the pink of his suit evoking spring's
bounty, his smile detached and engaging at the same time. He had
on a cream-coloured panama hat with white trim. His entire get-up,
his style, felt Parisian, or Venetian, certainly not English. The
oblique admiring looks aimed in Lucy's direction spoke of his effect
on some of the passengers. Stuck to his side, it was attention Shiv
felt he could do without. His eyes were red-rimmed from lack of
sleep, his pin-striped suit looked staid and dull. Even the small
touch of flamboyance he'd reached for—a yellow tie—failed to perk
up his general appearance. How did he seem to them—a lackey, a
paid servant of some sort, a rajah for hire? He sat next to Lucy with
mounting anxiety.

The compartment was full of young men in suits and top hats,
women in dresses that were calf length or ankle length. Dressed in
sensible garb, the women had accessorized with pearls, the flashier
ones with diamonds and emeralds, but they all seemed dowdy and
fusty compared with Lucy. Some of the women were in high-heeled
shoes; others in wellies. "Wellies?" Shiv asked.

"Yes, they're the knowing ones. There's going to be a lot of mud in those fields."

"So you wore white!" Shiv said, laughing and shaking his head.

The animated women kept up a spirited conversation about nannies, cooks, children, horses, housekeepers. The men discussed amenities at their clubs, the dull concert season, new actresses in musicals playing in the West End, and where they would be shooting grouse at the start of the season in August.

Lucy said, "You're going to hate us all by the end of the day. Even I find it intolerable and I've been listening to this stuff with a half-shut ear since I was a child."

"What do they do?" Shiv asked.

Lucy laughed. "Nothing. They're pretty good at that. Some of them collect art; some breed horses. They don't have any real interests. They meet one another—the men, that is—at their clubs, at shoots, and at the races. At the theatre, they are nodding acquaintances. It's essential to have eyes you can meet and heads you can nod at across boxes."

"I find that impossible to believe. Such ruddy specimens of humanity doing nothing! How do they live?"

"It's largely inherited. Invested heavily—telephones, electricity, diamonds, steel, coal. The Empire. You see why industrialization of the colonies is so important to this lot. And horses, of course, which is why the races are a huge social event. They do money quite well. Some make it; some blow it. The ones who do well cannily opine on world affairs with an eye on their checkbooks. Service is for Boxing Day."

"So what do they really care about?"

"Society. To never breach the rules of society, which are unwritten of course, and inherited largely at birth. It's the sure knowledge of these that allows them to walk into a room with a confident air and to take their place within it. Violate those rules, and you're out. There: a short course on English society."

Shiv saw someone who looked like Lady Sophia. Dressed in a crimson cape, crimson court shoes, her neck bubbling with large pearls, waving fingers studded with stones, she came eagerly towards them. "Oh, it's Polak's lodger, isn't it? I thought I recognized you! Fancy meeting you here, dear boy!" Her lips had been smeared thickly with lipstick and it sat like cream on her smile. Shiv got up from his seat, shook hands. "Meet my friend—"

"Oh, Lucy," she cooed. "Naughty boy, hiding behind the newspaper. I didn't see you! His mother and I were at school together. I've known this boy since he was a babe in his nanny's arms."

Lucy cut in, "He's my guest." He went back to his newspaper. Lady Sophia blinked several times. "I would never have taken you for an opera fan."

Shiv said, "It's my first."

"Ah, you lucky man," she purred. "You're beginning at the top. Mozart. *The Marriage of Figaro*. It doesn't get better than that. We are all giddy with excitement—marvellous Mr. Christie, to have pulled off the event of the season in the middle of pastureland! He's got the best singers in the world to come. Simply extraordinary!"

"So I've been told. The danger, of course, being that nothing else will ever come close again."

"Well, I hope you enjoy it." She appraised him again, surprise never leaving her face, and then gave him a broad smile, her ivory teeth flecked with bright pink lipstick, her cheeks already a bright tomato red. "Henry Polak was right. Young man, you bright natives will have the run of the colonies after we're gone. Perfect wogs!" Lucy's newspaper crackled furiously behind him. He had been paying attention.

Shiv felt a chill run through him. Again. That inevitable comparison, are you wanting or not, are you capable or not, are you one of us or not, can you be trusted to be one of us when we want you to be one of us, and not one of us when we don't want you to be one of us. He bowed stiffly, not saying a word.

"Tell your mother I insist on meeting Harry." She turned to Shiv. "It's her new obsession—a new breed, Bichon something. Quite a charmer, I've heard."

Lucy flicked his newspaper aside. "Frise. Bichon Frise. He's had a name change yet again—Hector, after Greece. Poor little fellow! Doesn't know if he's Greek or English now."

She laughed. "Funny boy! I see you're just as witty as ever! Well, cheerio! See you at the concert," she said, moving back to her seat.

They sat in silence as bright green countryside shot past the windows. "Cat got your tongue?" Lucy, his face bright pink with rage, lowered the newspaper and glared at him.

"What?"

"She called you 'lodger'—did that just sail past you? She called you a *'perfect wog.'*"

Shiv shrugged. "Yes, I've been called those names before."

Lucy shook his head. "I wish you'd fight back. You take it. It's bloody infuriating. You make me want to be a monster for you." He put his newspaper down. "The French have a term for it—*avaler les couleuvres*—to swallow grass snakes."

"What?"

"Yes, when insults are so deep, one's stunned into silence. Was that it?"

"You would have wanted me to make a scene? Here?" He puzzled over Lucy's words.

"Yes, *here*," Lucy said, going back to his newspaper.

Bit it off, he wanted to tell him. Bit off that tongue, didn't I, when I was told my opinion wasn't worth a penny. Mr. Polak's enraged face swam into his consciousness—*lie low, don't question, don't offer your opinion.* I bit if off to make it. *Here*—his eyes swept the green fields of early summer. Lucy would never have understood.

"Wish I had some of your irreverence," he said to Lucy.

"Is that a challenge?" Lucy gave him an impish smile. "Because it won't take long, I promise!"

As the station came into view, Lucy got up. "Right! Off we go," he said, pulling their bags off the racks as the train pulled in.

At Lewes Station, as Lucy had predicted, the giddy crowds disembarked with their luggage, their picnic baskets, their bottles of champagne and packed boxes of caviar sandwiches. "It's as if we're going on a picnic," Shiv asked.

"We are! Grassland, meadows, sheep! It's tradition, old boy. Tradition. If the outdoors are involved, there will be picnics—catch the British departing from that one little bit. But I predict: after we've lost India, they'll be eating curried chicken sandwiches on the grass here. Washing them down happily with Moët." Shiv laughed.

Small green vans awaited their arrival and as they all piled in, Lucy said, "It's promising." He was watching his people with amusement, anticipating their next moves as cannily as a bookie calculating his bets. As their van drove into the Christie estate, there was a palpable rise in temperature in the bus. People were training their binoculars on the farther reaches of meadowland, where sheep grazed. Lucy said, "This is the part of the country I love the most. These hills, the cows, the blue skies. A lone church rising out of a green landscape. . . . Even the bloody sheep. What a marvel it is."

As FLUTES OF champagne made the round, and the garden began filling up with guests, some of whom had booked rooms at a hotel nearby and were just entering the grounds, Lucy said, "Come and see this." He started walking towards the garden's edge.

"Calthorpe!" a man shouted.

Lucy turned around. "Ah, Cameron! Good to see you!" The man came forward with his pretty companion, champagne flutes in hand. "This is Sylvia, my fiancée. We're getting married in September, in Pembrokeshire. You'll get a stiffy and you must come!"

"Hello, Sylvia," Lucy held out his hand. "He's a lucky man! Meet

Shiv Advani, newly minted barrister. I'd behave yourself around this one if I were you!"

She laughed pleasantly. "How lovely to meet you," she said, holding out her hand. Shiv said, "Charmed," and bowed slightly. She withdrew her hand with a puzzled look. He hadn't taken it.

They began talking about the other people there, people they knew, people they were hoping to meet. The highly anticipated performance, the dinner menu, the gorgeous evening. Then Cameron spied someone else and moved off with Sylvia. "Bye, bye, see you soon," and off they went, easy, intimate, touching, as Lucy and he could not.

"What's a stiffy?" Shiv asked.

"Ah! Yes. The much awaited stiffy. It's a serious invitation, unbendable, printed on very thick card paper, the thickest stock available. It's saying, you're one of the chosen few."

Shiv laughed. "I don't have even one."

"No, Shiv, seriously. Certain people estimate their social worth in stiffies—if you've a good number, you're blessed indeed. High society considers you a coveted guest!"

Lucy took his arm and steered him away from the crowds. "Let's get out of here before someone else comes." At that moment, he spied a couple walking towards them. "Oh Christ, Mother's friends. I'm supposed to say hello. Look the other way, they may avoid us."

But it was too late. "Calthorpe!"

"Lord Windermere! And the charming Princess Hohenlohe!"

"Your mother said we would find you here. Beautiful day for it, isn't it? How are you, young man?"

"On a day like this, with the Sussex Downs for a view, and sheep for company, one can only reply well, very well, indeed."

"Yes, quite. And who is your Indian companion?"

"Shiv Advani," he said. "Just out of the egg at the bar."

"Ah! Yes, someone's got to look after the colonies after we've gone." Lord Windermere laughed broadly, cheeks aflame already, while Princess Hohenlohe looked at Shiv and said, "Mr. Gandhi is a dangerous man, we believe. He must be stopped in his mission. India will languish without the British." Shiv tried to look supremely bored, and turned his attention to the crowd, as if he spied an acquaintance there. She turned to look at Lucy.

"Oh well, your employer would say that," Lucy said. "The Führer is an evil little man. Happily, there are plenty of people in Britain rooting for a free India. And you can tell Herr Hitler that."

Princess Hohenlohe, stung, moved backwards, feigning horror. When they eventually pushed off, Lucy said, "Such humbuggery! And we put up with it. She's Hitler's spy. And Lord Windermere, who's engaged her here in Britain to serve as his consort, I imagine, is a sympathizer. She's always at these events, looking for new recruits to Hitler's cause. It's not commonly known that she is Jewish herself, and has convinced everyone otherwise. The British, I think I've told you, can be stupid. As you've no doubt noticed."

Shiv stared after them, astonished. Hitler's people moving about as heralded visitors in English society, despite Britain's anti-fascist stance. "They're welcomed here?"

Lucy rolled his eyes. "What do you think?"


THOUGH HE KNEW the story by now, and there was a libretto in English to follow, Shiv couldn't understand what all the fuss was about. Everyone wanted someone else, not the one they were with, and they complicated their lives endlessly to come up with elaborate schemes to ensnare the objects of their desire. It was exhausting just watching the cross-gender dressing, the constant changes in costume, and keeping up with a plot that depended entirely on ruses. Reading, looking up, reading, looking up.

It was when he gave up and concentrated on the music that its beauty came to him. How voice carried in this space—every note heard perfectly in all its fullness, surrounding them like an enveloping cloud and yet so clear, each note like a drop of water falling on glass. In the darkened space, Lucy reached for his hand. Shiv turned to look at him. Lucy was no longer sceptical, or even judgemental. His enraptured face and glistening eyes conveyed pure emotion. It was exquisite to see him as vulnerable as this. Shiv squeezed his hand, then relaxed it into a caress. He was deeply moved, too, but he didn't know why. The music had fused with the place, his experience of it, and the waves of desire that came to him from Lucy and which he was sending right back.

At the interval, they went towards the dining room. "We're not taking sandwiches," Lucy had said back in London. "Picnics are for the middle-aged."

The maître d' came forward with a smile, which vanished as he led them to their table. They had choice seating, by the windows, overlooking the lush summer gardens. "Mother would not accept anything but the best seats. They have complied royally." As they looked over the menu cards on their plates, Lucy said, "Traditional. But fitting."

Shiv pondered the choices in French, trying to make out a word or two. Useless, really. He closed the menu and pushed it to one side. Lucy said, "Well, I expected the trout and the leg of lamb, but the asparagus soup is a nice surprise. And the pineapple pudding sounds quite refreshing." He always did this—translated from the Italian or the French by making it seem as though he was pondering his choices. He knew Shiv did not know French or Italian. Shiv looked at Lucy as he continued to examine the menu, touched by his thoughtfulness. His face softened into a half smile.

"What?" Lucy said, looking up, his eyebrows raised in surprise. "Why are you smiling?"

"Oh, nothing," he said. "I'll have the trout."

"Comes with herbed green beans. Rather nice."

"And you?"

"The leg of lamb."

The wine list quoted Homer in Greek, with accompanying translations, and aphorisms:

No lover of good wine can be wicked.

Wine makes the weary wondrously whole.

When you ask the Gods for something, you have to be
    prepared to give something up.

Wine is heaven's best gift to man to drive away dull care.

Gods worked on a quid pro quo basis, he was aware of that—ask and you shall receive, but what are you going to give up? He knew, with certainty, that the one thing he wouldn't give up was the man whose hand had cradled his as they heard the music, who wanted good for him, from whom he never wished to be parted. Lucy looked at him, as if sensing his thoughts, and said, "I feel most at one with you when you're thinking." They were connecting so deeply that evening, Shiv saw no distance between them. How could anyone object to it, to their right to love? Seated across from Lucy, Shiv felt a frisson run down his back every time their fingers touched—so slightly, accidentally, or on purpose. Tiny brushes of want, desire that lit a deeper flame. How could anything this vital not also be natural?

Lucy ordered wine for them both, a half bottle of a red and a half of white. The waiter took their orders.

"So what did you think?" Lucy asked, as soon as the man left.

"I'm reeling with so many impressions. It's fantastical—I can't believe this is the world you live in. To have this at your command . . ."

"So please put some of those impressions out there, so I can feel them."

"Of *Figaro*?"

"Of everything. But let's start there."

"I've never heard music like this before. The sound of it, it feels subterranean, as if you're in a cave, and the music's coming down the walls like water. For once, it isn't hyperbole. I began hearing it only when I gave up on the libretto."

"Yes, I saw you put it down finally. Glad you did or I would have snatched it out of your hands. Your head bobbing up and down from the page to the stage was beginning to distract me. Mother wants to write an adoring letter of congratulations to Mr. Christie but insists on having our report first. I'm afraid I've lost my usual knack for biting sarcasm and wit. It's simply spectacular."

"I noticed," Shiv said.

"Don't underestimate it, or Mozart. The play on which it's based, Beaumarchais's *Figaro*, was making a point—and the point was about equality between servants and their masters. Mozart's opera was banned until it was rewritten to fit court sensibilities. This is how Revolution comes, slowly, through a back door, a spark that catches the spirit of the time and sets it ablaze. Just a few years before the French Revolution, so you can imagine how dangerous it was." Shiv was only half listening; his eyes were quickly sweeping the dining room. Across from them, a young couple sat at a table. Snatches of their conversation reached him clearly. "It's outrageous. Appearing here on a night like this with your rajah in tow. In pink, no less!"

"Is he a rajah?"

"I expect so. Or he wouldn't be here, would he?"

"Are they—"

"Yes, most certainly."

Shiv froze as he realized they were talking about him and Lucy. Lucy smiled at him. "It's a beautiful evening. I'm delighted to be here with you." His hand stretched out across the tablecloth, as if to grasp his. Oh, how they shone, his green green eyes.

"Lucy, I—" Those people are watching us, judging us, interpreting us, he wanted to say.

"What is it?" He drew his hand back; it had nearly reached Shiv's.

At that moment, the maître d' appeared at their table. "Sir," he said, addressing Lucy. "I'm most sorry, but I have to ask you to move."

Lucy said, "What? Why?"

"I brought you to this table in error, sir. It was already reserved."

"I see. And your other guests refuse to accept any other table, is that so?"

"I'm afraid so, sir."

Lucy turned behind him to look, and there were Lord Windermere and Princess Hohenlohe. "You can tell Lord Windermere we're not moving."

"Sir, I would be most obliged to you if you and your guest would take another table. It's most awkward as Lord Windermere is a patron. We would be very happy to send over a complimentary bottle of our best champagne." The man was pleading with Lucy.

Shiv said, "I'm happy to move. Let's sit elsewhere."

Lucy's eyes filled with anger. He shook his head. "Let me handle this." He looked at the maître d', making a supreme effort to bite back the words he wanted to utter. His face was flushed. Shiv said quietly, "Please, Lucy, a scene would be awful." He could hear his heart thudding. "Please," he begged.

There was a long pause. "All right, we'll move," Lucy said to the host. "And you can keep your bloody champagne!" He got up. "Where do we go?"

"Thank you very much, sir," the man said, bowing deeply. "Please follow me."

He could do that, Shiv thought, as he pushed his chair back and followed Lucy. He could speak in a tone heightened by anger to the maître d' of a grand establishment like this one and, aside from some throat-clearing and eye-rolling from some guests, it was like a frisson that had merely pinched the room and died out as it reached the doors. Shiv would have been carted off to jail, or at least handcuffed and led away by officers to his great humiliation and shame.

———

AT THEIR NEW location in the room, Shiv sank down in his chair. Butterflies raged in his stomach. He couldn't understand why the trout looked so unappealing. A small dry-looking piece, surrounded by small potatoes and French beans thrown carelessly on the plate. Lucy's lamb looked succulent, juicy, and the scalloped potatoes surrounding it were carefully placed and perfectly browned. Shiv's first bite proved his eyes had correctly estimated the texture of the fish. It was chewy. Fish only got chewy if you overcooked it. Why, in a place like this, with a French chef who reputedly caressed the ingredients before cooking them, would they overcook the fish? A mistake, of course. He tried to eat the rest of the food on his plate but had lost his appetite.

Lucy looked at his plate. "Oh, that's terrible. I wouldn't tempt a cat with that. They've overcooked it."

When the waiter came over to refill their glasses of wine, Lucy said, "Can you ask the maître d' to come over, please?"

"Certainly, sir."

But the maitre d' was nowhere in sight. They waited and waited, drinking all the wine. Lucy's face had gone white; he was ice cold, blanched white with fury. Then he said, "Shiv, listen to me very carefully. This is atrocious. We're getting up, and we're leaving."

"What about the bill?"

"It's all been taken care of. Get up and walk towards that front entrance. We're leaving, do you understand?" Lucy was speaking very slowly, with deliberation.

"What about the rest of *Figaro*?"

"Do you seriously think we're going back in there after the way we've been treated this evening?"

They both rose together and as, in lockstep, in perfect sync, they walked towards the entrance, all eyes turned to look at them. It was like a dance, like that first time at the Red Hart. Two as one. Shiv felt

the sharp triumph of retaliation, the sheer strength of it. They belonged, as Lucy said. Let the vipers talk. Outside, Lucy said, "Let's go
home."

On the train back to London, they sat in silence as the late evening
countryside flew past the windows. Shiv spooled the scene through
his mind. It must have been the usual—his had been the only dark
face in that crowd. Still, the manager's behavior was inexplicable. The
man had gone out of his way to create an uncomfortable situation
for them. Why? Again it reared its head, the blot on an evening that
should have been memorable for all the right reasons.

Lucy said, "Forget it, eh? First night hiccups. It had nothing to do
with you. And those damned fascists had dug in their heels and had
to have their way."

But he knew it, Lucy knew it. That's why it had to be said. How
could he not blame himself? Lucy had been humiliated, too, Shiv
realized, not a social setback he'd likely experienced often. He'd let
his lover down in front of his people. He'd failed him. Shiv looked
away, his shame almost unbearable. A few lines of Pablo Neruda
came to him as he stared out the window. *I love you like certain dark
things are to be loved / in secret, between the shadow and the soul.* He
threw Lucy a quick glance. Would it always be like this?

As the train neared Victoria, Shiv said, "I think I should carry on
to Gloucester Square tonight."

"Why? Why not come home with me?"

"I'm craving sleep," Shiv said. He was smarting and needed to be
alone. This was territory Lucy could not enter. Lucy needed the assurance of love as much as he did. They were unable to help each
other. "I'll be fine tomorrow. Are you going to Bayswater?"

"Yes." Lucy looked out of the window. Shiv longed to ask him
what he was thinking. Unusually, he didn't know. This was the most

painful effect of the evening—the sudden separation between them. But at least Lucy was going home to *their* home, not to his mother's, which was reassuring.

At Victoria Station, they both stood on the pavement outside, waiting for cabs to show up. It was a chilly evening. Shiv pulled his coat tighter around his body. "Hey," Lucy said. "Come here." In a second he had his arms around Shiv's waist. "Fuck Glyndebourne," he said, raising a finger to Shiv's lip. His touch was blistering. "One of our kings said it best. 'I know no ways to mince it in love but directly to say, "I love you."'" Lucy's heart was thudding, like his. A policeman was watching them from across the road. Shiv said, "Later. There's a cop on the other side of the road." Lucy lingered then took his finger away. The cop seemed to be debating whether to come across to them. A cab drew up. "You take it," Lucy said. "Till tomorrow."

Which king had said that, Shiv wondered, as the cab sped off through darkened streets. Which one? A little voice inside whispered, in agony: why is this so hard? For Lucy wanted nothing less than to be seen in public with his lover by his side. What had he said, just the other day? "The line between what's acceptable and what's legal is now so fine, we can be open, we can flout the law a little without risking Reading Gaol. It's 1934, Shiv, we don't have to live in fear." The truth, as a barrister knew, is that the law is the law until it's changed. Rules had to be obeyed. The noncompliant would suffer. But the want, dear god, the want. How did one cope with it?

As the cab drew up outside the Polaks', Shiv turned to the cabbie. "Can you take me to Bayswater?"

"What? You're not getting off here? Yes, all right. What's the address?"

Shiv climbed up the stairs, phrasing it all in his mind. It would shock him, but he had to tell him, had to get it out. His footsteps lagged as he saw the door ahead, as if this would be the last time.

Lucy was lying on the sofa reading, a drink by his side on the table. He turned his head to look at him as Shiv entered the room. He was surprised; light rushed into his eyes. Shiv stood by the door without taking his coat off.

"I had to come back because it's now or never." He paused. "Gosh, I've been wondering how to say this for so long. And now I feel tongue-tied. This is so hard."

"What is it?" Lucy scrutinized him. He moved his feet to the floor and patted the space next to him. "Come here."

Shiv went over to the sofa. He took his coat off and threw it over the arm of the sofa. He sat down. Lucy moved closer, then put his arms around his torso in a hug. He drew back, then took Shiv's face in his hands and leaned forward to place a tender kiss on his lips. Shiv flinched as an intense wave of desire shot through him. It was getting harder, not easier, to tell him.

"I have to move," he said, shifting away from Lucy. He turned to look at the shabby rug beneath the coffee table. He couldn't look at Lucy. "Look, I should have told you earlier."

"What is it?" His face wore a worried frown. "Have you murdered someone?"

Shiv shook his head, tried to smile. "It's hard to explain. In India, people get married very young. So young that they don't know what they're doing. Their parents decide what should be done for them. They have no choice. None."

Lucy nodded. "Horrible practice that, but it's relatively well known. . . ." He gave Shiv a puzzled look.

"Yes, but, you see—when I was leaving for England, my mother . . ."

"No!" Lucy said, drawing back as it hit him. "You're not married!"

Shiv nodded miserably. "She was sixteen and I eighteen when it happened—three months before I left. My mother insisted. He'll come back for a wife and child, she said, if for nothing else. And then, just as she had hoped, Seher got pregnant before I left. The child, a boy, was born in my absence. He's now nearly three."

There was utter silence between them. Lucy got up and poured some whiskey in a glass. He brought it over to Shiv, who took it, and downed the contents in one gulp. "Careful," Lucy said. "That stuff doesn't sit well with you." Shiv cracked a smile.

Lucy stared at him for a long time, his eyes raking his face. Finally he spoke. "You look like a guilty dog who's been up to no good somewhere and come back home, expecting a hiding! I'm not going to give you one, so calm down. You're weighted . . . you're not free. Your obligations are enormous—duty, country, family. I knew it, of course, but I hadn't expected this."

"I'm sorry," Shiv said. "I should have told you that first night at the Red Hart."

"Why didn't you?" Lucy asked, the angles of his face sharp, his eyes probing.

Why hadn't he? How could he have? He'd never been swept off his feet like that. Long before their bodies had come together, mere touch between them was ignition enough. It was there from the moment they met. The truth shocked him: he had wanted Lucy, still wanted him, as much as Lucy desired him. Sex, beauty, electric power, a hunger that only the other could satisfy, had bound them both.

"I didn't know you well enough that night."

"That slid off the tongue easily," Lucy said. "Go on, try again."

"I couldn't," he said lamely. "I was a dusty scholar, combing through cases in the Middle Temple library. I'm still there, researching cases. I don't know what you ever saw in me. A boring barrister type. But you've made my evenings magical. How was I going to risk that?"

"So why are you risking it now? The truth, please."

"Because of you. I was lost, really, before you came along. I don't know what love is. But sometimes I think this must be as close as one can get to it. I mean, people like me." He looked away from Lucy's eyes. "And we're in a deeper place. If we're going there, you have to know this about me now."

It was more than he had wanted to say but Lucy deserved it. If he was to be shown the door, which is what he deserved, he wanted him to know how he had transformed his life. Shiv reached for his coat.

"Oh, stop being so theatrical!" Lucy said. "Leave that coat alone."

Lucy got up again. He came back with a leather folder. Opening it, he took out a sheet of thick paper. "Look at this!" Shiv moved closer to the lamp to examine the paper Lucy had handed him. He looked at it carefully. It was a beautifully executed drawing of a naked man by a window. The man had large eyes that stared luminously out of the charcoal drawing. His vitality, his stance, leaning forward slightly into a world he wasn't certain about, was captivating. He seemed fragile and virile at the same time. The movement of the entire composition was riveting. Shiv drew in his breath. "You did this!" he said.

Lucy nodded with a proud smile. "Look at it carefully!" he commanded. Shiv looked again. Then he saw. The man was him. Lucy had captured him as he was—wrestling with longing, desire, ambition, and drive. All of it was in there. The tearing behind his eyes told him he was very vulnerable. To have been seen as he was, that was what shook him. It told him Lucy was as moved, no, deeply affected by their love as he was. There were many sketches in the folder; some of park scenes, some of buildings, some of other gay men on benches. But the ones that spoke loudly, passionately, were the ones Lucy had made of him. "I did them in Greece," Lucy said.

Shiv was speechless.

That night, they were especially tender with each other, their gestures substituting for verbal communication. Shiv, relieved, wondered how his lover could forgive so much, not punish him for his revelation by turning away from him. Lucy, realizing how vast Shiv's fear of rejection had been, touched him protectively, reassuringly from time to time, letting him know that he wasn't going to hold it against him, or use the newfound knowledge about him in some way as leverage. Shiv was aware of his lover's body differently that night. Lucy had shown him his nurturing side, that he could be playful and also supportive. Perhaps it was true that when you truly loved someone, you had no fear. He felt Lucy's cold feet warming as he rubbed them with his warm ones. Shiv's arm lay across Lucy's midriff. The blanket covering them both had slipped towards him. Very quietly, not wishing to wake him, Shiv inched the blanket across so that it now covered Lucy more than him. Towards dawn, he woke, freezing. The back of Lucy's neck, its tender eggshell skin, was close to his face. He moved towards it, kissed it softly. His lips felt cool as they brushed Lucy's skin. Lucy's hand immediately reached back for his, tightening around his fingers. His heart lurched. He breathed the moment in slowly, wanting it to last forever.

As he dressed in the frigid temperature of the room in the morning, he saw Lucy's body curled like an orange peel under the blankets. His mouth was slightly open. He looked defenceless, vulnerable, in a way he never was when awake. His rhythmic breathing and half smile told Shiv he was probably in the middle of a pleasant dream. This is when intimacy is deepest between lovers, when our faces speak of the dream worlds we're in, and when we wake, we clutch dream fragments, searching for words to know them, to share them. Resisting the urge to embrace him, he made his way out of the flat, avoiding Mrs. Parnell's cat, who ran in front of him down the stairs, as though blocking his way.

∽

It was a rainy afternoon in Bayswater.

Lucy said, "We're working today."

Oh yes? At what?

Your diction, Lucy said. "You're one of the select few now—a Templar, about to impress our courts with your brilliance. Your speech must match!"

"My speech?"

Hmmm, yes, your speech. Displaying a talent for teaching with flair, Lucy asked him to list seven different reactions evoked by seeing a person (a) you knew very well and liked; (b) you knew somewhat; (c) you knew as a passing acquaintance; (d) you didn't know at all, but said person was with someone you knew; (e) an elderly lady you didn't know; (f) a young woman among the guests at a party you'd been invited to; and (g) a well-known person, but one you didn't personally know, on meeting them at a talk, a gallery, or a shoot. *One, two, three,* Go. Lucy handed him a piece of a paper and a pencil. Puzzled, and slightly miffed, for he had been expecting an afternoon in bed together, Shiv said all right and began making a list. He wrote, chewing at the end of the pencil occasionally as he stopped to consider: genuine pleasure; hesitation; the urge to flee; curiosity; indifference; guardedness; irritation. He handed Lucy the list.

Right, Lucy said. "Well done. We're in business!" Wondering what was coming next, Shiv sat looking at him, slightly suspicious. Was this a new prelude to making love?

There followed a course on English society behavior.

"So first bows, handshakes, nods, hats, and smiles. The English have a subtle road map of signs to be able to read one another—it gives us something to do. We must know how to take in the person we're looking at, or whose hand has been extended towards us. So bows first."

Bows: once you've started bowing to someone, you can't stop. There's no changing your mind. You will always have to bow, in precisely the same way, every time you see that person. Forewarning: choose carefully. A bow is formal, not much practiced these days. If you bow, it will be taken very seriously.

When would I bow to someone? Shiv asked.

"A professional higher-up—say, that senior bencher who's known for winning a very difficult case, someone you admire. You bow when you're introduced. And if that relationship has stayed static, no movement at all, then you continue to bow to each other for the rest of your lives. If you've been for a drink with the man at your local pub, then, of course, the bowing stops. Then there's the nod. Nods are reserved for public places. At the opera, you spy someone you know in their box. You angle your opera glasses—lazily, indifferently, mind you, not looking desperate to find a nodding acquaintance—and when you've confirmed that it is the same person, and when his eye catches yours, you nod, acknowledging him. It's important to have people to nod to in public places. It shows you're a man about town. People can go through their entire lives as bowing or nodding acquaintances. It involves nothing other than a slight turn of the head and a head movement.

"At memorials, burials, funerals, a grave nod, directed generally, is required, whether you're deeply invested in the person's death or not. It's acknowledging the situation."

"Show me!" Shiv said.

Lucy's face instantly assumed a stiff, grave expression as he moved his head slowly. "It's the nod for when you do what you have to do." He nodded gravely again.

Shiv laughed. A pantomime this—English courtesies and civilities! Indians went for the hug, a catch-all for every social situation.

"And then the handshake. You already know touch is offensive to the English. We skirt around one another in every conceivable way, when one touch would do it. But an outstretched hand must be taken. There is no question of turning away from it unless you're mortal enemies. Limp handshakes aren't interpreted well—you can't shrink from a handshake: you either meet it full on, and shake the other hand vigorously and if gripped, then gripped equally in a strong hold, moving it up and down to convey enthusiasm, or you nod to avoid the vigorous handshake. When someone is being effusive, a prolonged pumping of your hand, say, you must interpret it. Is it a genuine large and generous personality; or is it a social climber, who is eager to make your acquaintance for what it can do for him. Flee from the latter, unless you, too, want to play the same game. Quid pro quo. But know it for what it is. A woman isn't expected to pump your hand up and down. Return it in kind, a bare touch, fingers meeting, then falling away."

Lucy reminded him of that moment out on the lawn in Glynde-bourne when his friend James Cameron introduced his fiancée, Sylvia, to Shiv. "She held out her hand. You returned the gesture with a stiff bow, ignoring her outstretched hand."

"Did I?"

"Yes"—he looked at Shiv's list—"it conveyed, let's see, both the urge to flee, and hesitation. I knew you were playing it safe. But she didn't. It came across as a rebuff. She was being warm and friendly and expected the same reaction from you."

"Oh dear. Did I embarrass you? Is that why we're doing this?"

Lucy laughed. "No. It's because you're going to be trawling through the courts now and I want all those pompous judges there to think Advani's one of us. Knows the ropes, how things are done." Bristling, slightly humiliated, Shiv recognized the information he was being given was invaluable. As a learner, he hadn't needed to show this kind of know-how. As a practitioner, it would be expected of him.

"Raising your hat is by far the most eloquent way of conveying all the reactions you've listed here." From buoyant uplifts and abrupt doffs to the coolly indifferent slight raise, and the imperious mechanical lift, Lucy ran down every conceivable social situation. "What's the impression you want to make? Let your hat speak for you." In a few minutes, he had assumed several personalities—from the pleasant to the best avoided. "Meet chilliness with an imperious mechanical lift—like this"—raising his hat a bare inch from his head, with his nose slightly up in the air—"and mutual enthusiasm like this"—raising his hat in a forward springing movement a good four inches above his head, and smiling pleasantly—"and, if you want to convey sympathy (to a spurned lover, a sorrowing husband, a person whose horse lost at the races), you nod as you slowly raise your hat to him."

"It's only men, is it, that you can raise your hat to?"

"Yes, it's a male thing to do. You smile at women and nod, but control it, and let it match your relationship. That's what it always is. Match your gestures to your level of acquaintanceship."

"But you don't follow any of these rules!" Shiv said.

"No. I make it a point not to."

"Then why—"

"I'm not a barrister in court, whose every move is being interpreted to disqualify me from the job, possibly from court. Darling, what you don't understand is that if you want to be one of us, you have to show you know the rules. Even when you get to be in a position where you can ignore them. Trust me, I know my people well!"

Being overdressed, he explained, was worse than being underdressed. You work towards less, not more. To appear uncaring of what people think, even though you cared deeply, was what you wanted to convey. Even appearing underdressed is a mark of independence, he said. "You know the rules, but this is how you've chosen to interpret them, or to skirt them. And that invariably produces both cattiness and admiration." Lucy was sharing his Lucyness with him, and Shiv stood there helplessly listening to a way of life he could never follow.

"But surely that's because you know the rules," Shiv finally said. "You don't understand. People like me can't ignore them."

Lucy said, "We're getting you there, don't you worry."

———————

WHEN IT CAME to words, Lucy presented strictures he'd never observed, never even been aware of. "You'd be surprised at how many rungs down you could slip in someone's estimation simply by mispronouncing a word."

"A word?"

"Yes, words aren't there just so you can express yourself. Your choice of words conveys who you are. How you say a word, how your tongue shapes itself around it. How it sounds in your ear. How it leaves an effect on your listener. How it conveys your feeling at that moment. Words change all the time, along with your feelings. They aren't frozen, they live, but they live with how you say them." He said that not many people knew the secret language of words—a word could mean so many things.

Shiv frowned. Was he having him on? "No, Shiv. Listen. Listen to the coloration of the word *pleased*. It can go from the palest pink to a screaming magenta." He went through different iterations of the word—from expressions of joy, to satisfaction, to an official confirmation of something granted, to an acknowledgement that someone had seen sense on an issue, to a marriage proposal happily accepted. Pleased. What a simple, almost vague word. "But look how it changes with every situation, how it means different things." Despite himself, Shiv was fascinated by the complexion of a word. "Say this absurd word, Shiv. Try it. It's from the French *élégiaque*." He wrote it down—E-l-e-g-i-a-c—and handed him the paper. Shiv looked at it, tried to imagine his tongue shaping itself around the word. "Eee-lee-gee—"

Lucy clapped his hands around his ears. "Stop!" And then went on to say it: ell-e-jy-ack. As in jive. Ell-e-jy-ack. Say it, Shiv. He did. He got the damn word under his tongue and spat it out with impatience. "There!" Softer, softer, not such harsh syllables. They should blend into one another, with a word like that.

"I doubt I'm ever going to need a word like that in the courts," Shiv said.

Lucy laughed. "You never know. 'That was an elegiac cross-examination,' said the judge!" They both burst out laughing. "Listen to this, Shiv. 'That was paarful and irreff-you-tible, an excellent adjoo-dication, your honour.' Paar, contraction. Irrref, not ir-re-fyoo-table."

And so his elocution lessons continued. "Don't say home, say house. Not mansion, but big house. Don't say never never, say never ever. Dinner isn't lunch; drinks, not cocktails, will do very well for every kind of gathering involving alcoholic libations. Don't say toilet paper when you mean lavatory paper. Lav paper is even better. Not rug but carpet, not cycle but bike. Spectacles, not glasses. Not raincoat but macintosh. Bag, just bag for anything that transports things. Luxuriant, luks-yorient, like it's spelt, not lughzyor-ient. And it's *lam*-entuhble, emphasis on the lam. Not le-*men*-tuhble.

"Now with dress: Don't wear anything that looks new, or as if it's been bought especially for the event. The slightly used look is always preferable to the shiny new one. This goes for everything—the older, the better. Never look as if you've dressed for the part. Never mind that you've been fussing with every braid, ribbon, and medal for hours, you must look as though everything was just casually thrown on. So scuff those shoes a little before you walk into court."

Shiv said, "This is beginning to sound like a joke. I think the preoccupation with performance, with ritual, with every inflection of speech, with how much dirt there is on your shoes, or how new your hat looks, is truly tedious. I can't imagine this is taken very seriously by people every single day of their lives."

"Listen to me, Shiv. You're not really hearing me. You want to be recognized for your skills and talents. Do you seriously think people are lining up to come up to you and say, my god, you look so brilliant—you must be brilliant. No, of course not. We're—the British, I mean—used to sifting wheat from chaff. We invent new rules all the time in order to exclude people, not to include them."

"Precisely. You *are* a toff. You were brought up in toffness. These are your people. I'm an outsider."

"And you'll stay one if you don't adapt. I mean it. You're going to have to infiltrate the places where there's bound to be work aplenty for you. Lady Lavina's monthly garden parties are lavish affairs—everyone who's anyone is invited. It's where exclusive London circles do a star turn on the first Saturday of every month. You want an invitation because you know you'll meet one of the three Ds, possibly all, there—Death, Debt, and Divorce—the mainstay of all court cases. You're not going to get it sounding and acting middle class. They'll say he's not quite the right colour, but the other attributes make him nearly good enough. I mean he must be a rajah, otherwise why is he here? And he's got style. That's going all the way—you've won acceptance."

"So I not only have to become a toff like you, I also have to be a rajah?"

"'Fraid so, my heart. These aren't my rules. If you're not one of us, you've got to have the money. You'll still be marginal but at least you'll be seen at those lavish affairs because you have tons of money. This is how they think and they're the ones who're going to be giving you work in the future."

"So some rules must be followed, and others must not only be disregarded but shown, displayed, as being disregarded."

"Yes, you're understanding it now. The rules you follow are the unwritten ones. The rules you blithely ignore are the written ones."

"You're all lunatics!" Shiv said. "I'd rather know what I'm dealing with than step into your quicksands. Stop trying to make me into a dusky version of yourself!"

"I'm trying to ease your path forward!"

"You're showing me how wide the gap is between us. With every word, you've widened it. I hadn't thought we were such poles apart."

"We're not," Lucy shouted. "Just show you know the game so you can play. No one's asking you to bare your soul. It's a game. You do understand, don't you?"

Shiv threw his hands up in the air and walked away from Lucy. *Savoir faire* again, wasn't it? His lover was probably ashamed of him, hence this elaborate education in the manners and mores of the upper classes. He stood by the window. Rain was sheeting down, hitting the pavements hard. Trees shook in a rousing wind. It wasn't enough to dress, talk, think, even smell like them, to guzzle champagne like them; to train your binoculars with equal enthusiasm on horses galloping across turf at the Royal Ascot races; to pretend you were enjoying everything they did as much as them; to have passed their exams with flying colours, to be recognized for his brilliance by those who came to know him professionally. You also had to show that you were the same egg really, just that you were a deeper tan than them. To be accepted on his own terms—that's what he wanted, and that's what he would fight for.

Shiv was thinking of Indian chameleons, how deftly they changed colour in tune with their backgrounds. As they clambered up the morning-glory-covered garden wall back home, he observed their attempts at blending in in order to survive, their skins going from brick red to a neon green to a violet blue as they met each impediment in their path. This is what he was expected to be, as seen through shifting lenses—as English as they come—"One of us," yet Indian, so he could be categorized as a misplaced exotic or a faded aristocrat from a bygone oriental age of splendour. He didn't want to just make it into their world under a guise they chose. He wanted to carve his own place within it.

Lucy shook his head, then came over to him with an air of resignation. "Look, forgive me. I was teaching you to be the very things I hate. Hypocrisy, for example." Shiv stood silently by the window. When had hypocrisy become a social asset? He'd seen it back home, of course, the constant discrepancy between what the British publicly said, what they did, and what they said in their clubs, in front of the Indian serving staff, who related every word to the community at large. But Lucy was showing him the true price of equality. *Think like us* was one thing. *Speak like us so we know you think like us* was another. Lucy said, "I know I'm being overprotective. I fell in love with you the way you are. You do see that, yes?"

Shiv didn't answer. Lucy's arms went around him. "Just forget it, eh? What was I trying to do, make you one of us. When you're the rare one."

It was at that moment—as they both saw the glittering garden parties, the evening soirées, the places where Lucy was a regular, and where he twinkled like the brightest star, fade away—that Shiv saw their destinies had come together in a dance. He is not they, just as I am not them, back in India. In a world where like was paired with like, they were as unfathomable a coupling as could be imagined. Yet together they shone. That was their truth.

As they walked past Mecklenburgh Square one evening, Shiv said, "Why is no one ever in those gardens?" Beautiful, private enclosures around which grand, imposing houses stood looking imperiously down at passers-by. "There's never anyone in there."

Lucy laughed. "Those gardens aren't for being in. Gautier put his finger on it. Only foreigners see these things for the oddities they are. All these residents have keys, and the gardens are private, but it's not the gardens people living here care about as much as keeping other people out. It's sad, but perfectly true. It's our snobbishness, our need for exclusivity. You saw it in unbridled form at Glyndebourne, didn't you?"

"That was an unusual situation," Shiv said, not wanting to get into it.

"No other country fetishises royalty as we do," Lucy said. "Anything to do with the House of Windsor is worshipped. And royalty is tied to the Anglican church. Worship involves ritual. Your Inns of Court, for example, are highly ritualized houses of learning, there at the pleasure of the Crown. Those precincts were once occupied by the Knights Templar but different reigning monarchs at different times, Henry VIII, as you can imagine, chief among them, got rid of the Knights and the legal profession moved in. The King's Counsel, Middle Temple Hall dinners, Silks. The Royal Opera. Guild Halls with their white-gloved dinners. Once a place is invested with the imprimatur of the Crown, it is instantly fetishised."

"So you hate the king?" It was a naïve question, and Shiv knew it as soon as it slipped out of his mouth.

"I'm not an anti-royalist, far from it. I happily trot along to upper-class society's celebrations involving pomp and circumstance, everyone eyeing the entrance for a glimpse of HRH, His Royal Highness. It's laughable, really, but few of us can resist it."

"What a strange pair we are, you and I, you with your ermine-clad kings and tiara'd queens, we Indians with our loincloth-clad leader."

Lucy burst out laughing. "He's got true taste, your man. Gautier called us 'varnished barbarians' who would buy taste if we could. And I rather fear he's right. We're not artists. We're tamers, conquerors. We build bridges and railways, we manufacture goods, we arrive in dusty lands and erect beautiful churches and tranquil hospitals there. But we're not artists. It's only in architecture, and specifically in the building of cathedrals, that we excel. Our cathedrals are sublime—ethereal what we've managed with stone. Spires, belfries, naves, and vaults are our poetry. Even the smallest country church, coming into one's vision out of a field of green, shows grace, is a paean to form." They walked on in silence.

"India has its palaces, its forts, too, and, of course, the Taj Mahal. . . ."

"Now if anything was a paean to form, to grace, to radiant beauty, that would be it," Lucy said. "I read somewhere that a rare light-reactive marble was used to build it. The stone changes hue to reflect the many colours of the sun. I think it's called makrana, or something like that, that translucent marble. I'd give anything to see it. Take me there someday, won't you, Shiv? I want to see your home," he said, linking his arm through Shiv's.

"Nothing would give me greater pleasure." He suddenly imagined them both there, Lucy's arm around him. He sighed; they could no more be open about their relationship in India than they could here.

As they walked, Shiv thought of how Lucy had laid his world open to him; had invited him in; had taught him how to navigate its shoals. Could he do the same if they were back in India? Could he show him all the delights of his childhood, could he walk along his Indus as they walked along his Thames, sharing thoughts and opening their hearts to each other? Sadness filled him. So much separated them, from their resources to their circumstances. There were a few pounds left in his bank account and it was only Mr. Polak's thoughtful loans of money that showed up quietly on his dresser or at the breakfast table, sparking humiliation and gratitude, that were keeping him afloat.

Lucy's reserves were boundless; he chose to live like a bohemian. For him, their cold water flat was an aesthete's delight—for all aesthetes occasionally long to be ascetics—and a tolerable place for their trysts. For Shiv, the flat was an enchanted place. That was where the dividing lines faded, where doubts and fears receded. And in the pulsing intersections where their hearts met, there were gifts that only love can bring: bright flashes of clarity, the radiance of true care. He knew it would have to end at some point. But not now, a voice from within cried out loudly. *Not now.*

"My mother wants to meet you." Lucy gave Shiv a quick look. "She thinks you've been very good for me."

His mother. So here it came, finally, the conversation he'd been awaiting and dreading.

"What are you thinking?" Lucy asked.

"Oh . . . yes, yes, of course," Shiv said. "I've wanted to meet her."

"She's trying to make a decision about her flat in Grosvenor Square. She can't stand the thought of us living in such Spartan digs together—thinks she might let us have her place. She prefers her pile in the country, in any case."

Shiv felt a breathless heaving in his lungs, a worried gnawing in his stomach.

"It's got four bedrooms, two full bathrooms, a beautiful drawing room, and there's room for everything—we could have the most wonderful dinner parties, and you'd meet all my friends."

Lucy's world, opening its doors wide. He wasn't sure he wanted to go through them. "What's the matter?" Lucy asked.

"Nothing. I'm just wondering about the Polaks. They've been so kind. I don't think I'm quite ready yet to say goodbye."

"You wouldn't be. We'll have them over. Every bloody Sunday."

That could never happen, he knew. Late one night, as he and Lucy stood at a street corner across from the Polaks' house saying goodbye, Shiv looked up at the upper floor, alerted by a curtain twitching across a window. He saw a bathroom light go out, and knew that Millie had seen them both. He said a hurried good-night to Lucy and went quickly across the road and let himself into the house. As he went up the stairs, he smelt Millie's Yardley lavender soap scent on the landing between their rooms. Powdery and austere, it filled the space in aggrieved puffs. He knew then that she was aware of his nocturnal jaunts but would keep them secret. Millie Polak was as deep as a hawk. She knew joy, and tragedy. Her face, lit like mother of pearl, shone with knowledge. She didn't speak much at their lunch dates at the Middle Temple Fountain Garden, but those meetings were all the more special to him for the largely wordless communication between them. Her mutterings—*Hmm, yes . . . , Ah . . .* , or *I thought so,* or that mock incredulous *Really?*—would tell him that she had understood all that he wished to tell her.

At dinner once she said, "This city is such a dangerous place at night for young men."

Mr. Polak said, "That's odd. You mean for young women, surely?"

"No," Millie said. "I meant young men." She knew.

Now Shiv looked at Lucy, hating him for forcing him into a predicament that seemed so unnecessary. Lucy looked diffident but Shiv could hear his heart, beating as loudly as his own. "So what do you say?" Lucy asked.

"All right."

"Mother wants us to meet at the flat. She wants to picture us living in it."

"Yes," Shiv said. It was an innocent enough remark but being seen in that way by an aristocratic lady with money to burn—as a titillating spectacle, a brown-skinned man living with her son, her only child—made him deeply uncomfortable. Would they become an amusement for her and her kind? Was she seeing him as her son's caretaker? *She thinks you're very good for me.* He frowned.

Lucy looked at him again. His lips were fashioning words, but he left them unsaid.

It hadn't been a quick fling, the kind a man needs to get out of the way so he can get on with the real stuff of his life. No, Lucy was like Prospero waving a magic wand in his life.

It was one of those freezing Bayswater mornings. Lucy was up before him. He brought a breakfast tray to bed with him, and they ate leathery eggs and toast together, drank the tea quickly while it still had a faint steam. Lucy's face was set hard, as if he'd come to some sort of decision and needed to get it out now. "You're not enthusiastic about meeting Mother, not excited, at least not the way I am, about the flat in Grosvenor Square," he said.

Shiv looked at Lucy, feeling a growing emptiness inside as Lucy spoke. He was playing with the fork, moving it about this way and that. Shiv reached for his hand, cupped his tenderly over Lucy's.

"No!" Lucy said, taking it away.

"What's wrong?"

Lucy got up and stood by the bed in his silky flowery Japanese kimono, his graceful body now rigid, his eyes mocking and scornful. "You're not on board. You want to be but you're not. You—you're so much more of an innocent than I had thought. I imagined you were confused, it was new to you, but you were all in it. And now, you're not."

"I was, I am," Shiv cut in. "I mean, I am! I am in love with you, you have to believe that. You do, don't you?"

There was a long silence. Then Lucy said, quietly, "I'm not sure, Shiv. It's knocked you sideways. I don't want to sit around, waiting for you to find out how far you can go with it." The kimono had slipped off one shoulder, and revealed his thin, delicate neck bones, his pale eggshell skin.

"Please, Lucy!" Pain knifed through Shiv.

"Look!" Lucy said. "You've got pressures I don't. You're a man with a destiny. Very grand, that. I believe in you—you're going to kick us out of India—I'll be cheering all the way. You've got a wife and a son, and they're waiting to have you back, I'm sure. But there's also what we have, what we've created here. I can't go on like this. I need some assurances from you—that you're not going to let this— our life—go." Not a trace of irony, not one, could he detect in Lucy's response. He was deadly serious.

Shiv couldn't bear it. "I'll be the bad boy for you," Lucy had said. And he had. Not once had he pushed him to choose between him and his family back home. Their love was stronger than ever. Lucy was London, Lucy was life. It was Lucy's face he saw just before sleep claimed him at night and the face that greeted him in the morning, whether he was physically there or not. "I can't let you walk away from me," Shiv said. "I think it would kill me."

Lucy gave him a sharp look. "No," he said. "You'd live. I don't know why I know that, but I do." He'd seen what he wanted, for the ironical stance was back.

Shiv couldn't speak. His head was a blur, his eyes couldn't focus. All he saw was anger. He had failed the person he loved most in the world.

The longer he stayed silent, the colder Lucy became. "Why don't you seduce a woman and see what that's like? It's been a while. You probably don't remember fucking a woman anymore. Seduce one, why don't you? I suspect you're not really a 'bugger-boy.' You wanted to see what it was like. Now you know. So just shove off." His hollow voice echoed off the walls.

To Shiv's stunned silence, Lucy offered only a shielded mossy stare. Disappointment clogged his eyes. The more Shiv dilly-dallied, the angrier Lucy got.

Shiv didn't want to fuck a woman. It was Lucy who had inspired everything he had come to know as passion, as love, as sex. "No!" he cried, angrily. "It was you, your beauty, your enchanting terrible beauty, that made me risk finding out. And then I fell in love. I wasn't expecting to, but I did." He shouldn't have used the word *terrible*, he realized. It told Lucy how threatened he was by their relationship. "I'm sorry," he cried. "I didn't mean that the way it sounded."

Lucy's eyes gleamed. "What did you mean, then? There aren't many ways to slice the word."

He'd focused on it—*terrible*. Shiv couldn't speak, his eyes were glued to the pulse in Lucy's throat, its erratic throb.

He sat on the bed next to Lucy, put his head in his hands. "What do you want me to do?" he asked quietly.

Swift came the reply. "Live with me in the Grosvenor Square flat. Move in with me, *live* with me so we can be a couple." Alarm bells began ringing within. Just the past week, Mr. Polak had given him good news: Gandhi was so pleased with him, with how far he had got so quickly. ("Remember that only a fraction of colonials who register to read law in this country are actually passed. To be called to the bar is a singular achievement for Indians, and Gandhi knows that better than anyone.") He had great plans for him. "You're front-line, Shiv. You, and gifted ones like you, will free India! Think on that. Free your country from its oppressors!"

Elated, Shiv had joined his hands together, trying to stop joy spilling out of him. "You heard from Gandhi?"

"The man himself," Mr. Polak replied.

How could he risk it? How could he give up his future now? His mind flew back to his ten-year-old self, telling Gandhi he wanted to be just like him when he grew up. "Can you give up desire?" Gandhi had asked him. Yes, he had said, hardly knowing what desire was. Now here it was, the ultimate test. Shiv couldn't look at Lucy, the beauty of him, the raw, biting, angry, stunning beauty of him. He couldn't speak a word.


LUCY GOT UP and opened the closet. He pulled out a few clothes and left the room. Shiv heard him dressing in the drawing room, the crunch of clothes being hastily pulled on, the jamming of feet into shoes, the heavy pull of coat against body. Paralysed by indecision, he couldn't move, couldn't think of what to say to stop him. In a few minutes, he was gone, leaving the front door of the flat ajar. For a tall man, he was exceptionally light on his feet. But his footsteps, usually elfin, seemed heavy as he went down the stairs. Even the way he turned towards you, with one smooth liquid movement, had the grace of a swan. Nothing stuck or jerked, as if there was no internal agitation to him. "Do you ever hesitate?" Shiv had once asked him. "Of course," he replied. "But you mustn't show it. It's interpreted as fear." Shiv could see him in his mind's eye, standing there by the side of the steps, that endearing bent, like a reed in the wind, when he reached for the knob on the front door, about to push it open. There was a long pause, as if he was hesitating. "I'd move in with him if he came back," Shiv told himself. "Whatever the price, I'll pay it." He held his breath. Then he heard the loud creak of the front door being opened, a bang that told him Lucy had gone. Shiv rushed to the window, watched him cross the street. Why should someone as fabulous as that give me the time of day in any case? he thought. He deserves something so much better.

Lucy had told him about some fabled beaches in the Greek islands where waters of many colours, some so complex they have no names, wash over stones, drenching them with their hues. This is how we hear the earth speaking to us about what we do not know, Lucy said. The inner chambers of shells roar in our ears, the colours on stones speak of the intermingling of waters from many different seas. "We're still in the dark ages about so much," he said. What did Shiv know at that moment? Desire. And also that it had fled because he was unworthy of the privilege.

Then the rat he'd always suspected was there, somewhere, in the flat, came scuttling in. It stood still, its whiskers quivering, looking at Shiv, as though knowing it was safe, that the enfeebled man before him was incapable of shooing off a fly. He had always said there was a rat in the flat. Lucy would say, "No, it's Mrs. Parnell shunting around her flat. Yes, she's keeping tabs on us, but she's harmless." To prove it, Lucy bought a rat trap and left it on the kitchen floor. Either they had a wily rat on their premises or . . . there wasn't one. The trap sat empty. Shiv sat there, in the pallid light, letting the chilly flat freeze him while the rat scampered about.

As he reached the front door, he saw Lucy's kimono, the last thing he'd grabbed on his way out, lying in a heap on the floor. He picked it up and cupped it in both his hands. It sank like a bird into his palms. He held the fabric to his nose. Lucy's scent still lingered there: violets and oud. He sniffed and sniffed, feeling dismembered, in tatters. Why had Lucy reached for this one thing as he left? Why had he wanted it, when his cashmere cardigans and handmade leather shoes, his silver jewelry and sapphire ring were still there in the flat? Grateful for the fabric in his hands, he folded it carefully and stuffed it into his coat pocket. Bits of the flowery material draped the side of his coat.

As he shut the flat door behind him, he heard a high-pitched squeal—it was coming from inside the flat. He put his ear to the door: urgent screams of agony filled his ears. The trap: the rat had succumbed.

He drew away in horror. The door to Mrs. Parnell's flat opened. Suddenly there she was, in the flesh. A tall, large woman in a blue plaid dress stretched tightly across her bosom, wiry grey hair surrounding a jowly face, blue velvet slippers on her feet. Mrs. Parnell! She was staring at him, expecting him to do something about the hair-raising screams of anguish filling the landing outside their flats. That small creature, the overpowering sound! He stared back at her; they locked eyes for a minute, then he turned around and fled down the stairs, racing out into the street, leaving the front door behind him open, not stopping till he reached the entrance to Bayswater underground station. There he leaned against a wall for support, and slowly sank to the ground.

Back in his bedroom at the Polaks', he shut the door and sat on his bed. Everything had changed. Everything, even the city he was beginning to love. He hadn't fought to keep him, he hadn't offered Lucy everything he had, as Lucy had to him. Shiv had precious little in material wealth, but what he had, and what he could give, went beyond wealth and status in life. They had made each other happy. He should have offered him everything he had.

WHEN THE MOON reshapes itself into a horseshoe, it is hungriest, glows at its brightest. It is unpredictable. It adds to your store or it takes away. He was like a lean hungry moon, beaming down streets where he and Lucy had roamed. He sat down on the same park benches, stopped at the same art galleries, the same bookshops. He went to parties he didn't want to go to, hoping for a glimpse of him. He even walked past the Bayswater flat, bracing himself for a sight of Lucy with someone new. As he began losing hope of seeing Lucy again, certain areas became no-go zones. Edgware Road, Regent's Canal, Hampstead, where some of Lucy's relatives lived. London was strangling him. Their embers had scattered far and wide, across such a wide swath of the city that he felt always on the verge of a panic attack.

He regretted his words, said in ignorance, in fear. He would never again know the kind of love he had known with Lucy. Their encounter felt like a dream, its tender moments floating into memory like stills from silent movies, fading back into oblivion even as you attempted to pin them down. When he tried to recall Lucy's face, it scumbled into many expressions, becoming remote, like the face of a beautiful stranger in a crowd. Perhaps that is how we remember our lovers, in bits and fragments; a racy night whisper; a lingering touch; a laugh; a phrase. "Humbuggery!" he could hear Lucy say, as he stripped someone privately of pretence.

And then the languid way he slid out of his clothes . . . Shiv's body juddered with the shock of isolation, of loss.

A city's doors are in its inhabitants, Shiv reflected. Each one is a key to its secrets, its inner workings, bearing a lifetime of knowledge earned through pleasure and pain. Like members of a tribe, we are marked by the cities where we live. We are the city, for it is in us, and we dwell within it. When we fall in love, we inherit our lover's personal markings, his tribal bearings—his world. And when your loved one leaves, you lose it. The doors are closed, the keys taken back, and you must survive as best as you can, or flee from its gates.

Where we once knew where we were when we heard pigeons warbling, park gates clanging shut, ambulances roaring by, a street busker blowing his horn, we now falter, our footsteps hesitant and unsure. Where scents of fresh tar being laid, of fruit and vegetable peelings rotting in rubbish bins, of roasting meats and yeasty beers drifting out of pubs, of perfumed women emerging from theatres and opera halls once placed us, now we recoil from the unfamiliarity of it all. We are grounded in our city when we can hear it cradling us, biting and wounding us with intimacy. Tourists don't slip—they're too wary of strangeness. It's the locals—the ones who have made a place home—who slip and tear tendons, break bones, and chip teeth as they keel over jutting stones in the pavements. Intimacy takes away self-protection. A barrier had gone up between Shiv and the city he loved. He could no longer smell or hear anything. Grief had completely deadened his senses.

He stared at the sparkling Serpentine with its little boats and gay people, heard the tinkling of laughter around him, the thwack of balls hitting palms as people played ball. But it meant nothing at all.

If he lived, it was at night, when, in his dreams, he saw Lucy clearly and woke up sobbing, his body intense with longing for his lover's physical presence.

Unfinished business, wasn't it.

## *The Empress of Scotland,* June 1941

Mairi gives him a surprised look as she enters his cabin. "Your face is wet," she says, coming to him with a napkin. "There were herons flying above while I was out on the deck. I think we should take you up there. Will you like that?"

"No, not today."

Something's bothering him. She goes to the chest of drawers and pulls one open. She takes out the tight knot of black silk in there and carries it to his bedside. As she shakes it out, gay butterflies flutter and dance between them. She laughs. "Where did you wear *this*?" she asks.

His eyes narrow as he tries to focus on it. Then he convulses, remembering. He reaches for it with both his arms and clasps it to his chest. "Oh!" he cries. "Oh oh." She watches as he buries his nose in it, breathing deeply. Tears are running down his face. She tries to take it away from him but he pulls it back, fierce and strong. He runs his hands over it again and again. "This will be here from now on," he tells her, lifting one edge of the pillow. "Here." She nods slowly. "Yes," she says, folding it neatly and placing it under the pillow. He looks away as his eyes begin to tear.

His eyes shift to the small bright hole in the darkened window of the cabin. Sunlight ribbons fly past flashing grey-blue sea.

"Grace Blackwell told me you were going to liberate India."

He raises his head from the pillow and looks at her. "Yes, she made me believe it, too," he tells Mairi. "Grace Blackwell was a friend as well as a supporter. I owe her a great deal."

"She was deeply concerned about your welfare."

"Her son died in Verdun but she didn't find out until much later. She couldn't give him a proper burial. She hates the British. I have never hated them. Neither does Gandhi. We just want them to leave our country and hand over its administration to us Indians."

The ship has hit some turbulence. He feels the lurching movements in his bed. It's a tug, not a gentle sway. "It's rocky in here," she says, straightening the lopsided mirror on the wall. He stares at her.

She glances at her image in the mirror, readjusts a hairpin. When there's a knock at the door, he knows it's the ship's purser calling. He shuts his eyes. She opens the door. "Miss Mairi, there's dolphins up there. Care to take a look?" She turns to look at Shiv. "He went off quickly this time. All right, I'll come up for a few minutes."

There's a liveliness to her step, Shiv notes, when she comes back into the cabin. He's with her, this Will, he notes. She's deep in thought. He immediately closes his eyes. "He's still sleeping," she says. The purser lingers a while, possibly because she's not shooing him away.

"So, what made you take on this job? It's a long way from home. And it's wartime." He's asking to make conversation, Shiv thinks. The young man doesn't really care. He's just glad she's on board so he can spend some time with her.

"Fair questions," she says. "I'm twenty-three and still unmarried. You know how they talk. I couldn't stand it."

"But why are you still unmarried?" Will sounds indignant. "I'd have thought any bloke with some sense in him would have made a play for you. I know I . . ."

"Oh, there were suitors enough. I wasn't ready," she says. "You make the wrong choice, you're stuck with it, aren't you?" Shiv knows then there's much more to it than that. It comforts him to sense that she has secrets, too. In that they are equals even if his battered body is no match for hers. They're both secret bearers. Will, sensing the conversation is at an end, goes to the door.

"That was lovely, Will," she says as he leaves. Shiv, his eyes closed, imagines the young man grinning from ear to ear and it makes him want to smile, too.

HE OPENS HIS eyes and looks at her, the attractive flush in her cheeks. She's pretty; Will could do a lot worse, he thinks. She says, "I've got some pea soup for you." He groans. More dishwater.

"Do the cooks here know what salt and pepper are?"

"There's rationing on board." She pours some of the soup into a bowl, picks up a spoon and comes towards him. "Salt is a luxury."

She has *A Passage to India* in her hands. "Where shall I start?" she asks.

"Open it. Where it opens, is where you begin reading."

She inserts her thumbnail into the book, opens it. She casts her eyes across the page and starts reading. How servile his countrymen were, how ready to please their arrogant rulers. Some phrases and sentences stay with him as she reads. "'But I want to see [Indians].' She became the centre of an amused group of ladies. One said, 'Wanting to see Indians! How new that sounds!' 'Natives! Why, fancy!'" . . .

"'Why, the kindest thing one can do to a native is to let him die,' said Mrs. Callendar."

Hah! Shiv cries. Hah! Mairi looks up from the book. "Are you all right? Shall I stop now?"

"No!" he cries vehemently, feeling the spark of fire within. "I'd forgotten . . . rage. I'm smelling it now again." Fury coiled like a rope bristled within him. "No, no, don't stop!" he says, raising one hand weakly.

She turns to the book again, flicks through a few pages, begins reading again. Phrases stick with him, fan the growing fire in him. "'Your sentiments are those of a god . . .'"

"'India likes gods.'"

"'And Englishmen like posing as gods.'"

"'We're not pleasant in India, we don't intend to be pleasant . . .'"

"'Why are you here?'"

"'England holds India for her good . . .'"

"'Even mangoes can be got in England now,' put in Fielding. 'They ship them in ice-cold rooms. You can make India in England apparently, just as you can make England in India.'" Ha, ha, ha, Shiv laughs, the surprising sound crackling through him like dry spiky leaves. Ha ha. Morgan: he had tried his best through his writing to tell the truth, but his views were discarded as quaint, as radical in a pro-monarchy empire. Mairi says, "Are the British as horrible as that out there?" They were too far gone in India, he reflects. Moral corruption, this, when such subjugation, once unfeignedly for plunder, now became "God's work" in the name of Empire.

When Will comes to visit her, Shiv closes his eyes, pretends to be asleep. It's strange how his keenly observant nurse hasn't noticed how he does this the minute Will steps into the cabin. It's his entertainment, the growing affinity his nurse and the ship's purser have for each other. Will always lingers by the door, ready to be banished if she wants him gone.

"I've been thinking a lot about India," she tells him. "You've been there before, haven't you?"

"Just a few days. Ship turned around quickly and went back home. But I saw a few things—crowds, lots of crowds, and markets, and hunger. We've got hunger in Glasgow, too. But these are children who haven't eaten for weeks, pregnant mothers starving for food. What are the British doing about it?"

She shakes her head. "It's dreadful, really." She's read *A Passage to India* from cover to cover. She says she reckons she's not going back to Glasgow. No reason to go back, she says. He nods, as if he knows what she's talking about.

"What's your story, Will? Why are you on this ship?" she asks.

"I was just a lad in Glasgow. Not much happening there. You know how it is. You can go from one shite job to another, just whiling away your time. Getting older, seeing the world around you shrink. My sister was the one who told me, 'Go see the world, Will. You're always looking at the horizon. Go see what's out there.' So when a mate told me they were hiring at the shipyards, I went to have a look. It was as good a life as any, I reckoned. I signed up there and then. And here I am!"

India might just hold him for a while, Shiv thinks. India might even keep him.

# London, 1934

On entering the chambers of Boothby and Edwards for his first six months of pupillage, he heard a man say, "You there, are you the new pupil? I didn't realize you were a black man. Well, go in there and meet your pupil master."

"Who are you?"

"Some would say, if you have to ask, you shouldn't be here. I'm Louis Scrimgoeur, the clerk. O-U, as the French have it, not E-W."

"I see," Shiv said. Better get that right after such clarification, he told himself, handing him a ten-guinea note as Mr. Polak had advised him to do. The man pocketed it without a word of thanks. "Go in," he said, gesturing at the door to the office before him. Shiv opened it and stood there, waiting to be asked to enter. An elderly barrister sat at a table behind mounds of files. "Ah, the new pupil. Well, I expect you to be quick and efficient. Here"—he handed him some files—"do get on with these."

"Yes, sir." Shiv took the files he had been handed and went out of the room. He would have to pick things up very quickly himself. No one here would show him the ropes.

⌁

In those first six months, his pupil master assigned him to help experienced barristers with research and preparing documents. In due course, after he had shown that he had something that could rightfully be called intelligence, he was allowed to accompany barristers to the courts, to see how they really worked in practice. Seated close to the judge, he heard arguments from lawyers and cross-examination first-hand. The most valuable thing he learnt from those months of daily court attendance was that the real business is never done in the open, in plain sight. People had reputations and their reputations preceded them. Words of caution were dispensed along the way—ways to watch and read the lay of the land so you came armed to court. Your fellow barristers filled you in over a drink or a game of tennis or golf. He had stayed at Boothby and Edwards for his second six—the second of the required two six-month terms of pupillage—and it felt as though he was finally being given a chance to prove himself.

It was his friend Morty Saxena who had made him aware of why literature had an obligation to be political. Compass and temperature gauge, it questioned human standards—of decency, of civilization, of our capacity to love, hurt, harm, destroy, and comfort one another. "If you're not making people think and feel the words on the page, you're not doing much as a writer."

Their friendship went back to when both boys were around fourteen. Saxena's family was living in Hyderabad Sind for a short while and the two boys formed a bond that became a lasting pact when Morty's mother died. Shiv's mother immediately extended an invitation to the boy to spend some time with them. Ramdas contacted Morty's father, who gratefully accepted. Shiv and Morty spent two perfect months together playing cricket, shooting quail, and discussing poetry. Hours in Thacker & Co., Hyderabad Sind's best bookshop, arguing about who was the better writer, Tolstoy or Dostoevsky.

Shiv claimed Tolstoy: "He creates scenes that play in your mind forever. Sensory feasts!" Morty went for Dostoevsky: "He gets to the heart of what makes us human! His sinners and atheists are deeply interesting!" Their passionate discussions revealed how they differed on almost everything, yet they cherished each other's company, preferred it to anyone else's. Shiv saw him as his brother and his closest friend. Morty became a regular fixture in their home until Mr. Saxena moved back to Calcutta, taking his son with him.

WHEN MORTY PHONED to invite him to go to a meeting of Indian students at Nanking's restaurant, he accepted with pleasure. Morty had graduated earlier in the year from Oxford and had finally made it back to London, where, he said, "you can live again." He was a committed socialist, the only scion of a very rich family, and had already given much of his wealth away. He was living in a room let by a Scottish woman, who was sympathetic and understood his politics.

Shiv felt so removed from his own kind, so distant from the struggle in India. Almost four years had already gone by without his knowing much about the other Indian students in London. There were clubs and places for colonial gentlemen but he had not gone to them, fearing additional expenses his paltry budget could not accommodate. The meeting that evening was the first of its kind for him. But he sensed it would be a farce, representing a knot of rival organizations and editors of journals all vying with one another in true divide-and-rule fashion. They wanted to work towards a common goal but you put three Indians in a room, and you get twenty opinions. Shiv braced himself for an evening of bickering.

Mr. Fung San, a left-leaning Shanghainese transplant, owner of Nanking's at 9 Denmark Street in Soho for some years, was the genial host. He generously allowed the Indian students the use of the cellar downstairs free of charge.

They walked into a packed house: Dissolute sons of maharajahs,

who played polo by day, shot grouse with the sons of India's oppressors, and downed whiskey with revolutionaries by night; the Calcutta socialists, seriously left, idealistic, the poetry of Tagore in their
veins and passages from *Das Kapital* on their lips; the Bombay Parsees, fully Europeanized and pining for their lost Persia, revitalized
by the freedom fight of their present homeland, and increasingly
communist, though their families back home were devoted Anglo-
philes and front-rank industrialists (airlines! steel! coal!); the Hyderabad Sindhis, administrators, lawyers, and merchants, loyalist by
nature, deeply against partition, and aware that in the heat of war,
their part of India was more than likely to get lopped off to become
part of an Islamic state; the Gujarati Muslims, deeply entrenched in
their land, their customs, their beliefs, equally aware that partition
would divide their community, too; the Indian Jews, part and parcel of an India that had given them refuge for over a thousand
years, committed to the cause of Independence for India; the Madras brains, communist-leaning, all scientific research, numbers
and equations and stats; the Punjabi agriculturists, landowners,
farmer-soldiers, fighters, unafraid of war, and ready to unsheathe
their swords as required; the Kerala lefties, doctors and mathema-
ticians, yearning for new hospitals and learning centres in their
community—all their tribal loyalties resurfacing as soon as they left
the precincts of their English colleges and settled down to a platter
of vegetable fried rice in Nanking's.

The meeting had been organized by the key leaders of the Indian
Writers' Progressive Association (IWPA), a newly formed group in
London, which was deeply concerned with the language of literary
discourse. It sought to address inequalities in representation of the
written word, which led directly to the heart of economic and class
inequality, and so to racial tensions in India itself. The flag bearers of
the new Indian literary movement were eager to look at their country in a fresh light, to focus on cleaning up at home.

In 1932, two years earlier, a couple of luminaries among the crowd at Nanking's that evening had published *Angare* (Embers), an anthology of short stories and poems that went against the grain of classical Urdu literature. It was a new departure in every way, its tone experimental, its politics progressive, its sympathies clearly with the downtrodden, the poor, wrong-caste outcasts of society. It was in tune with the gritty realism of Zola and Gorky but its celebration of the working-class hero was a challenge to the status quo—and a strong step towards equality for the untouchables in India. But the country was far from ready for it. The book was banned there, its editors and the writers anthologized were declared heretics, and the penal code was invoked to imprison writers. The entire effort was denounced as "dirty literature." Copies of the book were burned in public. One of the speakers, Sajjad Zaheer, said, "The time has come for us to reclaim our literary allegiances, to fight a war with the forces of darkness." He spoke of the refugees out on the streets of London, Jews escaping Hitler, Spaniards escaping Franco after his savage overthrow of the Anarchist uprising there, Italians fleeing from Mussolini, Russians fleeing from Stalin. "The one strong concerted effort against these lethal assaults on freedom, peace, and safety has been the factory workers' associations. Their fight against fascism has shown what a powerful force they are, and that if we are to fight, whether it is by words, by marches, by protest songs, and hartals, we must do it shoulder to shoulder with them. We must fight as one unit." Zaheer asked them all to read a copy of the IWPA manifesto on their chairs.

Shiv gave it a quick read in the dim light of the restaurant:

> Radical changes are taking place in Indian society. . . .
> Indian literature, since the breakdown of classical culture, has had the fatal tendency to escape from the actualities of life. It has tried to find a refuge from reality in baseless spiritualism and ideality. The result is that it has become anaemic in body and mind and has

adopted a rigid formalism and a banal and perverse ideology.

It is the duty of Indian writers to give expression to the changes taking place in Indian life. . . .

It is the object of our Association to rescue literature and other arts from the conservative classes in whose hands they have been degenerating so long, to bring arts into the closest touch with the people and to make them the vital organs which will register the actualities of life, as well as lead us to the future we envisage.

Class war, Shiv thought. This isn't going to go down well. One person got up and said, "The book burnings of last year should remind everyone that people aren't happy with the old order being abolished so quickly. Turning to the poor to make them subjects for literature is a bit like an apology—the poor don't want to be immortalized in literature. They need food, clean drinking water, medicine, and opportunities. Ask the untouchables what they want and they'll all say, to be like you."

"No one would argue with that. But that's a separate issue," someone else said. "We're discussing a path forward for literature. All across Europe, literature is aligning itself with the common people. Look at George Orwell, Aldous Huxley, H. G. Wells, Federico Lorca, Virginia Woolf, and before them, at Zola, at Gorky, at Neruda, at Dostoevsky, at Turgenev! Look at the legacy of the great Russian Tolstoy! Literature's true power today is in realist writing. We Indian writers are mired in idealism, not realism. We cannot continue to paint pretty pictures of societies we admire or platitudinize. We must mirror the flaws, we must show the corrosive undercurrents. We must aim for a more progressive literary form in our writing, one that is more representative of our times."

The crowd murmured approval. "Yes, this must happen." But they would never agree on how or what was meant by realism in literature.

In that room, with its brightly painted walls in vermilion, yellow, and green—Eastern, Asian, bringing home the banks of the Indus River—Shiv knew what was needed: a magazine, a journal, founded in London, centering on politics, literature, and art as igniters of change, with contributions from the greatest artists and intellectuals of their time, and from the "common people." Who were the common people? In the end, weren't we all the common people? he mused. The untouchables, the farmers, the engineers, the mine workers, the shipbuilders, the thinkers, the spinners of yarn and the potters, poets, and artists—all of them had a story to tell. India's war, a war that promised to erase class distinctions, needed to shift to the pages of a powerful journal, capable of affecting international opinion. Only artists knew how to really fight injustice, to insist on peace.

As the conversation around them grew louder, more excited, more combative, Morty said, "The evening's done. It'll be endless arguing from this point on. Do you want to stay?"

He was right. Shiv could tell the evening would disintegrate into aimless bickering from that point on. He had a vision and he wanted to cling to it.

A WET COLD whipped off the street as they stepped outside. The air came at Shiv in tufts, gripping his face. He stopped and stared at the pavement. Puddles of water spangled with bright colours from marquees, shop windows, and pub fronts nearly blinded him. He sensed a hand on his shoulder, the scent of violets and rose oud, rouge and face powder, a laughing voice, the lithe arm of a sensual young man slipping down his back to his waist, daringly resting there in full view of passers-by on the street. When he looked across his shoulder, he saw The Eclipse, one of the gay places Lucy had taken him to. They had danced on the floor there all evening, pent-up sexual energy radiating from one to the other. They hadn't touched—their dancing itself was an embrace. Other boys looked enviously at them as they flashed around each other, their energy creating ribbons of light. There had been reports of undercover policemen there that evening, scouring the crowds for the "nancy boys." Sons of well-placed government officials often dropped in—gay men in drag unsuspectingly chatting up plainclothes policemen sent there to entrap them. Reporters avidly wrote up stories for their rags the next day, naming and shaming all those who were there.

Lucy knew all the signals and had spotted the plainclothesmen early enough for them to beat a hasty retreat. Shiv recalled sweat trickling down his back though it was ice cold, and trying to still his fast-beating heart. That was close, a warning voice had cried inside him, as Lucy and he walked fast towards crowded Piccadilly, and entered the crowds gathered there.

Now, as he watched Morty walking ahead of him, he knew it was a haunting, a knife point raking a wound. He was gasping for air. They would never free each other, Lucy and he.

*Desire:* a word you had to lick around to know its richness. The god Janus's word: keeper of the keys to heaven, he locked its doors at night and unlocked them in the morning. Desire imprisoned and freed, it cradled opposites: the bite, the caress; the flame, the ash; the silken touch, the stiletto cut; the salt of tears, the red of blood. Desire's wounds you sucked for their exquisite pain. Ice cream? he had asked Gandhiji once. And got a knowing, deep-throated chuckle back in response.

Morty stopped walking, turned round to look at him. "What's the matter?"

"Go on. . . . I'll be fine, I just need to get my bearings."

"Nonsense. I'm taking you home. You're swaying, old chap." Back in his flat in Ladbroke Grove, Sen put the kettle on and poured himself a shot of whiskey. "What happened? You looked as if you had seen a ghost."

"Maybe I had," Shiv said, sipping his tea with honey.

HE LACKED THE essential quality Lucy had: self-knowledge. Lucy knew his world like a hand in a well-tailored glove. He had years of self-assessment, correction, interpretation, self-esteem, self-loathing, and misunderstanding behind him. He had got it just right so he could bask in its adulation yet mock it publicly for its most cherished rituals when he chose, its "humbuggeries" as he called them. And he was adored for his impertinence. Society chose to bestow on him the special favours it reserved for its beloved breed of eccentrics. He could do no wrong. London society's heralded hostesses made a beeline across crowds to greet him when he entered their salons or garden parties. He shone with virile energy at their affairs; he was no ordinary star.

People like him could not risk being earnest or show wonder without censure, or worse, being entirely misunderstood. But they longed to. Lucy's moist eyes when he was touched came to mind— Shiv felt his beating heart close to his often enough and knew how deeply he felt things. He was the one Lucy dared to be most himself with. But the adoration of his own kind fed him, gave him his power.

What could he have given his gold dark boy, who came bearing Chimborazo and Cotopaxi in his hands? Only his love and his unqualified support, and it wouldn't have been enough.

In the months that followed, he lost so much weight, Mr. Rayner's suits slipped off him. The shirts sat on him like gunnysacks. On the same streets where passers-by had turned to look in his direction, the smartly dressed dandy, now he cut a pathetic figure for whom no one spared a second glance. Mr. Polak chided Millie for starving him, but the truth was, he had no appetite.

# London, March 1935

One morning, some months later, Mr. Scrimgoeur, the clerk in his chambers, summoned him to one side. "There was someone here earlier today asking for you."

"Yes? Who?"

"A solicitor looking for a barrister to lead him in a very special case. It's"—he blew his nose into a large handkerchief—"a little delicate."

"Can you tell me a little more?" Shiv's excitement grew as he looked at the clerk's face. For the past three months, he had waited patiently, hoping that Mr. Scrimgoeur would finally settle his gaze on him, and tell him he had a case. His moment had finally come.

"It seems there's a domestic dispute involving a young Indian male servant and his master's daughter. The father is suing for justice—he claims his daughter has been violated."

Of course, Shiv thought. There's an Indian angle, which is why he had been approached. "And he thinks that because I am an Indian, I will be able to learn the truth better than anyone else and send the man packing off to jail as quickly as possible?"

"I think you might be right, Mr. Advani. I think that is the thinking."

"I am not sure I'm the right person for this case. The truth in rape cases is a very sticky business, and the highly political overtones—"

"They are offering a considerable sum for services. A. Very. Large. Amount. You will thank me once you hear it. And you would know the cab rank rule. You've been chosen. You can't decline it."

Shiv frowned. "I will never sully my profession, and do not intend to tarnish my reputation as a bought man. As for the cab rank rule, I am sure, in situations like this one, exceptions can be made. One Indian can't be pitted against another when there are only half a dozen of us around."

Mr. Scrimgoeur's cheeks went red as he stiffened and drew his shoulders in. "This is not bribery, young man. They are crediting you with the right sort of instinct and intuition for the job. I would see it as an extreme honour, instead of casting about for excuses to not do the work. Exceptions are not made where representation in court is involved. You cannot walk away."

"Not work? I want nothing else. But—"

"You can't say no." Mr. Scrimgoeur was frowning, as at an unruly child. "You cannot circumvent our system. Besides, they are offering one hundred guineas to the right candidate for the job. Mr. Snelling, the solicitor, has watched you clerk, has heard you speak to the judge you're shadowing. With firmness and integrity, he said—not words that get bandied about much, I can tell you. His client wishes to establish a relationship with someone who can be trusted in this case."

Mr. Scrimgoeur was looking at him with a mixture of amusement (these colonials are a prize lot, I tell you!) and anxiety (did he really think he could be an exception to the time-honoured cab rank rule?).

Shiv felt his eyes on him. He took a deep breath. "Does a decision have to be made this instant?"

Mr. Scrimgoeur said he'd try to buy him a day or two.

Mr. Polak, when he brought up the case with him, said, "You have no choice, you do see that, don't you? The cab rank rule is quite clear-cut. We don't choose, we are chosen. And must comply."

Shiv said, "But my being Indian is a little complicated. And it's my first case."

"What do you mean, Shiv?" Millie Polak asked.

"Well, I'd probably be even more aggressive with the defendant—I wouldn't want to be seen as though I'm favouring my own kind." That was only one half of it. Everything he believed in seemed to be at stake with this case. Justice would be on the line, and he didn't want to see it falter when it came to people like him.

Millie said, "But you know the rules now. Of course you wouldn't. That's why they've scented you out. They know you won't be partial."

He had misgivings. You had to be Indian to know them—his colour uniting him with the defendant in court, in a world where like was paired with like, from the start. His own knowledge that in this court, they were in an adversarial position to each other. His awareness of the man's likely impediments, his experience living in England, how he was looked at every time he entered a room. *Foreigner! Foreigner!* He knew the debt issue was a humiliating noose around the man's neck. His knowledge of how deeply his family was counting on him to preserve them from the worst misfortunes of fate would have haunted him day and night. Worlds separated Shiv from the defendant. Yet what they shared bound them. Both he, the figure of authority in court, and the accused in the stand woke up every day to feel a wall encircling them—excluded by their colour and the pressures of family back home, they lacked the privilege of choosing their paths in life. And this man was a domestic, a coloured servant in a white world. Shiv knew he was the better positioned one between them, yet they were both subservients, serving a master they did not fully trust.

Millie was right. How did you prove yourself in a world that had exempted you without being on a stage where you could display your skills? He needed a big case, one that would establish him as a discerning lawyer, a reliable, trustworthy man. This was what they had offered him. When Millie handed him a letter from India that evening, he felt his future was decided. Along with the usual complaints about not being able to see enough of her grandson and the stresses of everyday life, his mother spoke about their financial worries.

> Father has no time now for the transport business he had started three years ago. The buses are rusting, the drivers long gone. This is what had made it possible for him to do the legal pro bono work, to have meetings every few days, catered by our kitchen. Now all he does is pro bono and there's no money coming in. It is hard to see how we will manage to keep the house going at all in the coming year. Our entire staff are now down to two—the cook, and a part-time gardener. I do what I can . . . a lot is suffering, and we are now illustrious, but poor. You will have to be independent, son. We can no longer support you.

There was nothing to think about, was there? He needed to make his own way in life. Yes, he said to a relieved Mr. Scrimgoeur a few days later. I'll take it. Mr. Scrimgoeur rolled his eyes.

WHEN MR. HAWLEY, the solicitor, of Hawley and Carruthers invited him to his chambers and explained the facts of the case, Shiv saw immediately that it was more complicated than he could have imagined. A young man brought to London from India to continue serving his master as an indentured slave. Why? What were the circumstances behind that? A young white woman, daughter of the master. Rape was the charge. Who claimed this, the father or the daughter? Both? It was the sort of stuff that filled the pages of the gutter press and sold newspapers. Nothing could be guaranteed to inflame even liberal hearts as much as a criminal case involving coloured slaves, their white masters, the young children of the house. Mr. Hawley offered his version of events: Miss Emily Fleming, twenty-year-old daughter of John Fleming, formerly of Madras, India, now of Holland Villas Road, London, had returned from riding and wanted her boots, which were caked with mud, to be cleaned. She passed a maid on her way upstairs and told her to tell Ramesh Thorun, the valet, her boots needed cleaning.

It seems she waited for Thorun, the defendant in the case, to come up. When he didn't show, she rang the bell for him, as he often doubled as cook in the house. The call system registered in the form of lights on a wall panel in the kitchen, which lit up red by room when an occupant needed service. He was busy in the kitchen and failed to hear the bell. By the time he began going up the stairs—why? Shiv asked. I thought you said he hadn't heard the bell. Ah yes, Mr. Hawley explained. It turns out the maid delivered her mistress's message to him and Thorun confirmed it by glancing at the wall panel and finally noting the lit red light to her room. He went up the stairs and knocked on her door. He thought he heard her say "Come in." He entered the room. She had just emerged from the bath and was—let us say, in a vulnerable situation. Naked? Shiv asked. Yes, Mr. Hawley said. She screamed, "Go away, go away," the father came running, saw the servant in his daughter's room, saw her clutching a towel to her body. The matter speaks for itself. The police took a statement from Miss Emily, who was hysterical. When asked, did you call for the servant?, she replied no. Her muddy boots were outside the room, by the door. Why didn't he pick them up and leave? Why did he enter the room? Mr. Hawley said.

What sort of motivation might the man have had to risk his reputation, possibly his life? Shiv asked.

It appears, Mr. Hawley said, that he's homesick. "But he is bound by his contract to live here until the debt is paid off. It is thought that the assault on the daughter of the house was motivated by rage and vindictiveness towards his employer."

Shiv considered the situation. Would he risk that? Would any man from the colonies living in England risk being accused of rape? They were all watched by hawks—in the government, the police, the intelligence services. Ramesh Thorun would have known that. Perhaps something within him had snapped, unable to take any more. Had the police interviewed the complainant? And the defendant? Yes, of course, Mr. Hawley confirmed. "And the facts of the matter are clear. The man had no business being in his mistress's room, and the maid has now retracted her story and says she never told Ramesh anything. She refuses to testify and has left the Flemings' employ. Mr. Thorun refuses to answer any more questions, which speaks to his guilt in the matter."

"But where's the evidence that he harmed her, that he intended to harm her?"

"It's in the facts of the case, Mr. Advani. Servants, especially male ones, do not enter their mistress's rooms without being specifically asked to do so."

So he was being asked to conclude, on the basis of sketchy facts, the truth of the case.

When he brought it up with his mentor, Mr. Polak shook his head. "You misunderstand. You're not trying to prove guilt or innocence. Facts, supporting evidence, that's all you're looking at. You build a strong case for conviction or acquittal based on the facts."

"But there are things one senses, things that aren't conveyed by facts but are divined using intuition. I—"

"Mr. Gandhi and I had many talks on the subject. He, too, believed in intuition, in the sixth sense. It is part of the Indian system of belief. But while that may have a place in meditation, or even in the practice of spirituality in one's daily life, it has no place in a court of law."

"But there's gut feeling—instinct."

"Instinct and intuition are two different things. Intuition, that sixth sense, is subjective. Instinct is not, for it is honed and sharpened by experience and knowledge. Instinct is used as much by mushroom-hunting dogs as it is by predators of all kinds. You use it with caution, for to rely on it excessively would be detrimental to you as a lawyer."

Shiv put his head in his hands and released a long sigh.

"It is simple, Shiv," Mr. Polak said. "Impress the judge by presenting a thorough case. Be cogent, concise. Pay attention to details. Be sure and confident. Your summaries should reflect your intimate knowledge of the case. Plain words will do—it's not a poetry competition. Whatever you can do to convince the judge that you know everything there is to know about the case will work in your favour. Your case has one of two outcomes: acquit or convict. You must convince the judge and the jury that the only outcome possible, based on evidence and facts of the case, is the one you're fighting for."

But without believing in guilt or innocence, how was it possible to defend your client with conviction, passion, and authenticity? Shiv asked.

"You have done due diligence; you know the rules, you know the law. You know your brief so well, you could recite it in your sleep. That is conviction."

One fact stood out from his discussion with Mr. Hawley: "The accused man refuses to speak and has gone on a hunger fast."

"A lot of them do that when they have no options," Mr. Hawley explained. "They think it will win them some sympathy."

Ramesh Thorun, his face covered with a sheen peculiar to fasting people, gazed at them impassively. He was a handsome man, tall, with a sharply angled face. He was dressed in a suit clearly borrowed for the occasion. It hung loosely on his body. Hunger of many kinds showed in his face. He looked weary and emaciated. His coal-black eyes were filled with fury. He had no reason to think anyone in that courtroom cared about his fate.

They shared that, Shiv thought, this prisoner in the dock and he. They both had the language, the internal knowledge, the honed instincts to know them—the people they were working for and learning from—and to know what they were thinking. The prisoner had already taken stock of the courtroom; his demeanour showed that he expected nothing.

Emily Fleming wore a white frock with a pink hat. She had pearls around her neck. Her nut brown hair floated in becoming curls around her face. When she took the witness stand and said in a calm, sweet voice, "I am Emily Fleming," there was a perceptible shift in the jurors' attentions. They were already looking at her with compassion.

Shiv rose from his seat to invite his client to take a stand. Miss Emily Fleming had a case, but there was no strong evidence to back her claims. How would she present in court? Testimonies given aurally from a witness stand were wild cards and could substantially affect the nature of the case. "Thank you, Miss Fleming. Would you be good enough to tell the court how the accused man came to be in your father's service?"

"Thank you. Yes, it was in India, in Madras, that Ramesh Thorun, a young boy of twelve, first encountered my father, who was a district magistrate there. My father hired him to water the plants in our vast garden. He did a careful job and eventually rose in our household to become his valet, and now continues to work as a valet and a cook in our home here."

"So he has been working with your family for ten years, would you say?"

"Yes," she replied, "that's right."

"Has he ever given you reason to think that he might be capable of assaulting you?"

"In the past few weeks, the defendant gave me very strange looks. I didn't understand what he was saying."

The jurors now turned their attention to the accused, who looked impassively ahead.

"Has the man ever expressed a desire to return to his homeland?" Shiv asked.

"Yes," she said, "more than once. But he owes my father a good deal of money. He will be free to leave when he has finished paying his debts."

"And how much longer would that be?"

"I don't know."

"What is the nature of his debt?"

"He had borrowed money for his sister's wedding. His parents were unable to afford the costs of marrying her off. Daddy generously supplied everything they needed."

She was sure-footed when it came to answering questions about Ramesh's entrance into her room, about the nature of the assault. "He pinned me against the wall and ripped my towel away from my body." There was a loud gasp in the courtroom. "I was terrified of what he might do. He was on top of me and I had given up all hope when Daddy heard my screams and came running into the room."

It was at that point that he stopped believing her. But it was useless to hope that Ramesh Thorun would save the day. His impassive face stared at them all, expecting not one iota of compassion, empathy, or relief. Shiv could not help admiring him.

The father had been advised not to attend the trial on account of his weak heart.

The defence counsel began his cross-examination of Miss Fleming with a statement of sympathy. "However severe your sufferings, I hope you will see fit to answer this court truthfully . . ." Mealy-mouthed, Shiv raged inwardly, as he saw how empathy injected itself at every turn into his questioning. Truth spied a backdoor and went towards it, quietly sliding out of the room.

The case was open and shut after all. The man had been proven guilty already. It would not take much to get a conviction from this court. He was an alien, marked so by his colour, his attitude, his silence and defiance. *He must have done it*, was the unspoken verdict.

WHEN SHIV ADDRESSED the defendant, he did so with courtesy. "Mr. Thorun." The name, said correctly, unmangled, already had a ring of dignity to it that it hadn't before. "Sir, you need not fear anything. British law is just and fair—it relies on the golden thread, ha-beas corpus, presumed innocent until proven guilty. You will be heard and everything you say will be carefully considered. Please tell us what happened the night you entered Miss Emily Fleming's bedroom."

Silence. Shiv waited a few moments. Then he said, "There are few options in this court, Mr. Thorun. Either you refute the truth or you corroborate it. You agree, or you don't agree. You have already heard Miss Fleming's version. If you agree, you may stay silent. If you do not agree, you must tell us. You must speak." Shiv looked at him. He was pleading as much as one could within the strictures of court protocol, which prohibited biases of any sort. "Do you understand?"

Ramesh Thorun looked at him long and hard with his blazing eyes. He said nothing.

Shiv felt his pulse beat faster. What sort of man was this, willing to go to jail for a crime he did not commit? For by now, he knew the man was innocent. Then he saw that it was a deeper battle than the one being fought out in the court. The accused was unwilling to betray himself. It wasn't fear, Shiv saw. It was the knowledge that he was already doomed. Confronted with a language he could not trust, he chose silence.

*Guilty as charged*, as everyone in court that day expected, was the verdict.

Thorun received the words impassively. Then, perhaps from hunger, or the strangeness of the entire situation, he began swaying. "He's about to fall," someone said. A court aide rushed towards him, to steady him. But he had already slid to the ground, having lost consciousness. "It's that bloody Gandy, ain't it?" someone said loudly. "Egging them on to give up food. Don't like something, just stop eating. Madman, as they say in the papers."

As Shiv left the court, while people muttered their good wishes and congratulations, he heard a man in the crowd assembled outside call out, *Traitor*. Shiv whipped around. *Traitor*, a brown-skinned man with blazing eyes—another fasting Indian?—said again. Who was he? A friend of Thorun's? Should he attempt to speak to him? But the die was cast.

This was victory? A silent, emaciated brown man, an eloquent, pretty white lady, a barrister who knew the truth but was obligated to fight for its opposite.

*Traitor.* How well the word fit him, he thought.

It stayed with him, a hair shirt of a word, tormenting him every time he saw the man's glowing eyes, his lips form the word: *Traitor.*

MR. POLAK AND Millie were waiting to toast him. They were beside themselves with joy, Millie smiling at him warmly as he sat down beside her. "Here's to our rising star," Mr. Polak said, raising his glass.

"What?" Shiv stared at him in amazement. "It didn't take much. The scenario was presented, the jury cast a verdict. It spoke for itself. Anyone could have handled it with the same results."

"No, not anyone. It was well fought and well won. You've impressed everyone. It was a test, as I rather feared it might be. But you were fair without showing favour. I see a very busy time ahead for you, Shiv, and I couldn't be more delighted to share the good news with your family."

As Mr. Polak had indicated, that first case seemed to pave the way for others. He took everything that came his way—from divorces and insolvencies to illegitimate children claiming shares of estates. "This is what you're supposed to be doing, learning how British law works in practice, how it is fought over in court cases, how judgements are made."

As Shiv's reputation grew, Mr. Polak, surprised and proud, and perhaps a little taken aback, said, "It's as though you were born into it—true, your father's a renowned pleader back in Sind, but for you to achieve that kind of reputation in our English courts, and in a relatively short period of time—you are a marvel, my boy!" Shiv basked in his mentor's admiration. But he knew it was more than that. He remembered now how Lucy had tried to coach him so he could avoid some of the hurdles that awaited him as he stood around like a racehorse snorting steam, throwing up clods of earth, waiting to be chosen for a case. Without his being conscious of it, Lucy's tutelage had branded itself in Shiv's consciousness. He had an internal guidebook that provided meanings for every judicial nod, smile, facial expression. He couldn't see a hat leave a man's head without interpreting it, reading its implications for a possible case outcome. While still in pupillage, he could smell condescension a mile off, and knew from a man's glance how he was seeing him. Lucy would never know it, but not one hour in court passed without Shiv realizing the advantages of knowing what he knew. Long before a man opened his mouth, Shiv had interpreted him by his gestures, his facial expressions. It sharpened his instincts, brought persuasiveness to his briefings, and when he spoke, people straightened up in their benches and listened. Only someone who had truly been born into it could have shown him how to decipher that code for success.

As he had left for Temple one morning, Millie stopped him on his way out. "We're having guests for dinner this evening," she said. "We'd like you to be there."

"Of course," he said. "I'll be back by six."

Just as Millie had known about his evenings and nights with Lucy, she knew now, of course, that his nocturnal trysts were over. She often gave him quick glances of concern. He didn't need to speak with her. She didn't need details. He knew she knew.

The pavements were slick with large wet leaves from plane trees that lined the street. He skirted the leaves cautiously, knowing how they stuck to shoes and could send you flying. Now that Lucy was no longer in his life, his evenings yawned before him in long, lonely stretches and even the thought of dinner with the Polaks' friends was pleasant. Barristers' friends were other barristers and their wives. He braced himself for an evening of legal talk.

The sharp acidic smells of cured olives and amontillado sherry met his nostrils as he came down the stairs. "Ah, here he is," Mr. Polak said, as he walked into the drawing room. "Shiv Advani."

Henry turned to a woman seated on the sofa. "Mrs. Woolf," he said.

She gave her hand. He looked at her and shook it. What had Lucy said? Touch it, and let it go. It was a long, slim hand, a beautiful hand. Renaissance artists working with marble had spent lifetimes perfecting the sculpting of hands like these. He wanted to hold it, turn it around, examine its fineness—it was as if he had known her. What had inspired that? A tall thin man, with a sharply angular face, was introduced as Leonard Woolf. He stretched out his hand and felt it grasped quite warmly.

There was another woman there, a younger woman by her side. "This is Mrs. Georgina Chesley, an old friend of Millie's, and her daughter, Julia." He shook hands with them. He gave Julia a closer look, feeling sure he'd seen her somewhere before. "We're having sherry," Mr. Polak said. "What can I get you?" Shiv said he would have the same.

The Woolfs held everyone's attention. The writers; the publishers. Their manner, the atmosphere that floated around them, was charged with a different kind of energy. Their dress was ordinary, shoes scuffed, clothes that seemed nicely worn, even a little shabby. "I spent some time in Ceylon as an administrator there," Leonard said by way of introduction. "Where are you from in India?"

"Sind," Shiv said. "The cradle of civilization. Or an inferno. It rather depends on which lens you turn on it."

"The British were determined to conquer the province. The Indus, that mighty river, is what they desired. It was their last major annexation and when they finally overcame resistance in 1843, they took it with both guilt and admiration," Woolf said.

"Guilt?" Virginia said with a half smile. "Not an Imperial trait, is it?"

Leonard Woolf told them how Sir Charles Napier, recently appointed to oversee operations in Sind, and determined to retire comfortably, had surprised the Talpur ruler of Sind while he and other members of the royal family were in the middle of wedding celebrations for his daughter and the army was given time off. Not organized for war, they were easily overcome. The British bombarded Sind, winning it handily, and they began looting the fort in Hyderabad immediately, making off with a million sterling. "A million?" Virginia said. "Leo, can that be right?"

"Yes," Leonard replied, filling his pipe with a wry, slightly disturbed expression on his face. "A cool million. Napier had Sind, of course, as he coyly punned in a telegram to the prime minister. 'Peccavi.' I have sinned."

Everyone laughed a little uncomfortably. "There's a sequel to that," Leonard continued. "Possibly not true. It's said that when Lord Dalhousie took Oudh in the 1850s, not a large province like Sind, but a conquest all the same, he said, 'Vovi,' I have Oudh. Say the translation from the Latin quickly enough and it sounds like 'I vowed.'"

Virginia's mirthful hoot . . . Shiv smiled, hearing it. "It's quite clever," she said. "Though deplorable. . . . The rapaciousness and low morals of these men out in the colonies!"

Millie was shaping her lips around the words, suddenly getting it. "It's quite clear the Eton boys were playing chess with one another," she said, with a disgusted look.

"Yes," Leonard said, laughing drily. "Chess!"

"Where do you find all this information?" Millie asked.

Leonard turned to her. "Hughes's *Sind Gazetteer* recounts the skirmishes that finally led to Sind's capitulation. Mind you, the ruling Mirs weren't a saintly lot either."

"That's no justification for raiding another country. Would you call our people saintly?" Virginia asked.

Leonard snorted. "Hardly!"

"They came, they saw, they conquered," Shiv said. "When they first came to India in the seventeenth century, they were like everyone else. They dressed like the natives, ate their food, joined in their entertainments, jolly good fellows they were. The moneylenders lent them the money to stay so they could trade along with everyone else. But then they got into conquest and subjugation."

There was a tense silence in the room. Mr. Polak threw Shiv an anxious look. Shiv realized he'd gone beyond the edge of civilized chat in polite society.

Virginia, her eyes blinking like the click of a camera aperture, said, "Shiv is right. Veni, vidi, vici. Nothing's changed. History repeats itself. It's no wonder Indians hate the British so much." She delicately spat out an olive pit into the palm of her hand.

"Oh, but we don't blindly and collectively hate the British," Shiv said. "To want them out of India is not to hate them. Yes, there are people, individuals, we all collectively hate."

"Reginald Dyer, Michael O'Dwyer, others in that lamentable history, the history of conquest. What did you say the other day, Virginia? Dog collared, you said. History and future generations will dog collar us with the words 'For God and the Empire' around our necks." *Lam-en-table, emphasis on the lam.* Shiv heard Lucy's voice as shivers went down his spine.

Millie, one ear attuned to the kitchen, said, "I remember the astonishing foresight of your lines, Virginia—'The Empire is perishing, the bands are playing, the Exhibition is in ruins. For that is what comes of letting in the sky.' On the Wembley Exhibition of Empire and its goods, wasn't it? In the early twenties?"

"Yes," she said musingly. "It wasn't hard to see even then."

Leonard Woolf had accepted another sherry from Mr. Polak, who was walking round the room, refilling glasses. He adjusted his spectacles before taking a sip. "We dislike the kind of people you refer to as well," he said, turning to Shiv. "The playing fields of Eton produce their fair share of narcissists intent on leaving their stamp on the world by fair means or foul. But they don't speak for all of Britain." His long legs were crossed, the baggy trousers and tweed jacket a little shambolic, his air that of a distracted philosopher. His eyes were penetrating and sharp.

"It's the motto of the Knights and Dames of the Most Excellent Order of the British Empire, who vow to defend God and the Empire equally," Georgina, who had been talking to Millie and her daughter, turned to them. She chuckled. "You are right, Virginia, to hold us women to a different path. We mustn't accept the male hankering for loot and plunder, for subjugation, or, as is common these days, to 'bear the white man's burden,' which means nothing other than mass conversion to Christianity."

"You've been there, haven't you, Georgina?" Virginia asked.

"To India? Yes. I stayed at the Gandhi ashram. To be there, surrounded by his followers, all enacting the Gandhian doctrine of self-sufficiency in their daily lives, their discipline and passion, their industry with spinning, defying British bans on producing cloth at home—it was quite astonishing. I was very happy there. I felt closer to God."

"Admirable man, really," Virginia said. "I do wonder about him. He's such a curious phenomenon, bizarre ideas, but he does somehow seem perfect for our time."

"He is a man of many moving parts," Georgina said. "But the wonderful thing is that they all come together—the strategist and the philosopher, the activist and the spiritual leader. It's a combination that speaks deeply to the Indians. His message, which is, nonviolence is the only way to wage war; disarming your enemy is an act of love—these are all truths deeply embedded in Hindu spiritual texts." She turned to Shiv. "Do you believe what Gandhi says about *ahimsa*?"

Shiv thought for a moment. "As my father explained it to me, *ahimsa* is the stage just before *satyagraha*, or soul-force. *Ahimsa* prohibits violence but you're still struggling with hate, to conceive ways of showing up your enemy, even harming him. But this can never make you strong. Strength comes from the harder part—from *satyagraha*, when hate has been burned out of the equation. It comes when you learn that love is the most powerful way of over-coming hate. Seen in that way, it is both self-mastery and mastery over the actions of others. Your abnegation of hate strengthens you because you no longer want to hurt another. Gandhi says, how can you hurt someone you've trained yourself to not hate, perhaps even to love?"

"It's extraordinary," Virginia Woolf said. "While the fascist ideo-logues in the West preach hate and violence, here is the leader of a colonized people preaching love and nonviolence. It remains to be seen if we in the West can stomach his ideas, for we come from war-ring nations. When mothers lose their sons, and husbands perish on the battlefield, that is when we here might be ready to hear him."

"Gandhi got us out of jail in Johannesburg," Mr. Polak said. "When he and I were locked up in 1913, it was his daily fasting and praying that got us both through it. He was always cheerful—even when the guards tried to beat him up. He astonished them really. Henry, we're getting out, he would say to me, even when it seemed to me that the South African government was intensifying its attempts to keep us confined for as long as possible. And then one day, we were out."

Leonard Woolf was refilling his pipe. As he tamped down the tobacco in the bowl, he said, "I've heard it said over and over again that anyone who spends some time with him is bound to go over to his side. They call him a saint, but I think he's a canny, knowing pol-itician who has come up with the perfect formula for waging war—

nonviolent war—in India. And, for that matter, here. Good luck to him! I'm all for him, as I know you are, too, Henry."

"I am, of course. But I don't like religion-based politics. Gandhi does go over the edge sometimes. Self-mastery over desire is a personal dialogue, surely, between one's own reasoning, the body, and the soul. It cannot be transferred to a political movement. He goes too far with all that chastity, self-denial business. Hinduism's proper home is the temple, not Parliament. And not all of his followers will be vegetarians."

"I couldn't agree more," Leonard said. "But he is making an impact in the halls of Westminster. Hurrah to him!"

"So to turn the Hindus from their ancient Indo-Aryan origins to Christianity—that's got to be going down well in India," Georgina said. "The sheer arrogance of it! We women must disengage from empire building if we want to avoid dog collaring."

Mr. Polak laughed. "Forgive me, but aren't we all already dog collared thus? Defenders of the faith?"

"I think you may be right, Mr. Polak," Virginia said. "I was thinking the other day how cosmopolitan Bloomsbury is becoming. Living and working there, one is bound to see the influence of Empire everywhere. And our so-called subjects are now beginning to affect us as much as we have influenced them. When the British Museum opens, races from all around the world can be glimpsed there—London is a truly global city now."

She had an extraordinary voice, Shiv noted. He could hear words humming as she spoke. It wasn't a high voice; it wasn't a low voice. It was a well-moderated voice, with inflections that came from meaning, not from a sense of drama, and with her distinct finely boned face, the wry, wide lips, her deeply hooded eyes, her high, arched eyebrows, she clasped your attention like a vise. Pigeonlike, he thought, a cooing, come to think of it, but structured and laced together by her sensibility, the peculiar meaning she brought to her words. He felt he could listen to her forever.

At dinner, he was seated next to Julia Chesley, who told him she worked at the Hogarth Press with the Woolfs. "How lucky you are," he said. "I could listen to that voice forever."

She laughed. "Don't hear it much at the press, I can assure you. She's a writer, above everything else, always in the back room banging out sentences on her typewriter. You might hear her hoot of a laugh from time to time, but that's all."

Then it came to him, where he'd seen her before. At the party in Maida Vale, across the room, a single pearl hanging just below the hollow in her neck, her hand outstretched as she reached for a glass on a sideboard. He had been walking towards her, the poet who worked at a publisher's, when a man barred his path. Halt! Verboten! Wog! He closed his eyes as the humiliation of the evening washed all over him. She gave him an anxious look: Are you all right?

He nodded. He prayed she wouldn't remember it. He hated the fact that the memory of the evening had come to him now, devastating, threatening to tangle the evening before him. Seated next to her, watching her lips widen as she smiled at him, or laughed at something someone else said, he felt terror. That evening, in the company of like-minded liberals, of the easy talk and companionship that is exchanged between equals, he had forgotten he wasn't one of them.

His mind went back to that evening, when he had first seen Julia Chesley. As he had walked away from the party that night, skirting Regent's canal, moths' wings gently batting his face, he remembered the intense humiliation that burned him as Lady Sophia's *Loddgger* rang in his ears, and the face of the angry Englishman who had barred his way towards the perfect feminine vision of English peaches-and-cream across the room. Men like Shiv were not even supposed to look at someone like her. That searing sense of emasculation filled him now, as he sat beside her and saw her pretty lips move, engaging him in conversation. Had she seen him leave the party, mortified, and in shame?

Millie had roasted a chicken, served with a mushroom gravy.

"Cèpes! Wherever did you get fresh Paris cèpes?" Virginia cried with delight. Accompanied by mashed potatoes and minted peas, it was a hit at the table.

Julia charmed him with her smile, her laugh, her enthusiasm when she spoke about literature. She was reading Katherine Mansfield now, she told him. "A writer from New Zealand. How clean her prose is, how unaffected. I've noticed that about writers from the so-called dominions and colonies of the British Empire. The details and the humour are delightful, and then there's her sly observations, the sideways glance that picks up everything. She's economical, too. There's a lot in her small, spare sentences."

Leonard Woolf, who had turned his attention to them, piped in. "It's Mansfield you're talking about, aren't you, Julia? Yes, we're great fans of Katherine Mansfield's. She's frightfully observant. Her ear for language is extraordinary. And she's a good translator."

Virginia glanced at Shiv. "I hear you've been called," she said. He noted the way her delicate hands were poised above the chicken leg on her plate, like a pianist's composed elegance before striking the piano keys. Her wrists arched as she cut into the meat and placed a perfectly sized piece into her mouth. She chewed thoughtfully.

"Yes. I've begun practicing." He smiled at her.

She nodded. "The best barristers read literature—by women, by men, by poets, by painters on their craft. Some are even excellent writers. Dickens and Wilkie Collins attributed their attention to plot to the time they spent in solicitors' offices. And wasn't it Sir Philip Sidney, Leo, who said that lawyers and poets share one art—the art of persuasion?"

"Yes," Leonard said with a short laugh. "I'm not sure what the poets would feel about that."

Virginia turned to Shiv again. "Reading literature shows us what's behind things. That's what we're interested in, isn't it? We writers, and artists—yes, and barristers. We make patterns of things that come to us at random, in a disconnected way."

He said, "I was always a devoted reader. I intend to continue being one."

"Very good. And perhaps you'll come by and help us with some of our Indian submissions." She frowned and looked at him. "To be perfectly honest, they're often mired in a nostalgic look backwards. . . . For a while, I thought it was the oppression of colonialism that had produced a persistent collective dream of a past golden age, but it's difficult to ignore when you come across it so often. Mirza Ghalib was a poet from another era. Is it the lack of a vision, or is classicism truly a resting pillar for the Indian literary imagination?"

"Indian literature is only now learning that it must be political to be relevant," Shiv replied. "The challenges of the present demand a new form and style in literature. I don't know where it will end up. But there are growing calls . . . and influential people are taking note."

"Come and see us when you're in Bloomsbury," Leonard said. "We'll find something on our list to fill up your hours on the benches."

Morty Saxena phoned to say he was talking to a publisher named Allen Lane about a paperback publishing company. "Indians are readers, but they can't afford the high prices for books. Paperbacks are cheap. Everyone can afford them." The publisher wanted him to start working with them once the company got off the ground to learn the ropes. He would later return to India to begin an Indian subsidiary there. Shiv said, "Congratulations. He's picked well."

They made arrangements to meet at the Grenadier, a pub near Hyde Park Corner. He had a glass of pale ale before him. Morty was drinking whiskey.

"You caved in," Morty said accusingly. "You weren't fair." Shiv knew instantly he was referring to the Thorun case.

"How? I followed the rule of law."

"You did what you were told to do." Unmistakable, the censure in the expression on Morty's face. His triumph, all his friends at the bar said. But he felt a lingering sense of shame that he couldn't quite explain. He had hoped Morty would raise a glass to him but there would be no "Cheers, mate" at this meeting. "We're still their slaves, Shiv, like it or not."

"Come on, Morty, you got a coveted first-class degree at Oxford. Let's raise a glass to that?"

"No, because I did what I had to. I toed the line. I wasn't controversial. I steered clear of troublesome areas. I asked the right questions, and gave answers that pleased. I didn't ruffle any feathers. I suppose that made me a deserving candidate."

"You mean that, do you?"

"Well, when you toe the line so assiduously you give up something of yourself. Tolstoy called it. He asked, 'What does it mean that thirty thousand men, not athletes, but rather weak and ordinary people, have subdued two hundred million vigorous, clever, capable, and freedom-loving people? Do not the figures make it clear that it is not the English who have enslaved the Indians, but the Indians who have enslaved themselves?' And we're still doing it—still enslaving ourselves."

Shiv sighed. "As if there's a choice."

Morty looked up from his drink. "They're fantastic builders, I'll give them that. They approach the earth with ownership, it's theirs for the taking—so they alter it, and mine, and extract whatever they can. It's the personality of a warring tribe. The bridges and railways weren't for us," Sen said. "They were to transport goods, to make India traversable."

"But English, it's our language of communication. Even you and I, Morty, wouldn't be here conversing like this. You'd be speaking Bengali, I, Sindhi, and we wouldn't have a word in common."

"True. But you forget that Macaulay's intentions weren't to get us

Indians talking to one another. They wanted civil service officers and administrative employees to be fluent in English so British government could be run efficiently in their colony. They weren't gifts."

"And we can't pull back. . . ."

"No. We've been trained to be like them. Their culture is now ours. We're the lost generation, you and I, so enslaved, even infatuated, that we now voluntarily adopt, we choose, our oppressors' ways."

"Infatuation?"

"Yes, that's what happens when you give up your sovereignty and embrace the ways of your oppressors. A kind of rot in our aristocracy and in the richer classes led to this subjugation. Watch the rich boys here, princes all, or sons of wealthy industrialists in India—they're not going anywhere. They don't need to. They're not going to be lifting their pinkies to get the Brits out of India. They're here to party and play polo, sow their wild oats, return home to a life of debauchery and privilege. Their warring families have brokered protection for plunder. Welcome to our land, take what you want, but just make sure your army fends off the maharajah next door who covets my F & C Osler crystal four-poster bed and crystal windows, my Rolls-Royces and my Arabian stallions. Oh, and while you're at it, could you send over some of that Highland malt, and those Cuban cigars?"

Morty sat back, exhausted. They stared at each other. There were no comforting words to share. Just Gandhi. "Yes," Morty sighed. "As if we need a saint!"

"Better than a dictator!" Shiv retorted.


It was a pleasant evening, not too cold. Birdcalls filled the air in Hyde Park. The croaking of frogs grew louder as they neared the Serpentine. The water shimmered molten silver.

"Was it worth it?" Morty turned to face Shiv. "The fellow's been locked away for life. He had an entire family counting on him back home. The English don't have much sympathy for tribal loyalties, but they know they run deep in the natives. You could have made something up and exempted yourself."

Shiv flinched. "After months of waiting . . . I had to take it," he said miserably.

"Debt?"

"Not yet. But it was knocking at the door. And barristers don't choose."

Morty looked down at the ground as he walked, tense and uncomfortable. "Poverty is the devil we've made a bedfellow of, we colonials in England. Only the rich ones can really afford this country. And they're paying for it, too—the daily attrition of pride, self-worth, that in their eyes we will never be good enough, always slaves. We go back poorer in the end."

One evening, as he came out of 24 Gloucester Square, a man followed him into Hyde Park. Shiv kept going, not wanting to alert the man that he had picked up his scent. Just as he reached Long Water, he saw the man approach from behind. "Stop!" the man commanded. Shiv did a double turn and faced him. He looked Indian but in the darkening evening light, Shiv couldn't be sure. "Sir, I did not mean to scare you."

"You did!" Shiv said, in a wavery voice. His hands were sweating.

"I will tell you something." The man's English was perfect. "He never did it. The young woman found every pretext to bait him. He wanted to pay his debts and leave. He wanted to go back home. She told him she missed India, and he was all she had to remind her of her childhood. He never gave in."

The man tightened his lips and stared at him. "Those *behnchods* are torturing him in prison. If you saw him now, you would not recognize him."

"I will look into it. If it's true, you can rest assured that justice will be done." Shiv had barely finished speaking when the man turned around abruptly and was gone.

Shiv left the park and sat outside on a bench. His head swam with his assailant's claims. Torture. Not possible. Yet he was trembling. *Calm down*, he told himself.

Dusk: the enchanted hour of calm between day and night. He heard the city winding down. Keys turned in iron gates as parks were locked for the night. Birdsong filled the air. He heard rather than saw the marsh creatures who lived on the lake close by—ducks' wings skittering across water; frogs plopping into its depths; the sussurating branches of surrounding trees; the shriek of a low-flying owl. A hushed silence settled on the exhausted city. Irritable and anxious, he thought Thorun was wrong to have stayed silent. He should have told everyone the truth. He chose prison instead of a language he couldn't trust.

Why would Thorun's friend have come to seek him out, the traitorous lawyer, if there wasn't some truth to it? In India, dissidents, activists of all kind, journalists, were routinely tortured. One law for Britain, another for the colonies. His father was constantly bailing out journalists who spoke the truth and pointed out dire injustices. But this was England. They wouldn't torture, even a coloured man, here.

Mr. Polak said, "You can't turn the clock back. This case is over." When Shiv insisted on going to see the prisoner, Polak said, "It's better, then, that I try to see him. You will only implicate yourself further."

"Sir, I have to go with you." Shiv's voice was commanding, so insistent that Mr. Polak said, "I warn you it is sheer folly. You stick with your side through thick and thin. You can't be suspected of speaking from both sides of your mouth. You do understand?"

"I understand. But I'm a lawyer, I must see the facts for myself."

Henry Polak threw an imploring look at his wife. But Millie

didn't say a word. She only gave Shiv a slight nod that escaped Po-lak's eye and that told him that she would not stand in his way.

Ramesh Thorun had been severely beaten. Even the prison guard who led them to his cell had to look away. They both went pale as they looked on a husk of a man. Thorun's eyes bulged out of a shrunken face; the prison clothes he wore hung on his frame. He held on to a wall to stay steady. Shiv walked over to him. "Mr. Tho-run, you would not speak in court. But please speak to us now. They have been severely torturing you?" Still silent, Thorun stared at him in that unnerving way he had had even in court. Finally, realizing that they had come to examine the truth, the man lifted his shirt. They gazed in horror. Shiv wanted to vomit. There were thick bloody welts across his chest, his stomach. "Turn around," Shiv said, in a steady voice. "Please turn around." Thorun's back had been as deeply disfigured as the front. Mr. Polak was muttering under his breath. "It reminds me of South Africa. The abuses of apartheid. Battered and charred bodies are routine there. But this is England." Thorun was hardly breathing but, in the cold air of his room, his breaths hard-ened and hung in the air like ropes, speaking of a body in severe crisis. He didn't need to say a word.

"Why are they torturing him?" Shiv asked.

"A white woman was involved," Mr. Polak said, giving him a grim look.

As they left Thorun's cell, Shiv said, "I'd like to fight for him."

"You can't." Polak's face was firm. "There's no turning back now. I will lodge a complaint with the bar and inform his lawyer. That is all we can do."

Two weeks later, Mr. Polak came back home and told them that Thorun was on a ship bound for home; he'd finally been deported.

"What?" It was splendid news. "How on earth did this happen?" Shiv asked.

"Lady Sophia made it her cause. I confided in her, knowing she has a strong sense of justice and a long reach. She got people to pay attention. Put up all the funds required to get him out of jail, and to ship him back to India. I've always known she was a good soul."

"Ultimately, the law sits in the laps of the well-placed and wealthy ones," Shiv said.

Mr. Polak said, "I wouldn't go about making statements like that. The law is sometimes fallible, but it works ninety-nine percent of the time. That's the best we can hope for."

In the end, Shiv pondered, you pulled strings to preserve the hypocrisies of the legal system. You had to call on the rich and powerful to step in and make a wrong right. Was this the system he wanted to fight for, carry back home to implement as the rule of law in India?

Councillor G. T. Hughes in *The Times*, 30 March, 1935:

Letter to the Editor

Sir:

I was present at a lecture given by Mr Shiv Advani, Esq., last week at St. Martin-in-the-Fields Church, Trafalgar Square. I went to hear this "brilliant young lawyer" make a case for independence in his native India. As there was little time at the end to interrogate him, I address some of my concerns here. His lecture was an ill-informed presentation that bore the hallmarks of naïvety and childishness we have come to associate with our subjects.

Queen Elizabeth I's charter to the East India Company in 1600 for global, but particularly Indian exploration, resulted in the arrival of the first British ship on Indian shores in 1603. By 1637, the British had founded their first settlement in India: Fort St George Madras. India's future was charted when the foundation stone was laid there.

The British arrived in a land populated by villagers— a land blessed with innumerable valuable resources but lacking the leadership necessary to control them or mine them for nation building. The ruling Mughals had little vision for the country. Had the British not arrived when they did, India, surely, would have disintegrated into a loose entity of warring states, subject to famine and disease. By 1858, we had colonized it. We brought bridges and railways, we built dams and trains, we gave them trams, electricity, and automobiles. And we gave them a language, the noblest of them all: English. We brought agricultural equipment— tractors and threshing machines—and we built schools and hospitals. Prosperity and tranquillity were the consequences. It would not be an exaggeration to say that we brought them the idea of nationhood and nationalism—the very concept under which their misguided and eccentric leader, Gandhi, seeks to unite them now.

For Mr Advani to imply that public works and nation building would be greatly improved by using the extra revenue gained (80 percent!) by getting rid of the British is mendacious and shows gullibility of the worst kind. The Congress Party, touting itself as the leadership party of Independent India, lacks the basic rules of governance and statesmanship. Its methods are primitive, its analyses simplistic, and its understanding of the skills, talent, and political expertise needed to rule a country like India virtually nonexistent.

The only way forward is cooperation with the British. Any other strategy is bound to fail.

Cllr. G. T. Hughes
Folkestone

LETTER FROM SHIV Advani, Barrister-at-Law, in response to Councillor Hughes:

To the Editor:

Sir,—I thank you for the courtesy you extend to me in publishing my reply to Councillor Hughes's letter. As his letter contains many misleading statements, I hope you will permit me to offer some corrections.

I am surprised that Councillor Hughes, instead of carrying on a reasonable argument, has imputed malice and falseness and unnecessarily called one of my statements "childish." Wherever I have spoken in this country, I have been complimented on the fair-mindedness and moderation with which I have stated my case and many British people have told me that, under similar circumstances, they should not have known how to keep their tempers.

Councillor Hughes is defending a bad case, but it is no use covering up lack of material by personal remarks. I feel that British people have a conscience in this matter, but as it is against their interests, they try to stifle it by finding all sorts of excuses for continuing their rule in India. I do not appeal to prejudice, which has been engendered for over a hundred years against India, but this country has a very strong tradition of freedom and democracy, and I ask for my countrymen the same privileges which people enjoy here.

In 1833 an Act was passed by British Parliament laying down that in appointment to high offices, the East India Company would make no distinction of "race, caste, colour or creed." No effect was given to this provision by the Company, and the promise was again repeated in Queen Victoria's Proclamation in 1858.

Indians appreciated this declaration of equality, but it remained a dead letter for nearly half a century. Some effect has been given to it since 1919, but still a good deal of discrimination against Indians is made when appointments for "key positions" are filled.

Repeated promises of self-government in India have been made in Royal Proclamations and pronouncements of responsible ministers, but up to now there has been no fulfilment of these. Particularly during the war, the hopes of Indians were raised, when India helped generously (what better example of cooperation could Britain expect from India?), but these were dashed to pieces by the reactionary policy pursued afterwards.

Whatever advances in giving "Reforms" to India have been made have come ten years too late, after a great deal of agitation, and Britain has always appeared yielding with a bad grace. We are, indeed, grateful (!) for all the Royal Proclamations and promises spreading over a century, but we want to see them implemented into deeds in our own time.

Of course a Britisher regards his own rule good for Indians, but there is also the point of view of the governed. In spite of so much peace and tranquillity, why has there been a widespread revolt of a nonviolent character (it might have been violent but for Gandhi's saintly character), if the people had been content?

India is tired of the slow pace of progress and large profits for the British and wants to take her own affairs in her own hands now, to put her house in order for her own benefit. If after a hundred and fifty years of British rule, only 7 percent of the people are educated, and an Indian earns 4 pennies per day (out of which he pays taxes), it is high time that Indians took control.

It gives me no particular pleasure to say the above things. I myself believe in cooperation between the two countries for the mutual good of both, but before that becomes possible, the Indian point of view will have to be understood and appreciated in this country. It is no good telling India that she must accept whatever you choose to give, or, worse, to regard her as being in tutelage. Indians naturally resent this attitude. You will have to treat India on a footing of equality if you want her friendship.

As a lawyer of some standing, I have observed there is a discrepancy between what is professed and what is actually followed even here in Britain. Having just returned from a visit to a prison, where an incarcerated Indian was shown absolutely no mercy, flogged to the bone, left bloodied and disfigured and unable in any way to plead his case, I see that standards are just as brutal, when applied to the coloured races of this world here at home, as they are elsewhere in the world. Britain cannot continue on this path. Believe what you say or revise what you say, so you can believe it. But to act in bad faith is not a form of conduct anyone, anywhere in the world, can subscribe to.

If the British give up this high and mighty attitude, one we consider patronizing and condescending, they will find that the Congress people are quite reasonable. Among them are men who have given up their careers and fortunes for the ideal of a free and regenerated India.

Congress is unnecessarily maligned in this country, but that will not solve the British predicament, for the Congress will continue to be a force in India.

A reasonable attitude will be to understand our viewpoint and to explore possibilities of mutual adjustment and friendship.

Shiv Ramdas Advani,
Barrister-at-Law,
Inns of Court

"AN ADMIRABLE RESPONSE," Henry Polak had said, when Shiv showed him the letter before it was published. "It hits all the right notes, except one." He took his pen out of his jacket and began editing it. By the time he handed it back, the entire paragraph on Ramesh Thorun and their visit to his prison cell had been excised altogether. "You can't say such things in print," Polak said. "Some of us will have a good discussion about an issue like this but it cannot be stated in public in this way. And I'd lower the temperature throughout in the letter."

Shiv said, "I'll take out that one paragraph but the rest of it is going just the way I have it. It's high time someone put the Indian point of view out there."

Mr. Polak raised one eyebrow as he looked at Shiv. He opened his mouth to say something but then quietly shut it again, as if he'd thought better of it.

A WEEK AFTER it was published, there was a telegram from Gandhi. *"Brilliant. My utmost faith, you have rewarded it."*

"I don't believe it," Shiv said. He was smiling from ear to ear. "Gandhiji read my letter!"

When he got home one evening, Millie Polak told him Muriel Lester of Kingsley Hall had just returned from India, after a stay with Gandhi. "She wants to hear from you immediately."

Muriel Lester. One of Gandhi's most esteemed supporters in London. "I look forward to my meeting with her."

"You must ring her immediately." Millie read the number out as he dialed. A high-toned, rather businesslike voice answered his. "Hello, Muriel Lester, please," he said.

"Yes," she said. "It's Shiv Advani, I imagine. You must announce yourself before you ask for anyone on the phone. It is only polite."

After he'd apologized, she told him she had a letter for him from his father and a small bag of gifts from his mother. She gave him the address and told him she would receive him at six p.m. the following day. "How are my parents, Miss Lester?"

"They are well. I think they miss you terribly, but they know you have important matters ahead of you. We will speak when I see you."

THE TALL, IMPOSING red-brick building looked just as formidable as its owner had sounded. He craned his head, looking up towards the top floor. There was where Gandhi had lived for three months. This place had been his home. Shiv whistled a little nervously to himself as he went to the front door, fearing several further breaches of savoir faire and possibly being booted out of Kingsley Hall as a ne'er-do-well.

In person, Muriel Lester was everything her voice told you not to expect. Dimpled cheeks, pale amber-yellow eyes, teeth that endearingly jutted out, a warm smile. It was how she greeted him, hands stretched out, expecting him to take both of them at once, which he did. She looked like a missionary and a troublemaker at the same time. He warmed to her immediately. Millie had told him it was her sister, Doris, whom everyone adored. Muriel is a thinker, Millie said. "She wants to change the world, like Gandhi. It's what makes them both such close friends, two peas in a pod."

"Would you like to see the place first?" she asked.

"Yes, please," he said.

"Follow me." She showed him the dining room with its long table, where residents ate communal dinners, and the kitchen, where meals were prepared daily by the cooks "in our community." The smell of cocoa and something he could only think of as bones boiling, a thick creamy collagen smell and dish rags used past their prime, lingered in the air. "We are a mixed crowd, like Gandhi's," she said. "Our residents are all from the East End—seamstresses, plumbers, fitters, teachers, singers, flower girls, navvies, artists, doctors of law—all living together like one family. I knew he'd be comfortable here, and he was."

"Where did he stay?"

"I'll show you his room and the porch outside, where he welcomed fellow delegates. The people of the East End loved him. He visited them in their homes, you know—he wasn't going to sit here and wave to them. People told me he was like a light that had walked in. Can you believe it?"

"He told Mr. Polak he walked by the river every morning because he met so many people there."

"Oh yes. He loved the riverfront. He would get to the canal by six thirty a.m. for his daily walk, and meet the local workforce on their way to their jobs. He loved cockney wit, and gave as good as he got, I can tell you."

Shiv laughed. "Loincloth and all?"

"Of course," she said. "He wouldn't be Mr. Gandhi without his loincloth."

She showed him the guest book, in which Gandhi had written *"I was surrounded by love here."*

"He really was," Miss Lester said. "He felt he had found his home in London."

She excused herself for a minute and brought in a tray containing a pot of tea and two cups. "It's so close to supper, I don't imagine you'd like teacakes or biscuits now, but a cup of tea never goes amiss, does it?"

"No," he said, longing for a shot of whiskey instead. "Miss Lester, tell me more about my parents. My little boy—"

"Yes," Muriel Lester sighed. "I did make a trip to Hyderabad to see them. Your mother's fine. Your father is working too hard. I recognize the strain of fatigue when I see it. He is working much too hard to—" She flicked her fingers in the air.

He cut in. "To support me here."

"Yes, it is a constant worry for him. But I think relief is in sight."

He looked at her, wondering what she meant. "And my son?"

"Your mother said he was away with his mother to visit her parents. I did not see him." She continued, "Your father asks that you either return home or find a place of your own, one that you can afford with your earnings, as he's uneasy about your staying with the Polaks any longer. He feels they have been kind enough."

"Of course. I am well aware of their extended, gracious hospitality. I intend to move as soon as I can find a bedsit of my own."

She wanted him to see Kingsley Hall for what it was—a place sought out by leaders and thinkers from around the world. "Gandhi really changed life in our little part of the world here, I mean, in the East End. He left such an impression on us with his daily routine, his kind words for everyone, his natural openness. He had no airs, no pretensions, as the leader of his people. And he was loved for it. 'There 'e goes,' they'd say, watching his bald head and stooping frame ascend the steps to his room every night. 'Uncle Gandy.'"

Shiv laughed. "I wish I'd come to visit him here at that time."

"He met you at the Polaks', didn't he?"

"Yes. It was an unforgettable meeting." His cheek burned, remembering Gandhi's touch.

"Let's go upstairs. You should see the place." He followed her up the flights of stairs to the top of the house, where there was an open-air porch with a day-bed swing and fragrant flowering bushes. "Just as it was when he was here. I leave it like this—you never know when he might want to pop in for a visit."

Shiv laughed, remembering his own long journey to England on the SS *Rajputana*.

"And here's his room." To the side was a small room with a mattress on the floor. "This is where he slept. But on warm nights, he'd take the mattress outside."

Shiv felt the man's presence in the space—it was his, so much his that even now, four years after his visit, it wouldn't have surprised Shiv to see him come out onto the porch and take his place on the day-bed swing. He stood there for a few minutes, then followed her down the stairs. "I'll be back," she said, going down a passageway.

When she came back, she handed him an envelope. "There's a letter for you from the Mahatma in here."

His heart did a quick catapult. Muriel Lester watched his face eagerly. "He read it out to me," she said. Did every recipient of a letter from Gandhi feel like this? His pulse was racing, his eyes blurred.

As he removed the paper from the envelope, she said, "We all read your letter to Councillor Hughes. It was brilliant. You stated exactly what the Indians think of their oppressors. Gandhi was so impressed by your courage. I gave your parents cuttings of it and Councillor Hughes's preposterous rejoinder. They were so proud!"

He looked at her. "Truly?"

"Yes," she said. "And they know Gandhi thinks the world of you." Shiv felt himself growing hot under the collar. Such high praise from someone who had charted his destiny since childhood. He smoothed out the single sheet and read carefully.

My dear Shiv

You will not be surprised to receive this letter from me. Your letter to the *Times* editor was an act of tremendous courage. You spoke to the British as one of them, as a cultured man whose sense of outrage was therefore not to be pushed aside, and had to be taken seriously. When we met at the Polaks', I had already told you I would reach out to you when the time was right. It is now, my dear boy. Your talents, your spirit, your passion, your devotion to the cause, are needed by your country. I have discussed your future with Muriel, who will explain to you in greater detail. You are now called to bring your special flame to the sacrificial fire. Muriel has many contacts and much knowledge of the corridors of power in Westminster. She will guide you. With each passing day, our determination to regain our sovereignty grows stronger. Our fight with the British will grow more intense. We must never forget our duty or our passion.

> Yours with affection,
> Bapu

The sacrificial fire had sent out its call. "How did Gandhi receive the news of the letters so quickly?" he asked.

"Imperial Airways carries mail and newspapers to India now in a week. People there know all the news here almost as soon as we hear of it."

"You have been summoned," Muriel said. She watched his face carefully. "You must obey."

He took a deep breath, sighed. "What does Gandhi have in mind? Does he want me to return?"

"Oh no, quite the contrary. He has a new mission for you."

"And that is?"

"He would like you to begin a magazine, a cultural journal. It will involve full entrance into the political, intellectual, artistic, literary community in London. You must win their support."

"What?" Once, sitting in the bowels of an eccentric Chinese eatery, while people clamorously spoke of classicism versus realism, he had sensed the magic of such a creative effort, of art and politics coming together. Was this the chance to shake it out from the folds of a dream into reality? There were growing sounds from the kitchen, the clatter of pans, of cutlery. His thoughts began scattering. "I don't understand why Gandhi of all people wants this," he said finally. "He's always encouraged me to excel at British law so I can be of use in the Ministry of Justice in India, when she is free. He now wants me to be a journalist?"

"Oh, he reads more than you'll ever know. And he's canny. People don't realize that about him. He sees that real change has always come when the artists and intellectuals of the world band together in a cause. Many people wrote to him to suggest that you should be the voice of the movement in London. While there may be other journals here run by Indians, he feels your voice, your presentation of ideas, is how he would like to reach that world."

"But it's a closed world, with limited, some would say exclusive, entrance. I don't have those connections."

"No, not at the moment, perhaps. The point is that there isn't much to unite us these days, but apart from the warmongerers who thrive on it, war is hated by almost everyone, in every nation, and the longing for peace is cherished by most inhabitants of this earth."

"But nonviolence, in the Gandhian sense, is a discipline, a way of life. Resistance in the West isn't nonviolent, Miss Lester. People are making bombs in their cellars even as we Indians speak about turning the other cheek."

"There is no need for such formality. Please call me Muriel," she said, with a smile. She took a sip of her tea, which was probably cold by now. He hadn't touched his cup. "You are not being asked to enlist a band of *satyagrahis* here in England. You are being asked to help artists and intellectuals understand what is happening in India so that they lend their voices, their art, their minds, to the cause of Indian independence."

"And in practical terms, how do I achieve that?"

"You'll gradually work away from being in court, tending to cases there. As you meet more people in the literary world, you will cultivate contacts that will be essential to you as you set up. You will have to pick things up quickly—the language of intellectual discourse, getting to know up and coming artists, thinkers, and writers. You will dive deep into literary circles to know who is doing what, who you want to cultivate. You will become a trusted ally whom they will then want to support. Oppression is not a difficult word or concept to understand. Everyone has felt it in some way in their personal lives."

Shiv sighed deeply. "The world of art and literature has always seemed to me a preserve of the wealthy, the privileged. Its doors are closed to people like me. . . . And the family doesn't have play money . . . there's no safety net."

"I know your situation, Shiv, how hard everyone is working for you, to give you the wind in your sails so you can fly. Mr. Gandhi realizes this will take time, and energy. He suggests you form a political society that will then publish a magazine—a political one with strong cultural leanings. It should be called something like 'Friends' Association,' or something like that. I know you are already in touch with the Woolfs, the Polaks' good friends. They know everyone. You couldn't have had a more fortuitous starting point. Georgina Chesley as well, and there's Grace Blackwell in Edinburgh, who knows everyone in the literary world. There will be help."

"What sort of help?"

"You will be put in touch with all the leading lights in these fields in Europe and in Britain, and freedom, guided by *ahimsa* and soul-force, will be its focus. You will be a torchbearer lighting the way to India's freedom—a bridge between Mr. Gandhi's thought and the world of creators, artists. Gandhiji feels your work as a barrister, your knowledge of British law, is a strength. It will root your editorials in the basic tenets of British law, the force behind British rule in the colonies. That will give your words weight. This should be a very exciting venture."

Muriel Lester was like a lit ship cruising down blue-black waters. He couldn't see land, only the lit ship. Was he prepared to follow it? They were asking him to be a bridge.

He glanced at her. "I don't think Gandhiji understands my position."

Muriel nodded. "I see your concerns quite clearly. He knows your family situation. He will support the effort himself. There have already been fairly substantial donations from people in the West as well as Indians for this cause. You'll be paid a monthly salary. Modest, of course. But it will enable you to find a place of your own, one that is suitable as both accommodation and a home for the journal."

"I'll have to think about it. The Polaks—"

"I think Henry Polak will see the sense of this arrangement. You can't run a journal from his home."

"Yes, of course. That is true."

When Muriel Lester went back into her room again and brought out a fuchsia silk bag, he recalled his mother tenderly, her quiet dynamism, her flowers, her garden, her candour. It was her favourite colour, fuchsia. He longed to smell it, that scent of roses from her garden it was sure to have. He took the bag from Muriel. Even as she handed it to him, he caught the first few transporting whiffs. "Thank you. This has been a most interesting visit."

"There will be others from now on," she said.


His mother's letter brought shocking news.

Come home. Immediately. I will explain everything to Mr. Polak.

You must return when you hear what has happened here. About six months ago, Seher went to Thatta with Sher to see her parents and grandmother. She told us she would come back within a month. Months went by. We were missing Sher. Father wrote to her father, asking what was happening, when would they come home. He wrote back to say, "Never." Never, can you imagine! What sort of answer is that? Father wrote again, asking what was meant. Her father wrote to say his daughter had no wish to return to a home where her husband had been gone for so long, where her position as a married woman was laughable since she had known her husband for just three months before he left. She was a widow already. He says Seher believed her husband would return after earning his degree. "But that is not happening. So our daughter wishes to be with us. She will not be returning to your home." Father then wrote to say, "But what do you mean?" Her father said, "This is a meaningless marriage." Then Father, you know what a stickler he is for clarity, said, "If I understand you correctly, you are saying that this marriage is now over." He wrote back and said, "Yes, over and annulled." Father, in anger, sent him a formal letter, stating that as far as he was concerned, the marriage between our son and their daughter was terminated. There has been silence since then. Over! Annulled! Terminated! Such words—I have never heard them used before in relation to a marriage. I fear she has ambitions, and these will take our grandson far away, and we may never see him again. If you come back, you can exert pressure on her family for custody of your child.

There was a small grainy cameo portrait of Sher. He sensed rather than saw the little boy in his loving smile. The pull, the noose, the love, the need, the harness, the guilt—he felt them all. This would not have happened had he been there.

He had a son who knew nothing about him. A son who was approaching four. He stared at the grainy portrait again. His heart went out to the little boy. A wild thought then came to him: could he bring him here to London, to live with him here? But even as he considered it, he saw the impossibility of running a journal, a political society, attempting to enter exclusive London circles while trying to raise a son, alone. It couldn't be done. He sealed his heart against whatever hope had fluttered there, if only for an instant, and looked away from the portrait. Someday he would find him, when all of this was behind him.

It dawned on him then: he was now no longer a married man. But he had a son, who probably didn't even know his name. He sighed a long, helpless sigh.

> Dear Father and Mother, Your news has been most
> distressing to me, especially because my son is no longer
> under your loving and watchful eye. I am saddened to know
> Seher was so unhappy. But she is young, and beautiful, yes,
> and ambitious, and must strike while the iron is hot. My
> future, precarious at best, unstable at worst, must have surely
> caused her discomfort and anxiety. I wish to reclaim my son.
> But it will be some time before I can return as I must now
> gain as much experience as possible working as a barrister in
> the courts.

He said nothing about Gandhi's new plan. He paused, considered: Could he make a short trip back, just for a few months, to reclaim Sher? The costs alone hobbled him: £2000 for a moderately priced cabin on the SS *Ranchi*, according to Morty Saxena. That represented four times his father's annual income in his most prosperous years. They had dipped deep into their savings to send him here. The figures, when written down, had a steel-cold sharpness to them, quickly aborting the thought before he could take it any further. Would Gandhi make allowances, if appealed to by Mr. Polak?

Millie said, "Not one for emotions, our Gandhiji. He would never let them get in the way of business. He always complained about his wife, Kasturba, who seemed to him to let hers run amok when it came to the children. He's a stickler for control, as we all know." She added, "I've been putting aside a little here and there from the household budget in case you needed it, but it wouldn't pay for a square inch on the SS *Ranchi*."

Deeply touched, he turned away. Emotions: how did Gandhi imagine you could fight a war involving such distances, separation from loved ones, for such long periods of time, without fighting for emotional stability every single day? He remembered how Gandhi always came back to desire with him, as if he considered it a serious flaw and knew it would be a sticking point for him someday.

He returned to his letter.

Gandhiji has written through Muriel Lester and expressed his delight at the letter published in the newspapers here. I don't know what he has told you but he wants me to start a cultural/literary journal here in London. Plans are being put into motion now. Gandhiji will fund it and the rent for a small flat of my own here. I will write more as soon as I can clearly see my way.

Not a day passes without my worrying about how much I have cost you emotionally, psychologically, financially, how much you're paying for it even now with worry and anxiety. I know you want me home. I can only say that when I return, you will be proud of me, for I will never stop working for India, and for freedom.

I send my deepest love and gratitude to you both.

Mr. Polak was quick to point out flaws in Gandhi's thinking. There were enough magazines already, he said. No one needed another one. What was lacking was leadership of another kind: men trained in British law, who understood the rules, the principles, and had walked down well-trod ways. "It is folly to make a journalist out of a barrister."

Mr. Polak spoke to Muriel Lester, who confirmed what Gandhi had in mind. She and Mr. Polak had never seen eye to eye on Indian independence issues. She was like Joan of Arc, with a torch held high in her hand; he, a reactionary who waited and watched for the right moment to stake a new route or plan. "He is a fine barrister. He will make a fine journalist," she told Mr. Polak.

Millie spoke to him privately and said, "He was a journalist once. That's why he wants to protect you. The *Indian Opinion* was fiercely anti-apartheid, and he was the editor. Both he and Gandhi were imprisoned for speaking the truth in its pages. Your father knows all about that, and Henry knows the beating heart of a journalist well."

As SHIV SENSED the doors to the world of ideas open, his mind, embedded for years in the cases that had laid the groundwork for British law, began moving towards the present and the future, where creativity, not precedent, ruled. He saw new ways of thinking everywhere, fresh interpretations of the world and of human behaviour, in art, literature, philosophy, and poetry. To witness change while it was occurring, to see first-hand the fruits of creative effort, filled him with an excitement he had not experienced before. And to be in the centre of the greatest capital in the world—London! Streets that had once dwarfed him now invited him in, became a setting for dreams. "Gemme of all joy, jasper of jocundities, / Most mighty carbuncle of virtue and valour; / Strong Troy in vigour and in strenuytie / Of royall cities rose and geraflour." A rapturous voice from the sixteenth century, that of the Scottish poet William Dunbar, filled his head.

He walked towards the bright light of his future with reverence and awe.

# London, May 1935

Just a few streets away from the Polaks at Gloucester Square was Lancaster Gate, a run-down area surrounded by the more established enclaves that directly bordered Kensington Gardens and Hyde Park Gardens. Where some streets displayed sophisticated living, smart houses that had thick red velvet drapes in the windows and bright chandeliers on their ceilings, Lancaster Gate attracted revolutionaries and troublemakers. So Millie Polak said.

As they walked past the street sign one day, he looked up the street. "It's an interesting corner," she said. "I don't think I've ever been down this street before."

"Shall we?" he said. She nodded.

They passed Christ Church with its long needle spire shooting up into the sky. A sunny day it was, as they stopped by the stone walls of the church. While they stood there, looking over the railings into the churchyard, a hedgehog came out of the garden patch and trotted across the street. Shiv looked at Millie. "Perhaps he knows something we don't," she said, an invitation to follow it. At a certain point it stopped and went down a hole. He looked up at the building across the street: 46 Lancaster Gate. It was one in a long row of white-painted stucco terrace houses, built in a grand baroque style, but clearly down at the heels now. *Shabby* and *decrepit* were good descriptive words for what met their eyes—the peeling paint, broken bits of plasterwork on the ground, dented pillars. A man was opening the door. Shiv ran across the street and got there before he could shut it. "Ah, glad to see you're here," the man said. He came out with a suitcase. "Go on in. Second floor."

"What?"

"Second floor, isn't that what you're here for? The flat upstairs?"

Without hesitating, Shiv replied, "Yes."

"Up you go then. Owner's from the Midlands, doesn't really live in London. But quick to respond if there are problems. Heat's all right, but you'll need him to get the gas going again. And there's a fireplace that you'll need to feed in the winter. High ceilings, so you'll freeze your arse off without a steady supply of logs."

"What's his telephone number?"

"You don't have it?"

"He said you had it." Shiv surprised himself by how quickly the lie came to him.

"Ah, yes, Park 2193."

"Is there a phone in there?"

"Yes, it's ancient and raspy. But it works."

"Thanks!" He waved at the fellow. "Cheerio!"

"Good luck!" the man called back.

Millie's expression clearly said, "Yes! Let's investigate!"


As they went in, he noticed a sign on the ground floor, just on the right of the door. Friends' Meeting House it read. He wondered what sort of club it was—its warm invitational lettering set the tone for their trip up the stairs. From the moment they walked into the flat, he knew. This was the place. His home. Some inner part of him leapt out and embraced everything—the walls, the large sash windows with clear, slightly uneven rippled glass, the wood floors, the smell of wood ash and toast, the intense quiet. He walked through all four rooms, slowly, taking it all in.

High ceilings, drafts that streamed in through the fireplace and the thin smell of London damp. The flat had that abandoned air spaces have when all the things that had once filled it—carpets, lamps, sofas, tables, and chairs—have been removed. Shiv took in the grey walls, the small damp patches. Paint would brighten it— bright, restful colours that would reflect the sunlight as it streamed through.

The sinking sun cast long shadows on the grey-white walls; dust motes spun like sequins in its rays. He felt as though the house was speaking. Is that how you come to know that a house is yours? When its walls radiate light, and its grained floorboards tremble, and the sun oozes orange out of cracks in the wood frames of windows like marmalade.

"Let's ring him," Millie said. "It's a little down at the heels but might be cheap for that reason. I can smell its potential."

There was a gas stove and a large porcelain sink with brass faucet knobs. There was a small table and chair in the kitchen. An old-fashioned candlestick phone sat on the table. He went over to the table and picked up the receiver. A faint crackly sound came out of the mouthpiece.

"Park 2193," a clipped English voice answered after three rings.

"Good evening, sir. My name is Shiv Advani and I'm speaking to you from my—sorry, your—flat. I'm interested in living here."

"Yes. You're not the lad from London University, are you?"

"No, sir. I met the previous tenant as I came up to the building. He mistook me for the other chap and ushered me up the stairs."

"Ah, that explains it. And how long have you been in the flat now?"

"About an hour."

"Righty-ho. Well, no sense waiting for a pot that isn't going to boil. The other fellow I spoke to probably changed his mind. He should have told me. Rude, as so many of those young fellows are these days. Tell me who you are and what you do."

"I'm a barrister, sir."

"Congratulations! Middle Temple?"

"Yes, sir."

"Good chap! My father was a Middle Templar. What was the ditty he used to recite? 'Grey's Inn for walks / Lincoln's for your call, / the Inner for a garden / and the Middle for its hall.'" The man laughed. "And where are you from?"

"India," he said. "Sind. My father's a barrister there."

"Runs in the family, then. I like that." He paused for a moment. "It's going fairly cheap as it's not in perfect shape. And the area. But you can ring me if there's any problem—water, heat, electricity, or whatsoever, and I'll get it taken care of."

"What is the rent, sir?"

"One pound and sixpence per week."

"I see." He mouthed the amount to Millie, who nodded approvingly.

"Payable every Monday. What is your current address?"

"24 Gloucester Square. In care of Mr. Henry Leon Solomon Polak."

"Very good. I'll send on the papers you'll need to sign. And I'll require the first two weeks on signing as a mark of goodwill."

"Yes. I understand." He put the receiver down, turned to Millie with an elated smile.

Millie said, "I feel you're going to be happy here. It's a place that makes people dream."

Millie had gone with him to a shop that sold Little Greene paints and they picked Boringdon green, a pale green, for the bathroom walls;

ultra blue, a vibrant lapis lazuli, for the kitchen; Dorchester pink for the bedroom; and a colour called Sunlight for the living room.

"Pink?" Millie said. "It's pink you want?"

"It's tranquil—it reminds me of the pink of my mother's garden."

"Ah," she said, as it made sense.

It was the exact shade of the rose-pink Lucy had insisted on for the walls in the bedroom of the Bayswater flat. That pink. That "sexy, come-and-get-me, sensual pink."

For a week before he moved in, he went by every evening. Morty Saxena often dropped by to paint the walls with him. "The place is in fine nick," he said. "Just paint. That's all you need."

When Shiv reviewed their handiwork after it was completed, he remembered caravans, the caravans of his youth. In winter, mountain people from the upper reaches of Balochistan and Afghanistan left their homes and came down to the plains for work as coal miners and itinerant farmers. They led a long line of camel caravans down the far bank of the Indus River. The camels' humps were loaded high with goods—flour, rice, embroidered fabrics, wool, dried fruits—and colourful fabrics covered their backs. The procession ribboned across the river's surface, painting it red, yellow, blue, green. He had brought those caravans from the banks of the Indus to his chilly flat in Lancaster Gate.

Two weeks later, the empty shell of a flat became liveable. Millie brought rugs, sheets, and towels. Pots and pans, plates and glasses. A teapot. Cups, saucers, a lace table cover and napkins. A cookbook, *Mrs. Beeton's Cookery Book and Household Guide*, where she had pencilled in stars next to easy recipes. White sauce. Cheese sauce. Custard. Most of the book was useless, as it contained too many recipes he would never attempt—lark pie? roast snipe?—and dishes for banquets and celebratory dinners. He would likely never need to consult the sections on how to coax rebellious sitting hens, lamp trimming, or how to spend the half hour before dinner. Certain passages, though, brought a fine gloss to the understanding of how the class system worked: Here was the housekeeper, whose position was one of "very great responsibility" and involved, "Like 'Caesar's wife,' being 'above suspicion,' and her honesty and sobriety unquestionable; for there are many temptations to which she is exposed. In a physical point of view, a housekeeper should be healthy and strong, and be particularly clean in her person, and her hands, though they may show a degree of roughness, from the nature of some of her employments, yet should have a nice inviting appearance." Got that, Mrs. Beeton, he said out loud. Scrub my floors until they shine but you must have nice hands!

As for her mistress, no greater paragon of virtue had surely yet existed, he thought. For she must be "like the mistress in *The Vicar of Wakefield*":

> The modest virgin, the prudent wife, and the careful matron, are much more serviceable in life than petti-coated philosophers, blustering heroines, or virago queens. She who makes her husband and her children happy, who reclaims the one from vice and trains up the other to virtue, is a much greater character than ladies described in romances, whose whole occupation is to murder mankind with shafts from their quiver, or their eyes.

Oh my. He put the book down. Virago queens did something else— they made your blood sing. Mrs. Beeton would never have got that.

He curled up on the sofa into a comma. Could they have lived here together, his virago queen and he? As much as Shiv told himself he is not they, his people would have claimed him in the end. Perhaps what they had once was all they could have ever had.

Up in the sky, now seen from cleaned windows, clouds were scudding by in an ice blue sky with the urgency of racehorses on turf. He felt their surge in his blood. He had been living with ghosts, with teasing shadows the departed leave behind. It was time to start living, he told himself. *Time to make this city my own.*

It was a fine summer's evening, when the trees hung low over the street in Lancaster Gate, and the light was cream yellow. He saw a young woman accompanied by an older one walk into his building. He recognized one of them, or thought he did, by the shape of her face and her hair, which was a light brown, like maple, and curled across her shoulders. As he got to the front door, the younger woman, noticing him behind them, held the door open. "Good evening," she said. "Are you going to the Quaker meeting?"

Ah yes, the Friends' Meeting House. "I live here," he replied, smiling at her.

"Oh my goodness," she said. "We met at the Polaks', when the Woolfs were also there. Julia Chesley," she said, holding out her hand. She seemed delighted to see him. He took it and shook it warmly. "Mother, you remember Mr. Shiv Advani from the Polaks' dinner?"

"Yes, of course!" Georgina's face lit with recognition. "When Virginia and Leonard were there, too. What a pleasant surprise! It's a talk on Gandhi this evening. Will you join us?"

"Yes," he said. "I'll just run up for a few minutes."

HE PUSHED THE door open as softly as he could and slid into the room. Julia and her mother were in the front row, their eyes glued to the speaker. The leaflet on the chair told him that Wallace Butler, a young man from America, was studying common ground between the Quakers and Gandhi's nonviolence movement and he had found a great deal of overlap. Reginald Reynolds, who led the Quaker movement, said, "I've been out-Quakered by a Hindu," and endorsed his protégé's findings. "We must work together with those who think as we do and overcome the hatred and violence that is, at the present moment, destroying our way of life, our countries, our people, and our civilizations. We must fight to preserve what we know to be true and good."

Shiv put the leaflet down. He listened to the young man explain beliefs he had grown up with at home in Hyderabad Sind.

Wallace Butler was a committed Gandhian—he spoke of him with reverence and deep admiration. "We Quakers are nonviolent in nature, but what Gandhi is trying to do—to subdue a youthful population that can be sparked instantly into violence with homemade explosives and other native instruments that have been used for centuries in violent confrontations between people—is extraordinary. They are learning *ahimsa*, nonviolence, by giving up hate. That is no small feat. When generations of British authorities in India have exploited and injured a people, and for that long, it is no small thing to ask them to give up hate. Yet this is what the Mahatma has achieved."

Butler's talk was anecdotal and inspiring. He spoke of men who travelled from across Europe and the United States to Wardha, where Gandhi lived in his ashram. "I met Arnaldo Cipolla, a well-known Italian journalist, while I was there. He said that Gandhi today is indeed the one champion not only of India, but of all Asia against Europe; he called him the standard bearer of the coloured peoples of the world in their struggle with the Caucasian race. 'All the Asians—Chinese, Japanese, Malaysians, Persians, Arabs, and the people of Indonesia—regard him as such, and were he to go to North America and to Mexico, he would find twenty million Negroes of the United States and sixteen million Indians of Montezuma's country ready to look upon him and revere him as a Messiah.'"

When it came to question time, many raised their hands, asking Butler what his meeting with the Mahatma was like, what his thoughts were on fascism in Europe, on Hitler, on Mussolini, on the threat posed by General Franco's growing power in Spain, on what it was like to live in Gandhi's ashram. It was at this point that Butler saw Shiv in the audience. "Sir?" Shiv looked at him. "You are Indian, I take it?"

"Yes."

"Are you a follower of Gandhi's thoughts and principles?"

"My family back in India is deeply connected to Gandhi. I am still trying to understand how his principles can be turned into practice." By now, all eyes had turned to him. But Butler was not going to let him off that easily. He said, "Tell us how Gandhi is affecting life in your community, how the cause of active resistance is being served by his way of thinking." Shiv groaned inwardly. Julia Chesley turned her head and gave him an expectant look. Partly from manliness, from seeing a chance to redeem himself, and from wanting to impress her, he rose and took his place on the raised platform beside Wallace Butler. "I must excuse myself for not being able to provide any deep insights that relate to the present moment as I have been away from India for over four years now and the news from home is always grim. We're at a cusp. As Mr. Butler said earlier, angry young men in India want nothing more than to take up arms and expel the British from our country." He looked around the room, at the intently listening faces there. He wanted to be helpful. "But we'll never win by conventional methods. We can't bear arms; we've been forbidden the right to defend ourselves by the British."

A man raised his hand. "And how do you think you can expel the British if you can't or won't use arms, and if you do not attack your enemy?"

"It must be done, as Gandhi says, by overcoming them. You disarm your enemy not with arms, not with violence, but with your

self-mastery. You could use violence, but you don't. You could use
the weapons of destruction at your command, but you don't. By not
using these things, you have already begun disarming your enemy."

"But how does this overcome hate?" another man asked.

"Yes. You see, your enemy is at first puzzled, then irritated; in his
irritation, which soon develops into frustration, he intensifies his assaults against you. But you do not cave in to reciprocal violence. You
no longer bear him hatred, which is the impetus for violence. And
even if you don't bear him love yet, you aim at him the truth that you
are as human as he is, that you are equal to him, you are, just as he is,
a member of the human race. In this manner, we persuade our enemies—we don't kill them."

There was silence in the room. Shiv felt his own power as he had
begun conveying ideas that he had known since he was a child. He
felt his words had been formed by inner knowledge, by deep conviction, and belief. To rise to his feet to express his thoughts on how the
leader of a colonized country had devoted his entire life to fighting
for the basic rights enshrined in British common law—equality, fair-
ness, liberty, justice—was thrilling; he brought his training as a barrister to explain what was at stake in the freedom struggle. "You take
these things for granted," he said. "We can't."

Georgina Chesley raised her hand. "If I could add to that . . .
Gandhism is, in its essence, very much like our inward light, which
makes us strong, and gives us power over evil. Conciliation is a form
of *satyagraha*. I have often believed Gandhi is the living Christ."
Several members of the audience murmured agreement.

"I have a simple statement of faith from Gandhi to share with
you all," Wallace Butler said. "When I took my leave of him, he said,
'A love that is based on the goodness of others is a mercenary affair;
whereas true love is self-effacing and demands no consideration.' It
is a profoundly Christian statement. His words were a gift to me and
so I pass them on to you. This kind of love is the path to fearlessness,
to truth, and to strength. Go in peace, dear friends."

As they left the hall, Georgina Chesley turned to him. "How long have you been living here? It's strange that we have never seen you here before."

"I moved in only a short while ago."

"Ah, that explains it."

"I would love to offer you both a cup of tea," Shiv said. "If you have the time?"

Georgina said, "We'd love to join you."

"Come on up." He led the way. He was lit inside; passion, the thrill of a rapt audience, the attentions of a beautiful young woman, came together to bring a spring to his step as he reached the front door. "Please come in," he said, motioning with his hand.

THE FLAT SEEMED sparse and unfamiliar to him as he ushered the two women in, its few pieces of furniture solitary and lifeless. They surveyed the room. "Do sit down," he said. Georgina sat down in the reading chair, and Julia pulled out one of the two chairs at the dining table. He prayed it was the sturdy one. He went straight to the kitchen to light the stove. He had no matches, he remembered, suddenly feeling despair. The place overwhelmed him. He pulled open every drawer, looking on top of the kitchen cupboard, even under the stove. "Can I help?" She was suddenly there, in the kitchen, looking at him as he stood on top of a stool running his hands along the top of the cupboard.

"Sorry." He got off the stool and said helplessly, "I can't find any matches!"

"Oh, I'll just run downstairs and see if the Quakers have any!"

"Where are you going, Julia?" Georgina said.

"To find matches," she said.

"Oh, I have some," Georgina said, pulling out a strip from her bag. "For the occasional smoke, you know."

"Oh, Mummy, you said you'd given that up."

Julia went back into the kitchen and rummaged around. "Is this what you want to use for tea?" She held up a silver teapot.

"There's nothing else, as far as I know. The Polaks brought over things they didn't need. It's a bit of a mishmash."

"And there's this." She held up a knitted elephant-shaped tea cosy and waved its trunk at him.

"Where'd you find that?"

"I have my uses." She threw him a delicious smile.

Over mismatched cups and saucers, and tepid tea, Georgina began talking about her trip to India. "My Quaker relatives in Philadelphia had heard of Gandhi's nonviolent movement and had begun mentioning Gandhi in their letters—I'm American, incidentally, Jewish on my mother's side, Quaker on my father's and as a practicing Christian, I was familiar with Gandhi's name. In our circles, he was already a name. But at the beginning of January 1931, the world got to hear of Gandhi when *Time* magazine declared him Man of the Year. Who's he, we all asked. I was immediately drawn to the meditative figure on that cover. He was draped in white shawls, and he sat with one hand pressed against his cheek, considering our furious world. Later, I heard him speak at the Quaker meeting when he was here in 1931 for the Round Table Conference. He'd been released from jail in India to attend the conference. He brought us all to tears. I will turn my suffering into resistance, and that is how I will conquer you.

"It was a new language, this language of nonviolence. We all felt he was one of us, for his teachings were so familiar. It inspired me to seek him out, and I went to his ashram in India. It was marvellous!"

"We have been too passive!" Shiv suddenly cried out. "We should have fought the British from the moment they came to our shores."

"But look at how the Gandhian method is working, Shiv," Georgina said. "Already the British fear him. His method is so strange, so unusual, they don't know how to deal with him or his followers. He's disarming them by not reacting—they're helpless. You've never met the Mahatma?"

"Yes, most memorably as a young boy. He came to our house in Sind as my father's guest. Such power! He reached everyone. He gave me his shawl!"

"Oh my goodness," Georgina said. "He has never, to my knowledge, parted with his shawl—Muriel Lester used to try to take it off him to wash when he was here for the Round Table Conference. But he wouldn't give it up. 'I'll turn it around and wear it on the other side if it looks grubby,' he told her. So that shawl means that—"

"You've been anointed," Julia said. "By the great man himself! Not to be taken lightly."

A stately word, rife with authoritarian implications. It said, you're mine. No, not anointed. Simply called. His right to obey or to refuse.

"It remains to be seen if I'm up to the challenge," Shiv said.

She raised her eyebrows and rested her gaze on him. He held her eyes for a moment then looked away. "Mummy, I think—" Julia turned to Georgina.

"Yes, definitely. We're in danger of overstaying our welcome, and we'll be late for dinner," Georgina said, looking at her watch.

Julia helped Shiv carry the tea things back to the kitchen. He watched her stack the cups and saucers neatly in the sink. Her marvellously straight back, her sharp neat silhouette. She turned around, her blue eyes like irises. "Thanks for a lovely tea. Do you need help washing up?" There was that smile again, warm and uplifting.

"No, no," he said. "I'll do it later."

Should he, shouldn't he. Yes, he should. "And what do you like to do, besides helping inept men find matches to light stoves?"

"Dance." Her face lit up. "I love it." It stumped him. He didn't know how to dance. Where were the dancing places in London? He had no idea.

Georgina had already put her coat on and was by the door. "Off we go, dear," she said. "Time flies when you're having fun." She turned to Shiv. "Do meet us for lunch, Shiv," she said. "I'll have Julia arrange it with you."

After they left, he went to the gramophone, Lucy's madly extravagant gift, and took off the nest of papers that had been gathering dust on its hard case. He opened it and stared. The last record he and Lucy had danced to rested on the turntable—"Stompin' at the Savoy," Benny Goodman and his band. He put it on again. As the music filled the space, he heard Lucy say, "Go knock 'em dead!" as he gave him the gramophone, proud and happy. "We're competing with the Bailey Boys at the Kasbah next month!" he joked.

Here he was now, with the same refrain singing in his ears. *Let's dance.* He reached for a 78. Should he try? He slid Ray Noble's "The Very Thought of You" down the slim chute of the player and waited for the music to begin. His body stood stiffly even when Al Bowlly's tremulous voice crooned seductively and the music, lilting, soulful, filled the room. He needed an instruction manual. He felt the rhythm but his legs felt tied to a wooden stake, as if he were in a three-legged race.

"Dance?" The man at Foyles in Charing Cross Road looked him up and down. "What sort of dance, sir? Ballroom, ballet, jazz? Swing, Lindy Hop? The Charleston? The Balboa? Or perhaps you're more the fox-trot sort of chap? The waltz alone fills a book. What were you looking for?" The bookseller's eyebrows were raised in inquiry.

Shiv didn't know one from the other. "Dance in general," he said. "Just dance."

The man said, "I'll take you to General, sir. The pictures will help you find what you're looking for."

"Yes, thank you," Shiv said, resisting the urge to leave the shop.

"Follow me," he said, walking ahead.

Confronted with shelves of books on the subject, he settled on a slim pamphlet entitled *How to Dance*, by Arthur Murray. It had been recently published. The illustrations showed men stepping about solo and the diagrams were clear and seemed easy to follow.

"Good choice," the bookseller commented as he paid for the book. "It's quite popular, that book. I've sold five of them this week alone." Shiv thought of young men all across London teaching themselves to dance in their lonely flats, their heads filled with images of beautiful women in their arms. It made him sad even as it brought a smile to his lips. He wasn't alone—others were trying, too.

The mirror was surprisingly hard to find. Morty Saxena again proved an indispensable ally. "What do you need a full-length mirror for?"

"It's impossible to see how shoes look with a certain outfit if you don't have one."

"Shoes are shoes, man."

"No, they're not. Trust me. And when you're trying to make an impression—"

Morty raised his eyebrows. "Ah. A girl?" Shiv looked away. "All right. If Whiteleys has them and will deliver, I'll get one for you as a housewarming gift. A bloody mirror! Are you sure? Want to know what my picks were?"

"All right. Tease me!"

"A bottle of single-malt, your favourite poison. Dinner at Veeraswamy's, where you can have all the chicken tikka masala you want. Or a trip to Brighton, to pay our respects at the Chhatri at the Royal Pavilion there."

"The Chhatri?"

"Yes, the memorial for Indian soldiers who fought in World War I. My uncle died in the fields of combat in France. It would be a good getaway, cold sea air, fish and chips on the pier, shoes crumbling on British pebbly sand. How about that instead?"

"I need that mirror, Morty."

"Accha, achha, accha. I rest my case."

The mirror arrived. Two young men carried it up the stairs and placed a stand on the floor. Morty had insisted on choosing it himself. "You'll go for something cheap and utilitarian. Let's make it a solid piece of furniture if it's going to mean so much to you." Beautifully carved in yew wood, the glass had bevelled edges that radiated light. Morty had splurged.

It took a while for the men to set it up on a stand. "Thanks, lads," Shiv said. They stared at him as they left. Bit of a preening rooster, wasn't he? the bemused looks on their faces said.

Which was exactly how he felt as he stared at himself in the glass after they left. Did he really want this unforgiving thing in such a prominent place in his flat? It noted everything, even the crumbs on his shirt from a biscuit he'd eaten earlier. One day of not running that razor across his stubble and a dark fuzz instantly showed up when he looked in that glass. He turned away from it abruptly.

Don't say mirror, say looking glass—Lucy's teasing voice came to him as he stared at it. Looking glass? No, for dolls' houses, that. Mirror, that's what it was, that big, grand thing in his drawing room.

He arranged the paper cutouts he had already prepared from Arthur Murray's book. Left and right feet, dotted lines for the left foot, unbroken outlines for the right. Pairs of them were strewn across the floor. His heart skipped a beat as he inserted the record onto the spindle. The last time he'd done that, Lucy was behind him, his lips hard against his neck. His hand trembled as he set the arm on the record. The needle jumped and settled into its spiral motions through the etched grooves on the vinyl. Sound began filling his space. *Ahhh.* He had memorized the steps in the book and now placed his feet onto the paper cutouts and began moving around the room. His hard, stiff body clicked into motion like a piece of machinery. It felt silly: a useless man who had nothing better to do than to hop around the floor on pieces of paper. It was foolish, foolish. He slumped down on the sofa, already defeated.

Once Lucy and he had lit up the Bayswater flat with their energy, the wooden floors reverberating long after they had thrown themselves, laughing and flushed, onto the sofa.

Like a Qawwāli, where call and response controlled the music, their dance had been directed by desire. Desire powered graceful, lithe movements. The body alone could never have managed it. How could he hope to find that again?

He went back to the emotions he had felt listening to classical music, which played in the Polaks' home every evening on the radio. That feeling was more like the German *Sehnsucht*, the longing for something once known but now transformed into a yearning for something new, an absence crying to be filled. He had felt it in their home, as they sat and listened to Bach or Beethoven in the evenings, after the day's work was done. How their faces filled with what persistently flickered within, the memory of what had once been there, of what was no longer there, of richness and the absence of it. Memory seeks out the burning ember within, quickens it to a blaze. Life-giving sap to a tree, memory feeds our senses, and our senses, thrilling to life, seek desire. Only through longing and desire can we claim, and reclaim, what is ours. Through the pain of remembering, we repossess that moment in time that had once filled us with joy.

The music he had on, this ragtime—joyous, born on the banks of the Mississippi River, this fiercely soulful music, full of pain and joy both, was not melancholic. It spoke of freedom and liberation. It urged you to break off shackles, find your true spirit, *his* inner spirit. Lucy had helped him feel comfortable in his skin. Now he was what the French called *deraciné*. Not at home—gone missing.

As the music filled the room, he stared at his listless feet in despair. What was happening to him? This paralysis—the reaction of a body in shock—frightened him.

His self-education, in preparation for the editorship of a new cultural magazine, now began in earnest. He knew his knowledge of art was skimpy and that he would need to be not just conversant but capable of judgement, founded on knowledge, of what was groundbreaking, what mediocre. Every illustration in the magazine would have to show taste. In the National Gallery, he stood before Monet's *Waterloo Bridge*, which juxtaposed evanescence and solidness, mist and stone, the mysterious unknowing fog that he, too, had felt surrounding him in those early days at the Inns of Court. He had seen even then that the stone was what he had to grasp, that it was there. Monet's fellow painter and friend James Whistler had told him about his old room at the Savoy Hotel, room 611, which, he claimed, had the best view. Monet booked the room on his first visit and painted Waterloo Bridge in there until he realized that the floor below had the better perspective. It was there that he completed the series of paintings of the bridge. One of the senses, sight, is said to come through mists. Milton, blind poet, spoke of spots on the moon, vapours that lay undigested on its face like clouds, obscuring and concealing its true face. Monet uncovered that bridge surrounded by fog and mist until he saw its true colours, until he had made it as light as air. Shiv went to the Savoy Hotel and stood outside the hotel, imagining Monet walking in through the entrance doors every day, going up to his room on the sixth floor, then later the fifth, to paint what he saw outside his window. Monet saw beauty through fog, the thicker the better. In the *brouillard*, as he called it, he saw a variety of colours, from lavenders, pinks, and deep purples to greens and blues. That's what good artists did. They uncovered and pared away until they got to the truth, knowing it was there, that it just had to be seen. Then they showed you fullness.

But everyone saw differently. Vision—affected by squints, slight irregularities in the eyes, wateriness, blurring, sensitivity to light, to heat, to cold, to a fondness or dislike of certain colours, to size—was unique; perception—subjective, peculiar. Perfection in art, as truth, spoke less to Shiv than the deeply flawed. How did an artist paint emotion? What was the coloration of despair, and of ecstasy? How did pain transcribe itself into the features of a character so you could touch and see it? A curve could be the emotional charge in a sculpture; the slope of an eye in a painting its story.

Every evening he would return home after mining paintings in the British Museum or the National Gallery, becoming increasingly sensitive to the line of beauty in a sculpture or form in architecture. He realized that it all came down to a work's truth—that its power was dependent on it. Even the grotesque had wonder, had mystery; and beauty, so insistent on admiration, could sometimes repel.

Then came the self-tutorials. After a quick dinner of sardine sandwiches and soup, or a piece of chicken and mushroom pie he'd picked up from the baker's on his way home, he'd reach for a record and slip it onto the spindle on the turntable. In two weeks, he had mastered some steps, could slide his feet into the required positions to simulate the basic steps of a fox-trot. Lucy used to say, "You've got all the moves, you just won't let yourself go enough to feel them!"

When the doorbell rang, he thought it was a mistake. "Yes?" he said, ready to shout out "Wrong address," or "XX doesn't live here now."

There was a pause. Then he heard a voice saying, "It's Julia Chesley."

He opened the door wide, mystified. Even in the dim light of the entry hall, he could see her flushed face, her awkward stoop as if ready to spring away. "It's the Quaker meeting. Mummy's downstairs. I wanted to say hello."

His floor was littered with paper cutouts, the gramophone was blaring, the place hadn't been dusted or swept in weeks. His skin prickled, a reaction of extreme discomfort. Deeply embarrassed, he stared at her. She was looking at him expectantly. Then he remembered his manners. "The flat is a mess but I'd love to offer you a cup of tea." The teacups, he remembered, were dirty, old congealed milk coated the bottoms, and he didn't want to start washing them up now.

Relief broke across her face. "Thanks," she said, stepping in. "For a moment I thought you were going to turn me away."

Then her eyes caught the paper cutouts littering the floor. "Am I interrupting?"

"No, of course not." He felt a fine prickle of sweat break across his face, looking at the paper cutouts as a woman would. A silly man learning how to dance.

"Oh, I see," she said, a smile breaking across her face. "You're teaching yourself some dance steps."

"Yes," he said, softly. "It's a skill I don't have."

He put the kettle on and when he returned to the living room, she was holding up a record. "It's Ellington's 'Take the A Train.'" He took it from her and slipped the record onto the spindle. As sound filled the room, she put out her hand. "Let's dance." His hand hung by his side like an iron limb. "It won't hurt, I promise," she said.

He took her outstretched hand. "It's a swing, so here are the steps. Watch me! I'll be the man, you can be me—it's easier to teach it as a man. Follow me, watch my shoulder line, and if I move a bit, peg your body to that, so that you move, too, along with me. So: rock forward on your right foot, turn your left foot back, then move one-two-three steps to the left, then four-five-six to the right. Forward, step back, then step to the side—one-two-three, four-five-six. Forward back—great! You're getting it, Shiv. Once again, forward, back, one-two-three, four-five-six. Forward back, one-two-three. . . ." And they were off. He hadn't noticed his hand in hers until they started moving around the floor. She smiled encouragingly at him, as if this was something she did every day—teaching stiff puppets like him how to move their bodies across a dance floor. The partnership with her, the deepening connection with the music, lessened his fears about bumping into her or treading on her toes.

When the record got stuck in its final groove, she said, "Let's play it again, and now you lead!" He began reversing the movements in his mind, and she said, "No, you're thinking now. Here, take my hand, and lead me across the floor in reverse. Let your body guide me." His body responded. As the joy of fluid movement took over, he looked in the mirror and his heart surged as he saw how perfectly their bodies fitted, how easily they moved together. It felt as effortless as water gliding over stones.

"Oh gosh, the kettle," he said, running to the kitchen to turn it off. By the time he came back, the mood had changed. It was as if they had been inside a snow globe, cut off from the world, spinning within it to their own music and rhythm. The whistling kettle reminded him of the intense loneliness that filled his evenings, when every sound pierced the air, roared like thunder in his ears. Inside the snow globe, those sounds faded, and he could hear his own heart again in its connection to the world. He said, "I bought a book. But it's not the same thing as having someone—I mean, you—teach me."

The doorbell rang. "Oh, that's Mummy," Julia said. Then, hurriedly, "Shiv, do let's go dancing. The Orpheans are playing at the Savoy on Saturday. I'm dying to go. Please let's!"

The Savoy? Did he have the money for it? Was he good enough to dance at the Savoy with her? Would he crush her toes? Could he afford to make a fool of himself so early in their relationship? He stood stock-still and kept looking at her expectant face. Monet's hotel, an inner voice spoke. Where beauty came out of struggle. He couldn't turn it down, he couldn't walk away. "Yes," he said. "You may have bloody toes by the end of it, but by god, I'll do my best not to let that happen!" Relief flooded her face.

Georgina walked into the room and stared at the paper-littered floor. "What a ruckus! You could hear it all the way down the stairs! You've been dancing!"

"Shiv's been teaching himself."

"Yes, I see the paper patterns on the floor!"

"I thought I'd help him along a bit!"

She gave him a warm smile. "How are you, Shiv?"

"Very well, Mrs. Chesley. And you?"

"Oh, I'm perfectly all right. You should have come to the meeting this evening. People from Kingsley Hall had come to talk about life there. It was all very interesting."

"I will pay attention to their weekly offerings. Please come for tea next Sunday."

"That would be lovely, yes, thank you. We'd best be going now. Bye, Shiv," she called out as she started walking down the stairs.

"Saturday, then?" he said, turning to Julia.

"Yes! I'll come over." There it was again, as she flashed a smile at him—that radiance, so peculiarly hers.

He would have liked to pick her up in a cab. "Good night," he called out as she walked down the stairs.

After she left, the encounter played itself over and over in his mind in slow motion: an elegant heel turned back, a pointed shoe going forward, the swish of her skirt, the way strands of her hair escaped from a clasp and framed her face, the thin line of sweat above her lip, the challenge in her sapphire eyes, the creak of wood under their steps, the scraping of papers across the floor, the whirr and scratch of needle against shellac—*bump bump bump*—as they stood still, looking at each other. He wanted to capture it forever. Their snow globe. Perhaps this, then, was what the Germans meant by *Sehnsucht*. Longing.

Millie Polak had come to eat lunch with him in the Temple Gardens. Surrounded by flowering bushes, a fountain that gushed water in unpredictable spurts, they sat on a bench between two mulberry trees. She unpacked ham sandwiches and put a flask of tea down on the bench. "How lovely," he said.

"Henry and I used to do this every spring. It's one of the best spots for a quiet lunch outdoors in London. You barristers don't use these spaces enough. Oh no, I've forgotten the napkins!"

"Oh, that's all right," he said, laughing. "I'll try not to ooze mustard all over my shirt."

She asked, in her quiet way, how he was getting on. "Georgina told me you invited her and Julia up for a cup of tea after their meeting. That was kind of you and very much appreciated. She's a lovely girl, Julia."

"Yes, I've promised to take her dancing at the Savoy."

"The Savoy?"

"Yes, it's what she suggested. I don't know where to go dancing in London."

"No, of course you wouldn't. Well, that's going to cost you a pretty penny."

"I couldn't say no. It was her suggestion."

Millie frowned. "It's extravagant. She's living on a budget, too. Georgina's not spoiling her. Be careful with your finances, won't you?"

He nodded. "What is it they say about women and money?"

"Quite a lot," Millie said, laughing. "And you'll be wise to heed what they say!"

"I've been terrible about coming by to see you and Mr. Polak. I miss our Sunday dinners!"

Millie gave him a delighted smile. "Let's have you come to us for dinner! You know nothing would please us more. See you this Sunday, then."

"Yes, lovely."

Later he remembered Millie's disapproval. The Savoy: it had represented a hive of artistic achievement to him. Now the hotel reared its head as a battleground. He had no appetite for it but there was no backing off.

She looked at him carefully as she stood at the door, sizing him up—ah, that perfect suit tailored by Mr. Rayner, how it hid his flaws, how it recast him as a man of the world. But it wasn't the suit she was looking at. Her eyes searched his for signs of nervousness. She wanted an evening of ease and relaxation, he imagined. And he, with his hot neck under his collar, his heightened sense of everything that could go wrong, was jittery and on edge.

"We should leave soon," she said. "But if you wanted a drink before we got there, that would be fine. We have time for it."

"What will it be?"

"What have you got?"

"No champagne, I'm afraid. But there is whiskey and some brandy."

"Brandy, then. A thimbleful." Lucy's drink. That was what rushed into his mind. Lucy's drink.

But as she sat down beside him on the sofa, and he thought how pleasantly restrained, how paced, their moves were, he began sensing some of the joys of courtship that lay ahead of him. This always-guessing place, the building anticipation, this was new. He liked it, the challenge of it. She sipped her brandy, he drank his whiskey in one shot, as Lucy had taught him to do.

"We should go soon," she murmured.

From the windows of the cab, London appeared glittering, aflame with light. It was mid-July and night and light played together on the streets. Dusk turned the trees olive green and fanned the asphalt in long silver planes of light. The shops of Bayswater, Marble Arch, the windows of Fortnum's, Hatchards bookstore on Piccadilly, sparkled like jewels. The lions of Trafalgar Square, their paws tensed on stone slabs during the day, now looked like toys ready for play. He felt the mystery of the streets as their cab sailed past them like Prince Firouz Schah's magic horse in the Arabian Nights. A light drizzle spattered the taxi windows. He gave her a quick look. Her face was relaxed. She was staring out of the windows like him, absorbed by the shadow play of people in motion. He became aware of her scent—a light creamy rose. The evening's seduction, its uneasy blend of terror, beauty, fascination, and potential had already got him in its grip. He grew warmer, uncomfortably aware of sweat pooling on the back of his neck, the prickly damp.

While he paid the cabbie, she was already going up the red-carpeted steps, where a guard doffed his red hat and said, "Good evening, madam." Shiv followed. The evening had begun.

She was so beautiful, he thought, as she removed her coat and handed it to the attendant at the cloakroom. Her royal blue calf-length dress had full sleeves, pin tucks that flared neatly at the waist. A necklace of moonstones hung around her neck and tiny stones flashed from her ears. Her brown hair showed its red tints in this light. Her full lips were painted a bright strawberry red. She looked like Hedy Lamarr, as young and fresh and beautiful as her. She said, "Shall we?" leading the way in. The music pounded out as they entered the ballroom. The Savoy Orpheans in full swing. They were led to a table, where their waiter handed them cocktail menus.

"I'll have a Jabberwock," Julia said. She turned to Shiv. "The captions here are clever. This one reads: 'This will make you gyre and gimble in the wabe until brillig, all right, all right.' Who could resist that?" She smiled at the waiter.

He would have to choose right then, he realized. "A Quelle Vie, please." The accompanying caption seemed tailored for his nerves: "Brandy gives you courage and kummel makes you cautious, thus giving you a perfect mixture of bravery and caution, with bravery predominating."

"Excellent choice, sir," the waiter said. Shiv wondered if his nervousness was showing. When their cocktails arrived some minutes later, he raised his glass with a bravado he did not feel. "To a wonderful evening."

She raised her glass. "Thank you for indulging me and agreeing to this."

The drink emboldened him and he felt he'd somehow make it through the evening. He looked around at the cosmopolitan crowd—there were expensively dressed black men and women, perhaps from Cape Town or Sierra Leone or Mombasa, far-away lands where men and women as beautifully dressed as these couples swayed to the music of bands and enchanted one another; there were Indian maharajahs with sultry bejeweled Frenchwomen on their arms; and Englishmen with lithe Englishwomen in sequined calf-length dresses and high-heeled shoes kicking up a storm on the floor. All rubbing shoulders with one another, almost like the gay clubs he'd been to with Lucy. There it was a sanctuary; your ticket in guaranteed equal treatment. Here, you paid heavily for egalitarianism. He waited for a fox-trot and when it came, with "Love Walked In," he held out his hand. "This one's ours."

She took it and followed him to the dance floor. Weeks of solid practice showed as they connected on the dance floor. He led, she followed, the steps flowed into one another and they quickly recovered the fluidity and grace he had felt in his flat. It was going well. A long slow exhalation, as he took in the words:

*Love walked right in and brought my sunniest day,*
*One magic moment and my heart seemed to*
     *know . . .*

As the song ended, he led her back to their table. He could see she wanted to continue dancing but the tempo had picked up, moving into a swing, a minefield he felt no urge to cross. He savoured the moment, his success with their first dance together on the floor. Something had shifted between them. They sipped their drinks, and she said, "Oh, do let's go back."

He anticipated trouble but hated to disappoint her. "All right," he said, taking her hand, immediately stepping on her toes. It happened twice. He saw her face cringe with pain. Mortified, he said, "I'm sorry, I knew this wouldn't work."

"No," she said, brushing up against him. "Let's continue." After a few further clumsy moves, his feet seemed to be speaking to him. Now, they said, back, forward, back, forward, 1-2-3, 4-5-6, and the floor at Lancaster Gate replaced the Savoy ballroom as he saw his steps in the full-length mirror at home, her shape against his, their fast glide through the room and back. She was delighted—he could see it in her smile. He, seeing what she was seeing, regained his own pleasure in the dance. He wanted it to go on forever, their closeness, their connection.

And just as he relaxed his arms by his side, another man cut in. With a sense of horror, he realized it was about to happen again—that *Halt! Verboten!* Anticipating the same set of circumstances he had encountered when he first saw Julia at the Maida Vale party, he lunged out this time.

"Oh no, no, you don't," he said, pushing the man away. Hardly aware of what he was doing, he said, "*You* bugger off! Go away!" His hand was out, about to swipe across the man's face. Julia said, "No, Shiv, don't do a thing! Stop!" He turned towards her, saw the horrified look on her face. His arm dropped to his side. The other man led Julia into the dance, a slow waltz. Shiv stared at him, at the two of them gliding across the floor. He felt helpless. When the dance was over, Julia rejoined him. The other man approached them again with a smile on his face. Shiv couldn't believe it. As the man reached them, he lunged out at him, the back of his hand hitting the man's face in a loud thwack. "What the hell do you think you're doing?" the man cried. Shiv caught Julia's look, an expression of dismay and perhaps even fear. Or was it horror, of him? He didn't know how to interpret it. "Stop interfering! Leave us alone! You had absolutely no right to do what you did!" he said to the man. The man's arm struck him hard across his face. Shiv reached for his nose. It was bleeding. "Oh, hell!" Julia said.

Everything went into slow motion after that. The band stopped playing. Julia was trying to explain to the hotel manager, who came to take both men away to his office, that no one was at fault. Shiv kept looking at her as she said the words. She had seen what had happened. How could no one be at fault? She saw how the other man had insulted him, butted in to their dance. What right had he to do that? He didn't know what to think. Was everything against him, even the woman he was beginning to care for?

The hotel manager, used to foreigners of all stripes crossing their dance floor, calmly ordered coffee for them all. "What happened?" he asked Julia. She said in a trembling voice, "I'm with him"—pointing to Shiv—"and we were dancing when this gentleman cut in."

"That is a tradition, madam. Men are quite within their rights to cut into another person's dance."

"I'm aware of that, but my partner isn't. He felt insulted by the action. There was no need for any of it. He thought we were being attacked. It's quite understandable if you don't know the custom."

Shiv looked at her with surprise. It was allowed then, in this strange country, to cut into another man's dance with his partner. "I didn't know or I would not have embarrassed you," he said.

The other man unexpectedly held out his hand. Shiv drew back. "Look, old chap, I'm sorry. You could have cut in and had your partner back whenever you wanted to. I'm sorry—I hope I haven't broken your nose."

Shiv took the man's outstretched hand. "I'll be all right," he said. The hotel manager was visibly relieved. As they left his office, Shiv said, "I'd like to pay the bill. If you could ask the waiter for it—"

"It's all right, sir," the manager said. "It's been taken care of."

"By whom?"

"The other gentleman insisted on picking it up."

"What?"

"Yes. It's all fine. Good night, sir, madam. We look forward to seeing you again!"

Out on the streets, a grim silence fell between them. He was suddenly at sea. He felt he'd lost the ability to read her. She must think less of him now for having failed her. The other man's generosity had humbled him. His first time at the Savoy—the hotel where Monet had painted *Waterloo Bridge*—and he'd made a complete mess of it. He couldn't bear it.

"How's your nose?" she asked.

"What? Oh, my nose. Yes, it's fine. It's stopped bleeding."

Another long silence. Then Julia said, "He was even worse than you on the floor."

"What?"

Then it struck him, how funny that was. Two men awkward with women and their bodies bloodying each other up because they couldn't dance. He burst out laughing. Then she began laughing, too, and then they were both laughing loudly, screaming at each other through their tears. "You should have seen his face when you lunged towards him and he began imagining the worst."

"And yours, when you realized your worst nightmare—two crazy men fighting in public over you."

"And the manager's, when he realized he had two deranged men on his hands. Coffee wasn't going to help! He needed a shot of brandy!"

"And the Savoy Orpheans, when their nice waltz became a shindig with stomping men on the dance floor!"

With each memory of the evening, they laughed harder.

"His face, when you thwacked him!"

"What about mine?"

His stomach hurt from laughing. There was a time when he had laughed like this. Belly laughs from the pit of his stomach, waves crashing through him, escaping as muffles and uproars, the body surprising itself with its own glee. He gave her a surprised look. She was the last person with whom he thought he'd be laughing like this.

Tottenham Court Road, brilliant with lights and people, was like a breath of fresh air. Laughing men and women, lit and boozy, were leaving a dance hall. The Dominion Theatre, with old advertisements for *The Phantom of the Opera*— the first film he'd seen in London a few years ago with Morty Saxena, starring Lon Chaney and Mary Philbin—still pasted on one wall. A different, forbidding London it was then, a London he didn't know.

He didn't want to go back home; he didn't want to end their evening. They passed a pub he had been to with Morty. He remembered the friendly, pleasant bartender. He glanced at the pub door and at her. "Go on then, let's go in for a pint of ale," she said.

He nodded and led the way in.

Over drinks, he felt a sombre mood returning. "I went to meet Muriel Lester."

"Mummy's friend. She's a true force. So, you met her finally."

"Yes. I realized you don't have to know Muriel Lester. The important thing is that she knows you. She had a letter for me from Gandhi himself. He had told me, when he came to the Polaks' for dinner in 1931, that I would have my calling to the sacrificial fire, as he put it, when the time was right. I was to qualify at the bar, and then he would let me know my destiny."

Julia was staring at him, fascinated, a little anxious. "What a grand concept that is!"

He gave her a quick look. "It's quite terrifying."

"What did the letter say?"

Shiv told her he had been expecting it for a long time, that he had been picked in his childhood, first by Mr. Polak, then by Gandhi himself, to be one of freedom's warriors. His training in England was all to serve India's cause. Now that the call had come, he felt unprepared for it. He had been called to the sacrificial fire. To burn, along with others, in the flame that would win India its independence. "Do you realize how absolutely terrifying that is?"

Her eyes were warm with understanding. "You have been called," she said, touching his arm. "You have a calling." The edge of her sleeve was on his jacket and he noticed her slim wrists and tapered nails, like marble under the intimate counter lights. She said, "I can see why you're terrified." But he sensed a slight withdrawal, as if speaking of her own unease.

He nodded slowly. "Yes, I don't think I understand what it means yet."

"It's been some time since we were all at the Polaks' for dinner. You should visit the Woolfs again. They know everyone in the literary world and will be helpful. I heard Leonard say once when poets start talking revolution, governments get nervous."

"Yes, I think he's right. It's now the intellectuals and literary personalities I must reach out to."

She reached for his hand. Surprised, he turned it palm upwards, and took hers in his. It felt like some sort of pact.

People began staring at them. Even the bartender seemed a little shocked. He sniffed from time to time to let them know he wasn't happy about it. We're holding hands, Shiv thought, not making love!

Julia seemed not to notice or didn't care. He felt worn out—it was exhausting having one cyclopean eye always alert to signals in a crowd, preparing for trouble, picking up signs, sensing danger everywhere. Julia's pale cheeks had turned rosy, but he did not know if it was the ale or the looks people were throwing in their direction. When Shiv signalled for the bartender, the man came quickly. He was as anxious to get rid of them as they were, by now, to leave. It was only ten o'clock. Perhaps it was his bloodied nose, Shiv thought, that was making the bartender uncomfortable.

"Come, Julia, I'll walk you home."

A companionable silence fell between them. As they entered Bloomsbury, a quiet hush descended. Leaves riffling in the breeze, swaying tree branches, the steady light of street lamps, long shadows across the pavements, quivering movements in mounds of dead leaves. The serene black-and-white landscape of London's park-bordered precincts.

By Russell Square, she told him she had been to her mother's hometown, Philadelphia, only once, as a little girl. In her memories there were a lot of old aunts and uncles who lived in large musty houses with endless stairs, and paintings of ancestors she had never known about on the walls. "I was taught their names by an uncle, who quizzed me the day before I left for England. 'It's your heritage,' he said. I wonder what that means when there are relatively few connections with that part of the family now. I haven't seen any of them since I was ten. He called it heritage. I call it history."

"But someday, when you have your own children, it will mean something, that heritage. You'll want them to know it, just as your uncle wanted you to know."

There was a long silence. He heard their feet step over fallen twigs scattered on the pavements from a recent windstorm. He could hear her thinking. "I imagine you're right," she finally said. "I would, I think, want them to know. I think of myself as English but Mother's side, though I hardly know them, is important, too. Heritage—it's where we've come from, isn't it?" She gave him a quick look, as if struck by the novelty of a strange thought. "What's your heritage, Shiv? Where do your people come from?"

"Family lore says they came from Mesopotamia—they left their original lands, which may have originally been Iraq or Persia, and perhaps they took the trade route to northern India—the Silk Roads, as they're known—and got there by caravan."

"People leaving home—even when it seems like a choice, it isn't. Mother left Philadelphia because she couldn't bear being confined to her narrow circles there. She felt the world calling to her." Shadows flickered across her face. He liked the pensive expression on her face as much as he loved hearing her laugh. She was solid, real.

Julia asked, "Where did your family settle?"

"In Multan, a city so ancient it was the centre for solar worship until the eleventh century. Generations of our family had lived there. But when mandatory conversion to Islam began in the seventeenth century, they fled, along with many other Hindu families. They crossed the Thar Desert by caravan, and arrived in Sind about three hundred years ago, around 1650. Our family records from the seventeenth century establish us as being warriors."

"A warrior!" She laughed. "Fighting in the cause of nonviolence!"

He laughed back. "Yes, going against the grain, you could call it."

"So you're the first barrister in the family?"

"No, my paternal great-grandfather was a judge, my maternal great-grandfather, a native of Sind, a fisherman. My father is a pleader and a judge."

She said, "That's much more interesting than my background. I wish I had pleaders and fishermen in my gene pool."

He laughed. "I suspect everyone has a fisherman in their gene pool."

As they turned into Mecklenburgh Square, she said, "That's my flat up there, right at the top"—pointing to the third floor of a tall, elegant building. "And there's the glorious garden. Come visit me during the day and I'll take you there." She inserted the door key. Her hand lingered on the knob, not quite turning it to open.

He was awkward again. How did you say good night to a girl you've spent such an evening with? He looked at her helplessly. "I'll ring," he said, and turned instantly away. He heard the click of the key in the lock as he crossed the silent street. Then she'd gone.

He stared at the locked garden gate, remembering Lucy telling him that the keys were there for exclusivity, to keep people out. But here was a garden to which a beautiful woman had keys, and she was inviting him in to join her in marvelling at its glory.

He waited for a few days. She might reject him, but he would be a fool for not trying to see her again. He tried to get up the courage to phone her. But his fingers went into freeze mode as they reached the dial. When it rang one evening at nine p.m., he sat glued to his chair, making no move to answer it. Millie Polak would never ring so late. Nor would Morty, pickled in scotch by this time. It rang and rang. He raced across the floor to answer it. "Am I disturbing you?" Julia's pearly voice.

"No, of course not. You're not, I mean."

"Oh, good. How have you been?"

"Busy. Working twice as hard at chambers because two are out with the flu." Pedestrian, boring. He could never tap wit when he needed it. The French had a useful phrase for it, *l'esprit d'escalier*, for the quick-witted response you wanted to make, which came only as you were leaving, going down the stairs. He felt stodgy and prosaic. Why would she be interested in him? He nearly put the phone down.

She said, "The Woolfs said they would be happy to see you again."

"Really?"

"Yes, Virginia said she wants to ask you about Indian poetry."

"I'm hardly an expert there," he said.

"You don't have to be. She *will* steer the conversation round to mysticism, which interests her greatly these days. What *is* brahman? she might ask you, as she did Tom Eliot the other day. Poor man nearly ran out of the office! But you could field her questions, I'm absolutely sure."

"Gosh. Any advice on what I should not say?"

"You can say anything as long as it's not conventional," she said. "You'll be brilliant! Oh, and one more thing. Leonard has a marmoset named Mitz. She's quite a celebrity and the apple of his eye. She's peculiar. If she takes a liking to you, she'll have a painful way of showing it. They won't lift a finger. She's the celebrity that charmed their way through Europe and Nazi Germany as neat schoolgirls and burly guards all succumbed to Mitz's charms."

Shiv imagined his eyes being clawed out by an overly affectionate monkey. He shuddered. Julia laughed. "You have to pray Mitz doesn't like you. Otherwise, you'll have to sit quietly and suffer her affectionate outpourings without any sympathy from them!"

How unlike the patrician woman at the party, he thought, as she came out of the back room in a blue overall over her dress, a lit cigarette between her lips, grey hair falling across her forehead, steel-rimmed round glasses. She said, "Hello, I believe you're Julia's boyfriend." Surprised by her directness, he replied, "Hello." She seemed to have forgotten they had already met at the Polaks'.

Leonard Woolf looked curiously in his direction. "Sit down, sit down," he said. "How's Henry?"

Julia indicated a chair with her eyes to say "Sit."

"The Polaks are well, sir. They're preparing for their annual trip to Cornwall."

"Ah yes. It's that time of year," Leonard said. He turned his attention to filling his pipe.

Shiv sat down on a sagging chair. It was a hot day, and the drains under the house were letting out a stench that made him gag.

There was an uncomfortable silence. Julia had told him about Mrs. Benson, a sturdy woman with a round red face and large glasses who was seated at a neat desk in the other room; she paused in her typing and threw him an inquisitive look. Shiv grew hotter under the collar with every passing second. He felt his vocal cords dry up.

Julia stepped in. "Shiv has been asked by Mr. Gandhi himself to set up a cultural magazine here. He wants the intellectuals involved in India's struggle." It was at this point that Mitz, the marmoset, hopped off a ledge of books and landed at his feet. He cast a quick glance at his feet—Mr. Rayner's expensive trousers!—and watched in horror as the weird-looking monkey began pulling at the cuffs with its sharp claws. He glanced around helplessly. Julia seemed blithely unaware of the havoc the creature was causing. No help came, nor should it have been expected, he quickly realized, when he caught Leonard's bemused downward look at his ankles. He seemed almost approving.

"Smart idea," Leonard said. "We all know that when it comes to really winning wars, it's the intellectuals and artists of the world who make the crucial difference." A dog had jumped onto Leonard's lap. Leonard stroked him, as he puffed on his pipe. Pinker or Pinka, or something like that, Shiv couldn't remember what Julia had said. "Henry Polak believes that our government must be persuaded to relinquish its colonies through debate. I disagree with him," Leonard said.

"So what do you think is the answer?" Virginia said.

"I think the groundswell will have to be artistic and literary to have lasting impact, and also to widen the struggle and its appeal. Articles condemning British rule in India by writers and well-respected journalists—persistent coverage. Common cause is what will draw them. Our times are violent, rapidly changing. Fascism, as

Herr Hitler reminds us daily, has new recruits by the thousands every day."

"Muriel Lester said much the same thing," Shiv said. The moment excited him, made him see the magazine's potential. That a humanitarian philanthropist in the East End and a leading left-wing intellectual in Bloomsbury were thinking along the same lines indicated common ground and a larger swath of like-minded people that he could draw on.

"Herr Goering was at the Lutyens dinner last week, Vanessa reported, selling the Hitler brand," Virginia said. She put her freshly rolled cigarette to her lips, lit it with a match, and drew deeply on it. "He's such a snob, she says, but he convinces the British with his polish. You know how we iron things out. We never truly believe aberrant behaviour in people we consider refined. Old chap will come round, just a temporary loss of reason. All will be right again." Virginia's long, tapering fingers reached for a pouch of tobacco on the table. There was already a lit one burning in the ashtray next to her. Shiv couldn't help staring at her, her long, gentle face. Even in her utilitarian garb, with her stern glasses and worn shoes, occasionally picking up her knitting to fill in a line, or turning to roll her shag cigarettes, she seemed like a queen. Seated on her throne in the heart of the most exciting publishing company in the world, she managed the packing of books into boxes and contemplated the mysteries of the inner life in the same breath. "She sits in the back room near the fire tapping away on the typewriter all day," Julia had told him. "It's unnerving to hear her words coming out on paper like that. Another ground-breaking masterpiece that will speak to women all over the world—if not now, then someday." He watched Virginia roll another cigarette, hold it like a wand to her lips. Those marvellous hands. He was drawn to her every movement, a moth to a flame.

"Hah!" Leonard snorted. "But you're right, my dear. It is the British temperament to admire what it should sometimes detest. Oswald

Mosley and his British Union of Fascists are drawing larger crowds today than they ever did. Demagogues are inching closer to the reins of power. This is why Mahatma Gandhi commands our attention, even our reverence."

When Virginia asked Shiv what he thought was the essence of Gandhism, he explained it, to his surprise, lucidly. "Its four prongs are home rule—total independence—*swaraj*; homespun, homemade, *swadeshi*; nonviolence—*ahimsa*; soul-force—*satyagraha*. Four key elements that hold it all together." She seemed to have forgotten their earlier conversation—admittedly, from a few months ago, at the Polaks' dinner. These days, Gandhiji popped up with some regularity in the news, either as a crackpot, a genius, a menace, or a wily politician. So perhaps she was wondering about him again, what he was using to win millions over to his cause.

Leonard said, "Full marks for succinctness and clarity. But preceding this development of his thought was the most important prong of all: noncooperation. Gandhi says that noncooperation 'is a duty when the government, instead of protecting, robs you of your honour.'"

Shiv cut in, "It's extraordinary when you stop to think about it. It means that Indians now see noncooperation as a form of power, as a weapon: they will not recognize foreign government on their soil, they refuse to obey it, they will ignore its law courts, and stop paying taxes. It's called *purna swaraj*—no dominion status for us, we're fighting for total independence."

Leonard jabbed the stem of his pipe towards him. "Do you realize how unthinkable, and nothing short of revolutionary, it is? What you call soul-force is a natural extension of that notion."

"Well, you've put it quite well, I must say," Virginia said. "Except for that . . . soul-force. What on earth does he mean by that?" She looked at Shiv with her fine, hooded eyes.

Shiv took a deep breath. "It's neutralizing hatred so it can be *converted into love*, and in doing so, you disarm your enemy from wanting to hurt you. You create disarmament through love. It sounds trite, almost silly."

Leonard drew on his pipe. "It's anything but. Hate can only be overcome through love. This is what the Mahatma is trying to teach us, in circumstances that are difficult for him, his country, and the world."

"So then, *ahimsa*, or nonviolence, is akin to the Christian concept of loving your enemy," Virginia said, her cigarette midair, as if pausing midthought. "They do call him the chocolate Jesus."

Shiv laughed. "The chocolate Jesus. I've not heard that before. It's better than 'half-naked fakir.' Or madman. Or wrecking ball. I admit it's not easy to think in these terms. To work on hate so it can be defanged and converted into love is a lofty idea. But it's working. Gandhi once told me that nonviolence was strong enough to paralyse the mightiest government on earth. It was when he came to the Polaks' for dinner."

Pinka bounded over to Virginia and clambered onto her lap. She stroked his head thoughtfully. "I've heard he's written to Hitler to stop the madness in Europe." She shook her head. "We saw the pro-fascist crowds just a little while ago in Germany, Austria, the Netherlands. They're all for him!"

Leonard said, "Yes, that is true. But we've seen enough of war, of violence. The times are with Gandhi. I pray he succeeds." After a pause, puffing on his pipe, he said, "What do you intend to call your magazine?"

"I haven't given it much thought. But something suggesting a way forward seems appropriate."

"Call it just that: *Forward*. I like that," Virginia said.

"Does it need anything else?" Leonard said.

"What do you mean?" she asked.

"An exclamation mark for instance. Optimism and youth coming together?"

"No," Virginia said, shaking her head. "Too too. It's overreaching, and it becomes a slogan with an exclamation mark, and we all know how dangerous those are in our times."

"Talk to Morgan," Leonard said.

"Morgan?" Shiv said.

"E. M. Forster. He'll have some good ideas."

"That's a good suggestion. And who was that funny little man, Jewish Romanian, journalist who came to see us the other day? He has a literary magazine in Romania and is moving to London." Virginia's voice, like water over pebbles. "Don't you think, Leo?"

"Oh yes, Miron Grindea. Very smart, very well connected. You must get in touch with him. He's part of the anti-fascist literary brigade in Europe." He looked around on his desk and found a card. "Yes, here it is. He's your man." He handed it to Shiv.

"What about Bertie Russell?" Virginia said.

"He's fiercely intellectual but I shouldn't think that would intimidate you," Leonard said, turning to Shiv. "And you must meet the writer Mulk Raj Anand, who proofreads for us when he's in London. His novel, called *Untouchable,* holds a mirror to the caste system— it was published last year here but it had no reviews. He's gone to Gandhi's ashram to write his next one."

"I could review his novel for *Forward*!" Julia said.

"Excellent, my dear! I am sure that would please him," Leonard said.

"He speaks of Hindu gods and goddesses a great deal—it seems Hindu literature cannot be written without a religious base." Virginia looked at Shiv. "Do you think that's true?"

"I think he's right. The gods are given new relevance constantly— in art, in music, in drama—and I think that will continue. Even Gandhi's political message is fundamentally a religious one. But I believe there will be change—secular forces in India are pushing for it."

"We will arrange a meeting between you two angry young men when he's back," Leonard said.

Shiv smiled at Julia. She had brought him into the circle of people with whom you could discuss anything, even uncomfortable topics. They weren't mocking him; they weren't condescending; they weren't trying to upstage him; they didn't make him self-defensive. They had assessed him correctly for who he was. They made him feel part of the human race, no different, not other, just like them, in fact. They assumed he spoke the same language. Inclusion, until proven unworthy. Not exclusion, until proven worthy. And they were far more sympathetic to India's cause than he could have imagined.

Leonard said, "You should come to my club in Gerrard Street. I'd like to hear you address our members on this very theme: *Ahimsa* Is Love. We've heard enough about hate. Now let's hear something about love—in politics, as a pathway to freedom. Quite a star, your chocolate Jesus, isn't he?" He smiled at Shiv.

Virginia gave him a thoughtful look. "Creon said, 'Once an enemy, never a friend, even after death.' To which Antigone responded courageously, rightly, 'I was born to join in love, not hate.' And how she proved it." She rose and held out her hand. He touched it delicately. "You must come again," she said, smiling, as though he had something to offer her.

"She means it," Julia said as they closed the front door behind them and stepped out onto Mecklenburgh Square. She strode ahead of him, excited and happy.

He said, "Do you know a good tailor?"

"What?"

"Look!" She then saw the fraying shreds of his trouser cuffs and burst out laughing. "Oh, that Mitz! She's a scream!" Beloved English pets were a breed apart—they could do no wrong. Even if Mitz had fastened her sharp little teeth around his calf and bitten into it, no one would have batted an eyelid. He shuddered. "She loves you!" Julia said.

He grimaced. "It's a love I can do without, to be honest."

"Forget about the trousers for the moment." She turned and gave him a brilliant smile. "You just won another round with both of them. And they gave you introductions to others who can help you. You don't realize how marvellous that is." He basked in her appreciation. It hadn't cost him anything; that was what surprised him.

She told him that Grindea knew everyone in Europe. "Picasso, the young rising star Camus, Chagall, Miró, Gide—all friends and allies of his."

Shiv began to see how feminism, anti-fascism, socialism, and anti-imperialism had become close allies. For women felt the impact of war more than men. They lost sons, husbands, lovers to the battle-field. They watched their households sink towards poverty. They tended to the sick and dying in hospitals, in bombed streets, towns, and villages, and in their own homes, if they were large enough and requisitioned by the state for the care of the wounded. Women had led the anti-war movement; they had been the cheerleading team for nonviolence: Madeleine Slade, a.k.a. Mirabehn (a British aristocrat who had converted to Gandhism, taken on a Hindu name, and become Gandhi's right-hand assistant), Virginia Woolf, Grace Black-well, Muriel Lester, Georgina Chesley, their friend Sylvia Pankhurst, who led the suffragettes, Vera Brittain, who had written so movingly about the horrors of war, Annie Besant who had died two years ear-lier, had all, either directly or indirectly become supporters of the cause for Indian independence. It was this influential and well-heeled body he meant to target for the magazine. Its name seemed so familiar—*Forward*—both preordained and a significant word from the past. A different context, what was it? Then it came to him.

"*Forward. Let's dance to the stars and beyond! Your loving Lucy.*"

Call night. Malt and caviar. The gramophone. Grapes. His lips. Lucy.

He turned away from the memory—a radiant ember destined to burn.

From the moment Julia knew that the magazine was becoming a reality, she started him on reading the newest and noteworthy writers of the day. "Your reading of the classics is pretty impressive. Even I haven't read the *Odyssey* cover to cover. Or Dante. Or *War and Peace*. But the moderns—there are gaps." So began Julia's crash course in contemporary literature—every week she would assign him two novels and a book of poetry. By week 4, he had read Conrad's *The Secret Agent*, Katherine Mansfield's *The Garden Party and Other Stories*, Hemingway's *A Farewell to Arms*, Jean Rhys's *Voyage in the Dark,* André Gide's *Counterfeiters*, Henry James's *The Wings of the Dove*, Virginia Woolf's *Mrs. Dalloway*, Henry Green's *Living*, and F. Scott Fitzgerald's *The Great Gatsby*. He'd also managed to read some poetry by Mallarmé and Rimbaud, translated into English for the magazine *Adam* by none other than its editor, Miron Grindea, which, Julia explained, "is essential reading for a meeting with him."

At times he noticed her apprehension. A quiet intense look at him, as if she were gauging him. "You have so much on your shoulders," she once told him. "I don't know how you can bear it."

They were in Kensington Gardens one fine September afternoon. Ducks paddled the light-quivering waters of the Serpentine. A fine breeze perked up drooping heads of flowers and brushed the grass. It was getting colder; he could feel winter's breath already. In the distance, strains of a violin rose above the cries of children and came clearly towards them. How neat English children were, he observed. In their pinafore dresses, shoes and socks, their curls brushed and pinned back, marching alongside their nannies, who were briskly pushing prams containing sleeping infants. "No dawdling, come along now," he heard. Stern voices cautioned, kept the marching little ones in line. He thought of Sher, toddling along in the park like these children. For a moment, the image of a little brown lad with sparkling eyes in shorts and a neat shirt crossed his vision. Then, as swiftly as it came, it was gone.

He lay back on the grass. It felt like a bed of feathers, springy and light. A cool ceramic sun swished across his face like windshield wipers, its rays filtering through swaying tree branches, its touch barely warm. He had a sudden urgent desire to see his homeland, to feel its harsh heat on his skin. That sun, falling hard on his face and legs, was bright and hot; its ooze burned like hot wax.

"I don't understand Virginia," Julia said. "She says the most awful things sometimes."

"She's a writer. You can't expect her to mince her words."

"No. I suppose not. But there are limits. Not everything can, or should, be said. She can't stop complaining about her Jewish mother-in-law. It's pathetic, she married a Jewish man. Her day, she says, is ruined when Mrs. Marie Woolf comes to tea. Such disdain, such censure. I wonder how Leonard can stand it. She doesn't go out of her way to hide her feelings."

"It's possible to love someone without also loving their origins."

Julia looked at him curiously. "Yes, that's true. But marriage is complicated enough as it is—why stir the pot further with all this business about origins and ancestries. We're all individuals, unique in our own way."

"It's the area she's bound to explore—the place where all the tensions are. I'm just a novice but surely tension is what really interests a writer."

Julia nodded thoughtfully. "I love your readings of her, you know I do. But this is bothering me, her attitude."

He plucked at leaves of grass by his side and held them to his nose: breathed in fresh green earth smells and sodden mud. More and more he was beginning to rely on smell to place him, to orient him, even when deep in conversation.

She looked into the distance, away from him. "My grandfather was Jewish. So I suppose I do take it a little too personally." Shiv gave her a quick look.

"You must get this all the time," she said. "I remember the Maida Vale party when I first saw you. That big blustering bully who stopped you as you were crossing the room."

"You remember it?" he asked incredulously. "I was coming to you."

"I know," she said, giving him a mischievous smile. "You didn't make it. So I had to come to you."

It was his first real indication that she might have been thinking of them—him and her—as something more than friends. He looked at her, her flushed pink cheeks, the cherry lips, the fine furrow across her long brow, those blue, blue eyes, turquoise and sapphire and sky. The lilac-apple smell of her. Could she really be thinking of him in that way?

She said, "Virginia collared me yesterday. She wanted to know more about you. Mrs. Benson and Leonard were out doing errands and she seized the moment. Perhaps she was bored."

Shiv sat up. "What did she say?"

"She said, it was hard for her at first, with Leonard. He was a Jew and so foreign. Did I feel that about you, she asked? That you were foreign?" She went silent.

His heart lurched. He couldn't bear the suspense. "And?"

"I said, yes, but it wasn't something I disliked. She said she disliked Leonard's mother's Jewishness. She is an eyesore, her clothes are cheap and ugly, so Earls Court. It's a bit much! I was terrified by her intimate divulgences, which, even after some thought, strike me as ungenerous and unkind. To characterize an entire people by saying how impossibly out of place they are, how nosy and dowdy they are . . . this is how racism spreads, doesn't it? Yes, she'd been writing, and hated being interrupted by the visit. But it shows intolerance. A lack of understanding . . ."

"How did you respond to her?"

"I said that perhaps we English, with our need to conquer other races, had become adept at characterizing people in simplistic ways. She frowned but then nodded, as if she agreed. She said, Leonard is quite proud of who he is—his origins go back to Persia and Palestine. I know she's mostly Anglo-Saxon with some Gallic influences. So I suppose she assumes some superiority there. It showed me a side of her I'd rather not have known about. Let's face it, Shiv, she can be quite mean and she's an awful snob."

He thought of her in all her entirety then, the fullness of her, gleaming like a silver, lunular shape in the night sky. Virginia Woolf was a representative of her time, she contained it. That was the mysteriousness of her. "Curiosity, prejudices, notions of beauty, of love, of order, and the desire to understand all come bound up together in truly sentient people, and she is surely one of those. Like Jane Austen, she is of her time. And it makes her infinitely interesting," he said. He gave Julia a stern look. "I don't think she should, or can, be judged, off the cuff, like this."

"Are you sure you're not in love with her?"

He laughed. But like a stench-filled wind off the Thames, the conversation filled the air between them, a thick impenetrable fog he couldn't cut through. But there was no backing away now. The door had opened and he had to look at whatever was in there right in the face.

"I wonder if they have a happy marriage, Leonard and Virginia," Shiv said.

Julia gave him a surprised look. "We'd have to define 'happy' first," she said.

He gave her a quizzical look. "You first."

"Well, let's take her, for example. By her own admission, she was always lonely—and her novels have lonely female characters—Lily Briscoe, Mrs. Dalloway—and they say things lonely people think to themselves. 'For ever alone, alone, alone . . . Gorged and replete, solid with middle-aged content, I, whom loneliness destroys, let silence fall, drop by drop.' Bernard, in *The Waves*."

"What do you mean?" he asked, wondering where this was leading.

"I think Leonard has made her feel less lonely in life. He truly takes care of her. She is precious to him. He probably hasn't written as much because he's always so anxious about her. And he loves her. She knows he loves her. Isn't that a recipe for a good marriage—and yes, there are many but this one's so unique, so special—to be cared for, and to be, truly, companions to each other?

"And," Julia continued, "she said once that she can talk to Leonard about anything. For someone like her, and she is deeply reserved when you get down to it, that's extremely valuable. That's so essential to a happy marriage. It isn't all about jumping into bed with each other."

There are two kinds of happiness then in love, he pondered—the one that does thrill at a touch from your lover and wants more of it, and the one that notes it and is pleased to have the touch, regardless of whether it thrills or not, as comfort. The first is not necessarily based on closeness, perhaps just on lust, on a kind of aesthetic desire. The second on intimacy and on deep knowledge of the other. "She can say, 'Oh, Leonard's never going to wear yellow socks. He'll think them ludicrous—too Malvolio and his yellow garters!' with full conviction. She knows that based on her deep knowledge of the man. She's fascinated by bugger-boys, as she says, but would never refer to herself as a lesbian. If anything, she'd say she's androgynous, which she is and has been wildly attracted to women—Vita Sackville-West, Katherine Mansfield, others—but Leonard is her home base, her lighthouse. They don't have everything but they're not foolish enough to believe that any marriage can." Julia's flushed face told him that she was trying, as hard as she could, to say she wasn't expecting him to be the whole world to her. He didn't know what to think. He was deeply moved.

"What?" she said.

"Oh, nothing, particularly. Just—that blue sweater matches your eyes perfectly." A thrill filled him when he saw her smile, as if she knew what he was thinking. They were growing closer, he sensed it. And the usual red lights weren't flashing. He could see they both wanted the tightening bond between them.

"Would you do something I wanted if I asked very nicely?" she said.

He swallowed a groan. Here it came. Let's go dancing.

But she had something else in mind altogether. "Dorset," she said. "There's an old shepherd's caravan there in a field. It belongs to the family. It's where I spent most of my childhood, hiding from everyone and imagining other stories I was part of while people were looking for me."

It was a preposterous invitation, and she must know it. They were not a married couple, not even engaged.

He looked about uncomfortably, as though distracted by a moth or a cricket, and said, "Well, we'd really have to stay at a local hotel or something, wouldn't we? I'm not sure, with the magazine, and all that. Should we wait a bit?"

She went suddenly quiet, the way people do when they've been hurt. A tension settled between them. He didn't know what to say to her to soften it—it wasn't a rejection, but she, no doubt, would have seen it that way. Again that slight knitting above her eyebrows, apprehension, or at any rate, some disquiet.

He couldn't stop thinking about sex with her. The thought of disappointing her, of failing her, was paralysing.

Seher had been a failed experiment. Desire fled as soon as their bodies advanced towards each other and they had gone through with it as a necessary accommodation you made in the name of marriage and children. Imagining it with Julia drove him mad with anxiety. She hadn't taken her eyes away. A caravan didn't have room for flexibility, the moment's mood. Lucy—well, Lucy; they hadn't needed space or mood. Mere touch had been enough. That had been something else, almost unreal—a different matter altogether.

"We could take a room for you in Jess's old farmhouse, just up the road," she said, reading his thoughts.

He considered it. "What would we do there?" Things were moving too fast and a train leaving a platform had its own urgency. His agitation was making him sound boorish, unimaginative. One could come up with something to do in the most nondescript places.

"Well, let's see . . . there's Swanage, a village by the coast, and it has some incredible natural sights. There's the bay and Corfe Castle nearby. It would be nice to get away from grimy London."

She frowned, wondering which rabbit to pull out of the hat next to entice him. She had proposed something complex and was trying to simplify it. She was rooted in this land. He was unmoored. She had such bright prospects before her. Working with the Woolfs, she'd meet all the right people—literary people, her sort. "I think it's time for us to have a conversation we're both trying to avoid," he said. "To be utterly honest, I'm probably not your best prospect. I'm subsisting on pennies to run a magazine, and it will be this way for a while. And—"

She put out a hand as if to stop him. But he was on a roll and barged on. "And I'm an Indian. I doubt you've stopped to consider that. You've got such an open and inclusive way of looking at people—it's one of the things I love about you—but I think it stops you from seeing things." It was clear she'd never given any thought to the complex nature of being an interracial couple in London or she wouldn't have been with him. She wasn't Lucy, proud to walk into a room with his arm linked through his. Lucy was an iconoclast at heart—proudly, overtly homosexual. Lucy courted controversy: he flouted convention. Julia was proper in the best sense of the word.

She had bohemian aspirations but deferred to society's conventions. She would eventually notice, with love a little paler, and passion a little cooler, that they were different; her social world would constantly rub her nose in it. He didn't want to be hated for his race. He didn't want it to ever be an issue for them.

"What things?" she asked, her brow furrowed.

"Things that would be more to your advantage. I'm trying to say that a man with no prospects isn't a good match, and in addition to that, I'm, as you can plainly see, a very serious encumbrance. I go around smacking people if they display any interest in you. I mean, men, of course."

She began laughing, but then, her upper lip trembled as she reached for his hand and placed hers over his. She gazed straight into his eyes, shook her head slowly, and said, "I really don't care that you have no money, or the colour of your skin. I think you're opening all sorts of doors already. You hold your own. You're so smart, and likeable." Her eyes were like crushed violets, a little moist, prickly and shiny. He placed his other hand over hers, tightened his hold. "You win people over," she said.

She had never been more appealing to him. He needed the company of a woman like her, he told himself, a woman who would understand a man with a mission and not punish him for it. Julia, with her knowing, sensitive ways, would be a perfect companion. And yet.

Was she being kind? And how much kindness could a relationship take before it ceased to surprise? He didn't want to take her for granted. And yet, to be so, to be kind intrinsically, at a granular level so it was how you presented to the world, wasn't that the enviable state?

She said, "How far along are you with Chekhov?"

He could have cried with relief.

———

As CHILDREN, OUR secrets make us feel special. We're constantly forced to reveal our most intimate moments to our parents, caretakers, teachers, sometimes groups of people. The most minor event in our lives is subject to recall and disclosure because the adults around us demand to know, are armed with the right to know. A child isn't permitted to have sacred areas, where no one can go. All of him is available, open for mining, belongs to other people. So he learns to guard his secrets zealously. He'll take caning and spanking, and being beaten across the knuckles with rulers; he'll look impassively at being denied loved meals, treats, outings, the company of friends, and even books. He'll never tell.

As adults, our secrets burn inside us, weights that cause intense discomfort, that keep us awake at night. We think of the relief of having shared the burden, of having halved it in the telling of it. Then we think of the consequences and we are paralysed. If it means losing someone dear to us, we keep silent, though our mouths yearn to speak and our hearts long to be unburdened. The pain of loss is worse than the weight of a secret. We choose silence.

Until the day when the danger of being misunderstood strangles every fear, and we know there is no choice but to speak.

It came up again, the trip away, together, with everything that implied. He had been working in the flat when Julia rang. She said she had been given a few days off at the press and was thinking of getting away.

"Where?" he said. "Where are you going?" His voice had risen in alarm.

"It's just for a few days."

"But you can't go now. We're only just beginning with the magazine."

There was a pause. "I know you'll think I'm going on about it. But it's Dorset. It's the most beautiful part of the British Isles, it's where the bond between people and land is the strongest."

"Really?"

"Yes, I think so. Please come with me. We'll work really hard when we're back."

He said, "I have something to tell you." Perhaps it was his tone that put her on alert.

"What?" she said, suddenly sharp.

"It's not a phone conversation."

Silence. Then, "Shall I come to you now?"

He considered it. The flat, her presence there so strong already. "No," he said. "I'll meet you by the Albert Memorial in an hour. Is that all right?"

"Yes." She hung up.


HE SAW HER come down the path, looking preoccupied. He nearly fled, but knew he had to go through with it, whatever the consequences.

"Hello," she said as she reached his side.

He looked at her. She was dressed sensibly, walking shoes, a grey coat, a soft white woolen scarf around her neck. She had red lipstick on.

"Shall we walk a bit?" he said.

"Yes, all right."

She was going through something, too. He saw the irritable waves of her arm as they walked, as though flicking off raindrops. They didn't speak and then both opened their mouths at the same time.

"So what's—"

"I wanted—"

They both fell silent. He looked at her carefully as he started speaking. "I have to tell you something. It's been a secret for so long and now I want to get it off my chest, regardless of the consequences."

She gave him a worried look.

Shiv continued, "Julia, I'll get to the point immediately. When I was eighteen, just three months before I left for England, my mother insisted on a marriage ceremony."

She looked at him sharply.

"Yes, I got married to a girl two years younger than me, chosen by my crafty mother, and exactly as she had planned, I managed to get her pregnant just before I boarded the ship that brought me to England." He explained that it was unavoidable, and that his son was now four years old, the mother, distraught that he hadn't come back as promised, had left home, with his son, and now the marriage had been annulled by both sets of parents. "They got us married, they divorced us." He looked at her. "So even though I am no longer married, I felt I had to tell you. I know I should have told you earlier. But now, with Dorset in the picture—"

She kept silent, thinking it through.

"So if we go any further—" he added.

She looked away into the distance. "I have something to confess as well. All my friends have been warning me about getting in deeper with you," she said in a trembling voice. "They say Indian students are scrupulously watched in London, that many are suspected of being socialists, troublemakers. These same friends have painted dire prospects of my not being able to walk freely in the park for fear of being followed. Of losing liberties I now take for granted. And my father, I know, will completely disapprove. He's a white supremacist, if there ever was one." She frowned. What had happened since their talk in Kensington Gardens a few days back, how had she changed so much in her attitude towards him? She was unfathomable to him in her fears. She was no longer open to him.

They walked on in silence. She said, "I knew there would be differences, I didn't go into this with a blindfold on. But—the strangeness of what you're telling me. Another culture, that has rituals and beliefs so different from ours. You got married to a sixteen-year-old?

A child. Perhaps some cultural differences truly are insurmountable. I don't think I want to talk about this now. I'm sorry. I'll get in touch with you later."

Then she abruptly turned around and walked away. He saw her disappearing round a thicket of bushes and knew then that he had completely lost her. He had thought things were rock solid between them. The bitter cold shock of it, now that it had happened, so quickly, so without warning. Had she had doubts all along? Why hadn't he sensed them, he with his highly sensitive antennas? He couldn't understand it. Then he remembered how she told him about Virginia's opinions about Mrs. Marie Woolf and Leonard's Jewishness. She had probed Julia to know how deep her discomfort was about Shiv's being foreign. He shook off the memory. It was so much more complicated than he could have imagined.

Months went by. He never saw Julia and her mother at the Friends' Meeting House on the ground floor. He didn't dare phone her. Perhaps it was delusional to think that he could have a relationship with an upper-middle-class Englishwoman. They weren't looking for Indian princes, as some of the working-class Englishwomen were, men who could transport them away from their hard-working existences to lives of glamour under an Eastern sun. Julia and women like her were looking for people who were like them, a comfortable world where their children could all be friends, the parents, too, bonding at least over their children if not at dinner tables. She would want the predictable English childhood she had had—one of horses, and stables, and badminton, and summer cocktails tinkling around tables on the lawn while people played croquet. She would need a pile in the country and a town house in London. Her world came with built-in comforts and guarantees. He was hardly in a position to satisfy them. And then there was his colour. The minute you walked into a room, your exterior screamed, "Foreigner! Foreigner!" and others looked on you as an intruder. He had been utterly foolish.

The world quietly went dark around him as he pondered his choices with *Forward*. He had to get it going—it could not wait any longer.

Alerted by Leonard Woolf that Miron Grindea would be leaving for Bucharest soon, Shiv rang the number he had been given for him and when Grindea himself answered, said, "Sir, I am very keen to meet you." He added that Leonard Woolf had suggested he ring, as he was about to start a literary magazine himself and needed guidance.

Grindea paused for a minute and then said, "A fellow slave to the scaffold of literature. Why not? Let us meet by all means?" His voice—thin, shrill, but packed with urgency—energized Shiv. But when they met, he had only one thing on his mind. He wanted to talk about London, and how it had been for an "émigré like your-self" to settle down here. He and his wife, Carola, a concert pianist, had come on a short visit to London to see what his prospects were for grounding his magazine there. They had decided to move to London permanently as soon as they could get visas. "Conditions are wretched in Bucharest, one can no longer live there."

They were in a little café in Finchley. Grindea told him that his international magazine, *Adam*, was doomed in Bucharest now for the fascists had arrived and were making life intolerable. He said, "The magazine has a strong following all across Europe—in France, in Germany, in Italy. It is solidly cosmopolitan. But it has to take new root here even though Britain does not tolerate cosmopolitanism well. It will be a challenge to make *Adam* thrive here. But it will sur-vive. That is the goal. Carola's career may take off here. Europeans are far better tolerated in the world of music than in literature. We shall see."

Shiv said, "It's among writers and intellectuals that I've found fellowship—there's more curiosity and kindness with them. It is difficult for us colonials to be accepted here. As a barrister I find it very hard."

"Yes, of course, with you there is also the colour bar. Torture."

"I am learning how to make it tolerable," he said.

Miron's small hands with their long fingers knifed the air excitedly as he described the difficulties of keeping a magazine afloat. "Subscriptions, of course, but also being constantly noticed and talked about. You have to be provocative but not so provocative that you turn your main readership away. Appeal to the sensationalists so that they make you part of their conversation, charm them into helping you find a wider readership. But never sensationalise yourself. Be noticed but never be corrupted by the attention or the power. You must try to get the widest readership for your magazine without ever sacrificing your own standards. Once you let yourself become a crowd pleaser, you will lose your soul. Do not go down on bended knee when Mammon walks in through the door, with a plateful of gold coins in one hand and a list of conditions in the other. Rather, usher him out as quickly as you can. You must preserve what excites you. It is your magic token. Nurse it, pray to it, amuse it. Open the door when it knocks and be bold when you greet it. Preserve it as best as you can and it will honour you. Neglect it and it will come back to bite you."

"Yes," Shiv said, drawing in a long breath. Gods, foreign creatures, magic tokens, mission, soul—Grindea spoke a strange, mystical tongue. But it told him that this venture would take everything he had.

They were in the Dorice, a little *kaffeehaus*, Grindea explained, that was now home to the Jewish residents in the area. "A place like this is a haven for us, a sanctuary. Nearly twenty-five thousand refugees live in and around Hampstead, most in tiny, one-room apartments where cooking is impossible. Places like this are our homes, our kitchens. These refugees are 'Hitler émigrés,' a group which I, and my wife, Carola, will soon join, God willing, in the next year or so. I'm here now to make connections, to see how *Adam* can survive here. For survive it must. It is my lifeblood, my pipeline to the world." He spoke quickly, as if time was running out.

Grindea bit delicately into the biscuit on his coffee saucer. "We are fleeing for our lives," he said. "We are fleeing a killing machine behind our backs."

Shiv nodded. "Our decimation is happening at a cellular level— yours is at a survival level. We are being killed by taxation, sub- jugation, loss of self-identity, humiliation, the inability to defend ourselves. Long-term destruction."

Their talk was grim but the heavenly scent of the coffee brought a little luxury and homeliness to their table. He looked around: ani- mated men and women speaking German or Yiddish, Polish or Rus- sian. They were poor, their scuffed trousers and the worn elbow patches of their jackets spoke of their condition. Perhaps that cup of coffee and slice of cake brought back treasured memories of other lives in the homes they'd left behind. "Tell me more, Mr. Grindea, about the refugees here."

"Ah, yes. The interesting thing about this place is that you never know who you'll meet here. Some are here on visits, trying to arrange a more permanent move, like my wife and me. Some have already decamped here. Oskar Kokoschka drifts in, as does Piet Mondrian, Stefan Zweig comes in as do so many legendary printers, founders of publishing houses in Czechoslovakia, Hungary, Poland, Germany. They are typesetters and designers, scientists, physicists, Nobel Prize winners, dramatists, chemists, engineers, you name it. This is where they come—for solace, for company." His eyes swept the room. "And to remember. Do you know how much has been inspired in our *kaf- feehauses*? From art to literature to political movements, places like these are where ideas are born."

Miron looked up as a man approached. "Tibor!"

He got up to embrace him. "This is the finest typesetter in the world. He is from Romania—I know him well." The man's name was Tibor Schmidt. Shiv held out his hand, which was gripped warmly. "You should get to know Tibor." Miron turned to Schmidt and explained in Romanian what Shiv was hoping to do. Mr. Schmidt nodded knowingly. "He says he will help you. He also knows a very fine designer. He's your man."

Schmidt sat down at Miron's invitation. The conversation moved quickly to a format for *Forward*. Again the palpable excitement when the talk turned to literature, to art.

"You must have a dazzling first issue. The cover must catch people by the throat," Miron said. "Have you had any thoughts?"

"Yes, but you'll laugh me out of here."

"Try me." Miron had an impish smile on his face. "No one loves chutzpah more than me."

"I'm dreaming of Picasso doing a sketch of Gandhi," Shiv said. "Just a simple black-and-white sketch."

"That is big," Miron said. "Very big. I know Pablo but he is in the middle of a series of paintings right now. It is not the right time to approach him. If I find the opportunity, I will mention it. You never know," he said, with a fine shrug that conveyed hope and scepticism both.

Schmidt in the meantime had some thoughts. Miron translated Schmidt's conversation. "He says he will think about typefaces—nothing Soviet, which would appeal to the socialists but not to anyone else, or Bauhaus. None of that Comintern or Blaue Reiter stuff. No Victorian sentimentality, no Edwardian pretentiousness. You want something modern, now."

Shiv glanced at Schmidt, who was giving him curious looks. "He will think of the right typeface, the layout," Grindea said. "And he will find the designer. How many pages? How many contributors? Do you have a masthead? You must have a masthead, it shows others are involved, it's not a vanity enterprise. And *les sujets* will change, of course, but the themes must be different, unpredictable. Never showcase the same ideas. Be daring. Challenge, provoke, stimulate. Stand firm on your ideas. Never apologize. Be consistent, which is not the same thing as predictability. And earn your reader's respect." Grindea was on a roll—a new magazine. Did anything excite a literary editor more?

There was a lot to think about. Shiv said, "I wish I'd taken notes as you were speaking, Miron." Shiv took Schmidt's card. "You're lucky I have not moved my operation to London already," Grindea said. "Or I would have completely monopolized Tibor. And don't worry about communication. Tibor knows enough English to communicate. He's just not that comfortable with speaking it yet."

Miron would return in a few months. "It is a long journey but Carola and I know we must make it." His neat, dapper figure, his funny bow-legged Charlie Chaplin walk, his impish smile. "Travel well, and come back soon, Mr. Grindea," Shiv called out. "I'll be waiting." Grindea turned back to wave then disappeared round a corner.

But *Forward,* for all the much needed help it was getting, lacked its figurehead, its inspiration. He saw how Julia had already fed it with her spirit, her sprightly optimism. She had acumen and charm; she could make friends of enemies, and thaw out freezing temperatures around a dinner table to get people talking to one another. He had seen all those things when they had gone dancing. Would an Indian man have been treated so well had it not been for her charm, the way she had made two men who'd bloodied each other up shake hands at the end? How he missed her companionship. The days grew short and gloomy as he looked forward only to bed and to sleep.

When Morty Saxena, noting his friend's despondent attitude, chided him for "mental paralysis now that everything's coming together so nicely," Shiv said, "Perhaps I'm not the right person for this job. Perhaps this journal needs to be in different hands, more capable hands. Maybe I'm just a mediocre barrister destined to fight for gamblers and adulterers for the rest of my life." His heart sank as some of his least heartening cases came to mind.

"Nonsense!" Morty said. "I put good money down on this horse and I'm going to see it cross the finish line." He had, coming up with the first donation to *Forward*, a handsome hundred pounds, which had helped Shiv hire Tibor Schmidt as typesetter for the magazine. "How about a talk? On Gandhism? It's in any case needed as a foretaste to the journal's debut, and perhaps it'll oil the old machine. What about it, eh? At Nanking's?"

"Okay," Shiv said after a few moments. "Why not? I think I'll call it 'Soul-Force in Action.' How does that sound? God knows it's the most difficult part of his philosophy."

Morty agreed, and immediately set about inspecting Shiv's wardrobe. "My tailor is in Golders Green. He's absolutely first class. We'll get you dolled up for the occasion!"

As they went down Nanking's rickety stairs to the colourful basement hall, Morty said, "I had them put Gandhi's 1931 *Time* cover on the billboard announcing your talk. It sets the right tone." Morty was right. A half-naked man, the world's most famous fakir, in pensive attitude contemplating the world with the title of Shiv's talk under the picture. He felt a shiver run down his spine. He had somehow landed on the same billboard as Gandhi, fulfilling a decades-long pact. *"Like you. I want to be just like you."*

HIS AUDIENCE THAT evening was mostly white—the socialists, the British left, factory workers, bartenders from nearby pubs done for the evening, students from nearby colleges. Confident in clothes that now, after being altered, once again fit him, and groomed for the occasion, Shiv stood in front of a gathering close to a hundred people— they filled every inch of space in that basement—and began explaining Gandhi's call to action, the tenets of Gandhian philosophy, the four basic principles of Gandhism, why what was being demanded was nothing less than a transformation of self.

"No one should conclude that this philosophy is an invitation to retire to a cave and meditate. No, it's a call to action first and foremost. Gandhi is a consummate politician. He means to arm the Indian people fully in order to fight the biggest war the country has ever fought. But his arms are actions, actions that match the words he espouses. Nonviolence, truth, self-sufficiency, complete freedom, are his muskets, rifles, cannons, and gunpowder. 'Quit India!' is a bold call for British withdrawal from our shores and the name of the movement. These are not just pretty words," he told them.

But ahimsa should not be followed blindly, for then it would lose its relevance and its value in our lives. It would become a doctrine, pedagogy, not a way of life. You must demand the truth from your inner self: what is the greater violence? How does my action violate my creed? For instance, we must not kill, for that is an assault on creation, on the divine. But a sick calf is at my door, in agony from a terrible affliction. There are many practitioners of ahimsa who would say, never, it is unthinkable to kill, leave alone a cow, a creature sacred to Hinduism. But the creature's suffering is such, death is the kinder alternative. It's the negative aspect of ahimsa, because it involves taking life, but it is necessary. Gandhiji experienced this himself. He had a doctor administer a shot of poison to the suffering creature to end its pain. His followers were horrified.

The positive aspect of ahimsa, Gandhi says, "means the largest love, the greatest charity. If I am a follower of ahimsa, I must love my

enemy. This active ahimsa, or satyagraha, is about truth and fearlessness; it's about how to use love as a weapon, yes, but also about learning *how* to love." There were murmurs of approval from the audience.
As Shiv spoke, he saw people nodding, agreeing with him. Who
would not want to let that power, the sheer power of soul force, of
satyagraha, into your being? But ah, how difficult it was. He knew it;
his body, lanced with overt and subtle barbs and insults, knew it. As
for desire, he already knew where Gandhi stood on that one. He
wanted to believe the words, his mind believed them. But his body
rejected them. When did self-abnegation become a job requirement
for a revolutionary?

He ended with a quote from Gandhi: "Gandhi says, 'Satyagraha
works only when it arms people with power not to seize power but
to convert the antagonist to their own view until at last the antagonist lays down his arms, mends his ways, and becomes a mere instrument of service to those whom he has wronged. The mission of
*satyagrahis*, those who have achieved self-mastery, ends when they
have shown the nation its latent power, the power to conquer hate
through love.' May we all be successful in our own voyages to sweep
out the nests of hate we have built within us and replace them with
the seeds of love."

Morty stood up. "Any questions?" He addressed the crowd. There
was a healthy show of hands. "It's very New Testament, isn't it?" one
person said. "Is it possible Gandhism is an offshoot of Christian mo-
nasticism? That we are hearing the gospels of Christ in new form,
tailored for the battlefield, and not for the monastery?"

Shiv replied, "When it comes to love, are there religions, sects,
denominations? It's a conquering force that holds within it the constant threat of defeat. It's a force that can embrace and also destroy.
To experience it fully is to know what it is capable of, to use its power
to recover and to heal, to bring people to embrace the best in themselves. Love *is* universal soul-force." People began clapping, putting
an end to further questions. The room shook with an explosion of

sound; it was a standing ovation. At that point his eye, roving across the crowd, caught a gaze intently focused on him: he couldn't be sure, but perhaps, yes, just perhaps, it was her. His pulse quickened as his eyes met hers.

As he mingled with the crowd, there was a tap on his shoulder. "Shiv," she said. Her voice, that warm, lively voice; he turned around slowly to look at her. Her face—that upturned nose, those blue eyes, even in the dark speaking to him. He couldn't help himself—there and then, in front of an audience now deeply involved in the drama taking place in the centre of the room, he put his hands on either side of her face and pulled her close to him, then planted a full kiss on her lips. That sharp intake of breath that told him she had come back to him. He knew it, and yet, if it was not to be, at least he'd made it quite clear how he felt, how much he'd missed her. "Now that's a form of ahimsa I have no trouble understanding," one man called out. Everyone laughed. As her arms went around his neck, whistling and clapping broke out in the room.

Morty was by his side. "What's this?" he said, looking mystified. "Who's this young woman?"

"Ah, Morty, sorry, old chap. This is Julia Chesley, a friend of mine."

"Ah!" Morty said, looking at them both. "Shall we amble down to the pub together as planned, and would you join us, Miss Chesley? Or would you two rather be off on your own?"

"I'd love to join you," Julia said, which settled it.


AFTER THEY WERE seated at a booth with their drinks before them—cider for Julia, a single malt for Morty, and pale ale for Shiv—Morty raised his glass. "You made me feel proud to be an Indian, mate," he said. "I've been to so many talks on India before, but no one has made me feel Bapu's words as you did. I understood in a flash what he was trying to do. And you didn't undersell his canniness, thank god. That came through loud and clear. It's what might just win me over to his side. I don't want a philosopher-monk, a quasi-saint as my leader. I want a warrior. You revealed the warrior in your talk."

"Shiv, you were brilliant," Julia said. "You made nonviolence, a much maligned word, come across as the most powerful weapon in the world. And you made it clear it wasn't easy. But neither is fighting on battlefields, or dying in trenches. War is war."

As the evening wore on, Shiv saw how impressed Morty was with Julia, how at ease she seemed with him. It was comforting to him to know that his two closest friends were getting along as well as they were. When they parted, it was as a group of friends brought close by mutual affection and interests. "We will meet again soon," Morty said, as he shook hands with Julia.

"That would be lovely!" she said, giving him a warm smile.

OUT ON THE street together, he felt suddenly strong, powerful, able to meet challenges put before him. He looked at her. "Where are we going?"

"I don't know. Shall we just walk?"

It was already late, ten o'clock. "It's past your bedtime," he said.

"I'm not fussed."

"Lancaster Gate, then?"

She hesitated for just a second, long enough for him to think that was a bad idea. "Let's go home," he said. "And meet tomorrow, for lunch or tea, whenever your employers will let you get away."

"The Woolfs are away, in Rodmell. I may not be as free as a lark, but I could manage lunch."

He put her in a taxi and walked from Tottenham Court Road, past Marble Arch, and on to Lancaster Gate. Happiness and anxiety grew within him—was she here to stay? Would it last?

When he got home, she was there, at the door, waiting for him.

As they sat down to the spartan breakfast he'd put out for them the next morning, he told her he loved her and had missed her enormously. "I know, for I felt the same," she said. They ate bread and honey and drank orange pekoe tea. His thoughts went to the previous night as they lay together on his lumpy bed, after having made love for the first time. He felt strangely elated, as if he'd come through with flying colours. She had looked at him tenderly and said, "I've had a lot of time to think. And I'm not sure where we're going but we're in this now, and I'm willing to take it as it comes." He had been so touched, he couldn't think of a reply. His immediate response was relief at having met what had loomed so large in his mind, the impossible challenge.

# London, May 1936–1941

Waterloo Station: its depths criss-crossed by people with luggage carts and polite dogs on leads; its spatial vastness enfolding noise and sound so that a multitude of voices, the rumbling of carts across stone, melded and became a low hum; its four-faced enormous clock hanging from the ceiling; its glass-paned slanting-edge roof laced with iron, which let in just enough light to give the moving figures at ten a.m. a spectral quality. Misty grey-blue shadows moved through the space; morning's silence made their footsteps thud and echo across the stone floor. A dog's lone bark pierced the blanket of sound. The *Bournemouth Belle,* its steam engine a vivid malachite green, its bumper guard a bright red, its long line of brown and white painted wooden carriages filling up rapidly with passengers, awaited them at the platform. It was a splendid sight. They would change trains along the way, finally taking the Swanage branch line to their destination, Corfe Castle Station. "If Jess isn't there, we'll have to walk." It was two miles to Jess's farm. The entire journey would take nearly four hours. A woman's voice, even, monotone, but not without a sense of urgency, announced the train's departure on loudspeakers.

Julia sped on ahead, tickets in hand, the yellow pleats of her dress swishing from side to side as she moved briskly down the platform. Shiv followed with their suitcases, one in each hand, feeling wearied already by the trip. Trust the English and their devotion to the sod. The deep tracks of horse carts in the mud, the cackling of hens, milk in buckets, not city glass bottles, eggs gathered from roosting chickens at dawn, roosters owning the morning with their loud calls. Julia had tried to charm him with her amusing descriptions of country life, but he would have rather stayed in sooty old London, taken in gobs of sulfuric air, and eaten a ham sandwich on the run than make this trip to the hinterlands of England. But he had wanted to please her.

She shifted restlessly in her seat and couldn't wait for the train to take off. He took out a newspaper, intending to read, but the bustle outside commanded his attention. The urgency and energy of travel showed in the way people rushed down the platform; porters briskly trundled trolleys piled high with suitcases; lovers kissed each other passionately, as if for the last time, earning envious looks from passers-by. A ragtag group of prisoners, smoking and joking with one another, were being marched to the third-class cars by the police. Groups of uniformed children clutching toys waited patiently for the train conductor to help them board. London was London, wasn't it, the greatest city in the world.

As the train rumbled and whooshed out of Waterloo, Shiv said, "I'm not sure this was wise?"

"Too late now, love," she said, as the train began pulling out of the station. "You'll like Dorset, trust me."

THEY HAD FIRST-CLASS tickets—her splurge, despite his reluctance—and lunch was included. They sat in the dining car side by side in a booth, starched white cloths protecting the headrests of their seats, cutlery and stiff napkins, a nosegay of anemones in a small crystal vase, wine glasses at the ready, as the waiter took their orders. "Madam?" he intoned in a way that sounded supercilious to Shiv. Julia had already looked through the menu and made her choice— "I'll have the lamb," she said. "And nothing to start with?" She said firmly, "No, thank you," and turned to look at the scenery outside. He fumbled indecisively, his eyes scanning the menu as he veered between the chicken and the lamb. "The chicken cutlet, please," he said.

"Very good, sir." As he stepped away, he sniffed and picked up the napkin that had fallen off Shiv's lap to the floor. "I'll bring another one."

"Will you have white or red, madam?" The waiter was referring to the wine, traditionally a man's domain. Shiv gave him a surprised look. Julia turned to Shiv. "You choose, love." She put out a finger and touched the centre of an anemone in the vase before them. It immediately closed up. "Anemones do that," she said. "They sense threat."

"The red. We'll have the red," Shiv said.

"Right-o." The man still hadn't looked at him. Shiv stared at him.

Then a light went on. An Indian man with an Englishwoman, and the waiter wasn't having any of it. Tribalism had many faces. He felt assaulted, slightly nauseous.

She turned to him. "The food's usually good in first class." He didn't respond. A couple sitting in the booth across from them were quietly eating their meal. The woman suddenly spoke. "Disgusting to think of their children," she said, looking directly at him. It seemed part of another story, and so Julia seemed to think it was. But the pointed look at him, the loud voice, too loud for the dining car. He went cold. Julia reached for his hand. He let her take it though a tight fist of anger was already balling up within him. He could share every other emotion with her. Anger exposed him, got his wounds bleeding again. He couldn't let her see that—Glyndebourne all over again. Burn him, shrivel him, humiliate him. *Avaler les couleuvres.* Swallow grass snakes and don't blink while you're doing it. "Your hand's freezing," she said.

They sat in silence. The countryside rolled past their windows—the greening of summer festooning the trees, blossoms breaking into flowers, thin ripples of water shining in muddy ditches; grassy hillsides dotted with buttercups and daisies, profuse and gay. The low darts of unknown birds flashed their feathers. The odd lone cottage, as though part and parcel of the land. England's glory—its countryside.

When her lamb came, she smiled up at the waiter. "Looks delicious," she said. The man dropped the chicken cutlet onto Shiv's cold plate with a pair of steel tongs. Shiv could sense the hardness of the meat on the plate—its surface had a congealed layer of fat around it—and when he tilted the plate slightly, it slid across the porcelain surface like a leather ball.

"That does look quite awful," Julia said. "Have some of mine, Shiv. I can't really eat so much." He refused. The lamb looked quite pallid as well, the mashed potatoes grey, the green beans like slim worms slithering on the plate. They sipped the wine, and looked out of the window. The waiter had a mocking look on his face as he gathered up their full plates, as if he had won justification for his initial suspicion that they were London snobs who thought they were too good for the fine old British fare on board. When he brought them two small platters of trembling caramel custard, Shiv took one look at the brown pool of butter and sugar in the dent at the top and excused himself. She said, "What's the matter?" He said, "I'll be back," and left her sitting there as he lunged out of the dining car and into their compartment. Fighting back nausea, he lay down on the berth, wondering how on earth he'd get through the next few days. Leave London and this is what you got: English provincialism, pickled in a complex mix of fear, paranoia, suspicion, contempt for the refugees from Europe and most of all for the dark-skinned people their government had subjugated all over the world.

_ഗ_

The toothy ruins of Corfe Castle, majestic, crumbling ramparts, guarded the surrounding countryside like silent sentinels. Julia said, "When the Parliamentarians came to take over her castle, Mary Bankes, wife of the castle's owner—a Royalist—fought for her people, with help from her maids. Right there, at those ramparts"—she pointed with her finger—"bayonet in hand—and when the Parliamentarians won against the Royalists, they gave her the keys to the castle. Her courage was an inspiration to me growing up—" She stopped. "Oh hello, Jess. You're here!" Shiv turned to see a spry elderly man, dressed in baggy brown trousers, a blue-checked shirt, a light blue jumper, and muddy walking boots come towards them. "Jess," he said simply, holding out his hand.

"Shiv," he said. "Pleased to meet you." They loaded their suitcases onto the cart. It was a four-wheeled cart, small in size, with one bench in the front for the driver, and one behind, for two passengers. It was attached to a sturdy dray horse, black with a white stripe running down its face to its nose, and feathers along its legs, who was stamping the ground impatiently. Jess gave it a carrot, which it munched, while he pulled down a wooden step from the cart. He gave Julia his hand as she stepped up and sat on the bench. Shiv slid in beside her. "All right, then?" Jess called from the driver's seat in the front. He clicked the reins. "Harry's keen to take to the road," Jess said, pulling on the reins.

"Off we go, Jess!" Julia replied. Lone cottages dotted the fields, smoke unfurled through chimneys, and birds flew across carefully tended pastures. Horses grazed in the fields. Cows chewed the cud peacefully. After the humiliations served up by the train journey, Shiv felt his skin tingle with pleasure. The air was scented and pure.

It was not familiar. Back home, mustard, corn, and cotton fields baked under a fierce sun, crows cawed high in a cloudless sky, and the sound of cicadas sizzling in the high grass filled the ears. The countryside wasn't peaceful back home; it stirred the blood and lit passions. Hunger filled its spaces. Women were assaulted and raped in those fields; lagging children abducted by tigers slinking through the undergrowth. Young girls sent to draw water from wells never returned home. Men who had not been able to pay back their debts to moneylenders stared in distress at the deep furrows of drought-parched land and sometimes went down the same wells their daughters drew water from.

Here all was safe. The land soothed the mind and the heart. You could bathe in the green of this land. He imagined himself lying on it, its soft velvet grazing his cheeks. This must be happiness, or a state he could only think of as blessed.

Jess's house was a farm. The house itself was crumbling—his wife had been gone a long time and now his cats, chickens, and cows roamed outside, while inside, in a room that smelt of coal fires and cat piss, they sat on a chintz-covered sofa that had long lost its springs, and drank tea out of heavily stained mugs and ate short-bread biscuits Jess had picked up in town earlier that day. Buttery soft crumbs slipped down his shirt, but tea and biscuits had never tasted better, Shiv observed.

"It's the Missus' birthday today. I always send her a card on her special day."

Shiv looked at Julia. "That's a lovely thing to do, Jess," she said.

"I reckon it's worth it even if I don't get a reply. I know she gets my cards."

"You do?" Shiv asked.

"Yes."

"How?"

"She liked falcons. Would keep her eyes open for them. Every year, a peregrine falcon appears, goes round and round above the house, you know, like this, circling fast then flies away. So I know she's getting them."

As Shiv retreated to his bedroom in the attic that night, he noted its bare simplicity—a four-poster wooden bed, a small fireplace, a straw basket of coal to one side. A small rocking chair covered in a crocheted shawl. It was a bare room that made no demands, asked for nothing. It would do perfectly.

THE CARAVAN, WHERE Julia slept, was a diminutive world of its own. A black-canvas-covered wooden box with stairs leading up to its door, which opened outwards. Two small windows on one side, which overlooked the Purbeck Hills, a paraffin stove on the other side. Shelves with cups and saucers and a few plates. A kettle for boiling water. A copper basin. A fruit bowl on a small wooden dining table that you pulled up from the side and set on its wedges. A small cupboard. A sleeping alcove through another little door, which contained a bunk bed. A small wardrobe and a drawer for shoes. It was cheerful and compact and the heavy wooden floors were sturdy. In a portable home not unlike this one, his ancestors travelled through mountain passes high in the Himalayas and reached northern India, where they finally made their home.

They spent three happy days exploring the sights, and came home to put together a dinner from choice pickings in town. Cheese and ham, bread, eggs, apples and peaches, carrots and peas, which they cooked in local churned butter in a dented copper pan, and beer. Julia introduced him to the delights of the local Badger Brewery's Firkin Fox pale ale—he loved its fragrant flowery hops, waited for its flavours to scent the air once the top was twisted off. Their evenings were what he looked forward to all day—moths beating against the windows, attracted by the lamplight; their plates, local rustic pottery from Poole, simple and unadorned with uneven edges. He loved the thick wooden spoon sitting upright in the pot containing mashed potato, and the quick custard Julia made to go with their plums or pears or apples. They ate simply but it was all good, filling and wholesome.

On their second night, Julia gave him a sideways, expectant look. He knew she was asking him to stay. Their bodies were craving closeness. But the bed in the caravan would not have worked. He had a plan, and was building up to it with the patience of a snail. "Gunga Din!" Jess would cheerily call out every evening when he got back to the farm. "Fancy a drop of ale?"

On the day before their departure, they went to Swanage to see Lulworth Cove. It was a two-and-a-half-mile walk up hills and down to the coastline. Thatched houses, narrow village lanes, green overhangs where the trees arched into a lattice above, and after a long walk uphill there was the cove—its sweeping crescent curving into the sunlight. Blue water, fringed with a glacial green, shimmered and shivered with the breeze. The beach was deserted. The chalk downs sweeping into the cove on one side, the mossy green level meadows on their flatter tops, the strange sheen of puddled light sucking the waves in the sunlight, the seashore crinkled with crushed seashells. The sea is never the same everywhere. English seashores were heavily textured and wind, sea, sand, and a feebler sun produced images and sounds with different intensities than the tropical ones he had known. The delicate light and the high-pitched whistling sound created by echoing winds enthralled him. She must have sensed it; he felt her eyes on him as he stood there, and it seemed right to him that he should be there, and she by his side as he bonded with the marvellous land of her childhood.

As they walked back, stopping from time to time to look at a flower or a creature's nest, he stifled the urge to take her hand. He was on high alert, and watched her every move anxiously. Julia had a book with her, which she immediately consulted on spotting something unfamiliar. On one of these halts, she found a flower with gentian blue buds. "It's sea holly!" she cried. "I saw this only once as a child." As she bent to take a closer look at it, he pulled her back and raised her hand to his lips. There was a startled sharp intake of breath, and the book fell from her hands. In the bright light, he could see the fine blond hairs of her face; the tiny red mole by her upper lip.

"Finally!" she said. "You've been avoiding touching me since we got here!" It was then, on that heath—though his anxieties had already begun flapping about his head like a flock of crows—when he knew this was the woman he wanted as his wife, if she would have him, and that he would do everything in his power to deserve her. Before the clouds came back again, in that simple moment of clarity, he went down on bended knee, still with his hand in hers, and said, "Julia Chesley, will you marry me?" At first she seemed stunned. Then her face broadened into a smile. "Yes!" she suddenly cried— a cry of exhilaration, it seemed to him—repeating it several times, as if in astonishment. They kissed with the sound of waves breaking on the shore, the shrill high cries of terns tearing the air, the wind racing past them, and the magical sound of her yes, yes, yes, filling his ears to the exclusion of everything else.

As they walked back, he said, "I would like to formally request your father for your hand in marriage."

She stopped and stared at him. "That's very sweet, Shiv, but it's not a requirement, truly. It used to be but not any longer. I mean, not really, unless the family's frightfully old-fashioned."

"But I really would. It is the done thing, the right thing to do. In my book, it is."

She smiled and shook her head. "All right, Mr. Shiv Advani, let's do it by your book."

"You once said he would completely disapprove. A white supremacist, you said."

She gave him a startled look. "You remembered! Darling, don't let that stop you. He does believe in the supremacy of the white race, it's true. But he wouldn't dare say no. Mother's been working on him—and I've said yes, and surely that's all that matters?"

HE RETURNED TO Jess's farm that evening happy in the knowledge that he had found a loving companion to share his life with. Jess showed him a grey china bowl containing seven eggs in soft earth colours. "The hens reckoned they'd say goodbye. Tomorrow's dewbit!" Jess said. Dewbit, Shiv knew by now, meant the first meal of the day.

AFTER BREAKFAST, THEY loaded the cart and set off for Swanage. Jess dropped them off by St. Mary's Church. "You bring Gunga Din back soon," Jess said. "He's got a bed in my farm."

It was a sunny day and the beautiful old stone church she wanted him to see radiated light. They left their bags by the church's entrance and placed flowers at the graves of her grandparents. She removed fallen tree branches and twigs from the plot, then smoothed the plot with her bare hands. "I didn't really know them, but that's not the point, is it?" The dead seemed happy to him here, in this secluded spot, where nature was in charge.

"Why didn't you know them?"

"They both died before I was born."

Shiv looked back at the church. "Can we go inside?"

"Of course, let's." She led the way in. "This has been our church

for over two hundred years," she whispered. How he loved old English churches, the smell of must and myrrh and amber embedded
in the worn wood, the pitted stone floors, decaying books, and sput-
tering candles. He sat in a pew and watched the sunlight come
through the altar window, scatter jewels across the floor, and wished
he could have been alone in there to send up a prayer of thanks. As
they left the church together, her arm linked through his, he said, "I
hate to leave Dorset."

In the Wareham train bound for London, she pulled out Woolf's *To
the Lighthouse*.

"You've hardly put that book down," he said.

"I've got to get on with it." Virginia had asked her if she had read
it and if so, what had she thought?

"What will you tell Mrs. Woolf, when she asks, as she no doubt
will?" He couldn't call her Virginia again. The conversation she had
had with Julia about race and differences had shown him that for all
her liberal thinking, race was a factor for her; it was one of those
hidden lines in the sand.

Julia considered his question, one of the things he loved about
her. That abstract yet thoughtful look on her face, indicative of internal braille work, to find and put into words the harder parts of her
reply. "I think it's so extraordinary because it takes you deep into
Mrs. Ramsay's internal world. You inhabit her mind. It's such a privileged place, I'm not sure I've ever read anything like it before.
Women don't see themselves reflected on the page like this. A hundred chores and people to tend to and yet the rich inner life of the
mind . . . you're writing a book or a poem and rocking a baby to
sleep at the same time. The soul through turnip peelings. It's revolutionary. You can be that woman in the pages of fiction—that's what
she's showing us. And she sees beauty and has the words to show us

what she's seeing. It's bloody marvellous! I would worship her if I weren't working for her. It's hard to be objective."

"You're concerned about how autobiographical it is—but everything is, to some extent. I recognize things in your poems—things you've told me."

"Yes, but that's different. This is Virginia. Woolf. It's why I didn't want to read her books while I'm still working there. It's a tiny office. You can see her looking into the distance, balancing her typewriter on her lap as she smokes, then typing in an onrush, and sitting back to think again. She said once to someone who came in, I'm not sure who it was, perhaps Katherine Mansfield, that a woman thinks through the women before her, her mothers, aunts, her grandmothers, and literary mothers. She said that Jane Austen had achieved what Shakespeare had—"

"Shakespeare?" he said in surprise.

"Yes, she said that Austen wasn't writing out of fear, or hate, or the desire to settle scores. She wasn't emotionally involved—it helped her see more clearly. She said she wrote out of the same sense of detachment that Shakespeare has, too. That bitterness and rage was burned out of Shakespeare and that's why everyone embraces him."

"Can rage be burned out of you like that?"

"I think it can. It's exactly what Gandhi's saying as well, isn't he? Conquer hate and your aim will be achieved." She looked at him. "I mean, that's what soul-force is, isn't it?"

"Like Shakespeare and Austen."

"Yes. Gandhi's energy is feminine, he has nurturing qualities that are more associated with women than with men, and I think that's why Virginia's so interested in him. Crushing rage out of you is pure Gandhi."

"You understand him better than I do," Shiv said, laughing.

"It's because I listen to you when you talk about him," she said, laughing back.

"So back to the book." He was aware of Julia's wide arc for

intellectual discussion and it intimidated him. "I'd be curious to know how she portrays the men. . . ."

"They don't come off very well. Mrs. Ramsay's an earth mother. And he is a pedantic scholar. Their match isn't ideal, but it works. In some ways—not the pedantic scholar bit, but in other ways—he's a bit like you, how I think about you."

He was startled. "Not at all like me, Julia. Just consider his position in relation to the world. Mr. Ramsay is a very particular kind of Englishman—in his manner, his outlook, his authority. He is fully aware of his position in the world."

"But so are you," she cut in. "You've lost the Indian part—even the accent. For god's sake, Shiv, you're more English than I am."

He felt stung by her words. She felt pride in him, he could see it in her face. He didn't raise objections. Instead, he pretended to doff a cap at her. "Whatever Mrs. Ramsay wants, Mrs. Ramsay gets."

She laughed. "You're a much better Mr. Ramsay than this one," she said, pointing to the page she was on. "Do you know it's not been much of a seller for the press, though it's her most talked-about book to date? But I predict, a hundred years from now, it will be selling widely and new generations of women will see the confusions of their lives in these pages and think, How could she have known back then?"

She said the way Woolf wrote parallels how we remember. "We remember through desire, through lack, through loneliness, I think. And that's what she's showing. James, who is only six, can't wait to go to the lighthouse—it's his promised land—but the weather is never fine enough for them to go. And Lily Briscoe, the despairing painter, who is one of the guests that weekend, is waiting for the final vision that will bring her painting into focus. . . . And then there's Mrs. Ramsay, and Mr. Ramsay, their longings . . . there's this wonderful dinner party scene—you know, she loves food, and dinner parties, she told me this herself. Loves how food is presented, what's in it, what's on it. She notes what people are serving, how it's served. So she's got all these invited guests around her table, and she's worrying about so many things. And it's a jumble of thoughts and feelings and tensions—all is in flux but the lighthouse, that granite structure that they look out on every day, is the one thing of permanence in their vision. You described primal energy—or what Hindus call brahman—as a central energy that is caught in snatches in our lives. It's broken by how we see it. Perhaps it's not possible to see it any other way, but that's what the longing is, to see it whole, intact. . . ."

*Sehnsucht* again. The longing for something that goes beyond words, beyond expression. A taste, a feeling, a haunting. He thought of Sher, a year or so younger than James. What lighthouse did his little boy long for?

"Why don't you pick a passage?" He loved to hear her read. Like the keys to her garden in Mecklenburgh Square, she was taking him into a beloved, private place, where words, yoked to one another, breathed air, and radiated energy, filling the space around reader and listener with life.

"Sorry for that long ramble. All right." She turned to the book. He smiled as she turned the pages looking for the perfect passage to read out to him.

"So, for context. There's a big dinner in preparation. The centerpiece will be Mrs. Ramsay's *boeuf en daube*, her French grandmother's recipe, and they get through the soup, and the *boeuf en daube* is mulling in red wine and bay leaves and onions and must be presented at the right moment to be a 'perfect triumph,' but someone asks for more soup, so she's worrying about the beef and her husband's talking about square roots, and the unsaid things and all the chatter around the dining table, someone's arms upraised holding a platter, the noises and aromas. The novel is all about perspective— how things are seen, from near, from afar. And the emotional undercurrents . . . her husband at one end, she at the other. The lighthouse like a compass point in the distance. Through the jumble of talk, there are these moments of clarity, which rise and float above the others, when we feel with her, like her, that there is order, there is permanence. That the true things, the real things, are there all the time, that they needn't be said to be felt. A little later, Mr. and Mrs. R are in the drawing room. She's picked up her knitting, he's put down the book he was reading." Julia gave Shiv a quick, shy glance, and cleared her throat as if reciting in a school hall in front of an audience of anxious parents:

> He found talking so much easier than she did. He could say things—she never could. . . . A heartless woman he called her; she never told him that she loved him. But it was not so—it was not so. It was only that she never could say what she felt. . . . She knew that he was thinking, You are more beautiful than ever. And she felt herself very beautiful. Will you not tell me just for once that you love me? He was thinking that, for he was roused. . . . But she could not do it; she could not say it. Then, knowing that he was watching her, instead of saying anything she turned, holding her stocking, and looked at him. And as she looked at him she began to smile, for though she had not said a word, he knew, of course he knew, that she loved him.

She finished, closed the book. "It's extraordinary to me how people communicate so beautifully through what they leave unsaid."

Her eyes were like blue ice-melt when she looked at him. He reached for her hand. Though her gaze was steady, he felt her inner fluttering as butterflies in his palm. His touch seemed to calm her. He loved her searching silences, which often spoke more to him than words. He saw things within himself better—she created that space for him. He wanted to tell her, but it sounded so much like what she had admired about the Woolf novel that it might not have struck her as real, as meant. He stayed silent.

She looked out of the window, her fingers tightening around his as the smoking chimney stacks of London hove into view.

"I've not said much about my father, have I?" Julia asked.

"No. Should I be anxious?"

"No, not really. But it might help to know a little about them. He and Mother live in their pile near Castle Combe in the Cotswolds, Wiltshire. When Mother's in town, she stays in her flat in Holland Park but the home is in Wiltshire. It's not exactly a conventional marriage but that's how they've worked it out for themselves."

"How many homes do you have, Julia?"

"They're not mine! My father inherited the Castle Combe house from an uncle, and it's much grander than his own home in Dorset. Anyway, I rang Mother from Corfe while you were pottering about in the bookshop. She was very pleased but a bit guarded. I'm the apple of his eye and he'd be very harsh with anyone, she said. She thought your instincts were spot on about doing the conventional thing and asking him for my hand in marriage. He's conservative, with a very large C. He likes things done by the book."

Shiv said, "If you remember—"

"I know, I know it's what you wanted to do in the first place. I thought it was delightfully old-fashioned of you. Mother thinks you're right."

"And if it's a no?"

"It won't be," Julia said. "He knows me too well. And besides, he always goes along with what I want in the end."

"Oh," he said, "I remembered what I wanted to ask you. Who said, I mean, which king said, 'I know no ways to mince it in love, but directly to say, "I love you."' Do you know, by chance?"

She smiled widely, gave him a tender kiss on the lips. "That's so sweet, Shiv. Yes, of course. I know that play well. It's Shakespeare's

*Henry the Fifth."* He closed his eyes. The ride back to London after Glyndebourne. Victoria—the taxi rank outside the station. Lucy reaching for him with the words even as a cop's eyes were skimming them from across the street as they touched each other. Shakespeare, of course—he should have known. Lucy's bible.

The meeting was arranged in the old boys' club—White's. "Oh my," Mr. Polak said, and immediately advised against walking there. "The most exclusive gentlemen's club in London. Smarter to draw up in a taxi. They notice such things."

Millie said, "Henry, you sometimes overdo things. Those people are driven to their clubs in their own automobiles by their drivers. They don't take cabs. It would be better to walk there." She turned to Shiv. "He's a difficult man. Politeness, even if it's excessive, is the best way with such people." He knew he looked sharp—Sunday best, Millie said, and his hair was perfectly groomed. "Even a minute late is too late, so be on time," she added. At one minute before noon, he entered the club. In the entrance hall, well instructed by Julia, he announced himself and said, "I'm meeting Mr. William Chesley." He waited for his host to show up.

The oldest men's club in London was exactly as Mr. Polak had described it. A quick glance at the room to his side revealed leather club chairs, thick old dark blue carpets, the smell of port and cigars, chandeliers. A young waiter said, "You'll be dining in the Coffee Room, sir?"

Shiv nodded.

"Have a look at the menu, sir. I'll take your order when you're ready." The menu was on a lectern immediately to his right. Shiv looked it over.

The waiter offered, "There's grouse from now until December."

Other seasonal offerings are woodcock, teal, and Dover sole, and, of course, smoked salmon."

"I think I'll have the Dover sole," Shiv said, smiling at the man. He almost always chose fish—for it was easy to eat and sometimes quite edible. The scents of food mingled with cigar smoke came down the stairs. Mr. Polak, who disdained gentlemen's clubs, had said, "They wear the aromas of their clubs, these old boys of England, literally on their sleeves. They're pickled in it. Their jackets and coats announce them as club denizens before they've even had a chance to introduce themselves."

William Chesley came towards him. Shiv saw a short, stout man with a handlebar moustache, thick black hair, and sharp blue eyes. There was no smile or word of greeting. "Punctual, I'll say that for you," he said. "I'll go to the bar. What will you have?"

Immediately thrown off by the man's brusque manner, Shiv said, "Water, please."

"They don't serve water here," Mr. Chesley replied. Lucy might have said something like that, but it would have been a joke, an invitation to get intimate and cuddly with him, to share a drink together. He banished the thought immediately.

"Sherry, then, please," Shiv said, in a voice that sounded wavery, not strong and firm, as he had intended it to. Mr. Chesley gave him an irritated look and went to the bar. A man of his own social milieu would have ordered a single malt, Shiv suddenly realized—too late to be useful—not sherry, for such an important conversation.

"So"—Mr. Chesley came back with his drink, offered him a cigarette, which Shiv declined—"I hear you want to marry my daughter."

His carefully planned words upended just like that. Shiv stared at the man. He found his voice. "Yes, but I would have put it another way, sir."

"What did you say, boy?"

"Yes, I am here to ask for your daughter's hand in marriage." *Boy*.

A nothing. He could barely get the words out and fantasized about pushing his fist into the man's face.

Mr. Chesley laughed. It was a mirthless laugh. His small, sharp teeth were suspiciously white and glittered when he spoke. Superciliousness joined with scepticism in a face that seemed permanently rigoured in a posture of disdain towards the world. "You're not the sort I thought she would go for. She's solid, like her father. She's a horse woman, a tennis player, she plays the piano beautifully. She has gifts, beauty, charm," he said. "And she has money."

"I'm well aware of Julia's gifts, sir. We have known each other for a while."

Mr. Chesley swallowed the last of his brandy and got up. "Did the waiter take your order?" Shiv said, "Yes, sir." He gave Shiv a quick once-over and said, "Follow me." They went up the stairs to the Coffee Room.

As they sat down, a waiter brought a plate of steak and potatoes for Mr. Chesley, and another containing a moist, delectable looking piece of sole with a thin slice of lemon on it, accompanied by a couple of new potatoes and thin asparagus stalks, for him. He had seen asparagus at the greengrocers when out shopping with Millie Polak but forgot to ask how it should be eaten. He never dreamed he would see it on a plate at the most challenging meal of his life. Mr. Chesley unfolded his napkin and tucked it like an inverted fan under his chin. Shiv stared at the meal on his plate, suddenly starving. Then he picked up his fork and jabbed it through the potato. He considered the long stalks of asparagus, and decided to leave them untouched. The fish was cooked perfectly—it melted in the mouth, fragrant with butter, lemon, and parsley—and needed nothing else. After a few bites, he put his fork and knife down. Something desolate and cold had taken hold of him—he couldn't fathom it. He felt he was holding on to a precipice while the sea roiled and churned below him. Then he remembered that Lucy was a member of the club. "My mother wanted it desperately. I complied." At the thought of seeing him here,

Shiv's heart began pounding. His consciousness changed instantly as his vision, so far glued to the growing red blotches on Mr. Chesley's face, shifted to the door frame of the Coffee Room, from where he expected Lucy's lithe figure to glide into the room. In his nervousness, he dropped his knife onto the red carpet. Mr. Chesley's eyes had narrowed with amusement. As Shiv bent down to pick up the knife, Mr. Chesley barked, "Leave it alone!" He gave him an arrogant smile. When the waiter came round again with a bottle of red and one of white, Mr. Chesley nodded at the waiter and took a gulp as soon as the glass was refilled. Shiv placed a hand over his glass. "Had enough, boy?"

All thoughts of Lucy vanished. That *boy* again. He said, "I'm not hungry, sir." The waiter brought another knife and, in a smooth movement with his gloved fingers, swept up the errant one from the floor and placed it on the tray in his hands.

Mr. Chesley was digging in, deftly lifting segments of food to greasy lip. "Why did she not introduce you to us earlier? I understand you have already proposed to her." His voice had risen, just slightly, enough to tell Shiv he was annoyed. Mr. Chesley ate quickly, without relish, a man who expected not to be surprised or pleased. His plate emptied, he sat back, staring at his prey. He had uncomfortably round, devious eyes, the kind you see in greedy, manipulative children, and he stared with a mixture of condescension and disdain.

"I have, sir, but it is conditional on your consent. Both Julia and I would be grateful for your blessings." Shiv had not meant to say the bit about it being conditional on his approval but it had been said now, making him seem, to a man like Chesley, too deferential, lacking in power. It had also given the man authority he hadn't expected.

His cheeks enflamed, his eyes hostile, Mr. Chesley spoke in a clipped, angry tone, each word a further sharp turn of the dagger he'd already thrust in his opponent's heart. "Let me put it as clearly as I can. I do not approve. There have been marriages between wogs and Englishwomen, I am aware of that. But I'm not in favour of them. I must be plain with you. I pity the offspring of such marriages. They are outcasts everywhere. I do not want such a fate for my child, for her children. I cannot honour your request."

Shiv felt his blood run cold. He sat there for a few minutes, debating his options as a barrister might in a court of law. There weren't many. He could present his credentials, his family's standing back in India, his undying love for Julia, but it would all amount to an apology in the man's eyes for not being the right sort of man, the right colour, for his daughter. He could not risk further humiliation. He rose to his feet, said, "I thank you, sir, for your time," and left the way he had come. He reached for his coat, his hat, and his umbrella and on his way out said goodbye to the doorman. Was it his imagination or was the doorman actually smirking at him? Shiv didn't look twice. Out on the street, he noted the buttery lemon-parsley taste in his mouth, his tongue acid with humiliation. Again it had reared its head. His origins, his colour, his race.

When Mr. Polak asked, how did it go, he said only, "Terribly. He refused."

Millie Polak said, "But what will you tell Julia?"

Early the next morning, Julia arrived at the Polaks'. "I must talk to Shiv," she told Mrs. Polak, who answered the door, and took her to the drawing room. "I've tried to reach him by phone since dawn. He's just not answering."

"Wait here," Millie said. "I'll put the kettle on."

Millie reached Shiv by phone who said he'd been out for a long walk and so missed Julia's calls; he would come over immediately. When he appeared, Julia went straight to him, put her arms around him and said, "I am so very sorry." She hugged him hard, as if blotting him with her sense of outrage, of deep injustice, so he could feel it, too. He patted her back but she didn't move away.

Shiv felt his stiff body in her arms. He could not offer her the words she longed to hear. "It's all right. It doesn't matter." Julia was looking at him anxiously. "Mother wants to meet us for lunch today. Can you spare the time? We need to talk about this."

"Yes," he said. Why did he feel so empty?

Millie offered Julia tea, which she accepted. "He didn't have the right to humiliate you in that stuffy club of his," she said. "Mother was horrified when he described the lunch.

"It really doesn't matter what he said or thinks. He's living off my mother, anyway. Everything belongs to her—she pays for his wine, his cigarettes, his horses, even his club memberships. He doesn't really have a say. It was wonderful of you, darling, to brave him, but he can't really affect anything and he knows it." She hugged him hard again. Her outrage did nothing for him. He was sealed off. But she didn't move away.

LUNCH WAS ARRANGED at the restaurant in Fortnum & Mason's. Georgina Chesley gave Shiv an anxious look as he came up the stairs and greeted them. He had forgotten to check in his coat so draped it around his chair and sat down. Julia had said she hadn't slept all night, and would try to nap before their meeting. But her red-rimmed eyes spoke of exhaustion and misery. She gave him a wan smile.

Amid platters of poached salmon, roast lamb, and steak and onion tart, Mrs. Chesley reassured him that his request to marry her daughter had by no means been rejected by both her parents. "You should know that I approve," she said, "and I'm very happy that you have asked Julia to marry you. You make an ideal couple. I have spent time with you both—and I'm full of admiration for what you are trying to do here in England. You're a born leader and a wonderful man. I couldn't be more delighted."

Shiv stared at the poached salmon on his plate. What was the proper answer to this? A mother assuring him he was right for her daughter, a father who couldn't abide the thought of his grandchildren because they would be "mixed race." And yet again, his future, dangling before him like a sugared plum on a tree, shimmer and promise. Everyone was banking on it.

"You're very kind," he murmured as their eyes scanned him anxiously. "I hope I will be able to make her happy."

Georgina Chesley gave him a broad smile. "This calls for champagne," she said, slightly raising one hand as an attentive waiter responded.

Three thin flutes fizzed before them as they raised their glasses. "To you!" Georgina toasted.

"To us! And to you!" they responded.


JULIA'S OLDER BROTHER, Jason, and his wife, Gwen, threw an engagement cocktail party for them. "I'm not really all that close to Jason," Julia said. "Mummy must have asked them to do it since Daddy's being so impossible." Shiv explained that no one on his side would be able to make it—the journey was far too long. In reality, he knew they would not be able to afford the fares and he did not have the money to pay for them to come. But he had to inform them.

Beloved Father and Mother,

I trust this letter will find you both in good spirits.
    I write to ask for your blessing. On 5th August, 1936,
I will join hands with Miss Julia Chesley in marriage. She is
absolutely splendid and I know you both will love her as
your own daughter when you meet her. Henry and Millie

Polak think the world of her. Her mother has been to
Sabarmati and lived in Gandhi's ashram. The family is pro-
Independence. I wish you both could attend the wedding.
But it will be cold here and I know Mother will not be able
to bear it. And the expenses involved would be enormous.

He stopped at that point. Perhaps he should tell them everything, let
them burn up their disappointment in one shot. He continued:

I have only just begun to launch a new cultural/literary
magazine called *Forward*. It was Gandhiji's suggestion as a
way to reach the intelligentsia here and in Europe. Funded
by Gandhi and his many supporters, it is already riding a
wave of goodwill from so many who think it is time for such
a magazine. We are, however, limping along financially at
the moment. Or I would have arranged passage here for
both of you to attend.

I ask for your blessings and good wishes, though I know
I hardly deserve them.

Your loving son,
Shiv

His father's reply cut to the quick, though not a word was unexpected.

15th June, 1936

To our dear son,

We are heartbroken that you have taken this very important
decision without consulting us. You present the matter as
already arranged so there is very little we can say.

Mr Polak has spoken very highly of her and her family. His letter arrived days before yours. I have asked him and Mrs Polak to officiate on our behalf.

We look forward to meeting our new daughter-in-law here in Hyderabad Sind and send our blessings as you requested for your big day.

As for your new profession, I will only say this much: your years in London have involved enormous sacrifices. You have cost us dearly. I will write to Gandhi, whose train of thought is difficult to follow here, and ask him what his thinking is now concerning you. You were headed for the post of Justice Minister. Now you have become, to my huge disappointment, a bohemian.

> Your father,
> Ramdas Advani, Esq.

Through his deepening sadness and his wretchedness that his father's letter hewed so closely to what he had feared, Shiv saw that every act of independence, of free will, on his part would involve pain for his parents. There was only one way for a son to live life: to abide by the conditions laid out for him by his parents, to ensure they were honoured in their community, to live a life charted out so closely by them that he risked nothing, never flouted tradition, observed society's conventions, and thereby guaranteed that his parents would live out their days contentedly and with pride in their offspring.

The wedding took place on a sunny August morning. St. Mary's Church in Swanage glowed with light. His mind spiralled backwards. That sun-filled room, the smell of incense, that flute, the sound of it rippling in through the open window, the procession of turbaned men, the hazel-eyed bride, the bees. He shut his eyes. Not now. The musicians began playing Purcell's "Ode to Joy" and almost immediately, Shiv broke out in a sweat. Flute sounds coming like waves off the Indus River sounded in his head. What was he doing? Get out, go away. His first marriage was, by the most conservative estimates, a spectacular failure. What was he doing, getting married again? If there were a hundred reasons for getting married, there were a thousand for not tying the knot. He knew all of them.

The moment of panic subsided when Julia appeared by his side, and as he looked at her, his beautiful love, his heart swelled with pride. He felt lucky and blessed. She had agreed to marry him. Why? What could he possibly offer her? They sang "Lord of All Hopefulness" and he belted out his favourite stanza with as much gusto as the choir: "Lord of all kindliness, Lord of all grace / your hands swift to welcome, your arms to embrace / be there at our homing, give us, we pray / your love in our hearts, Lord, at the eve of the day." Julia gave him a surprised look, pleased he'd bothered to learn the verses. That was the most wonderful thing about her—she noticed everything. When the priest pronounced them man and wife and the organist began playing Mendelssohn's "Wedding March," Shiv raised the lace veil covering her face and her lips met his eagerly. He kissed them with passion. Her smile dazzled him. He had never felt more in love with her than at that moment.

Jacob, Julia's younger brother, fifteen, came over to embrace Shiv. "Hello, brother," he said. Shiv smiled and hugged him. Jason, Julia's older brother, and his wife were distant, but cordial. "You make a wonderful couple," Gwen said. Georgina, beaming, put her arm through Shiv's and said, "You are particularly handsome today!" He laughed. "I'm a wreck!" he said.

Later, as glasses clinked and they celebrated at lunch in the local pub, he turned to Georgina. "I know I must have represented some sort of challenge to you all. People like me are strangers, outcasts in this country. But you have opened your heart to me and welcomed me into your family. Thank you."

She said, "I knew you from our very first encounter. I knew you two would be good for each other. I wish we had been able to have someone from your family here. But we'll visit them in Hyderabad Sind at some point."

"Yes," he said, with a sinking heart. "We will all go together."

THAT NIGHT, THEY walked up the red-carpeted stairs that led to their room at the Purbeck House Hotel, and faced each other a little awkwardly. The day had been exhausting, and the quiet calm of the room brought on an urgent need for sleep. He looked at her, trying to gauge her expectations. She said, "I'm exhausted. Let's just sleep, shall we?"

He nodded. "We have tomorrow," he said, giving her a relieved smile.

"And the rest of our lives. You look bloody wiped out, too."

"I am," he said, reaching for her hand and kissing it. The temperature went down immediately. Without the pressure to perform, everything felt normal. She leant forward and planted a sweet tender kiss on his forehead. "I'm going to change," she said, pulling out a nightgown from her suitcase.

By the time she returned, he was already asleep.

As soon as they got back from Dorset, he was invited to the Hogarth Press again. Virginia had asked him to come and help her with a submission from an Indian writer. Julia said, "He says he's part of the Progressive Writers' Movement and she wants to know more about it and also what you think of the work. You don't have to read the whole thing, just look at a small portion of it and give her your opinion. Would you mind? She asked, and I said I'd ask you."

"I'm honoured. The great lady herself asking me what I think. How could one turn that down?"

"And they've asked me to join you. They are delighted about our wedding. They want to toast us!"

"Oh my," he said. "Shall I bring the champagne?"

She laughed. "No! Leonard's quite fond of me—he'll be the perfect host. By the way, I'll join you a little later. Something I need to research at the London Library. Leonard has some other appointment as well before, so both of us might be a little late. You'll have her all to yourself, lucky you!" He laughed as he watched her in their kitchen, putting away some bread and fruit he had brought home from the market. Julia's flat in Mecklenburgh Square had been too small for them both and she agreed to give it up and move into Lancaster Gate with him. In two weeks, she had made it as much her home as his. He marvelled at her knick-knacks, a matryoshka nesting doll that opened to reveal sixteen others, each one smaller than the last until there was just one pea-sized doll left. A Noh mask of a smiling Japanese woman, an old Indian temple bell that hung on the bedroom door, which Georgina had brought back from her trip to India. He loved not knowing what awaited him as he pushed the front door open—a new arrangement of chairs and tables, or vases filled with flowers, and always, enticing scents coming from the kitchen.

Virginia peered out of the small barred window in the back room and seeing him enter the office, said, "It's all right, Mrs. Benson, I asked Mr. Advani to come."

Virginia was holding a piece of paper in her hand and something in it had amused her. He heard her deep hoot of a laugh as he entered the room. She put the paper down on the table as soon as she saw him. "Congratulations, Mr. Advani. Leonard tells me you are now married to our dear Julia. I thought something was going on between you. When did you get engaged?"

"Some months ago, in Dorset."

"Yes, I remember now. Well, she's a lovely girl and I'm sure you'll look after her. You seem the dependable sort."

He muttered something about feeling very lucky to have won Julia's hand. She asked, out of the blue, "Do your parents have a happy marriage, Mr. Advani?"

"Shiv, please," he said. "I think they do. Mother's quite bossy, and he doesn't mind being bossed, so I think they are quite happy, yes."

Again that thrilling laugh. "Well, it has to be worked out, of course! Leonard and I are quite happy with each other but no marriage is without its pitfalls, is it?"

He was always surprised by the vividness of her. Tall and thin, with large brooding eyes, an austere, almost gaunt face with sharp planes, a long jaw, high ears, her marvellous tulip shell hand with which she pushed away locks of grey-brown hair that fell across her forehead or removed the stray crumb of biscuit or bread that had fallen on her lap. Perhaps that was her beauty, the glow that came from life and pulsed through her almost transparent skin. He had always been wary of her, knowing from Julia how she could turn, sometimes within the space of a conversation. Virginia had once spoken of caves behind people, and when she spoke, he heard her voice coming to him from afar, echoing melodiously against walls as it reached his ears. She said she was keen to publish some Indian poetry.

"I think the Indian poets draw on spirituality, they're pantheists, really," she said musingly, her shag cigarette burning down slowly to her fingers. "The English rather rudely describe it as mawkish and overly stylized, but I think it's a completely different way of inter-preting the world. I should like to know more about it. I'm always asking Indians to explain it to me."

"There isn't one style," he said. "We're too varied as a people."

When she asked him what brahman was, that feeling of oneness with the universe, and why it was so important to Hinduism, he pondered her question. He took a deep breath for it suddenly came to him as he sat there. "There are moments when you feel all the la-bels, and boxes, and separating barriers—all the sorting we do to put things in their proper places—are really obstructions, that behind them all is one cosmic force, one uniting rather than separating force. Understanding is not the same as interpretation. We need the separators to understand, to parse this from that. But we need to in-terpret what we're sensing, seeing. For that the separators need to go. But they are never removed, are they? So we feel it in snatches, we catch glimpses of that force from time to time, like flashes of a river caught between buildings, and it stuns us." And then he added, "Actually, it's there in your novels—in *To the Lighthouse*, and in *The Waves*—there's a force holding everything together, even though it abides in chaos, despite chaos, and I think that is cosmic force."

She gave him a sharp, penetrating look. "Yes," she said, thought-fully. "I hadn't thought of it like that."

He took a deep breath. "I'm sorry, that was just a spontaneous reaction to your question." He paused. "How would you define En-glishness?"

She seemed taken aback by his question, as though it was an odd thing to ask. She said that Englishness was a quality that defined it-self, above all, as being "without accent"—a pleasant, familiar stan-dard where everything was "unruffled" and organic. "An evening could stand out in your consciousness because of its familiarity, its pleasant time-worn rituals and civilities," she said. "You made a statement—in dress, in behaviour, in style, in art, even food—but didn't draw attention to yourself. You made it without exaggeration."

"Without exaggeration?"

"Yes. Unconventionality is more a spontaneous response than an attitude. Attitudes are boring. Spontaneity interests. It's not fussy, it's in the moment."

He nodded, but remained perplexed. "England strikes me as insular, hemmed in by its cliffs and moors and marshes. Its glance is inwards even though its ambitions are global, colonial, commercial."

"That's true," she said, giving him a surprised look. "We are an insular and somewhat eccentric people. Look at Jane Austen and the Brontës, landlocked in their rectories, writing novels that will speak to future generations all over the world. They managed a classic Englishness."

She went on to say that classic Englishness, its inbred, homogeneous quality, so dependent on social ritual and etiquette, was, perhaps, not interesting but its sameness was its appeal and its strength. "But we're bound to be influenced by the ways of the Orient."

"How do you think?" he asked.

"Well, take the British public's growing familiarity with Empire and its many dominions, and their laxer sexual mores. Already it's led to a greater social acceptance of the 'bugger-boy' here in London."

He knew she was referring to homosexuals, and quickly noted, "That may be, but the law remains draconian, social acceptance notwithstanding."

She gave him a close look, as if a light had gone on in her head. "Yes, of course, you would know about that."

Did she say that because he was a barrister and would know about laws, or because she thought he might be a bugger-boy himself? You never knew, in these tight English social circles, Shiv thought. It was a small island steeped in history. Unconventionality is what stopped England from being staid and boring. Though there were poseurs enough, true eccentricity wasn't staged, wasn't a pose.

Perhaps that's what she meant. Julia would surely have a take on what Virginia had said.

She turned to her desk. "I wanted to ask you to look at this new submission that came in yesterday. I don't know much about progressive writing in the Indian context and would be grateful to you for having a look." She handed him a manuscript that was held together by twine. "Take your time reading it. It's not urgent."

The lack of novels by Indian writers humiliated him. But novels had always been written by Indians, he assured her—though very few wrote in English and only a handful had been translated. "Not very good ones," she remarked. "But you've had a language imposed on you. The literary-minded among you will sort it out, I feel sure." Perhaps it was regret at the lack of Indian novelists that prompted her inscription to the copy of *Orlando* she had pulled off a shelf: "To Shiv, Go forward, torchbearer, and light the way for your countrymen, Virginia Woolf." As they meandered down the pathways of Sheikh Sa'adi and the Arabian Nights, the swashbuckling accounts of ancient cultures by orientalists like Richard Burton and T. E. Lawrence, he wondered again at the feeling she always produced in him, a feeling of intimacy and deep reserve.

Leonard came in with a bottle of champagne. "We must celebrate your good news. We are very fond of Julia"—he looked around the room—"is she not joining us?"

"She is, she's just going to be a little late."

"Ah, let's wait then." Julia came in just at that moment.

"Here she is," Leonard said. "Excellent timing." As the cork flew off and their glasses were filled, and the Woolfs drank to their health and happiness, Virginia asked, "Are there new developments in India? What is happening there these days?"

Shiv said, "I know that Gandhiji is in his ashram at Wardha—Mr. Polak mentioned that Lord Linlithgow has complained that he can't get hold of him as frequently as he would like to."

"Yes, it's quite true," Leonard said. "There is talk of Lord Linlithgow installing a phone booth at Wardha so he can be in constant communication with the Mahatma. It will mean pulling teeth."

Virginia said, "But that is astonishing. How does he expect to take care of politics from there?"

"Again, a shrewd move," Leonard said. "*You come to me.* It's his way of ensuring genuine communication. Do you know it's just occurred to me . . . when people want to dismiss him, they say he's a saint. Saintliness is suspect, somehow pie-in-the-sky. You reduce a force to irrelevance when you call it saintly. We're on high alert now here in Britain. Last year's peace ballot told the government they were skating on thin ice with Gandhi. When 11.5 million of your people vote in favour of the League of Nations and in support of world peace, as we did, it's not hard to see how far Gandhi's influence has gone. Young people in Britain don't want war. They're all for peace. Our government is aware people are listening to Gandhi via his shrewdly appointed, eloquent emissaries who speak for him here—like you, Shiv! Britain won't give in to Indian independence easily. But in the end, India will win."

Shiv felt as though he was staring into a clear lake, its crystalline depths. As a call to resistance, it was unprecedented in human history. Gandhi was making people reach for the best in themselves. He had united all Indians—a tribal lot, in the end, defined by caste, region, religion, and heritage—in one cause. He had opened the door to forgiveness and to love. Shiv's head was reeling. He had never felt more ready to answer Gandhi's call from the depths of his own heart.

Suddenly Virginia turned to him. "Do you know my great-great-grandmother, Thérèse Blin de Grincourt de l'Étang, was rumoured to be half Indian?"

Leonard looked at her in surprise. "Really?" he said. "You've never mentioned this before."

"Yes, a Bengali Hindu. Mother's side—the Pattles had deep Indian roots, Mother was born there. There's only one likeness of

Thérèse. It's the locket Vanessa wears around her neck—a cameo portrait of her, very detailed. She does look Indian to me. Very fine eyes, dusky, oriental."

"But this is quite extraordinary!" Leonard said. "Why has no one said anything about it before?"

"We don't know if it's true," Virginia said.

"Of course it must be true. Look at your lovely eyes!" Leonard said.

There was no time to ask any questions. They wouldn't have been welcome anyway. Shiv tucked the manuscript she had given him under his arm, and he and Julia both thanked them for a wonderful evening.

"So she's not a hundred percent Anglo-Saxon after all," Shiv said as soon as they were out on the street. "She has Indian blood in her."

Julia laughed. "No! She's always been proud of the Gallic strain in her bloodlines. But Indian? That was an absolute shocker! Coming out of the blue like that! She's part—however small a part—Indian. And her beloved mother, whom she immortalized in Mrs. Ramsay, was born there. Perhaps that's why she's so interested in spirituality and mysticism. I think I understand her better now."

An Indian woman's portrait hanging around Vanessa Bell's neck, Shiv mused. In India, everyone knew about interracial affairs; households that were half English, half Indian. Colonial gentlemen with their native mistresses, who bore them children. They came to be known as Anglo-Indians but few willingly identified themselves as such, fearing ostracism from both sides. Such talk was taboo in England. People whitewashed their Indianness. Fair Indians passed as whites. The dusky ones remained in India and were never united with their families in England. This was the tightrope he had bound himself to forever with his marriage to Julia—a slippery balancing act between belonging and being an outcast.

⌇

As they began planning for the first issue of *Forward*, Julia said, "You must ask Virginia and Leonard to be part of the advisory committee."

"Fabulous idea! Shall I write, or visit?"

"Write. They like letters."

"I will. Whom else can you think of?"

"Well, Morgan Forster, and H.D. And Muriel Lester, who suggested it in the first place, and her good friend Sylvia Pankhurst, feminist and socialist. I'll think some more, but there's a start."

The letter from Leonard Woolf said: "Yes, on my part, as long as there are not too many meetings. Virginia is deep in her novel and says she's sorry but she has no time to spare now. But she's delighted with your marvellous progress and sends best wishes."

Woolf's acceptance led to further yeses. Shiv wrote to everyone. Muriel Lester said, "With pleasure." Her friend Sylvia Pankhurst said, "Delighted!"

E. M. Forster said, "You must come and see me."

As it turned out, Forster was visiting Leonard Woolf in Mecklenburgh Square and asked to meet for a drink afterwards. Leonard suggested they all meet at a pub near the press.

They were both there already, sitting outside on iron chairs, under the trees. Shiv stared at E. M. Forster, hardly able to believe that the writer of *A Passage to India* was sitting across from him and Leonard Woolf at a pub in Bloomsbury. Forster put Shiv at ease immediately when he called out, "Ah, the enfant terrible is here!" It took Shiv a moment to realize Forster was referring to him. He laughed. "Not yet. But soon to be!"

"You're stirring the pot already," Forster said. "Leonard has been telling me about your new magazine." Shiv told them about early plans for the first issue, about Tibor Schmidt, who was turning out to be a priceless gift for the magazine. He said Miron Grindea had promised to tell his influential friends about *Forward*.

"European through and through, of course. He will have different ideas," Leonard said. "We're an uncultured lot compared to them. They discuss music and art, literature and drama, in the same breath. We keep things quite separate—they're different audiences. But he's aware of what's happening in the world of resistance, and he is brilliantly well connected."

"I should like to meet him," Forster said.

"You will, if he makes it here in a few months. In the meantime, our young friend here is off to a good start. He has a typesetter. All he needs now are articles and subscriptions."

"You've got gumption," Forster said. "I like that. A Daniel entering the den of lions. Be an agile little tiger with teeth. You show them, young man."

"I'm going to do my best. Teeth—"

Forster laughed heartily. "I'm counting on you to use them!"

Leonard said, "Yes, he's got guts. This is a painfully hard business, but I can't help applauding the effort."

"I'll write a piece for you on India and the colonial mind," Forster said.

Shiv felt his heart race. "Sir, I couldn't have imagined—"

"Brilliant idea!" Leonard said. He turned to Morgan. "By the way, Virginia's writing ferociously again. A new novel. The bloom's returned, with the intensity. It gives me great happiness that she's so deeply in again, and some hope, if one can call it that, to see her troubles recede."

"She's at the height of her literary powers," Morgan said, with a wry smile. "She shines. I'm glad to hear she's so richly employed." Shiv gazed in horror as thick heavy drops of some substance fell into Forster's beer glass. He looked up at the tree, at the pigeons cooing there. Pigeon shit! Even as he wondered what to say, they were getting up.

"Are you working on something?" Leonard asked.

"No," Morgan said curtly, and turned away. A shadow crossed his face.

"Sir—" Shiv wanted to alert him to the pigeon shit in his glass as he picked it up.

Forster turned to Shiv, drained his glass, and put it down. "No 'sir' business, please. Morgan will do."

"Morgan, once the magazine is on its feet, I should like to pay—"

"It's a gift, old chap. Don't look gift horses in the mouth!"

"You're a lucky man," Leonard said, turning to Shiv. "You've got a long way to go, but you've begun well."

He felt the shine of a bright star on him all evening. To have been accepted in that circle of literary luminaries, to have received their encouragement, their friendship, and, perhaps more important, to have held his own within it, seemed to him worth the struggle, the piercings of the past years. *His* ship was finally setting sail.


JULIA SAID, "LEONARD says you're on a winning streak."

Shiv went through every detail of his meeting with them—including the pigeon shit in Forster's glass. "It must have slipped into his glass from the trees. He didn't even notice."

Julia laughed. "There's a writer for you." She was delighted, he could see it. He had impressed people she cared about and the magazine was beginning to interest her greatly. He could see that, too. "Julia," he said. "Will you be my editorial manager?"

"What? Of course. Aren't I already?"

"Yes!" he cried, putting his fist up in the air. They laughed as he opened the last bottle of champagne from their wedding.

"Why do you think Forster went cold?" he asked her, describing the moments just before they all got up to leave. There had been a slight tension in the air as they all said goodbye.

"Well, when you're a writer, and you're not writing, it hurts, it's like being ill with a disease. You really suffer. Morgan's not being very productive at the moment. And he probably drew in a bit, reminded of how the creative juices in Virginia were lacking in him."

"It must be hell to be a writer."

Julia laughed. "Get used to it—it's going to be your life from now on. You'll be dealing with them all the time. It'll consume you. Just look at the Woolfs. I think sometimes Virginia would just like to walk away from it all. She's reading submissions all day—whenever she can, she escapes to the room at the back to write, but it's not enough. She's always complaining about not having enough time for her own work."

In October 1936, Julia told him, quietly, proudly, that she was pregnant. His heart stood still. Now? Now? He wanted to cry out with frustration. But she put her arms around him and said, "Our little baby, Shiv. She's coming!" How do you know it's a she? he asked. A hunch, she said. Just a hunch. Don't kill me if it's a boy, please. The excitement, her pride and joy infected him. He hugged her. "It'll work out," she said. "I know you're worrying about the magazine but we'll work it out. People have babies, and jobs, and everyday life to contend with. We'll manage, too."

That other child, the boy he'd never met, somewhere in India, made frequent appearances in his thoughts once he learnt about Julia's pregnancy. He'd never felt his touch, never knew the warmth of his brow, the shine in his "diamond eyes," as Leela had put it. His daughter, who seemed already to have made a place at their table for herself, fluttered vividly before Shiv every day. It would be an uninterrupted bloodline this time, he promised himself. No leavings, no absences. No snatchings, as had happened with Sher. This child would be *his*.

By December, the flat in Lancaster Gate was beginning to show its limitations. The dining table was littered with papers and there were books everywhere—Julia was book reviewer in addition to her other duties and she was researching and reading at a furious pace. Dishes piled up high in the sink every night because they were too exhausted to wash them. Correspondence sat in wicker baskets bought for storage. Mrs. G, the Polaks' housekeeper, came every morning to clean and tidy up, but she always put things in the wrong place, and Julia couldn't stand not finding things. "Please ask her not to touch any papers," she said to Shiv, who had begun yearning for the simple, spare existence of his bachelor days. The flat had seemed enormous back then; now it seemed every inch was covered with something. He couldn't find things either, so things sat buried under newspapers, and correspondence gathered in a huge pile by the door. They couldn't live like this, especially with a baby on the way.

He gagged as he looked at the mess in the sink. Something had to be done. He found Julia curled up on the sofa, reading *Tender Is the Night* by F. Scott Fitzgerald. "It's dark," she told him. "Tragic dark. I need to concentrate." He sat down next to her feet. She continued reading.

"Look," he began. "We've got to come up with something. We can't operate the magazine, live here, bring up a baby at the same time. It's a mess."

She looked up from her book. "What?"

"I said we've got to do something."

"About what?"

"This! All of this." He got up and swung his arm around the room. "This rubbish we've managed to collect in here in only a few months. We can't live like this."

She sat up, seemed irritated. He didn't take his eyes away. She sighed. "We don't have all that much, darling. But the magazine takes up a lot of space, doesn't it? The books I have to review, the proofs that need collating, design layouts. There's a lot, I agree."

He nodded. "It's an absolute mess. I can't stand living like this."

"Leave it with me. I'll talk to Mummy about it. Perhaps they can house some of our stuff for us while we sort ourselves out."

"That's only a temporary solution," he said.

"It's all I can think of for the moment, Shiv." She gave him an imploring, leave-me-alone look. He threw up his hands in frustration and walked away.

Georgina went one better. She said, "What about the flat on Catherine Street? That's at least twice the size, perhaps even larger, than what you have now."

The flat, which was near Covent Garden, was hers. She had held on to it over the years, hoping that someone in the family would need it someday. "It's the perfect solution, Shiv. You'll see!"

Nearly three times larger than his flat in Lancaster Gate, there were three bedrooms, two bathrooms, a study, a child's nursery, a maid's room, and an enormous kitchen. He loved its proximity to the flower and food markets and the area, which was like a quaint village and a bustling market town at the same time. "Mummy still misses it," Julia said. "When she moved here from the States, she found it the most exciting part of London. It's changing, they keep talking about moving the markets somewhere else, but for the moment, it's the Covent Garden she knows and loves, and she's happy we'll be close to everything we need."

⸎

They moved in a month later, in January 1937.

The Polaks came to tea and said the flat was perfect for a growing family. They were both deeply affected by Edward VIII's abdication in December and could speak of nothing else. Henry Polak said, "Something should have been done. I doubt he would have made a great king but it was his term and he should have fulfilled it."

"He's very much in love, the poor sausage," Millie said. "It's obvious just by looking at his face in the papers." She shook her head sadly. "The things people will do for love, which is usually not a reliable compass, is it? Well, one can only wish them happiness."

"Quite," said Julia.


WHEN TIBOR SCHMIDT came to see them with Alix Brodsky, the Czech designer who was now working part-time with them, he said Covent Garden reminded him of the area near the shtetl in Prague. "Families live here," Brodsky said. But they do everywhere, Julia said. "But you can feel it here," he said. "They are not hiding in their houses. They are out, on the streets, buying apples and cheese, bread and fish."

*Hiding*, Shiv reflected. They had all hidden in their homes, his Jewish friends. All across Europe they found basements and hidden alcoves in which to sit and wait out the time until they could emerge into the light. To buy apples and cheese in the market was freedom to Alix, it was what defined *living*. Families did live here—families with brown and black faces. You saw them on the streets, in prams, in macs and wellies, holding an adult's hand, waiting for the bus. Their family would fit right in here. There were cockneys from the East End, and Jews from Golders Green, Jamaicans unloading boxes of fruit and vegetables in market stalls, slightly dotty booksellers in nearby Charing Cross Road, and an assortment of people from all parts of the world living around them. Royal Opera House drew international artists from Europe, Africa, and Asia. Sadler's Wells Ballet was the mecca of dancers from all over the world. Georgina said, "I thought it the most international part of London." You could stand at a street corner and watch all the different faces go past. Here, perhaps, their child could grow up unhampered by her race.

TIBOR SCHMIDT HAD come up with a typeface for *Forward*. Baskerville: "classic, modern, and the cut is fine." When they did some mock-ups, it pleased them so much, there was no question of using anything else. From paper and binding, to the actual look of the page, Tibor proved himself the absolute master of type and design that Miron Grindea had vouched for. With friends already well placed in the business, he was able to negotiate excellent rates for the printing of the magazine. Alix Brodsky left them with a smile on his face—he was happy to be working again, to speak the language he knew best.

"This is so exciting," Julia said, as they sat down to dinner with Tibor.

Tibor, a sophisticated man, had much to share about the literary scene in Bucharest, in those days before the thugs came. "I taught classes in typography, design, and typesetting. We were in the cafés in the evenings, talking about creating a better world—ideas, and politics, and drama, music and dance—everything was being reinterpreted, refashioned. We were sick of the old, we wanted the new. It was a time of great energy and excitement and creativity. Then the fascist Iron Guard, suspecting us Jews of being pro–Soviet communism, started cutting off our hands, our livelihoods. Thugs! It was bad, so bad. We lost everything. I was lucky. I have my hands!" He held them up with a grin.

There was a long silence. Perhaps there really were no words for some things.

"Someday, I feel sure, you'll be able to return," Julia said.

"No. Everything is destroyed. There is nothing to go back to.

Home now is a place you will not be driven out of, where you can drink soup without fear, and converse with a few people who understand your language. Home is to know that your children will come back from school, to walk in the street without terror in their hearts. Freedom from fear is home."

Shiv thought about Tibor's definition of home. His own home, that other home, where sun sizzled across baked earth, where, in the monsoons, thick palm fronds susurrated rain as it fell, where colourful birds darted from trees with shrill cries—that world was not his any longer. Now home meant this place, here, with Julia, the magazine, Tibor, and Alix. This was home.

The literary world had shown him an egalitarianism he had not felt once in his time at the bar. He needed to find his feet within it—he knew that. He read everything Julia put in his hands—Rupert Brooke, Thomas Hardy, D. H. Lawrence, James Joyce, Siegfried Sassoon, W. B. Yeats, Ford Madox Ford, Aldous Huxley. . . . His reading was random, nonlinear, with no regard to epoch or school. Shakespeare one day, W. H. Auden the next. Soon he was reading things he never imagined himself reading, thinking critically about his reading, and discussing T. S. Eliot and Wyndham Lewis with their peers. "Imagists will have their day," he proclaimed with authority, and was believed. It was a new kind of power. It thrilled him. There wasn't much of this to be had in the courts. As one of the fiery young literati, you became a gilded species. People listened to you, wanted to hear you speak. This was an international language—you didn't have to know it very well, you just had to know it.

London was the world, and he was at its epicenter. He wanted nothing more than this—to be one of them, to walk on the same streets as them, to share their food, their culture, to be animated as they were animated, to love as they loved, to hate as they hated. He was becoming a member of this special league, a lighthouse in their sea.

A Londoner, not just by dress and manner, but in his soul.

Reading Ovid's letters from exile for a review, he experienced a flash of recognition when he came across the lines "*As a prison commissioner I justified my appointment, / in the probate division too: not one complaint / about my judicial verdicts in private actions—even / the losers conceded my good faith.*" Yet, for all his even-handedness as a lawyer, poetry claimed Ovid in the end. Perhaps for this: community with others who relentlessly pursued the act of giving form to the mysterious, of refining language till you understood and made our most elusive colorations known. Art was metaphor, he mused, for the ineffable could be perceived only through words. Cosmic energy, brahman, call it what you will.

In preparation for Iris's arrival, Julia and he bought a crib and splurged on a Nibs Chariot. "I'm taking the baby to the park as soon as the weather gets better," Julia said. The image that suddenly rose in his mind of his wife with their baby in the park brought on inexplicable anxiety. He prayed the child in the pram would be fair like her, blue-eyed like her, and not dark like him. He wanted her to look at their baby with joy and love, not with revulsion, to show her or him off to others with pride. *What are you thinking*, he told himself. *She loves the baby already, not because of its colour or lack thereof, but because the baby is ours*. It seemed trivial and petty to think of a child's looks before she or he even came into this world. Stop it, he told himself. Stop it.

Iris arrived on 12 May, 1937. Shiv stared at his baby, holding her in his arms. She was, as far as he could see, completely white. He examined her carefully for some light biscuit under the skin but she was strawberries and cream, like all the other babies in the ward. More hair on her head than the others, and the hair was a reddish dark brown, unlike Julia's honey brown. He felt relief that she was all Julia, so little of him. Yet, something of him, he would have liked her . . . to have had his eyes. No, she's better off with the violet-blue ones, he told himself. A replica of her beautiful mother. He sighed a long sigh.

"Her lips are yours," Julia said.

"Really? I don't see it," he said, running his fingers gently across them. His gorgeous baby.

"Yes, the shape of them."

Georgina's delighted face went a pretty pink as she realized the baby had been given her middle name. "Let me know when you want to go off somewhere on holiday. I'll happily look after her." She stared at the baby's face and kept smiling uncontrollably. She rushed to change nappies, and held her while she cried. She couldn't stop kissing her all over. It seemed to Shiv that his fears were unfounded. Surely this was the most loved baby in the world. Julia's father never congratulated his daughter once.


THEIR DAYS WERE now charged, their nights restless, alert to the baby's needs. Feeding, sleeping, trying and failing to calm down a screaming baby, gently burping the tiny thing, learning how to tie a nappy, washing, endless washing, with nappies hanging everywhere to dry. Julia lumbered slowly from room to room, her body bearing witness to the feat of childbirth. She often cried, her face and body contorted with a sadness she could not explain. "Tell me what it is, how it feels," he asked over and over again, placing his hands on her belly, imagining the pain that came from having just borne a child.

She spoke painfully, her face contorted, and said, "I don't know, oh, I don't know." It alarmed him to see his tough, jaunty, confident wife so disabled.

He held Iris in his arms, felt the wet of her dribbling on his shirt, her sweet little face compressed against it, her little hands clutching. His heart expanded with pride. This miracle, this tiny little cooing, gurgling, dribbling baby was his. He sensed she knew she was safe, because she would suddenly go silent, her eyes closed, deep in sleep. He clutched his little bundle protectively, his embrace growing tighter.

Julia's younger brother, Jacob, started visiting soon after Iris was born. Younger than Julia by nearly ten years, he was nearly seventeen and on his way to Cambridge University soon. Iris went to him as easily as she did to them both. The young man, his cheeks flushing with pleasure, held her gingerly as she snuggled against him, often falling asleep in his arms. "What's the secret, Jacob?" Shiv asked. "She's all girly and giggly with you, leaps like a frog into your arms. You've got some magic going on there." Jacob began coming to see them at least once or twice a week, often staying for dinner, helping them roast a joint or fry up some steak and potatoes. The night before his departure for Cambridge, he came to spend the night, and took over.

With relief, they both turned in early for a good night's sleep. "She slept all night," Jacob announced triumphantly the next morning.

Shiv groaned. Julia said, "Right, that settles it. You're not going to Cambridge, you're staying here with us. Just move in, Jacob."

"Ha ha," he said. "I'll tell my tutor."

The first issue of *Forward* was scheduled for publication in September 1937. They were all debating the cover—nothing Tibor came up with seemed right. Shiv had begun feeling despondent about the whole enterprise. "We have everything, and we can't get the cover right!"

Then came the miracle they had all been waiting for. Miron Grindea, that small, dapper, wand-waving literary magician, had snared Picasso's interest. "Gandhi is a much needed man," Picasso reportedly told Miron. "Do you know him? I want to meet him!" He started working on a sketch immediately. Miron said, "I dare not ask Pablo when it will be ready. But he is working on it."

When it arrived at Catherine Street, Julia and he unwrapped it very carefully. They had no idea what they would see. Against a background blur of yellows and oranges, and fiery slashes of red, there was a simple charcoal pencil silhouette of Gandhi in his loincloth with a walking stick. Coming slowly towards the reader, his thoughtful, unruffled expression propelled him into the onlooker's field of vision until he filled it. They both stared in wonder. At the bottom of the drawing, in capital charcoal letters, Picasso had written:

CAN THIS MAN SAVE US?

Julia shook her head disbelievingly. "This is it, isn't it, the piece of magic we were looking for." She seemed shocked and delighted, rather like him. He nodded slowly, unable to take his eyes off the drawing. "It's a masterpiece. It's captured our time. The yellow-orange background could be a world going up in flames, with Gandhi leading us out of it, or it could be the brilliance of understanding, of knowledge."

Tibor Schmidt whistled as he looked at it. "It is how they say, perfect. Perfect." He bunched his fingers together and kissed them with his lips. "We must hurry. Surprise the public! Now it's all on us—if we fail even with this masterpiece, we are no good." They got to work immediately, working on submissions that had come in from Morgan and Leonard, from Bertrand Russell and Muriel Lester. Each contributor was asked: What should be done now? We are heading towards another war, the fascists are intent on destroying the free world as we know it, we are plunging towards darkness. What should be done now if we are to prevail? Shiv's editorial focused on nonviolence as a coherent, if unconventional response to so much violence around us. He entitled it "Gandhi's War." In it, he used a quote from Virginia's 1924 essay "Thunder at Wembley": "The sky is livid, lurid, sulphurine. It is in violent commotion. . . . Cracks like the white roots of trees spread themselves across the firmament. The Empire is perishing; the bands are playing; the Exhibition is in ruins. For that is what comes of letting in the sky."

Tibor said, "There are too many pieces. You cannot publish them all in the first one. Leave some for the next."

"Can't you take out some more space between the lines?"

"You want people to go blind reading your magazine?"

"No, of course not," Julia said. "Darling, he's right. We don't need so many pieces. Morgan's yes, Leonard's yes. Bertie Russell and David Jones's poems, yes. Morty Saxena on Bengali literature after Tagore, yes—the next issue needs to focus on more Indian writers in our pages—Orwell on Burma, yes. That's too many already. Let's take out Huxley's long one on India for this one and substitute Mulk Raj Anand, whose piece is brilliant. And your editorial. That's a pearl diver's bounty for one issue."

They were getting used to the strange, almost mystical, language of type: Ascenders, descenders, kerning, leading, stems, spines, bowls, shoulders, eyes, ligatures, ears, apertures, stresses, loops, crossbars, links, gutters, bleeds, dummies. Each letter had its own identity. The art of making them dance together on a page was Tibor's gift, his genius. Shiv would watch him loosen up a line by adding the tiniest spaces between words and letters, or tighten it for focus—an alert eye exercises the brain, he explained. A weary eye puts it to sleep. When he pleaded for less content, they listened.

Tibor said, "The spaces are important. The margins add to meaning."

Alix Brodsky said, "The capital letters are like the lions in a zoo. You don't go to see only them but when they roar, the zoo becomes exciting, it has an edge. You must leave room for the capital letters to roar."

They were artists. They knew their craft. Shiv bowed to their better judgement.

When the first issue came in, Shiv opened it up and sniffed along the spine, as he had always done, with every new book from Thacker & Co. Glue, printing ink, new paper. How that almond scent had always opened up pathways to adventure, new life. *Forward* appeared in bold black lettering at the top. Picasso's sketch of Gandhi, with its primary hues of red, orange, and yellow, dominated the cover. A small box in the left-hand lower corner listed some of the contributors. E. M. Forster, George Orwell, Mulk Raj Anand, H. G. Wells. In small bold capital letters running across the bottom: Cover illustration: Pablo Picasso. ("It needs to be stated," from Julia. "Not everyone will recognize his signature.") It was everything Shiv wanted: dramatic, urgent, graceful.

Leonard Woolf was the first one to congratulate them. "You do have a lot but it's readable, well put together. There is an inner coherence, which shows the mind of the editor. Virginia said to tell you that you've avoided the young-hopeful-at-the-gate tone and achieved something quite sophisticated. She said it already has a personality. And she liked the fact that you quoted her passage from 'Thunder at Wembley' in your editorial. It now has another context, she said. I agree. Well done!"

Forster said the same thing. "Onward and Forward—you're off to a splendid start!"

Within a few weeks, congratulations and submissions poured in from influential Indian writers like Mulk Raj Anand, Sajjad Zaheer,

Rajani Palme Dutt, and new talents like R. K. Narayan. Émigré writers found commonality with *Forward*'s cause, and the exciting writers to be found in its pages.

Julia, who was handling subscriptions, announced, "We've got fifteen hundred and seventy-six now!" She was sparkling. "Nearly sixteen, darling! Up from six hundred at last count."

Shiv could hardly reply, his anxiety was so great. People wanted a different world; they were ready to listen to new stories, new thoughts and opinions on Empire, on freedom, on authoritarianism, and on the perils of subjugation. The magazine could not afford to slip. The world was entering a new phase. Dialogue had never had more value, enjoyed such prestige. People were waking up to the horrific consequences of ignoring government. They were demanding authenticity, truth. Indifference was no longer possible.

The blood ran on passion, but the soul was fed by ideals. Hope, truth, beauty, equality, justice. These weren't just words, as history had shown us. As essential to us as food and water, we could not exist a day without them. Over and over dictators had risen up, tried to crush the human spirit, smother creativity with a show of guns and brute power. But the human spirit had prevailed. A quote from Camus in an article he had recently read came to him: "We must mend what has been torn apart, make justice imaginable in a world so obviously unjust, give happiness a meaning once more to peoples poisoned by the misery of the century. Naturally, it is a superhuman task." Could it be done? Artists everywhere were showing that it could and he was determined to play his part.

With the subscriptions, they could afford to pay Tibor a real salary, and hire Alix as designer on a full-time basis for the magazine. But every month's offerings would have to be more exciting than the last one, he knew that. There was a price to pay for the embarrassment of riches in their very first issue. How could they top Picasso, Woolf, Forster, Orwell, and the haunting poems of David Jones ("*a showery night's fall in the thunder-nones of hot July*"; "*the cool,* even, after-light"; "'m' apricots big in the convent apron"; "Prone for us / buffetted, barnacled / tholing the sea-shock / for us"—fragments that lingered in Shiv's head)? The bar had been set too high.

For Iris's first birthday, Julia said, "I'm going to the park with her. I want to draw her as she is now. She's growing so quickly." At one, Iris was like a little queen. She bossed them both around. Very sweetly, with sparkling eyes and giggles, but bossed around they were. She'd purse her little lips and make farting noises, and her bright iris-blue eyes had mischief in them. On one of his frequent visits, Jacob said, "She's my queen, anyway, whether she's yours or not." Shiv said, "Can you come and take your queen away?" She wanted Shiv to fan her face with papers, giggling when he did so. Julia, trying to finish a book review in the other room, would come in running because she'd say, "Mamma, mamma," so plaintively, even as Shiv was holding her, and rocking her back and forth. "She's pure theatre," Shiv said. "Don't listen to her. Go back, and shut the door." But all she had to do was whimper, and Julia would be back in there saying, "Oh my darling, my little sweetheart."

At dinner, she'd sit in her little high chair at the table, looking at them solemnly, sizing them up. "I feel she'll scold me if I drop anything," Julia said.

Shiv watched her with pride, his knowing, observant child.

JULIA CAME BACK from the park saying, "What a terror! She grabbed on to this poor boy's ball when it landed in her Chariot and refused to give it back! Then a dog ran past, and she was distracted by his lolling tongue, thank god. I managed to pry the ball loose from Her Royal Highness's clutches."

Jacob came in with a large stuffed Peter Rabbit. It was twice as large as Iris but she held out her arms to receive it from Jacob as though it had always been hers. "Success!" Jacob cried with a delighted smile. Georgina had brought a camera and they had a strawberry cream cake and tea and blew out Iris's candle together. Shiv took pictures. Then Georgina took a picture of the three of them: they smiled and smiled until their cheeks hurt, waiting for her to make all the adjustments on the camera; then she said, "Now!" and they tried even harder and the result was comical. Shiv's teeth showing in a smile too broad and unnatural; Julia's mouth open in an alarmed "Oh!" as she tried to steady Iris from plunging her little fist into a creamy slice of cake. They laughed over the picture when it had been developed—"Ridiculous!" Shiv said; and "Mother's a hopeless photographer," from Julia. When Georgina gave them a copy, they framed it. Julia took it to her room when she worked. "I like having her near me."

She meant it. Drawings of Iris were everywhere on the walls in their bedroom. A curious child fascinated by moving things—birds, bees, butterflies, flower petals shifting in the wind. Julia was better than a camera—her drawings captured their child trying to make sense of her world. How things fitted, how they sounded, how they moved. Her movements as she reached for flying things, little fists curling around air, opening up empty-handed. But ah, the look on her face. Her expressions were often priceless; Julia captured them— the clever upward look of surprise, the crestfallen look of dismay. That light-bulb smile from a radiant little creature enthralled with the world. He gazed and marvelled.

At night he could hear Julia lulling Iris to sleep with a song about the church bells of London. "*Oranges and lemons / say the bells of St. Clement's / Pancakes and fritters / say the bells of St. Peter's / Old Father Baldpate / say the slow bells at Aldgate.*" On and on, until Iris's eyes would close. Julia's lovely lilting voice made him hear the pealing bells.

She had told him once about the belling of sheep in Greece—

"Each herd has a different bell sound, and within the herd itself there are variations. So a herder who comes across a lost sheep can tell by the sound of its bell where it comes from. They're all at different pitches. Imagine knowing the language of bells. It's an art the Greeks excel at."

Julia was full of interesting information—everything had a reason. Iris's room had sprigs of lavender on the window sill and by her crib. "Why?" he asked.

"It's to calm down our little lioness and put her to sleep."

"Really? Lavender?"

"Hmm. Lions like lavender. It is comforting to them."

One morning, when Jacob came down from Cambridge, they left Iris with him, and he and Julia decided to take a walk at dawn by the river. When they arrived, the Thames was a sullen, thickly plicated sheet, puckering and pleating with the wind. They had hoped to witness a hypnotizing sight they had seen only once before. "Let's chance it," Julia said. "It may happen again."

He watched the water writhe with the wind. This was a speaking river, defined by its many moods; when open, it sparkled and chuckled; when closed, it repelled with sucking winds that bit and chilled the bone. There would be no sun that morning, he considered. He looked at the moody river.

"We're out of luck today," Julia said, staring at it glumly.

The Indus, his river back home, was so different, he told Julia. It came down from the icy reaches of the mountains, had a roaring laugh as it crashed down to the plains; it was worshipped, it had gods dedicated to its every turn. People sang to it, confided in it, endowed it with heavenly powers, made offerings. It was where people came to ask for blessings, for long life, for health, for relief from sickness.

It was where they came to cry. Julia looked at him. "Will you take me there someday?"

"Yes," he said. "As soon as we can go."

This river, the Thames, knowing and wily, moved between its winding banks, host to a multitude of creatures who lived in its burrows and folds and told it what it needed to know. Where the Rivers Ock, Leach, and Cole conjoined with the Thames, people prayed and made offerings. When the tide was low, its loamy shores glittered with debris from earlier times—trinkets, bits of pottery, coins, and small shards of gold. Children hopped from treasure to treasure, exclaiming excitedly as found objects disappeared into their backpacks, each one a gift from another time. Reflections of the sky and the sun were mirrored in its mudflats. It was like Aladdin's cave; it yielded secrets slowly.

They watched silently as the sun surprised them by coming up in a full blaze. As they stood there, the miracle they had been waiting for happened in front of their eyes. At that point between London Bridge and Tower Bridge, there was a slight dip in the river so that light puddled onto the water like liquid sunshine. The sun's light on the water was refracted through rainbows, vivid stripes hovering above the water. They waited. Then suddenly there was a whirr in the skies as the swans came flying in on a magic white carpet made by their enormous spread wings. They stood aloft there for a moment, then they alighted, their wingspans thunder-clapping across the water in a blaze of sound. Julia said, "This must be the most joyful part of London, when the swans fly in." Here, in this spot, where light and sound and image come together is where she would like her ashes scattered, she said. "Take care of it, won't you, if I go before you."

He stared at her. "But you have the family plot in Swanage. At the church. Wouldn't they want you there?"

"Yes," she said. "You're right, they would. But this is what I want."

Once, in an earlier time, he had thought the Indus would receive
his ashes. Those blind dolphins that unerringly found their mark
without the benefit of sight had captured his imagination from an
early age. But the Thames had its mute swans, who didn't make
sounds through their throats but through their huge wings as they lit
on water. "Swans remain together," Shiv said. "They mate for life,
don't they? This spot feels like ours." Here he would go, in Old
Blighty's river, to merge, finally, with the one great ocean that received them all. Julia held his hand as they both looked at the swans,
now sedate and quite composed, floating down the river.

The second issue of *Forward* focused on the Progressive Writers'
Movements in Europe, India, and Latin America. He thought of
Morty Saxena, who had gone back to his beloved Calcutta. The
IPWA was strong there—Calcutta was paving the way for progres-
sive literature, showing how the language of literature could be en-
riched by political engagement. Would Morty contribute to *Forward*?
"How exciting!" Julia said. "You must write to him immediately."

*Forward*'s future was assured when Grace Blackwell, an influential friend of Georgina Chesley's, who lived in Edinburgh and
Glasgow, and Lady Sophia made large donations. "The lodger has
gone very far indeed. Dare I say it? I knew it when I saw it." Even
after all she'd done for Ramesh Thorun, and now this gift to *Forward*, his body remembered the humiliation, refused to submit to
the more charitable impulses of his mind. A slow burn, dissipating
energy and causing corrosion, the kind Gandhi's magnanimous ex-
hortations to forgiveness did not take into consideration, lay within
him. Still. How long would it take to burn these out of his system?
Anger was the holding pen between cockiness and complacency.
Anger would assure he never rested on his laurels. He needed it to

remember how hard the journey had been, how quickly a road goes from being smooth to burning holes in your shoes again.

"She came through though, darling," Julia said. "Give her that much."

"I do. I know she has a good heart."

"Listen to Gandhi and forget hate."

"You know that's the hardest bit to swallow. Gandhi's defanged the independence movement with his insistence on ahimsa."

"But you were the one who said ahimsa is love. Your talk was all about that. I thought it was pure genius and in tune with our times."

"I presented it as a struggle—I said that was the aim, the goal, but I never pretended that it was easy."

"No, that's true. But believe what you said. It is something to aspire to."

"I'm trying," he said. "I'm trying, Jule."

Iris's second birthday. 12 May, 1939: Julia suggested they begin the day with a trip to the market. Covent Garden was a child's delight in the early mornings, before larger crowds came in to shop. It was a cool May and they dressed warmly. Iris, all bundled up in her warm cardigan and shoes, her wool bonnet, gloves and scarves, beamed at them, her excited face aware it was her special day and they were off on an adventure. She got into her stroller with a minimum of fuss.

They walked through the flower market. The bright displays of flowers thrilled them—tulips, primroses, violets, roses, some cut and in bunches, some in long boxes—and dazzled them with their colours. One stall owner came up and gave them a small bunch of irises—*Match her eyes, don't they just?*—and Iris gave him an enchanting smile. "Ain't she lovely?" he cooed. As they walked through there were other gifts. Mr. Davies at the fruit and veg stand they usually went to had saved some small strawberries for Iris. He bent down to hand Iris the punnet. Thank you, Mr. Davies, Julia urged Iris. "'Ank you, Mizdees," Iris dutifully muttered. Julia put a few tiny strawberries in Iris's palm and tucked the punnet away in her shopping bag. Strawberrry juice ran down Iris's chin as she munched them one by one. And then there was a rare gift: an egg. "Just had a few of those this mornin'," Mr. Barr from the cheese and egg stand said as he put a perfect egg of the lightest blue in Iris's palm. Julia grabbed it instantly. "Thank you, Mr. Barr," she said. "I don't want to lose that." Iris's palm lay open as if she was still savouring the feel of the warm egg in her hand. Stall after stall, they stopped, chose cauliflowers from Kent and mushrooms from Sussex, cabbages, leeks, and carrots from nearby farming communities, strawberries and marrows from Gloucester, cheese from the Cotswolds, and fed on snatches of conversation—"You awright, luv?" "Watch it, you, where d'you think you're going?" "Feckin' hell, look at them peaches!" Women porters carried produce out to cars and vans on wheelbarrows. Everyone, it seems, was there that morning—restaurant owners, buyers for big stores, flower shop owners, West End street flower sellers. The scents of fresh flowers filled the air. A man bearing a bunch of large pink tulips beamed at them: "Jus' wait till the missus sees these!" Julia handed Shiv the basket of strawberries. He ate a few and said, "Lucky Iris! These are the sweetest strawberries I've ever eaten."

By the time they got home, Iris was asleep. "Let her sleep!" Shiv said. "We can feed her lunch when she wakes up."

IN THE EVENING, a friend of Miron Grindea's, a journalist by the name of Laszlo Popescu, came to see them. The Grindeas' long-anticipated move to London would be further delayed until September, he informed them. He was electric with nervous energy, full of horror stories he'd witnessed in a Europe fast succumbing to Hitler's rule. Austrian Nazis had already achieved a major victory, their long-awaited Anschluss, when Germany invaded Austria. "It is like an evil cancer; the eradication of freedom has begun," Popescu said. "Everyone reads newspapers, but they don't read the important bits; they avoid the truth."

"Did the newspapers have any inkling? Did they try to alert the public to the dangers?"

"Very few explained Nazi ideology. Nationalism is now patriotism in Europe. No one will dare to oppose it. Even here, in Britain, there are many rich and influential supporters of Hitler and his party." Still, Britain was the safest country in all of Europe and he was grateful to have escaped to London with his wife. Popescu's parting shot stayed with Shiv: "Cruelty has many forms. We humans have perfected all of them."

"We are not safe. Our daughter isn't safe," Shiv told Julia. He helped Iris blow out the two candles on her cake, but he wouldn't eat any of it. Julia, irritated that he had brought the storm clouds of Europe to their daughter's birthday table, said, "The magazine is taking over our lives. It isn't fair."

He'd heard similar talk in Finchley whenever he went to the Dorice to have coffee with Schmidt, the air thick with fear and a sense of impending tragedy. "After *Kristallnacht*, there are no more delusions. We have murdered innocence. Civilization is finished," Popescu said with a despairing look on his face.

A growing paranoia about foreigners seeping into the country was beginning to fill Londoners. Articles, even in the main press, began demonizing the foreigner—whether they were Jews fleeing the Nazis in Europe, Spaniards fleeing Franco's iron-fist hold on Spain, or students who had come from the colonies to attend university in England. Dark, shifty, dirty, untrustworthy. They don't wash and they lie. The anger and belligerence against non-natives could be seen in the suddenly hostile faces meeting his on the tram, on the streets, in the tube. Despite outbreaks of violence, refugees came pouring in—taking the dangers of head bashing and mutilation with stiletto knives at the hands of pro-Fascist thugs in London over extermination in a concentration camp; choosing an education rather than marginalization because you lacked the right tools.

Leonard Woolf invited Shiv to speak at the 1917 Club, a club he'd founded with Virginia for people to meet and talk about the arts and sciences. Now an informal venue after the club officially closed down four years earlier, it still drew prominent members of society to its gatherings. To Shiv's surprise, his talk, an expansion of some of the issues he had raised in his editorial "Gandhi's Way" and in the "Soul-force in Action" talk he had given at Nanking's, was covered by *The Times* and the *Guardian*, both of whom referred to him as an eloquent young firebrand and Gandhian disciple from India. "They make it sound as though I'd just stepped off the boat from India to give this talk. I'm a barrister, a Middle Templar, a Londoner. It's ridiculous."

"But look at what they say," Julia said, picking up the *Guardian*: "'Mr Advani did not shy away from the more complex elements of ahimsa. With remarkable clarity and passion, he explained that in order to disarm one's enemy one must offer him love. Love may be suspect—especially in an adversarial and unequal situation such as the one that exists between India and Britain. But the power of the offer is such that, in the end, the adversary will accept it, for it represents the only way forward. "We in India do not want to destroy the British. We do not hate them. We want them to leave our country," he said. Simple words, but ah, the complex issues they raise. He is a powerful voice we must all listen to for the sake of Empire and for the sake of peace.' They heard you clearly, Shiv, people are listening to you. This is what you've wanted all along." She began coughing.

"What's that?" Shiv asked. "Doesn't sound good."

"Oh, it's only a cough."

But then it came again, harsher this time. He gave her a concerned look.

"It's nothing. Probably all that late-spring pollen flying about in the park." Her cheeks were rosier than usual.

As if on cue, Grace Blackwell telephoned to say that she was in Edinburgh for a few months and her friends and acquaintances there were eager to hear him speak. She had a date in mind—a week hence. "It's too soon, Mrs. Blackwell."

"I'll make all the arrangements. Just get on the train. I'll meet you at the station. Some important Americans are here that week and they're coming to dine. They must hear what you have to say. I promised I'd try to get you up here. One of them is a columnist with the *New York Times*."

Gandhi, and his emissary Muriel Lester, would have encouraged him to go. Shiv said, "May I ring you back in a few minutes? I would like to discuss it with my wife. We have a little girl who needs a lot of attention." Iris's bad cold, Julia's disturbing cough . . . she was trying to finish a book review on J. B. S. Haldane's *The Inequality of Man*, which had been reissued by Penguin a few weeks earlier, for the magazine. To leave her alone with a sick baby . . . he needed to think about this.

"Oh yes, of course. I do hope you will come!" she said as they hung up.

"I can't leave Iris and you," he told Julia after dinner. "I'm going to tell Grace Blackwell so."

But Julia was already on the phone to her mother. "She'll come to be with me and Iris when you're away," she told Shiv.

"But Iris has a cold, and you're not looking well either."

"Let's see how it goes. You've still got a week. You can cancel with her at the last minute if things get much worse. But accept her invitation now."

He telephoned Grace Blackwell to confirm the invitation.

But the next day, Iris got much better, while Julia's cough deepened and came from deep in her chest; her eyes were blood-shot.

"I can't leave in a few days. I will cancel. That's what I should do as a good father, a good husband. You're both the most important things in my life," he cried out, in frustration.

"No, don't," Julia said. "Iris and I are both tough. We'll ride this out. You go to Edinburgh. Tell them what is at stake."

"You met an up-and-coming barrister; you married an activist," he said. "One maintains the status quo; the other fights it. I'm sorry. It worries me greatly that I'm exposing you and Iris to unknown dangers."

She looked at him carefully. "I knew what I was doing. Don't forget that apart from that party at Maida Vale, which hardly counts, Gandhi's featured prominently in our relationship. He's been our third wheel!"

He laughed drily. She said it was necessary to carry on doing what they were doing. "Iris needs a better world to live in and we're doing our part. We'll handle the thugs."

He was by her side, enveloping her in a bear hug. "I simply couldn't get luckier, could I? With you by my side . . ."

GEORGINA TELEPHONED THE day before his departure. "Strike while the iron is hot. Grace has the kind of social diary people in London can only dream of. It's a wintry spring, everyone has colds. You can't cancel on Grace Blackwell because Iris and Julia have colds."

He stared at Julia, her deeply flushed face, heard her hacking cough. "Please go," Julia said. "Mother will be here a few hours after you leave."

The night before his departure, Iris obligingly went to bed early and slept soundly through the night. He and Julia lay in each other's arms, relieved to call the night their own.

"What's your mother's name? You told me once and I can't remember now."

"Leela," he said. "Sweet. And she really is—sweeter than sweet. She doesn't have a mean bone in her body. She comes out of her garden in the mornings bearing scents of dawn jasmine and freshly plucked rose. Sweet, scented, kind, and loving. That's Leela."

"What a lovely name. Leela. I'd like to see her garden, her queen of the night. I looked it up in the *Encyclopaedia Britannica*. Blooms for a few hours on one night and by morning, it's gone. If you pluck it, it dies immediately."

"Yes . . . it's got the most mysterious scent."

"You've smelt it?"

"Yes. Hard to describe. A bit like jasmine and sandalwood together, and also that green milk sap from the twig. It's a haunting scent." In the white light of the street lamp, her face was silvered, faraway, dreamy. Her eyes were shining. He had tried so many ways to bind her to his home, and that's all it had taken, the memory of an exotic flower, for her to want to travel there and see his world. Her body was warm, too warm, he noted, pushing aside fears.

Then she suddenly sat bolt upright in the bed. "I know what we must do, Shiv. We must bring Sher home. We'll go to India and persuade his mother to let him come to England. He can live with us and be a big brother to Iris. God knows she needs some competition." She turned to him. "It's a splendid idea! Don't you think?"

He was speechless. Sher, his son, here, with him and the two people he loved most in the world. He couldn't speak. He pulled her close,
kissed the top of her head. She settled into sleep almost immediately.

The next morning, he rose earlier than usual to light a fire in the
grate. The house was freezing cold. It was late May, but London's fabled spring, bringing tight, perky blossoms to branches and trees, to
them brought only the bone-chilling drafts of winter that seeped
through the windows into their home. There was something wrong
with the heating—it was sometimes too warm and then, at others, as
cold as Siberia. Shafts of cold air whistled in through the cracks in
the window frames. There was a loud hiss from the radiators when
they cranked into motion and blazed with heat. Mr. Jenkins, the
handyman, promised to come and fix it but then never showed up.
Shiv made some toast and tea, and ate quickly. He went into their
room, and covered Julia with several blankets.

He stood there in the corridor that led to their room, considering
not leaving. It would put him in a bad spot with Grace Blackwell. Too
many arrangements had been made already on his behalf. He would
have to make the trip. He packed quickly and went to Iris's room. Iris
was sitting up in her crib, reaching for him. "Daddy!" He picked her
up, and held her close. He breathed softly into her face, then blew
harder, and she began smiling. It was a game they played. Giggles,
laughter. Julia came in. "I can't believe she slept all night," Shiv said.

"You'd better go." She reached for Iris. The blanket she had
wrapped around her body slipped to the floor. He picked it up and
wrapped them both in it. "You all right?"

"This bloody flat—it's freezing and damp." Their breaths lique-
fied into steam puffs, hung in the frigid air between them.

"I'll hound Mr. Jenkins as soon as I'm back." His eyes lingered on
her face, the red mole on her upper lip. The sleepy sapphire-blue
eyes. She was exhausted, weary, unwell.

"Yes, but do go now. What time's your train?"

"Ten fifteen."

"You don't have much time. Go!"

He gave Iris a kiss and put his arms around Julia. "Be good, please, and look after yourself."

"I will. Now go!" She practically pushed him out of the door.

The memory of her lingered with him all through his journey—their cold bed, his hand warm on her flushed face, her hand resting listlessly on his arm. What would she make of India? For the first time, he had noticed the enthusiasm in her voice. "I want to see it, everything you've told me about. And Iris needs to know her country, her other home. Let's make plans and surprise your parents." He had promised he'd look into it as soon as he got back. Sher, home, with them. He saw the look on her face as she said it. This is what the future could look like: not fractured, not bifurcated, not the awful equation he lived with daily—honour this, and you lose the other. Choices of such magnitude, it was no wonder no one raised them at the start of your journey, for who would walk up the ramp of an outward-bound ship if you knew what sacrifices lay in store?

London, with its dreary suburbs, its Victorian red-brick buildings and smoking chimneys, raced past. The Flying Scotsman would get into Edinburgh at 6:30 p.m., a seven-and-a-half-hour journey. He was to dine with Grace and her friends that evening, give his talk at 10:00 a.m. the following day, attend a champagne lunch reception, dine at Grace Blackwell's that night, and take the train back to London the next day at noon.

He turned to his talk. Grace had suggested he keep it very basic— "Most of these guests know little about India. It will all be new to them. They are fascinated by Gandhi, as are the Americans. The Indian struggle moves us Scots deeply as it reminds us of how we lost our own sovereignty."

"Make it personal?"

"Yes. Some of us lost our sons in the war—I lost my son Hugh—our memories are still raw and run deep. So talk about why Gandhi thinks this is the way to win the war for independence. Place his uniqueness within a context they can understand."

Grace Blackwell sent her driver to pick him up. At her home, a Georgian mansion in the heart of Edinburgh, she gave him an hour to freshen up and then come down to dinner. He was exhausted. He said, "May I use the telephone?"

"Of course. There is one in your room."

While the maid unpacked his suitcase, he placed a call to Julia. The phone rang but there was no answer. He put the receiver down. After five minutes, he tried again. Did Georgina not arrive, leaving Julia alone with Iris, who was probably being fussy because her daddy wasn't there to feed her? It was his job—preparing dinner for Iris, feeding her. He pushed away a growing anxiety.

"Anything else you'll be needing, sir?" the maid asked in pleasantly accented Scottish. He looked up in surprise, arrested by the maid's smooth round Scottish lilt.

"Thank you very much, no," he said.

"Good evening, sir." She left the room.

He tried Julia again. There was no answer. He dressed quickly for dinner, longing to be on the train back home to London.

THERE WERE FOUR couples there for dinner, close friends of Grace's, in additon to him and his hostess. "These are your bread-and-butter people," she had told him earlier. "The ones you have to convince to part with some of their money for a good cause. Tomorrow you will meet the journalists, the professors, and the politicians." Her guests were rich, liberal, with forebears who had made their fortunes out East. They were eager to give back. He recognized them immediately—people who owed their prosperity to their colonial pasts but were quite aware that Empire was now becoming a dirty word. The sun was setting, the decline was apparent. They were anxious to be on the right side of history.

He gave them enough to chew on. He told them about the impoverished farmers and the heavily taxed textile workers. He told them about the Jallianwala Bagh massacre in Amritsar, when General Dyer entered the park where Indians were peacefully protesting for the arrests of two community leaders. Locking the park gate behind him, Dyer ordered his men to fire ammunition at the crowds gathered there. He killed 379 Indians by his reckoning, over 1000 in the estimation of other Indian officials there. Shiv explained how General Dyer had become the most hated Englishman in the Eastern Hemisphere. "This betrayal, this unwarranted massacre of unarmed people will never be explained. Rudyard Kipling, who has given his fellow Englishmen a reason to be in India by dreaming up their mission, their high-minded duty to civilize the brown and black man and so bear the white man's burden, said Dyer was doing his duty. It was the last straw. Indians will dismantle the British Empire brick by brick. We will take our country back." Some of his listeners nodded, others frowned. The women were enthralled by Gandhi and wanted to know "everything about him."

"Patience, dear Lady Lytton. Mr. Advani's talk tomorrow will focus entirely on Mr. Gandhi," Grace Blackwell said.

There was no answer from Julia the next day either. He tried to reach Georgina, whose maid said she was in the garden with the master. So she hadn't left for Catherine Street as planned, and Julia and Iris would have been alone. He was restless and eager to be on his way home.

He had crafted his talk well—he provided interesting examples and drew comparison between the royal union of Scotland with England in 1603, when King James I of Scotland became King of England. "It took another hundred years to consolidate that relationship. Though you were never colonized, Scottish aristocracy and English mercantile interests forged your Act of Union and led to the dissolution of your parliament in 1707. You lost sovereignty, as we did. Our revenues and resources are controlled by Westminster. We were once the world's top producers of fine cotton and wool. Now, denied the benefits of industrialization, we have become mere suppliers of raw material." He gave examples of extreme poverty and high taxation, and said the protests were "as much about the right to defend ourselves and our borders from attack as they are about the cruel mistreatment of our people and the diversion of our wealth to enrich our colonizers." The audience listened and asked questions.

The American journalists were greatly interested in nonviolence and noncooperation as key elements in Gandhi's strategy, and he satisfied their curiosity and left them with plenty to think about. One of them, a young man with the *New York Times,* asked if he could come to London to interview him. "With great pleasure," he replied. At the champagne reception later, he moved through the crowd, answering all their questions. Never let your guard down; don't relax until you're on your way home. You must be on form throughout. You must never falter, never seem unknowing. Clear thoughts come from passion, and from knowing your material, not from trying to make an impression—advice from Henry Polak on how to present in court, precious advice he never strayed from.

And despite his increasing anxiety, or perhaps because of it, he had passion also later that evening. Iris was with him that day, giving him all the urgency he needed. Grace Blackwell said, "You've deeply moved us. People understand what you're trying to do with *Forward.* You will receive many donations from this group. I know you'll continue to enlighten us and change the conversation around independence." It was what he wanted. Gandhi could certainly withdraw his financial support at any time. *Forward* had to be financially secure.

He took a taxi from King's Cross. It was an extravagance, but his heart was heavy and anxious. As he reached the top of the stairs that led to their flat, he heard the key being turned in their neighbour's door. Mrs. Mallory came rushing out. "Oh, you're home, oh, thank goodness you're home." In her arms was a wailing Iris. "I've not been able to quieten her down. She's been so restless and angry. I made some porridge but she won't eat it." Shiv dropped his suitcase and went straight to Iris. His heart was thudding. "Mrs. Mallory, why is Iris with you?" He was trembling with a premonition of disaster.

She muttered something and put her hand on her doorknob. Shiv handed her the keys to his apartment while he held on to Iris with all his might. "Could I ask you to open my door, please?"

Mrs. Mallory unlocked the door and pushed it open. Cold air rushed out of the apartment. He entered with Iris in his arms. Julia's blanket was on the floor that led to their bedroom. He smelt camphor. He walked slowly to their bedroom. At the entrance he stopped. Julia was sprawled across the bed. He went towards her, then took Iris out of the room. "Mrs. Mallory, will you hold her, please?" he asked.

He placed Iris in her arms and went towards his wife. Iris, panicked, wriggled in Mrs. Mallory's arms and let out a loud howl. "Jule," Shiv said quietly. "Jule." He sat down by her prostrate body. "Julia!" he called urgently. "Wake up!" He reached for her arm, which was limp and lifeless to the touch. How long had she been lying there? He reached for the phone and dialled the number for St. Mary's Hospital. The nurse who answered said, "Good evening, sir. How can I help you?"

"I think my wife is dead," he said, before blubbering down the phone.

She asked for the address. "Sir, we'll send an ambulance there now."

He sat down on the bed and took Julia's hand, trying to warm it with his own. Iris said, Mamma. Then louder, Mamma. Mamma. Shiv closed his eyes. What hell was this? Georgina arrived soon after. Calm, ashen-faced, she took Iris from Mrs. Mallory's arms. "What happened?" Georgina asked. Her face was rigid with confusion and sorrow.

He shook his head, biting back tears. "I've just got back. I don't know."

Georgina told him their driver back in Castle Combe could not come in that day. She had decided to hire another driver for the day but William Chesley said he would not entrust his car to a stranger. She decided to wait another day before coming down. "I thought you could use the help even if she was better and it would have been easier for me to help out from Holland Park than from Castle Combe." She looked away, her face ashen.

Shiv went to Julia's study to see if there was anything there that might give them all a clue to her sudden death. All he saw was a small bottle of pills—the top was off and a couple of tablets lay scattered on the table by the bottle. He put the top back on and handed it to one of the ambulance men as they took Julia's body away. "Not sure what these are but you would be able to identify them," he told the man, who put the bottle into his pocket.

They stood there silently. "What happened, Mrs. Mallory?" Shiv asked. Mrs. Mallory stared at him as she stood there, her hair dishevelled, an unwilling accomplice in a drama not of her making.

Julia had felt very ill in the middle of the night before Shiv's arrival and had taken Iris to Mrs. Mallory, saying she would come for her the next morning. She stood there coughing, reeling, delirious. Mrs. Mallory said, "I offered her some tea, but she said no, and dis-

appeared into the flat. I knocked on her door several times throughout the night but she didn't answer. Might it be the Spanish flu?"
Mrs. Mallory asked.

Georgina, distraught, said, "We don't know anything yet, Mrs.
Mallory."

Shiv said, "She didn't answer any of my phone calls."

"She told me she had ignored the phone for fear of worrying you.
She knew it was me ringing because I did so when you would have
been in the middle of your dinner in Edinburgh to tell her I would
be here as soon as I could," Georgina said, bursting into tears. "How
can I ever live with this?" Her voice was trembling. "This freezing
flat. It's like an icebox in here. Oh god, my poor baby."

Mrs. Mallory, her face tight and anxious, left them, clicking the
front door quietly behind her.

The hospital identified the pills immediately and told Shiv it was co-
caine. She had probably taken too many in a short period of time,
the doctor said. "Where did she get those pills from?" Georgina
asked.

Shiv remembered she had once told him about a friend who
swore by some new pills that everyone was taking for anxiety: "She
says she doesn't worry about being anxious anymore." But he never
found out who the friend was and it had not come up again.

Jacob said he would get onto the next train from Cambridge. "I'll
take care of Iris," he told Shiv on the phone.

Iris knew something had gone from her and refused to stop crying. Her mother's comforting touch, the hand she loved to pump up
and down, which made her laugh just as much as Shiv's breath fan-
ning her face.

Shiv stood there, looking at her, looking at Georgina, who was
making tea. Could he have prevented this from happening?

⌘

Julia, in her state of confusion, perhaps from the pills, and despair, had covered the dining table with her illustrations of Iris. She had begun a letter to Iris, in which she explained the circumstances and setting for each illustration. "Here you are, reaching for a butterfly on a bush. . . . Here's a red ball in your chariot—you refused to give it back to the little boy to whom it belonged and I had to take it away from you. . . . Here you are with a blue egg in your palm—Mr. Barr at the cheese stand in Covent Garden gave it to you. . . . You are going to be a very adventurous young lady."

He looked at them all. She had written down dates and descriptions for all of them, except the last one—this was a drawing she had probably attempted soon after he'd left them both for Edinburgh, just a few days ago. It was of him, standing by the door, looking down the corridor. His eyes were searching—he was looking for his love, his companion, his best friend, his ally. Georgina's eyes were pinned on her son-in-law as he held the drawing in his hands. The paper shook as he sobbed, anguished cries breaking from him as he realized she must have wanted to freeze him right there, by the door, and not be left alone. "I shouldn't have gone to Edinburgh," he said out loud to Georgina.

"I should not have let William bully me. I should have hired another driver," she said. "I should have been here with my daughter."

Jacob came in and went straight to his princess. "My darling child," he said, embracing her. Iris looked up at him mutely for a few moments. Without any further hesitation, she held out her arms to him, as she had always done.

Shiv stood stock-still as he thought of Julia's last hours. Had she known she was dying? Is that why she had started a letter to Iris and begun captioning her drawings of her? Anguished by the thought of her sufferings, he kept repeating out loud: *Won't know. I'll never, ever know.* Every time he said it, a knife twisted deeper within him.

⸙

A simple burial ceremony at St. Mary's in Swanage. Shiv wanted to honour Julia's wish about being cremated and her ashes dispersed where the swans landed on the Thames. He told Georgina about their trips to watch the mute swans land on the water, how she had brought it up first—that watery burial place for her ashes. Georgina looked at him anxiously. "Please don't bring this up. William will insist on her burial in our plot at Swanage. There is no will—I don't see that she has left anything behind so we can honour her wishes. Unless you have something?"

He said no. "No one prepares for dying so young."

She nodded grimly. "I'm sorry, Shiv. This—is not something I can take up with my husband."

He took a deep breath and let it go.

Georgina, Jacob, Shiv, and Iris left several hours earlier for Swanage to make certain they would be there on time. The hearse carrying Julia's body followed them down the motorway. The journey took them over three hours. At the church, Shiv noted the same stained glass windows, their light beams patterning the floor. Once he had stood there with his bride. She had lily of the valley in her hair and bluebells in her arms. In her long white wedding dress, her arm linked through his, they chatted with guests in a queue waiting to sign the register in the vestry. Their life together was about to begin.

It was then that William Chesley came towards him. At the last minute, he had decided to attend the funeral and had come in a separate car. Red-faced, furious, drunk, he poked Shiv in the chest and said, "I knew you from the start, you guttersnipe! Murderer! Murderer! You killed my daughter!" Family members rushed to restrain the man and take him away. Jacob, who was standing next to Shiv, exhaled slowly. "Sorry, old chap," he said. "He's a fiend. No one wanted him here today but he insisted."

"It's all right, Jacob," he said quietly. "I deserve his wrath."

Jacob shook his head, putting his arm around Shiv's shoulder. "No. It happened. Let it go," he said. Shiv turned away, his mouth as papery as ash. Iris came towards him, her hand in Georgina's. "Dadda," she cried. Her exuberance stunned him; her radiant smile, so much like Julia's, demanded his attention. He held out his arms to her and she came to him in one simple move. How would they make it, he wondered. How?

As they began their life together without Julia, Shiv watched as the mounds of laundry grew, dirty dishes tottered in the sink, while Iris howled day and night. Her red face and angry eyes showed no change in expression no matter what he came up with to distract her. He thought he could handle it all, but it was becoming quite clear he couldn't manage it on his own.

He hadn't slept for a week, his rhythms bound to Iris's, not daring to take his eyes off her. At night, he would sit wrapped up in blankets with her in his lap and she would then fall asleep, her soft breathing lulling him to sleep. Then a small hand reaching out for his face, playing with the fresh growth on his chin, would instantly wake him up. "Oh my god, Iris, it's past bedtime." But he couldn't deny that for all their lack of routine in that week, he had become the one she looked to now for protection, for confirmation, for approval. Aware of how inadequate he was as caretaker, he shot her apprehensive looks, which made her sob. Their collective despair grew.

WHEN GEORGINA AND Jacob came to visit, they saw the mess everywhere. Georgina said, "Oh my, this is not sustainable. You're being very brave, Shiv. But Iris needs order and some structure back in her life."

"You must have a nanny for Iris," Jacob said.

Georgina agreed. "I'll start interviewing immediately." In a week, she had found the right person. "She's competent, not chatty, and can light a fire and prepare simple suppers. She's exactly what you need."

WHEN TIBOR SCHMIDT and Alix Brodsky came personally to offer their condolences, Shiv said, "I don't know how to continue with the magazine." He had for some time now stopped taking on fresh cases as a barrister, and his visits to the courts had become infrequent in order to devote all his time to the magazine.

Tibor nodded. "This is a difficult time. But you must find a way. You need an assistant."

Tibor's son, Julian, was nineteen; he was home for the long summer holidays, and looking for a job. "Do send him to me, Tibor." One look at the boy's keen eyes, his fresh-faced vitality, and Shiv hired him on the spot. The nanny/housekeeper Georgina had hired, Mrs. Emily Worth, arrived within hours of Julian. She went about efficiently finding her way around the flat, sorting out clothes for laundering and taking stock of food supplies. But even as the flat began displaying order, routine, and the rhythm of family life again, Shiv's grief mounted. He had lost the best thing he had ever had— his helpmate and friend, his love. His home had been ransacked, its most precious possession stolen. He dreaded every day, and the next.

Out on the streets, a ghost walked by his side. He remembered all the things he had loved about their walks together—her pull on his coat, her hand curling around his arm, the smile with which she turned to him as they walked to the bookshops in Charing Cross Road. It brought him the greatest pleasure for them to be seen together like this, two people who delighted in each other's company. Her smile was for him—in that crowd of people, *him*. He never knew whether people gave them second glances because they were a mixed-race couple or because they were so clearly in love. But people did stare. And some even smiled.

Lucy and he could never have had *this*—the public face of love, this particular pleasure of being *seen*. Their love had been like the queen of the night, a flowering beauty that needed the thick blackness of night to blossom and delight the senses. Daylight suffocated it. Much as Lucy yearned for Shiv to take risks in public, he knew Shiv would never bend there. The lawyer in him, the Indian son protecting his parents and their reputation back home, could not take on the kind of exhibitionism Lucy needed to flourish in public.

Now, ANCHORLESS AND vulnerable, he regarded the Janus-faced city he had come to think of as home. London had teeth—he knew it, waited for the baring. *Pattes de velours,* Lucy would say, when Shiv noticed how amiable someone had been. Claws of velvet. "You didn't feel them?"

One evening, after Mrs. Worth had put Iris to bed and left for the night, he braved Julia's closet. For weeks he had been avoiding it. Now he yearned to see her clothes again, imagine her in them, remember their times together. He pulled up a chair in front of it, poured some whiskey in a glass, and sat down. He edged the door slowly open with his foot. The clothes stared at him in mute confusion. Where is she? they demanded. Scents of her came from within. Lavender and apricot. Rosemary. He breathed them in. It was as though she were beside him. The smell of her was so overpowering, he began edging the door closed again. Then the tears came, paralysing him. Some of her clothes, the everyday ones she used to walk in the park or go shopping in, were in heaps, piled high in front. He stared at the wildness of it. Using his toe to pry out a cornflower blue blouse she had worn so often it had discernible holes in it, he brought it to his face. Holding it to his nose, he breathed her in. He howled into its creases, looking for the woman he loved. "Dadda," a small, frightened voice called. Oh god, Iris. He turned abruptly, upsetting his whiskey glass, which crashed to the floor and broke into pieces. "Iris, no." He saw her coming towards him, the sea of glass. "No, Iris, no, please stay," he shouted. "Stay!" But the child's bare feet kept coming towards him. He rose from the chair, skirting the glass pieces, and bounded over to her, picked her up in his arms. "Oh, thank god!" he cried. But even as he clutched her, he became aware of a blinding pain. Pieces of glass were lodged within his foot. He hobbled across to the door, crossed the threshold and shut it firmly behind them. "Oh, Iris," he exhaled, taking her with him into the kitchen. He put her in her chair where, red-faced and angry, she began squirming and howling. He sank down in a chair, pinched his fingers together, and attempted to pull at the pieces of glass. Blood gushed out onto the floor. As he got up to find a clean piece of cloth and water to wash out the wound, he saw trails of blood leading from their bedroom into the kitchen. The place was a nightmare. Iris was looking at him in confusion, her tiny hands fisted. He felt cruel, unable to comfort her. When her howls filled the room again, he made no attempt to hush her. She was howling for them both.

On 3 September, 1939, Britain and France declared war on Germany after Hitler's invasion of Poland. World War II had begun. The air was rent with the sound of sirens going off. But soon after, as the threatened bombings never came, and the sirens fell silent, life went back to normal. People gathered in the markets, buying fruit, fish, eggs, meat, and vegetables. The feared food shortages did not happen. Schools were open. Uniformed children waited at the bus stops with their mothers or their nannies, neat as pins, keeping to

their schedules. The sounds of war, though distant, were real—the Luftwaffe were raiding Shetland—but otherwise, life continued as normal.

When Muriel Lester wrote simply to say, "Can Kingsley Hall give you solace?" Shiv considered her offer. He took Iris with him one Friday morning, boarding the tram at Covent Garden to Bromley-by-Bow. Iris, overexcited by a completely new adventure, sat with her nose pressed against the window, pointing to people, things, as they flashed by. She said things he didn't recognize but he managed to smile and nod as though he did.

Muriel Lester met him at the door. Over tea, she came up with a plan that was to save his life. She said, "Come and live here with us. Iris can go to Children's House, our school, where the teachers follow the Montessori program, and she will meet all kinds of children here. Children of shipyard workers, factory workers, shop girls, cobblers, lamplighters, policemen, and yes, also the children of some liberal upper-middle-class families seeking a more diverse outlook for their children. I think Iris will be very happy here."

"I should speak to Georgina first," Shiv said.

"I already have," Muriel said. "She thinks it's a perfect solution. You've hired someone to help you with the magazine, I believe. Being here will allow you to go back to doing the work both you and Julia devoted your lives to."

"Where would we stay?"

"Here, where Gandhi lived. I've never allowed anyone else to stay here, even for a night. But you are like Gandhi's son. Iris can have her own room downstairs. When you've found your footing, you and Iris can return to Catherine Street. Until then, please make Kingsley Hall your home."

Iris and he moved in the following week. He had requested a

small bed for Iris in his room. "She can't be left alone at this point," he explained. Muriel had not only seen to the bed, but also placed warm, furry welcoming toys in it. Iris went towards them with open arms. Mrs. Worth was relieved of her job with two months' pay, as well as assurances that she would be contacted as soon as Shiv and Iris returned to Catherine Street.

*Forward* also now had a new home. Tibor and Alix trudged down to Bromley-by-Bow once a week, bearing proofs and covers. Shiv edited and styled, Alix gave the words form, and Tibor set them into clean, readable pages of type. Julian dealt with correspondence and subscriptions, one day telling his father with great excitement that there were now 2800 subscribers to *Forward*. Some of the new subscriptions were from across Europe ("It's Pablo! He did that!" Tibor said), others from Australia, New Zealand, Canada, and the United States. The enclosed cheques came with congratulatory notes on the success of the magazine. Muriel Lester, a teetotaler if there ever was one, twisted the cap on an old bottle of sherry and they all—Tibor, Alix, Julian, Muriel, and he—sipped it from dainty little glasses up on the terrace. After they'd left, and Iris was put to bed, Shiv sat on Gandhi's swing, with his glass turned to his lips, savouring each drop as it fell on his tongue. "Jule, you were with us today! And we're doing it, we're doing what we had always dreamed of!" It wasn't such an empty feeling after that—these were shared, combined victories, with her sparkling energy at their centre. He had to be present to avenge her loss in their lives. *Forward*, in her absence, could only go forward.

Iris was flourishing at Kingsley Hall's Children's House. She was in a state of high excitement every day, babbling on about things he could not understand, but which Muriel translated for him. "They made a doll's house today." Or: "They enacted Cinderella at school.

The children love the story!" One day, Iris came back tearful, agitated. She ran to Shiv and threw her arms around his neck. Muriel Lester followed her in. Before she could speak, Iris began an urgent call: "Jule! Jule! Jule!"

Shiv froze. His name for Julia. Iris said, "Dadda, cold, cold, cold." They had enacted Sleeping Beauty in class, Muriel said, her face somber. Iris had run up to the pretend sleeping girl and kissed her all over her face. "Jule, wake up!" she cried. "Jule, Jule!" In great distress, the child told Mrs. Kitchener, their class teacher, "Mamma cold, Mamma very cold." Mrs. Kitchener asked Muriel Lester to come and fetch her, to comfort her. Shiv stared at his daughter as Muriel told him what happened. She was too young to remember, surely, when, oblivious to Mrs. Mallory, who was standing by the door to their bedroom, puzzled and despairing, holding Iris in her arms, he slapped her mother's face and shouted, "Jule, wake up! Wake up!"

The icebox room, the terror of those days, came back to him now. She must have absorbed it all—her mother's death, the sudden going away of a body that had once crooned and sung to her, see-sawing her up and down as she sat on her legs, squealing with excitement.

Shiv said, "Oh god, I'm sorry, Iris!" and Iris looked at him with puzzled wonder. Muriel Lester came and took Iris from his arms. "I'll be downstairs," she said. "She'll be all right." When she left he realized tears were sliding down his cheek. He was a cracked vessel that could no longer hold anything; life, itself, had become tired of him and was seeping through every opening it could find.

There was so much he didn't know about those few hours between Julia's turn for the worse and Iris being handed over to Mrs. Mallory, their neighbour. What had happened that night? Iris *did* remember, impossible though it seemed. His baby would carry those memories for the rest of her life.

⚬⁀⚬

At Kingsley Hall, they had made a temporary home for themselves. But their mail continued to be delivered to their flat in Catherine Street. When Christmas came in a shiver of bright lights and tinsel, Shiv remembered their annual expedition to Piccadilly to see the shop windows. The festive season would be a little sombre this year, immersed in the atmosphere of war rather than of celebration, but Iris loved the lights. He told Muriel Lester he would go to Piccadilly with Iris one evening and stop on the way back at Catherine Street to collect their mail.

The war was on, but it was like a non-war. Some called it a "phony war," their bravado refreshing when everyone had come to fear the worst. Since September, life had remained relatively normal. Even as calm prevailed, imaginary fears grew as news of what was happening in Europe made the rounds. What was the Luftwaffe planning? He stood by the shop windows in Piccadilly with Iris, who pointed excitedly at things and waved her tinsel star wand at passers-by. In her pink plaid coat and hood, her cheeks flushed, her little pink boots, she seemed unaware that Julia was missing. Julia's laughter and delight in her daughter's discovery of Christmas haunted Shiv. She seemed close by, close enough to touch, when he heard her laugh. His face frozen, he watched his daughter with pain and anger. Was she hearing Julia, too?

Iris picked up on his discomfort, his lack of connection. He put her down and directed her steps to walk along with him. But she began crying and wanted to be carried. Where once she had been adventurous, a butterfly flitting across flagstones, now she showed anxiety and fearfulness. She cried constantly. "Dadda! Dadda!" He hugged her tight, feeling her estrangement from everything she had loved as keenly as his own.

Her face often seemed pensive and sad to him. What sorrow was she nursing? What did she know? As he carried her, she held on to his hand and looked at him with a searching look on her face. A child's sense of tragedy is induced by absence—she knew something big had gone from her. Her eyes carried pain he couldn't bear to see.

They had been ejected, Iris and he, and become exiles.

As he held her in his arms and tried to direct her attention to a fairy flitting a wand this way and that in the window of Fortnum's, Iris suddenly let out a blood-curdling scream. "Mummy!" And as he tried to hold her firmly in his arms, she yelled "Mummy!" again and lunged towards a woman passer-by who bore a striking resemblance to Julia. The woman's face filled with fear and pity. "I'm so, so sorry," he cried after the woman as she turned her back to him and walked away. At Piccadilly Circus, he sank down on a stone step on the island surrounding the statue of Eros. Iris was sobbing. He could not calm her down and that sent his morale to a new low. All self-restraint seemed to break down as he began sobbing. Iris was so startled that she stopped crying and looked at him curiously. She stuck her thumb in his mouth and said, "Dadda, no cry, no cry." She made him smile, her self-possession taking over, just as Julia's would in moments of crisis. "What a pair we are, Iris!" he said, picking her up and adjusting her weight in his arms for the walk to the bus stop. Just as he thought he would make it back to Kingsley Hall, a cop came over. "Sir! Can you produce identity papers, please? Whose child is this?"

He looked at the policeman. "Mine," he said. "This is my daughter, Iris."

"I see." He looked at Iris and then at Shiv. "I'm sorry, sir, but I see no resemblance. I will need to see identity papers for both you and this child. We're being careful with all the kidnappings going on recently." Yes, he'd heard about them, missing Jewish children who left their foster parents and lived on the streets. Did the policeman think

Iris was a mistreated Jewish child, sobbing for parents who'd abandoned her? He clutched Iris closer to him.

Acutely aware that the outcome of every such situation depended on how you handled yourself from the very beginning, he said, "Officer, this was just a quick outing for the child, to see the shop windows at Christmas. I lost my wife, her mother, recently and we have not recovered from the loss. Please accompany us to our home, and I will gladly produce all the identification that you need." Then, as he saw the policeman's unyielding look, he added, "I am a barrister. Middle Temple." He still was that, he reminded himself. A representative of the law.

Perhaps it was the word *barrister* or his deferential tone that had an effect and calmed the policeman down. "All right. Where do you live?"

"Covent Garden," he said. All their identification papers were in their flat, and he remembered gratefully that he had the keys to the flat with him, intending to stop by to check for mail.

The cop said, "You're lucky it's close by. Or I wouldn't have put myself out. I've got a job to do."

They began walking to Catherine Street—a twenty-minute walk. Shiv hugged Iris to him tightly. The cop hummed an unrecognizable tune as they walked; it was worse than silence. Would the evening end with Iris being snatched away from him? The cop began whistling. By now, Shiv's heart was thudding, and his arms felt weak. The fear of dropping Iris made him move edgily, as if he'd had too much to drink.

When they got to Catherine Street, he put Iris down and inserted the key in the door. The key wouldn't turn. He fumbled with the lock, aware of how it looked—a man unable to get into his own home.

Iris began howling. When the policeman picked her up, Shiv called out in alarm, "What are you doing?" His voice sounded powerless, a thin screech.

"I'm waiting for you," the cop said with a smug smile, putting out his hand. "I'll do it, shall I?"

Shiv shook his head, and then, as he gave the key a final desperate turn, it caught in the lock and he pushed the door open, suppressing a sigh of relief. While the man waited outside in the drawing room, he went to his bedroom and opened the small iron box inside the closet. He took out the identifying documents with trembling hands—Iris's birth certificate, his British passport, his marriage certificate, photographs of Iris's first birthday, her second. The evidence of life lived as stated was in these scraps of paper. Without them, he would be identified a kidnapper, his daughter a ward of the state. Shiv knew he'd reached a dead end of sorts. He couldn't carry on like this. To be suspected of being a kidnapper because his daughter didn't resemble him, appeared to be an all-white child, was a disaster he could not have imagined. "She's mine," he wanted to shout at the cop. "Whether you believe me or not, this child is mine!" He stifled his rage and went out to meet the policeman, who took the papers to a table and switched the table lamp on. He thumbed through everything, glancing at him, at the photographs, at Iris, at Julia's photo, at the photo of them all at Iris's second birthday party.

"All right, sir," he said. "I'm sorry but one just can't be too careful these days." Shiv watched him leave the flat as his body flooded with adrenaline.

He telephoned Muriel Lester and told her what had happened. "My goodness," she said.

"I don't know what the solution is. I can't live without my baby but I don't know how to do this." Later he thought he sounded contemptible. It was his duty, his obligation to Iris, to parent her. She had no one else.

Muriel sighed. "I will speak to Georgina. No one's living in a

stable world anymore. She may have some ideas, at least for a temporary solution while we're heading towards total destruction everywhere in the world. In the meantime, I think Kingsley Hall is where
that child can feel some sense of home."

He agreed and decided to return there with Iris the following day.

Jacob, about to graduate from Cambridge University, had been
working at the Colonial Office during breaks between terms. He had
chosen India for his focus, and when the position of assistant district
commissioner in Karachi opened up, Jacob's supervisor put him up
for the position. When he rang Shiv to say, "May I come over this
evening? I have something to celebrate," Shiv knew something big
was up. He walked over to Malin's and picked up some fried haddock and their famous thick chips, along with some beer.

As they ate upstairs in Gandhi's room, Jacob gave Shiv the news.
"It's very exciting, Shiv. I will finally meet Iris's other grandparents."
Of course. Karachi, not the end of the world. Just ninety miles from
Hyderabad Sind, where his family lived. Jacob said, "I want to be a
decent colonial administrator. I'm not interested in carrying the
white man's burden. Far from it, I want to know more about India
and Indians. I have Indian family already; now I want to live with
them, come to know them as friends and allies, live among them,
not above them. We should be serving their needs, not just selfishly
looking to fulfil our own."

He looked down at his plate. "I'll miss this. No battered haddock
and chips in Karachi."

Shiv was convinced that Jacob meant to make a difference, that
this was at the heart of his choice to leave England for India, but saw
already how impossible his task would be, how he would run up
against his superiors, how the only way to be a colonial administrator was to be like everyone else, to maintain distance, not to cultivate

closeness, to be dispassionate, seemingly just there to do the job to fill up a curriculum vitae. To be tough and look the other way when he saw injustice, to protect his own kind no matter what they were guilty of. The white man's burden, he told his brother-in-law, involves looking as though you're there under duress, carrying us, your heathen colonial charges, on your back. We're your burden!

Jacob burst out laughing.

"No, Jacob, I'm serious. There's only one kind of colonial administrator in India. God knows, India needs Britons like you out there. But these are very tense times and it won't be easy."

When Georgina came to lunch the next day, she expressed worries about Iris, about her granddaughter being brought up in a war-torn London, having lost her mother. "This is a brutal time for families. I am involved with the Kindertransport people, bringing Jewish children to England—it is heartbreaking work. I think Iris should be sent to India with Jacob to see her grandparents. Once this terrible war is over, she can come back. Think about it."

Shiv had felt for some time that Iris and he needed to work out a regular schedule back home, in their own flat. Living with Muriel Lester, they were shielded, but their own lives were also on pause. Accordingly, they had finally moved back to Catherine Street permanently and Mrs. Worth had returned to work for him. The constant interruptions to forging friendships at school for such a needy, precocious child were defeating. The atmosphere of war had brought its chill to childhood—children didn't run around on the streets anymore. The ice cream men on their tricycles ("Stop Me and Buy One") had disappeared, their cycles having been requisitioned for war use. A cold hard reality had filled the city. You emerged from your home feeling lucky to have survived another night. No one knew anything. You lived in a world where knowledge was personally learnt—you knew what you had suffered and sometimes, that was all you knew. At street corners, women gathered and told one another what they had heard, what they feared would happen next. Trust was hard earned, as people prepared themselves for the full blast of war. Was this the atmosphere in which he wanted Iris to grow up? Would it not take an entire generation to overcome the heartbreak of this time?

He considered Georgina's suggestion. It would probably be his parents' only opportunity to meet their grandchild. "You have a point," he told her. "I'll think about it."

He asked the Polaks for their advice. "It is the perfect solution. I will write and explain things to your father," Polak said. "It is a tragedy. He will never have met his wonderful daughter-in-law. Now he must at least meet his granddaughter."

Millie agreed. "Your father and Henry have a very close relationship. Let Henry do the hard work. You can write and ask for their forgiveness after he has heard from Ramdas. When does Jacob leave for India?"

"In three months."

"Plenty of time. Henry will do the needful."

His father responded to Henry Polak's letter immediately. "We knew something was wrong," he wrote.

Shiv's mother kept saying, "There is something going on with him." She was convinced of it.

We learn of good and bad tidings at the same time. We had a daughter-in-law, whom we have lost without knowing

her. With war raging in Europe, we are very anxious to meet
our granddaughter, of whom we knew nothing until your
letter came. Gandhiji has told us Shiv is doing wonderful
work for India with his magazine. But I do not fully
understand how a magazine will further India's aims, how
it will benefit our struggle? Have the influential, thinking,
liberals of Europe joined us? Have they contributed in any
way to our cause? If they have, I do not see it. Not yet. But
if Gandhi is pleased with our son, as you say, then he is
bound to continue. We would very much like to have our
granddaughter with us. We will welcome Jacob as our son.
And we will try to learn as much as we can about Julia
through her brother and our granddaughter.

"He's lonely," Millie said when she showed Shiv his father's letter.
"I don't understand why you kept both Iris's birth and Julia's death
from him. I don't think it was fair."

"Millie, you don't know how tight that noose can be."

She thought for a few minutes. "I think I do. But Iris needs the
love of her grandparents as much as they need hers. God knows,
William Chesley will never accept that child. Your father had a grandchild once, and lost him. He must be heartbroken about that. And
it's a way of having you home. You've been away too long." On her
face, Shiv thought he saw sadness, a wistfulness for her own sons,
one so far away, the other long gone. He would go back someday to
see his aging parents. Someday. One day.

"How will I live without her, Millie? I've lost the best friend I ever
had. And now Iris, too." He struggled to rein in the emotions he felt
were flooding his face.

Millie silently put out her hand and covered his.

&#8766;

On 12 May, 1940, two days before Iris's departure, Georgina, Jacob, Muriel Lester, and Shiv celebrated Iris's third birthday. They blew out the candles on the cake—whipped together from scarce eggs and flour by Mrs. Worth—and sang happy birthday. But Julia's absence cast a long shadow over their table and Shiv could barely crack a smile for Georgina's camera. Their false gaiety ran so thin, even Iris looked pensive. They had once known true joy, and of all emotions, it is the least reproducible, ill suited for hollow imitation. He tried to sing to her to put her to sleep that night: *"Oranges and lemons / say the bells of St. Clement's / Old Father . . ."* Oh, what was the old Father's name? He couldn't remember, gave up. He'd always meant to learn the song from Julia.

The next evening, Shiv sat her down on the sofa. "Iris," he began softly. "I want to tell you a story." She heard the word *story* and perked up, a solemn listening expression settling on her face. "Good girl," he said, smiling at her. "Your mummy, Iris, is gone. But I want you to remember her always. She loved you with all her heart, more than me, more than anything." Iris stared back with unblinking eyes, her fists curled in her lap, her smocked dress of gay flowers, her little legs with dimpled knees, her white socks and little black shoes. Her arms were around her beloved Peter Rabbit, his coat slipping off his arms as she held him tight. She was listening intently. He said, "I want you to remember that London is your home. This city is where you were born. Remember the pink light of dawn on the Thames by the Temple stairs—remember how we stood there, watching daylight break? And summers in the park, children jumping rope, ducks on the water, the clip-clop of horses' hooves on the cobblestoned pathways; and the sound of the violin rising above all the other sounds and coming to us as we talked, your mother and I, and your mother fanned your face to drive the bees away. And the fruit and vegetable stalls in Covent Garden, and Mr. Davies, who saved his best strawberries, the tiniest sweetest ones, for you. And Big Ben ringing out the hours—how you'd fall silent as you heard them and just listen. And Mummy singing 'Oranges and Lemons' to you every night to put you to sleep. And fish and chips from Malin's near Kingsley Hall—Mummy wanted you to have a taste for them and she always fed you a little of hers. You always wanted more! And your first sip of champagne from Mummy's glass, which you spat out. To tell you the truth, Iris, I hated champagne when I first came to this country. Now I love it. I'm sure you'll love it, too, someday."

When Iris burst out giggling, he knew she was somehow taking it all in, although it defeated reason. A three-year-old, after all, how was it possible? "Why?" she suddenly said, surprising him. "Why, Dadda?"

He stared at her, stunned. Was it a real question? "I don't know, my love. I just don't know." He held her, and sobbed.

JACOB AND IRIS boarded an Imperial Airways plane from Croydon Aerodrome—a journey that would take five days, with layovers all the way—Paris, Marseille, Rome, Brindisi, Athens, Mirabella, Alexandria, Gaza, Baghdad, Basra, Kuwait, Bahrain, Gwalior, Jodhpur, Karachi. Then the plane would go on to Calcutta, the final stop. The next day, she and Jacob would drive down to Hyderabad, a three-hour journey by car. "Bloody marvellous, isn't it?" Jacob said. "Even as you're thinking about us, we'll be there. Your ship took thirty days to get here. This is less than a week!"

Jacob's letter arrived two weeks later. Iris had been as good as gold all the way. She only cried once, when she'd left her beloved toy in the hotel, and they had to go back for it. Until she had it safe in her arms, she wept bitterly. They had held up the plane, Jacob said, but "she would have cried all the way to Karachi if we hadn't found her Peter Rabbit."

> Your parents have already taken her into their hearts. She's settled in beautifully with them. She loves her grandmother, who makes garlands of roses for her every day, and who has knitted small dolls for her to play with. Your father has ordered hard-to-find children's books for her from Thacker & Co. Ltd. in Bombay and it promises to be a frequent ritual—watching Iris's delighted face as she rips open the packages, removes the books, and piles them high in her room. They are very dear, and have accepted me as their son. But it is clear they miss you terribly. I am very happy here.
>
> They have mined me for information about Julia. I think they adore her, if it is right to say one can adore someone one has never met. They want you to bring all her drawings home with you when you come. "That is how we will come to know her ourselves," your mother said.

On 14 June, Paris fell to the Nazis, a scarce month after Iris and Jacob's departure, and marked the official start of the Battle of Britain. On 7 September, 1940, the Blitz began and for the next seventy-six days, London was bombed relentlessly. People gathered in underground shelters; above ground, the noise of shattering glass and flames erupting out of destroyed buildings spoke of death and devastation. Slogans began appearing on the walls of the shelters: "Dig for Victory" (which led to backyard farming, people astonishing one another by the tomatoes and runner beans they'd coaxed out of their own little plots of earth); "Coughs and Sneezes Spread

Diseases"; "Make Do and Mend"; "Is Your Journey Really Necessary?"

Across the street, you would see a neighbour's house blown away
in the middle of the night. "Where are they now?" you wondered.
"Did they manage to get away before the bomb fell?" Beloved
institutions—bookshops, pastry shops, the ironmongers, the fish-
mongers and greengrocer's down the street—gone overnight. The
never-ending shattering of the air created new losses every day—an
enormity that could no longer be accounted for.

The Barrage Ballroom drew more clients than ever as dancing
became the only activity that was still allowed and brought people
pleasure.

In December 1940, Shiv went to Piccadilly, as he always had with Iris
and Julia around Christmas. He had told Muriel Lester he would
stop by to see her later that evening. Deeply aware of Iris's absence,
Julia's as well for the past two years, he strolled around aimlessly.
There were hardly any lights or decorations. The city was braced for
war. Intending to return a few books he had borrowed from the London Library, he stopped to talk to the front desk librarian there. "I've
been braving the Piccadilly line," the man said, referring to the tube.
"Not very reliable these days. And full of shelter rats, bedding down
for the night. I'd use Victoria." It was rush hour already, five p.m. The
streets were filled with people trying to get home before the nightly
raids began. Shiv lingered, watching their determined faces as they
walked briskly to trams, buses, trains. The people's army, these men
and women, office workers by day, ambulance drivers, nurses, fire-
men by night.

He descended into the tube at Green Park. People were already
staking their positions for the night—the escalators and platforms
would be full of sleeping bodies once the trains stopped running

around 9:00 p.m. The most class-ridden country under the sun, the land of snobbery and privilege, George Orwell had characterized it, but gone on to say its emotional unity is what made it cohere and come together in times of crisis. British spunk at its best: we'll manage all right.

But tension, if not fear, was on display everywhere. People were withdrawn, their gazes inwards. The conductors with their unsmiling faces, civilians tense with anxiety trying to make it through another day.

At Victoria Station, he got off the tube and went up to the main railway station, intending to pick up some flowers for Muriel from the flower shop there. An overground train was waiting at the platform, filling up with passengers. Children carrying gas masks and clutching their toys, with small suitcases or rucksacks on their backs, stood waiting patiently. Their mothers waved stoically as they watched their children board. The great evacuation of children to the countryside had begun.

At the other end of the platform, he saw troops in clusters, smoking cigarettes, buoyant and carefree, cracking jokes. They were also waiting to board the train. The cadets' and sergeants' fresh uniforms were so new the folds showed. Their untried faces were optimistic; their feet tapped restlessly across the platform as they waited to board. Unaware of the dangers to come, they were like adventurers bound for new lands, impatient and eager to be off. Shiv glanced at them with alarm. Victory, if it came, would be a long time coming. Go home, he wanted to tell them. Flee. Life's dirty surprises are hard to bear, so live a little while longer if you can. He felt desolate as he looked at their shining faces.

As his eyes scanned the crowd, he saw a young man whose gait seemed to challenge the uniform he had on. It sat stiffly on him, too loose and baggy for his slim frame, the sleeves of the jacket slipping off his shoulders. He hadn't bothered to have it tailored to his body or the tailors had been confounded by his litheness and given up trying to make it fit. Shiv looked at him, then clutched his stomach in horror and recognition. No, he thought, not him, not Lucy. In the waning taupe light that drifted down from the vast station's glass ceiling, Lucy appeared ill and sealed off from the others, or perhaps it was indifference to his fate. Lucy, suddenly aware of the intensity of his stare, turned his gaze up towards him and his eyes met Shiv's. As they saw each other, as if for the first time, Lucy's face went rosy pink in recognition. The distance between them made it impossible to communicate. The clicking slats in the wooden departure and arrival boards, the men milling around, the banter and the cigarette smoke, the pounding of his heart, the milky light suffusing people's faces—every detail formed a tableau that froze in time. Shiv shook himself out of his stupor. He had to act. *Now.*

Shiv pulled out the book in his coat pocket—a new translation of the *Odyssey*, which he was reviewing for *Forward*—and quickly ripped out a page. On the blank verso he scrawled a note: *If you ever need me, contact Muriel Lester at Kingsley Hall. She will get in touch with me. Be safe, please, yours, Shiv.* He slipped the note inside the book, leaving a small edge of it showing on the top, and stepped out onto the platform. He did not want to put Lucy in danger so he strolled down the platform casually and approached an army officer who was shouting out orders: "Last call, gentlemen. Get your bits and bobs now, just a few minutes before we're off."

"Officer," he said, drawing closer to the man. "May I ask if you have a Lucien Calthorpe in your regiment?"

"You know, I think you're in luck. He's among the troops here—fancied I just saw him. He's here. Have a look!"

"I'm in a hurry, sir, but if you would be so kind as to give this to him." Shiv handed the book over. "Happy to oblige," the officer said, taking it from him. Shiv watched him walk over to Lucy and hand him the book. Shiv blanched, resisting the urge to step forward. His body was blazing with memory. Lucy stared at him solemnly but Shiv averted his gaze, unable to meet his eyes. Some deep sense of tragedy had overcome him. But his feet continued to walk towards Lucy, whose puzzled expression soon turned to panic. Yet the pull was so strong. He had nearly reached him when the officer in charge blocked his path. "Sir, we're going to be off now." He put his hand on Lucy's arm and shunted him out of the way. "All right, boys," he called out to the troops. "Off we go!" Shiv's body was on fire—so close, and yet so far, he thought as he stood there, feeling the palpitations in his body recede. The soldiers extinguished their cigarettes; Lucy looked back once, a long, lingering look. Then the shutters came down and he turned away and boarded the train.

"Good luck to your troops," Shiv told the commanding officer, who was scanning the platform for stray sheep.

"Thanks, sir. Afraid we're going to need it more than ever. But our youngbloods are ready and keen to be off. And who can blame them?" Feeling suffocated by the man's cheerfulness, Shiv slipped away, into the dark of the station, and away from those crushed mint green eyes.

As he went down the stairs to the underground, he realized he'd forgotten about Muriel's flowers. His body, still in the clutch of an exquisite desire akin to pain, was in mourning as he got into the District Line train that would take him to Bow Road Station, close to Kingsley Hall. It seemed to him as though all his fellow passengers were suffering loss—their faces spoke of other times, their eyes blurry with tears or lack of sleep, their faces lined with anxiety. Stoically, they carried their personal burdens as the train lurched from stop to stop. He couldn't stop thinking of Lucy in his pathetic uniform. You could love two people equally, and both could inspire the deepest affection. But only one would be able to reach you there, at the core, where you burn. Both their voices came to him now: her pleasing, medium-high register, alert, prescient, reflecting her gift for anticipating disasters. Sinks were filled with water before pipes froze; panes taped down before a strong wind forced them out; nappies changed before Iris could belt out howls. It was a cheerful daytime voice, and it brought order and stability to their lives.

Lucy's was a night voice. It had wit and rhythm, it was vibrant and velvety, it promised pleasure, purred naughtiness.

Yet you instantly felt his bite when it came. Lucy could hurt like no one else. Even before he swam into view, Shiv heard his voice. A deep-throated warble with honey in it. And there, in the undertone, the sheathed dagger, the ice pick.

It was the most eloquent calling card for his body.

"[H]er phantom / sifting through my fingers, / light as wind, quick as a dream in flight." Virgil's Aeneas, mourning for his dead wife, Creusa, who disappeared as they fled a burning Troy. Two loves he'd had, more than anyone deserved. Lost both, hadn't he, lost them both.

As his ship plows through serrated waters, the slight rocking movement from side to side not unpleasant, he flits from his memory of Lucy in soldier's uniform at Victoria Station to another sharp recall: of a vivid blue-green summer day. It was dark, cold, and dingy in the Bayswater flat. "On a day like this, we should be out on the river," Lucy said. It was the perfect day for it, Shiv agreed. He did not have to be in the courts that day and Lucy's social calendar was similarly unfettered. While Shiv washed, Lucy made some ham sandwiches and filled a flask with tea. "We can picnic off the river somewhere." They packed a small canvas bag with a tablecloth and napkins, their lunch and a half bottle of wine.

AT CRANFORD PARK, they rented a rowboat from a man who had set up a stall by the River Crane. "I'll row," Shiv said. Lucy looked at him, his eyebrows raised. As they slid the boat onto the water, Shiv picked up the oars. Lucy laughed. "That's a sight! I never saw you as the sporty type," he said. A deep calm filled Shiv as they took off. The full rush of an English summer framed a serene river. Vegetation bubbled on its surface, creatures slid off mossy stones and into the river. Sounds of croaking frogs and hovering bees, and the whirr of crickets in fronds on the banks filled the air. The light on the water, a cool lemon green, covered the water. A light breeze pleasantly ruffled its surface. Fish glided past, their silhouettes lacing the water with movement. The sky was a celestial blue, cerulean, the clouds without a hint of grey, and the grass sprang emerald green on either side of the banks. Bowed branches of willows brushed the water's surface; birds swooped low and came up with tiny fish in their beaks. Was this real, Shiv asked himself, remembering a tea towel the wife of a colonial administrator back home had given his mother—that perfect English scene of darting birds, serene river, and flowering nature in communion? He still didn't know. A day like this was a gift. That's why it was commemorated.

Not a soul around. No one to gape at them; no one looking to lock them up. It was a blessing and that is how they took it—as a gift from the gods.

"You're a good rower," Lucy said. It was high praise from a man who had been sculling on the Thames from an early age, rising to become one of the most powerful rowers on his team in the annual Oxford-Cambridge Thames boat races. He was sitting back like a pasha, watching Shiv with a thinking look, his hands trailing the water. He had stripped down to his underpants; his torso was bare. Shiv watched him, too, as he rowed. He had also stripped down to his shorts but had a vest on. Sunlight flickered on and off Lucy's skin, giving him a golden hue. They were alone on this stretch of the water. As the birdsong got louder the farther they got down the river, Shiv felt lulled by the calm, his body in tune with the steady rhythmic push and pull of wood against water. He felt alive and engaged; his senses were keeping up with his emotions. Smell, sight, sound, touch, movement, all were thrumming together. He wasn't fighting anything. It was a rare peace.

After some time, Lucy suggested they stop and explore the woods alongside the river. "I'm hungry, aren't you?"

"I could eat, yes." They tethered the boat and stepped onto the muddy shore. As they walked along silently, companionably, Shiv felt none of the anxieties that plagued him in London. Here, he felt as free as a bird. Hares stopped and stared then hopped off into the woods. Birdcalls floated out from the leafy canopies of trees, a woodpecker somewhere was drumming into the bark of a tree with satisfied grunts, pausing to trill luxuriously from time to time. "There's a stream ahead, let's stop and eat lunch there," Lucy said.

He set down a yellow gingham checked tablecloth and napkins, placed two plates and glasses on them, and opened the bottle of wine.

"A little early, isn't it?" Shiv asked.

"It's a picnic," Lucy said. "Picnics are by definition daytime affairs. What's a picnic without wine?"

Shiv watched him swirl the wine around his glass, sniff it. "Hmm," he said. "Well, cheers!" He held up his glass, Shiv raised his in return, and they both smiled at each other as if they both knew exactly what the other was thinking. Then Shiv saw a school of fish, the size of large sardines, wriggling in the water. He took off his shoes and socks and walked to the edge of the stream. The fish, their tiny orange-and-white double fins flapping against their dark grey bodies, drew closer. "Aren't they meant to be doing the opposite, running away from me, a big, bad human?"

Lucy nodded. "They're probably too young for suspicion. Look at them! Babies!" They were encircling Shiv's ankles, their flicking tails flashing orange around his feet. *Stay! Play with us!* Cloud formations were ingenious for self-protection—sardines curling into a ball, cutting through the water as one tight body; starlings rising in their murmurations; wolves hunting in a pack. These fish were nipping at his heels playfully, showing no fear. Shiv laughed delightedly, wriggling his toes in the cool water. He had never felt more carefree. Lucy had gone back to their picnic. "The other creatures here aren't going to be as friendly. Some of them have been sending rapacious looks at our lunch." A couple of squirrels were sitting straight up on their hind legs, fixated on their sandwiches. Shiv joined Lucy. They ate quickly. There wasn't a single footfall—not one human around anywhere. Sunlight sifted through tree branches like rain. After lunch, they lay next to each other. "Take off that damn T-shirt!" Lucy commanded. Shiv complied. Now they were both naked, and it was the most natural thing in the world to have Lucy's arms encircle him, their lips touching, then their tongues, and finally a deeper embrace that brought them together. This is what it means to be free, Shiv thought. Lucy murmured, "We should come here every day." He was light and spontaneous, his movements natural and in accord with his feeling and Lucy was fully aware of it, of his delight at newfound freedom.

IT WAS DUSK by the time they got back into the boat. Fireflies flickered in the bushes, cool, clean air filled his lungs, there were wet socks on his feet, and river chill coursed up his legs and into his body. English bone-chilling damp, but what he felt was happiness as he saw Lucy's strong arms, russet now under the fading rays of the sun, plying the oars of their boat towards home. Lucy was as light and happy as he. You could see it in the shine in his eyes. So close their connection was that evening, the need for words had disappeared. Shiv felt his words and thoughts were transparent to Lucy and Lucy's to his, and they were the same; there were no boundaries between them. They were communicating at a different level now—open in a way they had not been to each other. Same yet different.

The previous day, Shiv had been shopping and procured garlic and ginger, some spices, and with some substitutions, cooked a chicken curry, some lentils, and rice. He had remembered, as if by instinct, what to use, how to cook it. Lucy had never eaten an Indian meal before. That evening, after their idyllic day rowing on the water, Shiv laid the table and brought out the food. Their flat was filled with the aromatic flavors and scents of Indian food. Lucy said, "This is delicious, Shiv," eating everything with pleasure, it seemed.

"I've never cooked in England before, never mind an Indian meal."

"You're a magician."

Shiv watched him eat, his facial expressions reflecting the foreignness of the tastes in his mouth. He chewed thoughtfully, appreciatively, grimacing as he bit into a black pepperball. Was he eating the food just to please Shiv or because he liked it? It pleased him when Lucy asked for more.

It was the only time he was able to bring his country to Lucy.

On the eve of his departure for the talk in Glasgow in 1941, he went to visit the Polaks. Henry said, "I have heard disturbing reports of government surveillance of Indian students here, and by extension, of all those involved in anti-colonial activities. You're on their list, son. I've confirmed it and have it on good sources. Do be careful."

Shiv said, "But we've known this for a very long time. *Forward* is now seen as a flag bearer for the anti-war movement. It isn't just *satyagraha*. It speaks for resistance forces everywhere. But what is the alternative? Silence? A betrayal of everything we believe in?"

"Could you be a little less overt in broadcasting the magazine's political stance?"

"No, Millie. You beam broadly or not at all. We'd lose our readers' respect. Listen to the European exiles in Finchley talk about what the Gestapo have done to the Jews. We are at war now. We cannot stay silent. The only way forward is to fight them. We have to turn public opinion against them. It's the pacifists and conscientious objectors of our time we must listen to now."

Millie said, "You must be more restrained. It is very dangerous."

"He knows that," Henry said. "But he is on fire. This is exactly what happens when Gandhi wins the hearts and minds of people. They become zealous converts. Gandhi doesn't need violence. Words are his heavy artillery. You could aim low for hate, as Hitler has, or go high for love. Gandhi's arrow strikes at the highest point—where we can dream of a better world, a world without strife. He just has to set men on fire—best fighters in the world there." His pride in Shiv was obvious. His own people were being massacred in Europe. His firebrand "son" was doing his best to combat the forces of evil.

Shiv laughed. " 'Sacrificial fire' he called it, in my case."

"Be careful," Millie said.

# The Empress of Scotland, July 1941

He sees Millie Polak's face now, anxious, full of premonition. It was exactly as they had feared. He remembers the horror of the moment when he was shot—the aim, the hits, the collapse. But he had survived. He would return to London, and to his life there eventually. Tibor, Alix, and Julian would manage the magazine in his absence. He'd picked the pieces, the editorial changes had been discussed with the writers, the covers chosen for six months' worth of issues. After that, fully recovered, he expects to be back at the helm again at *Forward*. "No one ever leaves London," Lucy had once told him. "And if they do, they dream of coming back. The haunted ones return, like salmon, to the rivers where they were spawned."

It is this expectation that helps him endure the new ritual of being taken up to the deck by Will and Mairi. They hold on to him as he limps along and up the ramp, a slow unsteady step at a time. Up here, he breathes deeply. The vast sea stretches out before him. They take him up only when it is calm, the winds subdued, the sun flooding the deck. They walk slowly up and down; the cold air catches his breath, perforates his lungs.

The deck is deserted, apart from them. Gulls scream, swoop low, then high. They spy a heron—"Look! Look!" Mairi cries, pointing up at the sky. His dry lungs try to suck in the sea air, salt spray and wind making him gasp as he tries painfully to breathe. His legs are in better shape. Mairi makes him sit down on a bench, take slow, deep breaths, and lift one leg up at a time, gradually stretch it out. The effort is worth it to see the smile on her face. "You're getting better," she says. "You've strong legs." His spine hurts with the effort; his shoulders are like bars of lead; he's exhausted by these trips. But he must get better.

SHE's STARTED GIVING him sponge baths. "Your legs have some movement to them now. I can turn you around to wash you." He watches her squeeze the sponge in a plastic bowl of warm water, and begin mopping his face, his neck, his chest, his stomach. There is a fine line of sweat above her upper lip as she reaches between his legs, and runs the sponge over his private parts then under him, and down the inner thighs, down to his toes. She wipes him down in the front before inching him over to his side so she can wash his back. She doesn't say a word; it is work to her, and she wants to do it thoroughly. It's as if every crimp of skin has been examined and refreshed by her. She changes the sudsy water and washes out the sponge before beginning on his back. He wonders how she can stand it. His body feels worn and bony to him—the body of an emaciated refugee. Her care is moving to him.

"Right!" she says, as she finishes up. "We've got you ready for your curtsey to the king now!" He cracks a laugh.

When Mairi suggests she read to him, he nods yes. She places the three books she'd unpacked from the suitcase on his blanket. "Shall I continue with *A Passage to India*?" "Not that one," he says. That leaves the other two. He picks up Homer's *Odyssey*, turns to his father's neatly inscribed salutation on the title page. "To my son, who leaves India to embark on his own odyssey. May you return victorious, and earn the trust of your countrymen. Your loving father, Ramdas."

So like his father, who was sustained wholly by the universals that kept his world perfectly steady: trust, decency, loyalty, humanitarianism, worthiness, solidness. He never had to question his friendships, never had to look back at betrayal. He chose well. "If you can't trust a man's handshake, why would you trust his word?" There were the inevitable disappointments, which he would attribute to some misunderstanding or failing on his part. He wouldn't understand the deep dark undertow of love and desire, he wouldn't know how you could love one person, and yet give your heart to another, how the body, heart, and mind could all want different things, and how the war between them could tear a person apart. Not enough self-discipline, he would say. *Know thyself* was his life's maxim.

How would Shiv face his father, bearing not a laurel wreath but a body tattooed by the arrows and slings of love? He had no Telemachus, no Penelope waiting for him to return. No tail-wagging Argos would run up to him and know him instantly. No faithful swineherd Eumaeus would shelter him, no aged mother Anticleia would see through to his heart, no old nurse Eurycleia gathering his finest robes for his reunion with his queen. He had a son, somewhere, and a daughter who would not know him. What was he bringing back to them? A battered body and a heart shattered by loss?

He's not listening to Mairi reading. He likes the soothing sound of her voice but he's stopped paying attention to the words. He's thinking about his little girl, whether she'll recognize him. Of course she wouldn't—it has been more than a year since she left as a three-year-old; she's not even five yet.

He says, "I have a little girl I haven't seen for fourteen months."

Mairi stops reading, looks at him. "Your little girl?" She puts the book aside and picks up some sewing.

"Yes."

"What happened to her mother?"

He is silent. That cold room, the lifeless corpse. Her father crying "Murderer."

"She died."

She's eyeing him carefully. "Is your little girl there, in Karachi?"

"Yes. With my parents."

She nods. "They're her parents now. You will have to slowly, very slowly win her trust, become friends with her again. And then, after she's accepted you, you can be her parent. But it will take some time, you know that?"

He knows it. But his mind refuses to accept that she won't be waiting for him as he gets off the ship. "Dadda!" He hears her in all the places they've been—Covent Garden, Piccadilly Circus, Kingsley Hall, Catherine Street, Hyde Park, Thames Embankment. "Dadda!" That trill, ownership and delight both.

"So home. You asked." Mairi is repairing a tear in a bed sheet. How did it tear? he wonders. Did he create the rent?

"What?" He shakes himself out of his thoughts. "What did you say? Ah yes. I was asking you about your home." A thin slant of sun from the uncovered section of the porthole is on her hand as she works. He watches the shiny needle flash as it darts in and out of the fabric in her fingers. Tiny fish, their silver fins flashing, circling his ankles—where was that? Some river, somewhere in London. He stares at her fingers, feeling Lucy's arms around his shoulders.

"It's in Glasgow, by the River Clyde. It's like a person, that river. Deep soughing sounds as though it's crying. It's the winds coming off it. My mother used to say 'There's the river screaming.' It wailed during the long lonely winters when no one goes near it. Riverbanks are summer fairgrounds and winter graveyards."

"I grew up near a river, too—one of the longest rivers in the world. The Indus. Heard of it?"

She shakes her head. "River people are different, aren't they?" she says, biting off the thread with her teeth. "They hear things land-locked people can't. Those filthy gulls screeching, for example!"

He attempts to smile back but is exhausted. He closes his eyes and drifts away.

River. Desert. Wind. Rain. These are the elements that have

shaped us, inspired us, nearly destroyed us, he thinks. On the one side, the windswept Thar Desert. On the other, the fast-flowing Indus. At its widest point the river is one and a quarter miles; at its narrowest, no more than a yard. What a chameleon river it is—picking up the hues of the lands it soars past. Its intense movements are below the surface, where deep whirlpools suck in small trawlers. It is where the blind dolphin navigates its way and finds its food through a precise interpretation of the water's sonar waves. . . . He had dreamt of taking Lucy there one day, some day.

Rivers stem off the great oceans that cradle the earth. When they flow through our lands, we give them names: the Ganga, the Hudson, the Nile, the Amazon. But rivers belong to no one. The river brings its gifts to us, and some of us bequeath our bodies to it when we die, dreaming of our ashes scattering wide on its shimmering waves. For it has known our joy, and our melancholy, and calmed us when we've despaired. Who better to spirit us away on our final journey?

A few days later, Mairi bursts into his room, unable to contain her excitement. Face flushed, beaming a smile, she says, "You won't believe it! We are in Lagos, Nigeria! Shiv, we're here, we're in Africa." She's practically dancing around the cabin. "Will's coming down as soon as he can and we're taking you up there. It's warm, the sea is so blue—I've never seen it this blue. Aquamarine, emerald, turquoise, cobalt—all the blues and greens you can think of. But you know these seas, it's me, Mairi, from a cold, grey land, never been anywhere, never seen anything, who's so excited. Maybe I'll get you to laugh finally—at my madness. But I think you—no, even you will be amazed."

He laughs. His ribcage strains with the effort. Her enthusiasm kindles something in him, a need for the sharp broad rays of a tropical sun. "Is it sunny?"

"Blazing! Wait till you see it. Just wait till you get up there." She's by his side now with one of her rags, brushing off flecks, imagined or real, on his face, a comb sifting through his thinning hair. "No U-boats finally! Just tropical joy." His mind flashes a sunlit patch on Lucy's head—his unruly curls never settling, the wind and his own kinetic energy arranging and rearranging the frame around his face so that it was never the same. He could touch pieces of Lucy, never the whole. He remembers his hesitations now, the things he wanted to say but never told him—the way, elbows on the table, Lucy held one index finger by the side of his head as he listened, his full-beam look, the way his body appeared under the blankets those freezing mornings as he dressed to return to the Polaks'— defenceless, needing him. He had never told Lucy—unprovoked, spontaneously—how much he loved him. Lucy had craved the assurance. He'd never given it. His hand closes, as if over the lock of hair he imagines in his palm; his sharp fingernails cut into skin as he tightens his hold.

They lift him off the bed, Mairi and Will, and make him take one step at a time. Will is carrying all his weight and supports him as they walk up the flight of stairs to the upper deck. Shouts of laughter and clamouring people reach him.

Will sets him down in a lounge chair and props him up with pillows. His leg rests on a cushion, and he leans his neck forward, bewildered and excited by the scene before him. Men and women in rowboats come towards them, waving and shouting, "Welcome! Welcome!" They are like colourful prayer flags in their swaying boats, and their wide smiling faces and bright tunics and headdresses disorient him after the monotonous grey black and blue hues of sea and night that he has become accustomed to. Their children are laughing and shouting excitedly. The men and women in their boats have goods for sale: goats and chickens, papayas and mangoes. Small boys carrying string bags scamper up the rope ladder slung across one side of the ship to deliver purchases and take money from the passengers. Will buys a rooster. He forks over the money like a breeder at a livestock fair. "What do you reckon?" he says, holding it up and looking at Mairi.

"What? You going to cook it?"

"Nah," Will strokes the creature's head. "Charlie the rooster. He's got a name now. He can't be cooked. I'll keep him for company."

She laughs. "Much good that'll do you." The rooster stares back silently at them, its neck craning this way and that.

"So what'll you do, once you've dropped him off?" He points to Shiv with his chin.

"Don't know, Will, exactly. I guess I'll stay a while. See the country. I might even open a school."

"A school?"

"Yes, a school close to an Anglican church, maybe affiliated with it. St. Theresa's or St. Anne's School for Girls."

Shiv is hanging on to every word. *Now*, Shiv thinks. Now is the moment.

"Nah!" Will says. "Leave the saints out of it. I can see it now." He broadens his hands in the shape of a sign. "McNulty's School for Girls."

She stares at him. "Crikey! You reckon?"

"I can see it now."

She turns around, props her elbows on the railing. The wind is rustling her dress skirt this way and that, her hair's blowing around her face; she has an exhilarated look on her face. "Dreams, eh? This ship's a good one for them."

Shiv watches as Mairi, leaning on the deck's railing, turns to look at him with his eyes half closed, smiling as sunlight covers his face. Will has drawn closer to her, he notes. She faces the sea again. Is it the breeze carrying Will's words, for they reach Shiv clearly. "Miss Mairi, I have something to say."

Her head is taut, unmoving. He senses her nervousness, the butterfly wings of curiosity and desire.

"I don't want to say bye when we get to Karachi," he says. She moves a tiny bit closer to him, or is it his imagination. Shiv is glued to Will's back, watching for movement.

He says, "I've been thinking. I reckon you're going to need some help with that school. I'm good with building things. I don't want to go back to Glasgow. And we'll show the natives that not everyone who lands on their shores from Britain is an oppressor. That sometimes, they're friends. No rolling pins and knitting needles for your girls! We'll teach them to play rugby and sail. We'll give them bikes and cameras! What say you, Miss Mairi?"

She laughs. "You tickle me, Will Sinclair. You tickle the cockles of my heart!"

He's so delighted, Shiv can practically hear his feet tapping with joy. There is a long pause. Will he, won't he? No moment better than the present, Shiv nearly shouts out. He watches Will do the male dance—the drawing away, the steadying, the holding of chin in cupped hand, the firming of resolve, the deep breath. Then he says, "Miss Mairi, you would make me a very happy man if you would accept my hand in marriage." He goes down on bended knee and holds out his hand. There, he did it. Shiv lets out a long sigh of relief.

Mairi gives Will a long look, and then in full view of the crowds up on the deck, she leans forward, brushes past his outstretched hand, and plants a kiss on his lips. A huge round of applause follows as everyone up on the deck cheers the newly declared couple on board. When they come towards him hand in hand, Shiv gives them the thumbs-up. He can't stop smiling—his pretty nurse and the lively purser are engaged, and it's a match made under warm tropical skies, with soldiers singing and playing on their harmonicas, and papayas and mangoes as festive fare. Who would have imagined this a month ago?

THE ARAB MERCHANTS buy up all the fresh produce—fruits and vegetables. Their mixed-race children—a small group ranging from six to ten, blue-eyed and blond as well as dark-eyed and tanned—cling to their robes as they lean over the sides of the deck. The merchants peel their oranges and bananas, offer them to the children, and eat slowly, meditatively, as if considering what it has cost them to be without these things for so long. "Traders of spices and gold," Will says, looking in their direction. "But it's the war now. It's going to be a while before people have loose spending money again."

A group of men carry carpets onto the deck. They unfurl them and tamp down the edges. The kids are like wind-up toys, jumping up and down and playing hopscotch on them. "Why are they moving up here?" Shiv asks Will. He can't take his eyes off the children.

"Now that we're going south and it's turned warmer, they've been sleeping up here. Don't know why they do it. It's bloody freezing up here at night."

Finally, the ship sets sail again. There is a huge expanse of sea before them, and nothing else. Not one boat, not even a dolphin breaks its calm surface. Shiv watches as the British soldiers strike up a medley with their harmonicas. "Rule Britannia, Britannia rule the waves! / Britons never, ever, ever shall be slaves." Such is the rousing quality of the song on that lonely ship cutting through tropical seas that some men cry, and their voices, gathering intensity, rock the deck with their power. The Indian soldiers, from a sense of irony, or the need for correction, click their castanets and sing "Jana Gana Mana," a nationalistic song composed by Rabindranath Tagore. *"Jana gana mana, adhinayak jaye he / Bharata bhagya vidhata / Punjab Sindh Gujarat Maratha / Dravida Utkala Banga / Vindhya Himachala Yamuna Ganga / Ucchala jala di Taranga. / Tava shubh name jage / tava shubh aashish mage / gahe tava jaya gatha.*" Released from Britain, and not yet on British-ruled soil in India, the Indians probably think it's a neutral zone and therefore safe, on this ship cruising through the Atlantic Ocean, to sing their own rallying cry. The British soldiers pause, consider. But politics is not in the air; the ethos is of freedom, of joy. They say, "Nah," and smile blithely. It is a merry scene, Shiv considers. The need to sing and rejoice creates unexpected and surprising alliances. The British soldiers listen with bemused expressions on their faces to their singing trench brothers from the war fields of Europe. Some even cheer them along.

"What does it mean?" Mairi asks Shiv.

Shiv considers. In a few words, it was simply a reiteration of ancient religious beliefs: God is in everything. But Tagore wanted a huge sweep of the land and its people. "From the Punjab, and from Sindh, from Gujarat and Maharashtra, from the Dravidians and Orissans and Bengalis, and from the hills of Vindhya and the mountains of Himachal, from the flowing rhythms of the Jamuna and Ganges Rivers, and the chanting waves of the Indian Sea, you, Lord, are in everything." The vastness of the land, the diversity of its people, and the stupendousness of uniting them in one cause filtered through Tagore's exquisite understanding of what Gandhi was trying to achieve strikes him then.

She nods thoughtfully as he explains it to her. "Every Indian will feel the country's future when they sing it," she says. "Because it's about them, and they're all included."

Then, improbably, he hears a heart-shattering musical phrase sung by a soprano. It rises above everything, floats in the air. He cradles his ear trying to identify it. It is Cherubino's aria "Voi Che Sapete" from Mozart's *Figaro*. He stares in the direction of the music, wondering if it's his imagination or a real voice, in this place, singing. "Mairi!" he shouts in her direction. She comes running to his side. "What is it?"

"That music, do you hear it? Where. Is. It. Coming. From?" He's so shocked, he speaks slowly, one word at a time. Tell me what love is . . . she sings; the longing, the desire, the joy, the torment. He hears it in the voice drifting out of the window onto a delirious scene of caged birds let loose in a forest.

"Yes, I hear it. It's Miss Cecilia Stein, a Jewish émigré from London, who's going to Cape Town for a recital. The captain let her have one of the rooms up here on the deck to practice in, and it's so warm, she must have opened the windows. I like it," she says. "Don't you? She has a beautiful voice."

"*'Ricerco un bene fuori di me/Non so ch'il tiene, non so cos'è'*"— beyond me, beyond my compass, this feeling, I don't know what it is. . . . Miss Stein took him right back to Glyndebourne. That moment when he stopped reading, and listened. He listens now . . . *non so cos'è*. On this barren sea, filled with desire, he doesn't know either. . . .

"Don't underestimate Mozart," Lucy had told him after Glyndebourne. Banned until it was toned down quite considerably by Mozart's librettist so it could be performed in Vienna in 1786, the opera was a call for justice and equality. "Just three years before the French Revolution, do you realize? Lethal stuff this, for us toffs," Lucy said. "Equality has always frightened those who have much to lose by it."

As the Indian soldiers bring the last stanza of "Jana Gana Mana" to a close, the British soldiers pick up their harmonicas again. "Should auld acquaintance be forgot and never brought to mind?" they sing. Cecilia Stein, probably distracted by the noise on the deck, stops singing, and only the sound of the sea waves and the plaintive, high-pitched mouth organs break the sudden silence.


FOR DINNER, MAIRI has curry. "Where did this come from?" Shiv sniffs the air. "Curry?"

"Yes, goat. The Arabs let me have some for you," she says.

"They slaughtered a goat on board?"

"What do you think? This didn't come from Glasgow." She lifts a spoonful to her nose. "Ummmm. This smells delicious!" She's still feeding him.

His hands are too unsteady—he can't raise spoon to lip without spills. She doesn't like spills. "Too much work." So she feeds him, spoon by spoon. He notes everything—her face, the long angular shape of her fingers, the way her lips purse when she wants to tell him something but isn't sure she should, the arch of her fingers, how they tense as they draw close to his mouth.

He says, "Will's a good man. I thought he'd never have the courage to ask. I'm glad he braved it and you said yes."

She gives him a coy smile. "We're not going back home. We're already too big for Glasgow now."

"I see that. It's a good decision."

A week before they're scheduled to land in Muscat, Captain MacIntyre and his staff issue invitations to each cabin to a celebratory dance in the ballroom.

Will delivers theirs. "You'll come?" he asks Mairi.

"I wouldn't want to leave him alone."

"We'll take him."

Mairi turns to Shiv. "It's a celebration in the ballroom. A dinner dance. Would you like to go?"

"I heard. I'm not deaf yet. I can't dance, so no."

"We'll put you in a wheelchair and take you onto the floor," Will says.

"Oh, do let's go!" Mairi does a little click with her shoes and turns back a heel.

He's seen that look before, and he knows it wins every time. Determined, already decided. Julia, Lancaster Gate, the Savoy.

He frowns, stares into the distance.

"Well?" His nurse isn't going to hear no for an answer.

"All right." He exhales slowly.


IT IS CROWDED and festive with sparkling lights and brightly lit chandeliers. Everyone is up there, the Arabs on their way to Muscat, the Indians on their way to Bombay and Karachi, and the British soldiers and officers also due to disembark in Bombay on their way to their stations in India. Will wheels him in his chair to a table. A jazz band from New Orleans, on its way to the Taj Hotel in Bombay for the season, is on board and as they start playing, couples form— men with men and soldiers holding the hands of young Arab boys and girls as they take them to the dance floor. Will looks at Mairi. "Sir"—he bends low to speak to Shiv—"would you mind if I asked Mairi to dance?"

Shiv cracks a smile. What a delightfully old-fashioned young man this Will Sinclair is. "I do mind! She's my nurse, so bugger off!" Will gives him a stricken look. Shiv's jagged laugh makes Will stare. "Are you all right, sir?"

"Of course I'm all right! You silly lad—she's your fiancée now. You don't need my permission. Look at her face! Off you go!"

Mairi is like a ship, sails billowing, ready for takeoff.

They make a fine couple, Shiv observes, watching them dance. Apart from two women missionaries looking misplaced in calf-length tweed skirts, scarves tied around their heads, lace-up flat shoes, there are no other women in the ballroom. Mairi catches everyone's eye. In a green dress and high heels, a touch of red on her lips, it is as if Olivia de Havilland has been dropped on board. She's laughing and radiant as she rocks back and forth in a swing number. When they ease into a waltz, "That Lucky Old Sun," Shiv watches Will and Mairi gliding across the floor—and feels arms encircling him from behind. Oh Lucy, he cries. Stop, please go away. And then, *NO. Stay.*

By the time they circle back to him, his face is drenched in tears. "Oh hell," Mairi says. She doesn't ask him what made him cry. She shakes her head and asks if he wants to return to the cabin. "No, take me up to the deck," Shiv says. Mairi looks at Will, Will nods yes, and they leave the band and dance floor behind.

It's raining up on the deck. Within minutes, a full tropical storm is in play. Skies rent with lightning, thundering clouds, a sea rising in all its fury. "*Prone for us / buffetted, barnacled / tholing the sea-shock for us.*" A fragment. Who said it? He shakes his head in frustration, winces with pain.

"Will!" Mairi shouts. "Let's go back down."

"Just a few more minutes," Shiv pleads. They wait with him. He feels the sea's fury in his limbs, the lashing waves, the blinding streaks in the sky rock through his body. His eardrums are splitting with the noise. But he turns his face up to the sky and gulps down large drops of rain. Lit with lightning, the drops slide down his throat like fire. He's wet. They are all soaking.

Back in the cabin, she changes him, brings him a hot drink. He looks away from her, sips the Ovaltine.

"What happened up there?" she asks.

"I think I'll finally sleep tonight," he says.

# Sind, 1941

*The Empress of Scotland* has docked in Karachi. The excitement of arrival ripples through the ship, reaching their cabin even as Mairi does checks and rechecks to make sure they haven't left anything behind. Shiv is in a wheelchair. "I can walk," he tells Will.

"Barely," Mairi says. She wheels him out of the room.

They are waiting for him. He sees his mother, his father, little Iris. He reaches for his mother. Her eyes are disbelieving. He knows the stages of recognition from Odysseus's travails.

*Stage 1:* Stranger, who are you? Explain who you are. Scepticism. *Stage 2:* We see you. But seeing is not the same as believing. We can't accept you until we know you. *Stage 3:* The burden of proof. Show us you are who you say you are so we can see if you really are one of us. *Stage 4:* Acceptance of proofs given. *Stage 5:* Further persuasion through the honouring of the tribe—fitting back in. I am back here because I am one of you. Restoration at last. Ah, how hard he will have to fight for that one. He holds out his arms to his daughter. Iris looks at him, shields herself in the folds of his mother's sari. She is tall for four and a bit, and she eyes him curiously, without recognition. In his father's eyes there is coldness, an accusation he will probably never articulate: you have betrayed me.

He sees his old warrior-self departing from these shores, the battered ghost that has returned to them. They had reached for the stars. Now he is a lame man, drawing stares of pity and ridicule from all.

His mother reaches out to him. Her glad eyes, her smile—the uplifted corners of her lips, the relief on her face—tell him that she is happy he is home. Trust would be hard-earned and would come when she has assured herself that he is again one of their own. He will have to win the others over. That he should be planning a charm offensive on first gazing at his family after a decade's absence seems strange, ridiculous to him.

His mother looks at Mairi. Shiv says, "This is Mairi McNulty, my nurse. She took good care of me all the way here."

Leela reaches forward and embraces her. "Thank you, my dear." His father says, "Please join us at our hotel for tea."

Mairi says, "We—my fiancé and I—will be going to the crew members' hotel, along with some of the ship's crew who are disembarking here. Shiv is in good hands now." She smiles at them. Shiv knows she wants him to be alone with his family, after such a long journey home.

"But join us at least for a cup of tea," his mother says.

"Yes, all right," she says, giving Will a look. Will is standing a short distance behind her. She reaches for his hand. He nods assent.

They get into a taxi. Shiv's father gives the taxi driver their address—it is a hotel in Karachi, where they would spend the night before travelling home to Hyderabad Sind, a three-hour drive away.

Shiv is helped into the family car. When it stops at a traffic light, his eyes drift to a massive billboard advertising a Bollywood film. A beautiful young woman with luscious red lips and a beguiling face looks back at them. With a shock of recognition, he sees it's the young woman he had married eleven years ago. Seher, who'd found her stars after all, not through a telescope but through the full-wattage beauty of her smile. His son, he feels his son reaching out to him forcefully through his mother's bright eyes.

He turns back to look at Iris, his blue-eyed daughter, gazing at him as at a stranger. He would make sure she knew him, called him Daddy, and embraced him as she once used to. He would be there for her from now on forever. And she would know it.

THEY SIT OVER steaming cups of tea and Marie biscuits. Leela wants to know all about the trip, her son's progress from the time they left England to their arrival in India. "You'll have to feed him well," Mairi says. "Wartime rations were poor on board—I had to coax him to eat and force-fed him all the way here."

His father says, "He was always a poor eater."

"And when did he start talking?" his mother asks.

"He was hesitant in the beginning, as if I wouldn't understand him and we spoke different languages. But once he knew I was his nurse, he became quite a chatterbox! I know all about the Indus River now, and the blind dolphins, and the people who come down from the hills in their brightly coloured caravans."

"Yes." Leela laughs. "He loves the river."

The conversation went from the ship's arrival in Lagos, and the excitement of being in tropical waters, to the storms on board. "It was not a comfortable crossing then," his mother says.

"It wasn't so bad," Shiv cuts in. "It was a good journey." As he recalls it now, it appears as a soft buffer zone between two ports of tension and trouble. "Mairi left me to my dreams and I was grateful for it."

Leela wants to know her son's present condition. "He looks well but can you tell me what we should be careful about?"

"He needs time, that's all," Mairi says. "His recovery will be complete—but it will take a few months. He must walk to develop muscle strength, and have regular conversations with people to keep his speech patterns coherent and distinct. The effort to be understood leads to clearer speech." Shiv sees his mother's anxious eyes flit from Mairi to Ramdas. Something's going on. There must be something wrong with me, he thinks.

"So has he been stuttering, or does he have memory lapses, things like that?" his father asks.

"No, not at all. He's fully present, his memories are crystal clear. He is keen to bond again with Iris, and I know she will keep him very busy!"

Iris has been playing with her doll and she looks up as she hears her name. Leela purses her lips. Another point of tension, Shiv notes.

"What will you do in India?" Leela asks.

"Well, Will and I met on the *Empress of Scotland*"—she glances at him and smiles—"and we're now engaged. We were thinking we would stay in India for a while, perhaps set up a school for girls here."

Will, who has not spoken yet, says, "No good us being here unless we're doing something to help the country—education is prized here, isn't it?" He's quite terse, as if he doesn't know how to present as an engaged couple. Mairi will set him right, Shiv thinks. She has the touch.

Leela gives them a surprised look. "A school?"

"Yes. I don't mean a missionary school. I mean a modern school with a curriculum comparable with those in English schools, a real place of learning and personal development. I was a nurse at St. Thomas's School in Glasgow and often substituted for teachers, as needed."

"That sounds like a very good idea," his father says. "We will need more and more of them as time goes on. Indian parents want to educate their girls, give them the same opportunities as their boys. Things are already changing here, under Gandhiji's influence."

Mairi asks, "May I?" looking at Shiv's mother as she goes to Iris. Leela nods. The little girl looks up. Mairi takes her by the hand—Iris doesn't resist—and puts her on the chair beside her. Mairi takes out a small pad of paper with the *Empress of Scotland* emblem on it from her purse and tears out a sheet. She folds it several times, and it is a bird. The little girl watches as Mairi slips her index finger into the paper body of the bird, her thumb and middle finger into the two wings, and makes it fly. Iris wants to try. As her fingers slide into the body and Mairi shows her how to move her fingers, Iris beams and looks around at them all. "I can fly!" she says. They all laugh. It pleases Shiv that Iris and Mairi have bonded. Iris puts her hand on Mairi's arm and leaves it there. Then she turns her hand around, as if examining the feel of it, the coloration of it against Mairi's skin. Iris's white skin blends perfectly with Mairi's and the child seems fascinated by the lack of contrast. She looks up at Mairi, who gives her a hug. Iris suddenly bursts into tears. Leela rushes towards her and tries to calm her down.

Mairi says, "She's probably overexcited and we must be off soon. The ship's captain offered us an introduction to his aunt who has a house up in the mountains. We're going to explore to see if it's a good spot for the school. We leave tomorrow at dawn."

"You're really serious, then?" Shiv asks.

"Never been more inspired to do something," Mairi replies. Shiv's father says, "I can't believe I nearly forgot." He takes out an envelope and hands it to her. "It's the wages we agreed on and something extra to sweeten the pot."

Mairi takes it from Ramdas and thanks him.

His mother suddenly goes to Mairi. "I want to give you this," she says, taking off the gold necklace around her neck and holding it up to the nurse.

"Oh, Mrs. Advani, I couldn't possibly take it. You've both been generous enough already."

"No," Leela says. "I want you to have it. Thank you for bringing my son home."

Mairi sees Leela is determined. She bends her head. Leela slips the chain over her head and adjusts it around her neck. "There," she says. "It looks beautiful on you!" The gold necklace around Mairi's neck glitters like a snake—it moves with the light, removes her from Shiv in her radiance. He can't stand how it alters her.

He cringes. It's too much. It's probably making Mairi feel deeply uncomfortable. In his head, he hears Virginia Woolf's marbly voice saying, "Too! Too!" It is. But, he tells her silently, it's generous. It's large-hearted, even if it's too too. It's how we do things, we Indians. He suddenly experiences not revulsion but a moment of pride. He knows Indians can be insufferably cocky, ambitious, competitive, all-knowing—he's seen it in England at gatherings like the ones in Nanking's as their egos vied with one another, as each group tried to grandstand over the other. We are a tribal people, in the end, and that tribalism would be the fatal flaw. But for that one moment, pure, crystalline, he experiences pride in Indian too-tooness; applied to generosity, could anything be too too?

He's desolate as Mairi picks up her things to leave. Will gets up, at the ready by her side. She's found a new life, a life she cannot wait to start living. She goes to Shiv. "You're an old trouper, you old bean, you are!" she tells him, putting her hands on his shoulders. "I'm expecting great things from you!" They hug, holding each other close. "Don't let the morbs get you now!" she says as she releases him. Then she's at the door. He watches his last connection to the land he left behind walk away, Will's arm linked through hers. Sadness fills him; it had been a long journey, a journey that brought reconciliation and the space for mourning, and she, his quiet, efficient nurse pottering about in the background, had seamlessly worked herself into it, so that even now, the memory of the mango she cut into slices and put on a plate comes with sweet fragrant juice running down his chin, the tugging motion of a ship churning through water, an old soldier mouthing the prayers of the dead, the excruciating contact of steel blade and raw skin while she shaved him, a warm sponge moving in circular motions on his back, and Lucy's warm body next to his. Her quiet presence had made Shiv a miner of his memories, and they would now be the ballast against the onslaughts of his childhood home.

Back home in Hyderabad Sind, he is given his old room. As he is taken there, limping in with his crutches, he feels torn; everything is just as it was when he left a decade ago. The young boy who went away is not the battered man who has returned. He does not know who he is now. They have put out a tray of sweets, cakes, nuts, and a flask of tea. He is famished and eats all the nuts and milk cakes on the tray, sips the strong tea. A young male servant knocks on the door and comes in. He goes straight to the bathroom and begins filling a bucket with water. Bath time, Shiv realizes—his first bath in seven weeks. Mairi had given him sponge baths on the boat, her strong arms running washcloths across his face, his arms, wiping away the sweat of his nightmares. He looks at the steaming bucket of water. He is seated in a wheelchair covered with waterproof fabric. The servant lathers his body, his hands expertly washing his private areas, shampoos his hair, and showers water from a copper jug all over his body and head to wash off the soap. He dries him vigorously, edging the towel behind and inside his ears, his belly button, between his toes. They do not have a language between them even for small talk. Shiv tries to remember basic phrases—How are you? Do you live in the house? Instead he says, "Shukriya," the only Urdu word he can remember, "Thank you," over and over again, until the man's poker face cracks into a smile. He makes a gesture for sleep. The man helps him to the bed, and puts his hand behind Shiv's back as Shiv slowly lowers his body onto the sheets. The man moves Shiv's feet carefully, straightens his torso, his legs, adjusts the pillows under his neck and head. He pulls a blanket over him; then, satisfied that he has performed his duties to the best of his ability, nods his head and leaves the room. Shiv falls asleep immediately.

---

THAT EVENING, BEFORE dinner, his parents come to see him. His mother says, "You're looking better already. I am sure you will recover quickly here."

He nods. "Mairi McNulty is a wonderful nurse. She took such good care of me."

"Yes," she says. "What a lovely woman. I wish they had stayed longer—we could have had them visit us in Hyderabad Sind."

He's thinking of the moment Iris left her hand on Mairi's arm, as if the lack of difference was startling, somehow so odd that it sparked some emotional disturbance in his daughter. Did Mairi make her recall Julia? Iris's fascination with Mairi told him that the last few hours of Julia's life had left an indelible mark on the child. He would never know what had happened between them in the hours before she died. But that experience had branded his daughter and would always be there.

His father says, "I want you to see Gandhiji's letter to me." He hands him a sheet of paper. Shiv reads:

My dear Ramdas,

I have your letter. You have good news from Mr. Polak. Shiv is recovering well. The doctor's report does not disturb me at all. Naturally he has to be careful, and he has used an expression which need not frighten us. I am already in correspondence with Polak. Any letter going from me to Shiv is likely to excite him. Therefore, for the time being I shall confine myself to writing to Polak. I have already written to Mirabehn or Agatha Harrison, I forget which, that Shiv should be induced to return to India. When the proper time comes, I shall not fail to write to Shiv directly and press him to come back, because I am quite clear in my mind that if he came here he would be quite all right. If he remains unhappy here, he might later on go back.

Yours sincerely,
M. K. Gandhi

"We spoke to Mr. Polak," his father says, "and told him to make arrangements with Madeleine Slade for you to be sent home with a nurse on board. She was in daily touch with Grace Blackwell and sent us reports via cable. We were beside ourselves with worry."

"I'm sorry I caused so much discomfort, Father."

"It was not your fault. However, activism is often a bloody affair. I wanted you to stay as far as you could from that."

There is a long silence. "What is the expression the doctor used?" Shiv asks.

"Oh, we will have the doctors here examine you. I'm sure the British doctor was doing his job."

"What was it, Father?"

"Seizures," he says. "Due to cerebral damage. But there is no evidence of it so far—Miss McNulty has assured us that your speech, as you began your road to recovery, kept improving day by day. That your mind is sharp. We are not worried on that account."

"What, then?"

"Your mother and I are rather anxious about Iris, and how she will take this."

"I have come back home," he says.

"Out of necessity, not out of choice," Ramdas says, looking at him gravely. "As Gandhiji says in his letter, no one knows what you will do next. You must first get better. In the meantime, it is best that Iris not be told anything. Let's wait a little to see how you fare."

"Wait? Wait for what? I am her father, shouldn't she know this?"

His mother says, "We think that you should not rush it. She has her uncle Jacob. He tells her stories about her mother; she now speaks to her mother endearingly. 'Mummy, what do you think?' she says, as if she's in the room with us. You will confuse her now. Let her get used to you. She knows Jacob is not her Papa, knows we are Dadi, Dada."

"In time," his father says, "she will develop a relationship with you. We will see then. You must think about her welfare now, not your desires. She is a happy, normal child, despite her losses, and a great deal has gone into that, from Jacob's efforts to ours. You can gradually build a relationship with her."

He breaks like the mast of a ship hit by a tempestuous wind. His face feels hot with rage. His pulse is racing. His mother tries to bring the temperature in the room down. "Look!" she says, handing him a piece of paper. "Look at this!"

It is a cutting from the evening edition of the *Sind Observer*.

## INDIAN BARRISTER FASTS
## FOR THREE MONTHS IN LONDON

### FRIEND REMOVES HIM TO NURSING HOME
### WHERE HE STARTS TAKING NOURISHMENT

#### [FROM OUR CORRESPONDENT]

KARACHI, 7 AUGUST

The sensational news that Mr. Shiv Advani, barrister, and editor of *Forward* magazine in London, having finished a fast of 90 days there, has been received at Karachi by his father, Mr. Ramdas, a leading lawyer of the city. The fast was kept secret by him from his parents and others all these days and the cause of it is still unknown. It is, however, learnt that it was embarked upon him suddenly on his return from the Continent on completion of a tour of propaganda for India, after which he went to a small village in England in the company of a friend and commenced it. This friend was attending upon him for the whole period.

For about the first four weeks, Mr. Advani wrote weekly letters to his parents, but they were stopped subsequently owing to his frail health. On completion of these three months of fast, he wired to Mr. H. S. Polak, who hurried to his bed and removed him in a delicate condition to a nursing home where Mr. Advani has started taking nourishment and is progressing well.

Information of the fast was revealed for the first time by cables despatched by Mr. Polak to Gandhiji, and the parents of Mr. Advani.

Mr. Shiv Advani has been doing very valuable work in Britain and in Europe for the last seven years in the cause of freedom for India.

Shiv takes a deep breath. His eyes burn as he looks at them. "I wasn't on a hunger fast! I had just given the most important speech of my career as an activist and editor in Glasgow. The library halls were packed—my talk resonated with them. Mill workers, miners, builders, nurses, librarians—all joined in thunderous applause, and then I was shot."

"We know, son. Henry Polak has told us everything. Gandhiji knows what we know."

"Then how did this get published? It's utter rubbish. I'm not a defensive, hunger-fasting sort of protester. After years of being advised to keep silent, to accept what I was told without objection, I now speak loudly, from the pit of my stomach, and I abhor the idea of fasting to make a point. This simply isn't true!"

"Son, Gandhiji and the rest of our leaders are in a very delicate situation. After centuries of fighting the British on our soil, we are finally nearing our goal of making them quit India. Negotiations are taking place at a very high level now. No one wants this process jeopardized. You are being seen as a hero for all your work in the cause of Indian independence."

"Yes, but the truth is that I was nearly killed. And no one seems to know who tried to kill me. Why not state that? Why let the truth be distorted like this?"

"It is not the right time for insinuations, particularly if the public feels you're one of our heroes. Violence could break out at any point. Tempers are high—passions on fire."

"So it's best to blame me for what happened, is it? Father, I worshipped you for your adherence to truth. You were my beacon; all through those years in London, I referred to you in all my speeches as the lawyer who promised journalists bail if they would report the truth. How could you agree to this?"

"I did not," his father says grimly. "The reporters spoke to the Mahatma directly."

Shiv turns to his mother. "Why did you think this would make me happy?"

"They have acknowledged all the heroic work you've done for India. That makes me proud. I thought you would be proud, too."

AFTER THEY LEAVE his room, he sinks back on the pillows. He had come back—not to the loving bosom of a family, but to the authoritarian stronghold it always was. They would tell him what to do. They would take control, smooth out his rough edges, present him to the world again, transformed, worthy of being a hero to his people, the man they had all been waiting for to fulfil their destiny.

∽

In the days that follow, he maintains a tight-lipped silence, waiting for Jacob to arrive from Karachi. When Jacob comes for lunch, Iris, dressed in a lovely new frock, waits for her uncle to walk in. She sits quietly in a chair, her eyes pinned to the front door, humming from time to time and swinging her legs. Shiv feels a deep stab of pain. It reminds him of the times Jacob would come to visit them at their Catherine Street flat, and Iris, already alerted by some sixth sense to Jacob's approaching presence, would waddle to the door, waiting patiently for him. He was the only person who could comfort her when they were all in the flat together, assessing Iris's needs while he and Georgina tried to make sense of what had happened to Julia. "My princess!" he cries, as soon as he sees her. She jumps into his arms.

SHIV STARES AT his brother-in-law, scarcely believing that someone from his life in London, such a familiar person, should be in his house, with his parents, in India. Seeing it in person, Jacob's complete fit, his lack of discomfort and his embrace of his sister's in-laws, is pleasing. It's not Jacob's fault that Iris prefers him to her own father, Shiv tells himself. It is a while before Jacob can greet him for Iris wants her uncle's complete attention. She jabbers on and on, filling him in on school and her swing and her new doll. Jacob is mesmerized, as always. "Hello, old chap," he says, finally releasing himself and coming to Shiv. He envelops him in a bear hug. It's the first bit of real affection Shiv's felt since his return, that very warm, very Indian hug, and it's quite apparent that Jacob is the more native "son" at the table that afternoon. He's dressed in a linen achkan and narrow pants, summer garb for middle-class Indians, and is wearing open leather sandals on his feet. Shiv is dressed in a shirt and trousers, and is wearing a summer jacket, which would have been more at home in the smarter precincts of London than in hot, dusty Hyderabad Sind. His feet are in socks and brogues.

"I didn't see you as the fasting sort," Jacob says.

Shiv laughs. "I'm not, you know that."

"Right." Jacob doesn't probe him on what happened. He probably suspects the truth and doesn't want it confirmed. A delicate time, his father had said. In the halls of power, and in their own home, Shiv thinks, suddenly seeing what his parents were protecting—Jacob's relationship with Iris, which was stabilizing and loving. Later, out in the garden, Shiv thanks him for everything he's done for Iris. "I don't want to take the reins from you, old chap," Jacob says. "You realize that, I hope." So he says, but Shiv cannot help noticing how his eyes constantly flit to Iris, seeing where she is; and she, the sought one, smiles back, reassuring him that he's the one she will always turn to. She's as aware of him as he is of her. Her internal rhythm is set to his weekly visit from Karachi and she takes her place by the door awaiting his arrival knowingly.

It's Jacob's connection with his dead sister, Shiv knows. Their bond is deep, trusting, familial. Jacob will not give up his role in Iris's life that easily. And he, her father, muzzled and bound, cannot offer his child anything.

"Of course," he says. "But you're going to have to hold them for a while longer. My parents don't want me to tell Iris I'm her father."

"Why?" He has a genuinely puzzled look on his face. "Why would you hide it?"

"I don't want to. But Gandhiji's put it into their heads that I may not stick around long enough to actually have a proper relationship with my daughter."

Jacob asks if he was thinking of going back to London after he was better. The frown on his face tells Shiv that he doesn't see that as a good idea.

"I don't know, Jacob," Shiv says. "There's a war on, for one thing. And there's not much to go back to, other than *Forward*."

"That journal might have caused the trouble you're in, actually," Jacob says. Is he referring to why he was shot?

"Why do you say this?" Shiv asks.

Jacob turns away, making it quite clear that he's not going any further.

They are on opposite sides of the fence now, Shiv realizes, in a way they had never been in England. Jacob knows it. He knows it. Shiv dreads what it will do to their relationship.

"What has happened to you?" his mother asks, after Jacob leaves. "You went an Indian, you have come back a pukka babu, an Englishman! You were irritated when Shankar didn't come in to change the plates for fruit after lunch. I saw it! Jacob didn't even notice. You have more requirements now than the English!"

We go to foreign shores, charged with the directive to become like the natives, he wants to tell her. It's an uphill struggle but then we manage it, we become like them so we don't stand out, so we are accepted, and then our countries don't want us, our families feel betrayed. "What has happened to you?" they ask and we have no answers.

# Gandhi Ashram, Wardha, India

## April 1942

The invitation, characteristically, is direct and unspecific: "Come to Wardha to see me. I have much I wish to discuss with you." Shiv responds immediately, not knowing if he was going for the first meeting of the Quit India movement rumoured to be held there, or to experience true ashram life, the Gandhian way.

THE BUS TO Sevagram stops outside a walled compound with an open gate that reveals a simple dwelling within. A cement structure with a verandah and a shingled roof, it shows no signs of life. Suitcase in hand, he walks towards it uncertain of where he is, if this is the right place. The bus has sputtered away, leaving a dust cloud behind. A solitary goat munches on a bush outside the compound. He walks into the building and is in some sort of office area. There is a typewriter and a cabinet, there is a bench by the wall. There are two simple wooden chairs by the bench. The walls are unadorned, the floors bare, the windows have vertical iron rods in them, like prisoners' cells. But this is no prison. It is filled with a quiet presence, serenity. Encouraged by the sound of clattering pots in the adjoining room, he walks towards it. The kitchen staff are preparing a meal under the supervision of a small woman in a sari, its border draped around her head. Kasturba. Or Ba, as she was familiarly known. He goes to her. "Mrs. Gandhi, I have come to see Gandhiji from Hyderabad Sind. My name is Shiv Advani."

"I know," she says. "Bapu is expecting you. Wait here. He will come soon." And she continues doing her work without paying him any further attention. She is shy, Henry Polak had said. Doesn't speak much, though she has plenty to say, Millie had told him. Shiv stands there in that disconnected space, in awe of Ba, of her connection to his English guardians, to his American mother-in-law, Georgina Chesley, who told him she had spent the happiest time of her life there, and to India's history.

GANDHI ARRIVES AN hour later, during which he has been offered tea and wholemeal biscuits by the kitchen staff. Gandhi is in a meditative mood but his eyes catch Shiv standing there, suitcase by his side, and he comes towards him and envelops him in a tight embrace. "My boy."

SHIV IS TAKEN to a small shed and encouraged to freshen up. There is a pitcher and drinking jar, a small wooden table, a hurricane lamp, and the charpoy is a bedstead with woven slats. A folded blanket at one end and a slender pillow are the only pieces of bedding provided. An adjoining extension to the hut contains a bucket and a pail, and a simple commode. He takes a cold bath, puts his clothes away on the shelves in a corner of the room, and prepares for lunch.

THE BUILDING HE had first entered is now full of people. Everyone is squatting on the floor. There are brass plates in front of each person and pottery glasses made of red earth for water. A musician plays on a vina while Gandhi, with his eyes closed, his hands pressed together in prayer, begins chanting. As soon as he has finished, young men and women dressed in simple grey-and-white tunics over their white saris, with white fabric belts fastened around their waists, come with brass buckets of food. They go silently around the room, filling each brass plate with small portions of food, and another server comes out of the kitchen with a platter piled high with chapattis, flatbread meant to be eaten by scooping up the food on the platter. Everyone eats with their hands. He stares at them, and tries to imitate them, spilling food on his trousers and on the floor. In the end, hunger takes over despair, and he eats ravenously. The food is strictly vegetarian, and delicious. After they have finished, the servers come round to collect the platters. Then young girls holding fruits in their aprons come out again and offer the guests nuts, dried fruits or fresh ones—an apple, a peach, a plum, or a banana.

In the afternoon, small boys and girls from nearby schools affiliated with the ashram assemble before them and begin singing hymns, accompanied by a small band of musicians and their flutes, tablas, and violins. The children's sweet high voices are earnest, in perfect sync with one another. Look at us, they say. We are the future. It is a shrewd touch, a powerful reminder to all assembled there of what is at stake. After the performance, people leave and come back with their spinning wheels. Cotton yarn is threaded onto spindles and wheels begin turning clockwise, then anticlockwise, to make tight threads out of the yarn that can then be woven into cloth. The room is suddenly transformed by humming charkhas. Shiv watches with amazement as the energy of spinning wheels, of focused concentration, fills the room. Gandhiji is spinning, too, his wooden sandals to one side, his glasses perched on his nose. Shiv stares at the spinners, at their intent faces and their pedaling feet, wondering how their efforts fitted in with the world struggle for independence. In open defiance of the growing love of Indians for "foreign cloth," Gandhi practices *swadeshi*, hand-spun, handmade, locally made. It was one of the key prongs of Gandhi's thought and practice. Shiv had spoken about it often enough in England, but here it is in action, and in concert with the other three: *swaraj*, total independence; *ahimsa*, freedom from hate, nonviolence; *satyagraha*, the spiritual power that flowers out of goodwill and love. No words can describe it, the complex yet utterly simple bid for freedom that's taking place in that room.

In the evening, they walk to the river to watch the sunset. The vina player produces his instrument and in the gathering quiet of dusk, hurricane lamps are lit, and music floats in the air. Before Gandhi begins praying, he says, "There are some newcomers here tonight so I will say again what I say often enough for those of you who hear me speak every day. We practice five vows at our ashram. The first is the vow of purity. No woman should be insulted, her honour besmirched. We look upon all women with the same reverence as our mothers, our wives, our sisters, or our daughters. We honour them, we cherish them. The second is the vow of purity of the palate. We do not live to eat. We eat to live. We treat food as a precious commodity that sustains life, our lives. We use it sparingly and in need. We do not use salt, and if we must, we use it in very small quantities. Fasting is a remedy when you have a disease. And when you are sick, it is important to consume only half of your normal intake. Our third vow is ahimsa, nonviolence. We do not hurt others; we purge anger and bitterness from ourselves; we take care of the weak. We do not condone cowardice; instead, we show true courage by not returning a slap with another slap. For violence harms both the perpetrator and the victim. We support satyagraha, love-force, soul-force, in ourselves, in our families, and in our communities. Our fourth vow is non-theft. I do not mean do not steal your neighbour's chickens or goats. It is assumed that no satyagrahi would conceive such things. I mean that if you have more than you need, while others around you have less than they need, you are a thief." Shiv gasps, thinks this is why the press and his detractors refer to Gandhi as a lunatic. But given the world we were living in, where some had so much, and others not much at all, was it mad to say such things or was it the truth? Shiv does not know. It is enough to listen, and ponder later. It's the Sermon on the Mount, and Chocolate Jesus is speaking.

When it comes to the fifth vow, the vow of truth, Gandhi exhorts the audience to tell it clearly, without embellishment, without fear. People may not be ready for it, but it is important to speak it. You may suffer in your daily life, even experience a loss of reputation or stature, but speak it you must.

So why didn't you? Shiv thinks. I came back a hero, you made me out to be a fasting crackpot, who didn't know fasting was killing him and finally had to reach out to Henry Polak to save him. That's not what happened, dear Gandhiji, his mind cries. Yet that is what you stated to the papers. Anger fills Shiv again. It's his personal battle, and he must conquer it, he tells himself. His ego and hurt pride are small potatoes compared to the drama occurring between India and England on the world stage.

There is a hushed silence as they all walk back to the ashram, lamps swinging in the breeze and lighting the way. Amar Singh, that Indian soldier on the *Empress of Scotland*, who had lost his left arm while fighting in the Allied cause—he didn't get his due either, Shiv thinks. He came back a hero from the First World War, and returned to fight another, but no one would thank him for it. More than likely, his family would breathe sighs of relief and welcome him back as the family's breadwinner, not their hero. The laurel wreaths of heroism were for the stage occupiers, who beamed and bowed as they accepted medals and bouquets of flowers and statues, not for the real warriors doing the work at ground level.

The next day, Gandhi takes them to a temple nearby. Shiv learns that the kitchen cooks and servers are all from the untouchable class. When they have finished their duties they join the rest of the followers in other activities at the ashram. There is no segregation. "Gandhi's vision is of a classless, casteless society," one follower tells him. "I know," Shiv says, remembering how since he first heard that as a child, it has always been one of the key drivers in his embrace of Gandhi's thought. They arrive at the temple as one group. The chief priest comes to the door. He prostrates himself before Gandhi and ushers them all in. The kitchen workers are at the end of the line, identifiable by the way they wear their clothes, symbolizing their caste and their tribe. When the priest sees them, he says to Gandhi, "They can't come in." Gandhi says, "Then we will decline your offer, too," and, stick in hand, wooden sandals back on his feet, starts walking away. They all turn around and follow Gandhiji, who is leading them back to the ashram. Humanity kicks in. The priest comes running after them. "Bapuji, please enter," he says, going to the kitchen workers at the back of the queue and holding his hands up in supplication. "Please, all of you." Shiv watches as the greatest sticking point for most Hindus in Gandhi's thinking—that untouchables are equal and therefore have access to the same rights as anyone—is quickly overcome. That is his power.

On the eve of Shiv's departure Gandhi invites him to visit him privately. His room is possibly even simpler than Shiv's little shed. The bed has the same woven braids for slats, the pitcher of water, a table, a couple of chairs. This place was a monastery, a place for prayer and the struggle for the soul, not the national war room for winning a country back from its occupiers.

Gandhi gives Shiv that same look that had enchanted him all those years ago—of genuine concern, of kindness, of immense courtesy and care. This time there is also pride. Shiv smiles back at him even though just the previous day he had wanted to follow Gandhi to his room and interrogate him on what he had told the reporters about his return. Now Shiv sighs with relief that he hadn't. The country's future was in this hero's hands. "I am very proud of you, son," he says. "You have brought renown to the nonviolence movement. Your talks and speeches, your editorials, your exchange of letters in *The Times*, all have honoured my faith in you. Not to mention your call to the bar. I had stood there on my call day and signed my name in the same book you did. I know how hard it is, how impossible it feels to think you might actually succeed when so much is against you. I knew you would be a star for us."

Shiv nods. Gandhi's words are like rain to dry land. He nods again, smiles. "Now it is time," Gandhi says, "for you to come to Delhi, to experience life in government circles in the city. I want you to be Justice Kania's right-hand man. You will follow him, shadow him as they say in Temple circles, till you know his thoughts as well as your own. You will take his place someday if you do your job well. He is slated to be India's first justice minister. You would do well to learn everything you can from him."

They speak of his parents, of his return from England. "You will not be going back, I presume," Gandhi says.

"No," he replies. "I may have to take a trip to settle our flat—you may remember my wife died—and make arrangements for a new editor in chief for *Forward*—"

"Yes, very sad business. I was very sorry to hear the news about your wife's passing. But that is the other thing I wanted to tell you.

We cannot afford *Forward* now. Money is needed for so many efforts. *Forward* has done its job. The intelligentsia in Europe and the United States have been made aware of what we are trying to do here, and how they can help us. That is all it was supposed to do. And thanks to you, it has been done. Well done, my boy!"

Its work is only just beginning, he wants to tell Gandhi. Fascism is on the rise everywhere—the jackboots are out in full force. He doesn't challenge Gandhi at that moment but he knows the magazine will continue. It is on sound financial feet—but it must continue to keep those subscriptions coming. Gandhi may withdraw from *Forward* but *Forward* will continue marching ahead.

As Shiv begins his long journey home, he starts writing an editorial for *Forward*, on what his meeting with Gandhi and his followers at the ashram was like, and how the key elements in Gandhi's thought worked in practice. So many will be interested, he thinks. I'm not dislodging *Forward* so easily. There will be another solution, a successor.

Delhi beckons, its bright lights promise an irresistible invitation to the table to witness first-hand how power changes hands, how a subjugated country becomes independent, and how a nonviolent war is won.

# Sind, 20 April, 1942

My dearest Julia,

Nine months have passed since my arrival in India. We had talked, the night before I left for Edinburgh, about our visit here, together, showing you my India, the India you wanted so much to know. I am here now, without you. It is unbearable to think of what might have been had I not left you alone that night.

Our Iris is flourishing. She will soon be five years old. Do you remember the look of full engagement on her face in Hyde Park, how she would scrutinize everything, the shape of the buttons on her cardigan, the bows on her shoes and the petals of flowers, the holes in a piece of toast. Completely absorbed in everything around her. Mother and Father are enchanted with her. She spends every afternoon after school with them, playing with Mother, and distracting Father from his work. She looks so much like you. Her voice is like yours. When she says, "No, it isn't," in that firm tone, I hear you. She has your confidence. She even loves to dance—like you!

I taught her a song you loved—"Troubles are like
bubbles . . ." Now I am Uncle Bubbles to her. Her favourite
person in the whole world is her uncle Jacob, who has taught
her how to ride a bike—he somehow managed to get a royal
blue Colson Fairy Cycle from London for her. I've never seen
her so happy! Because of him, she hasn't lost her English
accent, and is full of things to tell him when he comes to visit.
Jacob tells her stories about you, so she knows Mummy well.
Dadda, it seems, will have to wait. My parents feel I should
delay telling Iris I'm her ne'er-do-well father. "Who knows?"
they say. "You might take off for London again." It doesn't
seem likely but I do want to take a trip back to dispose of all
our stuff in the flat. It will mean torture but it has to be done.
Gandhi will no longer support *Forward* so it is essential that
it move to other hands. I will have to find a successor.

I've recovered from my accident in Glasgow, thanks to
Mairi McNulty, the nurse who accompanied me back home
on *The Empress of Scotland*. Mairi married Will Sinclair, a
young purser on the ship, at the Anglican church in Karachi
soon after we landed here. She plans to set up her own
school for girls in India. She is bright and lively and I will
send our Iris to her school. It would give me great joy to
know she has Mairi's influence in her life.

As soon as Gandhi heard that I had fully recovered, he
requested a visit to his ashram in Wardha in Gujarat. I have
just returned from a visit to see him. Jule, you would have
loved it there. Your mother, recalling her time there, said she
had never been happier. I see what she means. It is a place
without pretension—I would describe it as a humble
monastery—and yet the longest war in history is being
fought there. He is a maestro—the elements that have come
together there are invincible and they will win. I thought I
knew Gandhism well, but Muriel Lester told me once that it

is only when you go and live with him in his ashram that you see what Gandhism truly is. His fan base now includes Stefan Zweig, Max Ophuls, F. Scott Fitzgerald, W. H. Auden, Bertrand Russell, Sylvia Pankhurst, André Malraux. And of course, Picasso. All have sent him their good wishes as he intensifies his mission. All due to *Forward*! He's offered me a key position, as assistant to the minister of justice. It will mean a move to Delhi but that is a thrilling prospect. How can I walk away from an invitation to see first-hand how all these years of struggle will lead to victory?

Once, soon after I returned to Hyderabad Sind, Father wanted to meet me alone in his study. He wanted to get close again, he wanted to know how my years in England had changed me. I said, when a soldier returns home, he is unable to describe the battlefield. He gave me a long look. He had dreamt of a bewigged barrister, what he got was a smoldering activist. He turned away. I was aware that I had caused him great sadness. He knows now that his world is too small for me. I know that my home, once my universe, had moved away from me. He has never tried to meet me alone again. But I see his eyes flit to Iris with love, and devotion, yes, but also with sadness. They know your name, they love Jacob, and they know you are Jacob's sister, that your mother loved India and was a spokeswoman for the Gandhi movement in England and in America. But they did not meet you. I am to blame for that and they will never let me forget it.

I miss you, Jule. I miss our life together in Catherine Street. I miss your touch, your look, your smile, our love. My heart is broken. Forgive me for not having spirited you both away from London when I could have.

Your devoted
Shiv

# India, 1943

My dearest Jule,

Another year has gone by. You would have been thirty-three today. I celebrated your birthday with Jacob. Iris blew out the candles on your cake and said, "Happy birthday, Mummy." We looked at pictures from Catherine Street, our celebrations there. She grabbed your photo and said, "Mummy!" I asked Jacob how she might have known, and he said, "She's a knowing child." Which didn't explain anything. Jacob and I played tennis and a friend of his made films of the afternoon: my parents in lawn chairs, a sunny afternoon, Iris playing and teasing them. She had found a baby snake somewhere and frightened the living daylights out of my mother when she opened her palms and flung it into her lap! It was the funniest sight, Mother flailing her arms hysterically and screaming while Iris laughed and ran around her. You were, as always, missing. I am sadder than ever.

Since last year, there has been a great change in things here. I have moved to Delhi. Father wasn't pleased ("Sind needs you more than Delhi does") but he accepted Gandhi's wishes in the end. I have now met Jawaharlal Nehru, who has, fortunately, taken a liking to me. Gandhiji was pleased that I met with his approval. Nehru, after consultation with Gandhiji, has appointed me practicing minister for justice and public affairs, which sounds like a fake title, almost nonsense. But what they mean is that I have been appointed an apprentice to the man who will be Chief Justice of India, Mr. Harilal Kania, and who will succeed Chief Justice Patrick Spens. For the moment, I trot behind Mr. Kania and make all the right noises. I am not required to do anything more or less than that. The right things, said in the right tone of voice, neither too deferential nor too arrogant, not ignorant nor too knowing, are very useful. *Savoir-faire,* the English call it, something Mr. Polak went to great lengths to teach me so I would adopt it as my modus operandi. I pass and blend in and that is all that is required of me at the moment. I never knew that doing so little could take you so far! Gandhiji says, "In time you will show us all how brilliant you are." But it is as it is everywhere: don't show your light until you are assured you can show it without being elbowed out of place. Muriel Lester says, "You must be at the top." She wrote, "Your vision of a classless humane society is exactly what India needs now, at this juncture of change. Your courage, your ability to ponder and reflect and debate key issues, the skills that made you a gifted and much-sought-after speaker here in London, will serve you in good stead now. Your compassion—which is as essential as boldness in a leader—is obvious. You are a born leader." Words that made me sit up and really pay attention to what was going on around me. It will be a long time before I am a "leader" or live up to any of her words, but I must stay the course. You would agree and encourage me, I know that.

Father is finally looking a little happier with me. He's pleased that I will find a successor for *Forward.* He's spent his life pulling journalists out of jail for going against the British government, and thinks it's the wrong way to fight a war. You do it from the seats of power, he says, not from the sidelines. You do it knowing which statute and by-law to throw at them. You don't do it from a position of ignorance. When I told him that Gandhi himself had considered the magazine effective weaponry in India's fight, he said, "Bapu has some strange ideas. Not everything that comes out of his mouth is gold." You can't win. I have come to realize that I must do the right thing by my standards eventually and not by anyone else's.

Our Iris is a joy to all who know her. She will be six years old next month. Freud says that by now, a child's emotional palette has acquired most of its colours and its tones. If that is so, what I see with Iris is golden yellow. She charms everyone she meets. She has them eating out of her hand. I feel there is nothing she cannot do. She might be prime minister of India someday! We both have every reason to feel proud of her. Or she might sail the waves and make her own mark in an evolved, race-blind English society.

I've tried to contact Sher directly, through his mother's film associates in Bombay, through government officials there, and through my boss Justice Kania's office. He is willing to help me locate my son and has offered whatever means he has at his disposal to find him. Every effort has been rebuffed. Seher doesn't respond directly but when Justice Kania contacted a film director school friend of his, she sent a message back through him to say that she does not welcome any further overtures. I am deeply saddened and fear I will never see my son. I will continue to try with the help of all my new acquaintances here.

But here's a brighter vision: Last year on your birthday, a strange thing happened. My mother came running into my room at around seven in the evening. "Come," she said, "hurry. I think the queen of the night is about to flower." It was pitch dark outside. We stood silently around the bush, barely breathing. So many thoughts were going through my head. The thing I missed most of all was you by my side, to witness something we had always wanted to watch together.

After an hour's wait, there was a slight movement in the branches, as if the flowers were shuddering, as you were when you gave birth to Iris. I waited, somehow anxious. And then the white flowers began opening, blooming with such grace and scent and beauty. There they stood, a stunning vision. A cluster of white petals, yellow stamens quivering in a burst at the centre, with a starlike burst of white beamlike petals radiating from the base of the flower. Their scent filled the air around us. Beautiful.

Later, I remembered Jess in Dorset—how he told us about the peregrine falcons his wife loved. How they appeared every year after he wrote her a letter. I think through the flowers you were telling me you'd received my letter and that you were happy with us—me and Iris.

Iris misses you as much as I do. She just doesn't know it. My mother asked me if it was cold when you died, and when I said yes, she said Iris keeps saying cold, cold, sometimes as if she's remembering something. She's remembering you, my love, as I do, every single day.

Your loving,
Shiv

Postscript: It happened again. The queen of the night bloomed tonight. I am overjoyed. You are hearing me, and I know you are here with us all.

# Delhi, 1944

It is June 1944. He has been in India for almost three years. Delhi has become his new home. He lives in quarters set aside for government officials—apartments that had been vacated by the departing British. It was as if they had all sensed that there would be no place for them in the new India and had begun beating a hasty, not altogether welcomed, retreat back to Old Blighty. Shiv's flat overlooks Lodhi Gardens, and the bridge with eight piers that crosses its lake. He wakes to shimmering dawns, with herons and geese flying out of the water, the ochre yellow stone bridge barely discernible through morning mists. He had moved to Delhi in January 1943. There is still no talk of him returning to Sind for the moment. Gandhi needs him in Delhi, and here he will stay, walking beside Justice Kania and "learning the ropes."

When his valet interrupts his breakfast one morning to say there is an urgent call from Bombay, Shiv assumes it's someone from the Bombay Presidency, with whom he had begun talks about the future of Sind after independence. A woman's voice says, "Hello, Shiv." It's a familiar voice, implying intimacy, and he draws back from the phone for a minute before holding it to his ear again. "Yes?"

"I don't expect you to remember my voice. It's been so long. Fourteen years!"

Seher. Of course, he realizes with a shock. "Ah yes," he says.

"You were expecting my call?"

"No. Now that you've reached me, I'll confess I'm pleasantly surprised." He suspects she has learnt something more about him, and now is keen to renew contact. Despite his great desire to know the reason for her call, he decides he will let her wait a little longer. "But I'm terribly busy and must ask why you've called. We can talk at greater length another time. I have a meeting—"

"Of course you do. Everyone knows you're the busiest man in Delhi at the moment. Your face is in the newspapers every day." She laughs. "I'm only teasing. But seriously, everyone's talking about you. Not just in Delhi circles, but here, too, in Bombay. You will be a force for the good, they say. I believe it." She's completely rebuffed his attempt to delay speaking to her. The implied intimacy, the instant warmth, puts him on guard.

Trying to respond in kind, he says, "Your face on a billboard was the first thing I saw when I landed in Karachi from England. That was almost three years ago. You dominate the billboards still. You used to watch stars once. Now you have become one."

"Thank you," she says. "But I wanted to speak to you about your son, who is now twelve. Sher is a fine young man."

*Your son.* He savours the words. *Mine, my son.* She tells him Sher looks like him. "He's tall, like you. His face is the same shape. He has your lips, your forehead. Only his hair is the same as mine—the colour of red oak." He feels cornered, defenceless. The thought of meeting Sher terrifies him, but his desire is stronger. What did it mean to become known to a child as his father? It had been so long since anyone had looked to him for help, for guidance, for support—was he capable of it now? That moment of horror in Catherine Street, when he sat bleeding on a chair from the broken glass that had lodged in his foot while Iris howled and he had joined her, comes to him now. *"Dadda!"* Now Iris was always on the lookout for her uncle Jacob, clinging to him every time she saw him, while he, the father, sat quietly, smiling indulgently, sipping his scotch and soda. Was this a chance at doing it right? As if reading Shiv's thoughts, Seher says, "His stepfather is supportive. He's always known about you. He's a movie director and Sher's influences are all from the film world. I want him to have other role models. Bombay's film industry isn't good enough." She laughs, that low, intimate chuckle, he remembers it now, as they had looked at each other, bewildered by their bodies, by what they were meant to do with them. "Yes," he says quickly, before either of them can change their minds. "Yes. Can he come here to Delhi?"

Plans are made. Sher will stay with her husband's relatives. They will arrange for him to be brought over to his office. They can go from there. When Seher and Shiv say bye, he feels indebted to her for bringing him this unexpected gift. Sher will be in Delhi in a week. Shiv prepares for it by thinking of nothing else.

The boy who enters his room is at the threshold of manhood. His finely planed face has a sheen, his cheeks a faint blush, his eyes sparkle. A milky tea complexion, a lean body, his mother's curly red hair, her hazel eyes. The build of his body is like his father's. He is wearing an achkan and churidars. His feet are, incongruously, in Keds— a boy's defiance against smart shoes. Shiv smiles as his son stands before him. They do not hug. They don't know each other. Shiv wants to give him time, give himself time to feel his son out.

"Sit down," he says, indicating the chair by the fireplace. He sits in the armchair across from the chair. "Will you have tea, or coffee?"

"No, sir."

"Coca-Cola?"

"No, thanks."

"That's beautiful," Sher says. He goes to the window to look at the lake. "We learnt about Lodhi Gardens only last week. Migrating birds stop at that lake every year—rare birds from the Russian steppes and from Tibet. Do you see them?"

"Yes. In the morning, it's a carpet of wings rising from the water—a beautiful sight."

The boy smiles—a curious, sweet smile. There is no accusation in it. "You have an English accent. My mother says you lived in England for a long time."

"Yes," he says. "I was there when you were born." The boy's face tightens—or is he imagining it? Shiv, imagining their talk would veer off to the trivial, takes the bull by the horns. "I could not come back to see you. Though I wanted to, very much."

"My mother says you became a famous barrister there."

"Not famous. But yes, I did become a barrister. I then started a journal on politics, literature, culture, and the arts."

"I know. It's called *Forward*."

"Yes! How do you know?"

"My teacher had a copy of the magazine. I saw your name on the cover. I didn't know you were—"

"What?"

"Related."

The boy's right. He's leaving it up to Shiv to designate that relationship.

"Your father, you mean?"

"Yes."

"When did your mother tell you about me?"

"About a month ago. I had pointed you out in a newspaper to her."

"What?"

He nods. "The article said you were a rising star in India. That you would be one of the leaders of a new and free India. It described your background. I told her that's what I wanted to do. Learn the law and become an editor of a magazine. She laughed and said, 'Like father, like son.'"

Delighted, disbelieving, Shiv says, "So you initiated our meeting?"

It hasn't occurred to Sher. He blinks and smiles. "I think I must have. Though I didn't know then that you were"—he pauses—"my father."

Then Shiv tells him how he had yearned to see him when he was born.

"Why didn't you come?"

"Because it was so far, and so expensive, and I was in the middle of my studies."

The boy looks away.

"Your name, Sher, the Lion's Mouth, harking back to the Indus. The river in our blood, which links us no matter where we are." Why is he blabbing on to cover a hurt? He turns to his sister, Iris, and Julia. "I married again, Sher. An Englishwoman who became my best friend, companion, managing editor of the magazine, and wife. Our Iris was born in 1937. She looks a lot like you, Sher. She's mischievous. She teases. Don't ever get into a fight with her. She will win."

Sher laughs uncertainly. Too much information, Shiv thinks. I'm scaring him. "Julia died of the flu and I sent Iris here to be raised by my parents. There is a war in Europe; and I was alone."

Sher nods. "I'm sorry you lost your wife." The second one, he's probably thinking. Shiv sees his son watching his face carefully, as if gauging him. Was his father to blame?

"What do you like to do when you're not studying?"

His face brightens. "In the evenings, there's cricket in Cross Maidan. And on the weekends, my father"—he stops, looking uncertain—"teaches me how to golf at the Willingdon Club. Until a few months ago, Indians were not allowed to join. But as he says, the British are now making efforts to let Indians join their clubs—not all, but some clubs—and he joined because he wanted to teach me golf."

As he talks, Shiv notes his diction—clear; his thinking—well expressed; his lack of nervousness—admirable; the clear indications that his boy was loved, and had been well taken care of. He senses no blame, no accusation in the young boy.

"How long will you be in Delhi?"

"A few days. My uncle here is going to Bombay on Friday and will take me back home."

"Can we meet again while you're here?"

The boy nods and smiles.

"Have you been to see the Taj Mahal?"

"No, not yet."

"I'll take you there," Shiv says. "All right?"

The boy nods.

Shiv cancels all his duties for the next two days. They go to the zoo, and laugh at the animals' antics—bears ham it up; chimpanzees, like lolling madams on couches in prostitute dens, beckon visitors up close; tigers snooze on the flagstones in their enclosures, occasionally raising their heads and yawning to reveal their fearsome teeth; peacocks, their tail feathers out, fan the air like regal monarchs in all their finery. It is an amusing time and lets out some of the air between them.

The following day, far more relaxed in each other's company, they pile into the back of a car bound for Agra, a four-hour drive away. It is 6:00 a.m., and the skies are just beginning to lighten. When Shiv asks Sher, "So what do you want to be when you grow up?" Sher says, "You. I want to be just like you." He wasn't joking. Taken aback, Shiv stares out of the window, unsure of how to respond.

After a tour of the inner chambers and tombs of the Taj Mahal, Shiv pays a roving on-site photographer to take a picture of him with his son in front of the iconic rose canal. They stand a little awkwardly as the photographer covers his head with a blanket and peers into his box, throwing off the blanket to shout directions, a little right, a little left, centre, smile . . . Shiv's arm tightens around the boy's shoulder as Sher smiles, and Shiv, looking pleased and proud, beams for the camera. Shiv pays for two copies of the photograph, to be delivered to his address the following day. They both turn back to look at the Taj Mahal. Its marble exterior is now a rosy pink under the evening sun. *Makrana*, Shiv remembers Lucy telling him. A special marble that changes hue with the quality of light. Its reflection in the canal is that of a vibrant, breathing rose. He sighs, again filled with a longing that cannot be quenched.

As they get back into the taxi, Sher says, "The Emperor Shah Jahan had the laborers' hands cut off after they built it so they could never replicate what they'd done."

There it was again. Beauty and pain. Love and torture.

On Sher's day of departure, the boy makes a quick stop at his father's flat. He goes in while Shiv is eating breakfast. Shiv jumps up and rushes forward to embrace his son. "Beta! I thought you'd already left!"

"The car is outside. I wanted to say bye again."

Shiv picks up an envelope and pulls out the contents. A smiling boy, his proud father. The photographs they had taken outside the Taj Mahal had arrived early that morning. He hands one to Sher. "To remember our lovely day together," he says. "I was going to post it but this is better."

The boy takes it from him, stares at it, then looks up at him with a smile. "I won't forget," he says.

Rich, so rich, that smile on his boy's face.

Shiv fights back tears. He puts his arms around his son, his son clasps him, hugs him tight, so tight all the air feels gone from both of them, and they are light, one in their embrace. Sher's eyes are moist. "I have to go," he says, backing out of the room. Memories were legacies—you drew on them for sustenance. There was one he would live by, and perhaps, in the future, his son, too.

A few days after Sher's departure, Shiv makes plans to leave for Hyderabad Sind to pay his parents and Iris a visit. Ramdas and his mother greet him eagerly. Delhi is the most exciting place in the world these days. The end of three hundred years of oppression; a new government—made up of brown faces, their own, leading the country. Talks have begun. "The end is still a way off," Shiv tells them. "There are endless negotiations. But it is in sight."

Not end, but beginning, his mother says, beaming. "We are kicking them out, finally!" she says, with satisfaction. "It's a new era!" She's prepared a special meal for her son—tender lamb biryani; shammi kebabs, raita, relishes and chutneys.

Iris is coy, doesn't want to come down to meet Uncle Bubbles. It's only when Shiv stands by her door imitating animal sounds that she opens the door and smiles at him. How tall she is. It's been six months since he's seen her. He picks her up in his arms and brings her down. She joins them for dinner, humming and singing, "Everything Stops for Tea."

*Boomalacka, zoomalacka, whee, whee,* she hums. Clocks strike four. *Whee whee.*

Shiv starts singing the words, and her small mouth shapes them, following his lips.

"You must have taught her this silly song," his mother says, smiling nevertheless.

Shiv laughs. "Of course. And she has a lovely voice." For the rest of the evening, to his great delight, she sits on his lap and plays with his chin as she once used to. He feels intense pleasure as her hands flit about, and when she pinches his face hard with her little fingers, he winces but laughs, delighted by her cheekiness.

LATER, IN HIS father's study, Shiv tells him his plans.

"Delhi suits you well," his father says.

"I see myself living there," he begins. "It's a beautiful city." He tells his father he has made good friends there, that his colleagues are smart and helpful. "I'm settling down, Father."

"Shiv, it is time to pin you down." His father explains that the welfare of Sind is of great importance to him. Gandhiji has assured him that Shiv could work anywhere—in Delhi, or in Sind, that his dedication and drive would take him just as far at home as in Delhi. "Partition is a big issue. Independence will come at a huge price. The British will divide us—unless cooler, brilliant minds prevail and deflect the course." His father says he wants him back in Sind. "We are a strong community here—it will take a lot to divide us and pit us against one another. All Sindhis, Muslims and Hindus, will fight it. But agitators are up for hire and can be brought in at any time to create violence amongst us."

Ramdas's eyes, his most expressive feature, are shimmering. Tears, Shiv realizes with a shock. His father continues, "A sword lies across India now. If partition comes, we will be a severed limb here in Sind. Bloodlines run deep, rooted in the land. We will achieve independence without violence but immediately afterwards there will be a bloodbath as we turn our weapons on one another. We will always be in mourning for the loss of our homeland. For Sind will go to the Muslims, the butchery will begin even here, where we pride ourselves on communal harmony, and we Hindus will have to give up our culture, our ways, our language, and our ancient history, to belong to the new India. It cannot happen. It must never happen. We are one people. Do you understand what I'm saying, Shiv?"

Seeing his father's eyes pinned to his face, Shiv says, "Sir, I need to consider this. It's not that I am not devoted to Sind but Gandhi does have plans for me in Delhi. I will always be deeply involved with Sind. In fact, I will come once a month to spend time with all of you. Until this difficult apprenticeship is over. Then I can come more often, perhaps live here part-time."

His father considers. "Nothing is more important to me than the unity of this land of ours. I cannot press you now. But when the time comes, I will," he says, finally.

Shiv says, "Sher, I was thinking, Father—" The look on his father's face stops him.

"Don't ever mention his name again, Shiv. We gave that boy all we had to give. Where is he now? Gone. Gone from both of us."

"But it wasn't his doing! He could—"

His father puts out his hand. "No. Enough."

Shiv nods. It's deeper than he had thought. His father's wound mirrors his, because it now means that to have a relationship with his son, he will have to break with his father.

As for the issue of partition, which was keeping his father awake at night, in Delhi, it was contemplated—gingerly, toe curlingly— with the insouciance of those who know that every war has its casualties. Someone always pays the price—in this case, it would be Sind.


BACK IN DELHI after his quick trip to see his parents and daughter, Shiv trembles before the front door of his flat, filled with a sense of foreboding. What a tenuous thing home is, he thinks: there one moment, a concrete thing strong enough to hold your dreams; gone, the next, like milkweed in the palm. He turns the key in the lock and pushes the door open.

The correspondence tray on his desk, containing letters and directives from the office that came during his absence, is full. Two envelopes catch his eye: one, from Calcutta, from Morty Saxena, his elegant, cramped hand instantly declaring its penman; the other postmarked Bromley-by-Bow. Muriel Lester. He reaches for Morty's letter first—probably an invitation to come meet factory workers in Calcutta, something he had promised to do.

It is as he had thought. Morty's open invitation says, "You will find Calcutta amenable. It is a literary city. And we all believe in you, in what you can do as India limps towards independence. Jai Hind!" Good old Morty. A forever friend, if ever there was one.

Muriel Lester's letter begins with a note of warning: "I hope you are sitting down, with a glass of brandy by your side."

> I never thought I would write a letter like this. It simply would not have occurred to me to sit on both sides of one fence. But so it is.
>
> My dear boy, yesterday, I had a visitor. Lucien Calthorpe has returned from the battlefields of Europe. You may not be aware that I know his mother well. She was at school with me, and we have remained friends. I suspect that is what made him come to me in the first place, as Kingsley Hall is a healing sort of place. He is fragile, exhausted. His eyes speak of torment. His road to healing will be long. But when he mentioned you, his eyes were lit with something I can only call love. He said he could not live without you, that the thought of you kept him alive, when so many by his side fell and succumbed to their injuries. As he lay there by his fallen comrades, he wept, cursing the fact that he was still alive, that he was able to make the choice between living and dying. He said he considered lying there in the open air,

waiting for birds of prey to come coasting by to pick his bones clean. Air burial, he called it, offering oneself up to the elements. But French villagers found him. They said he was as beautiful as Jesus and when he spoke in French and told them who he was, they took him to their farmhouse and nursed him back to health. He is not out of the woods yet but he will make it. He held up a piece of paper in his hands. "If you ever need me, contact Muriel Lester at Kingsley Hall. She will get in touch with me. Be safe, please, yours, Shiv." He said you gave it to him at Victoria Station as he was boarding the train for war. I felt he was handing me his heart when he showed me that piece of paper.

It is not up to me to judge. I am not God. I did not know the two of you were friends, and perhaps you were his closest friend, and he longs for you now. I do not wish to dwell on the nature of your relationship.

You will know what is best, what you should do. Gandhi will never speak to me again, I fear, if he knows I've written to you. But in the face of such pain and loyalty, I could not do otherwise.

Yours ever,
Muriel

He sits there for a long time, reading and rereading the letter. He looks up as night falls. He loves the city's ancient history, its architecture, its Mughal influences, its mystical grace, its grandeur. At dawn storks and ducks flew out of wetlands surrounding the city, the ancient towers and red brick of forts sailed into view through the parting mists like Spanish galleons.

Dusk is settling into the cracks and crevices of a city where people sit on the streets, huddled around coal fires. Hundreds of lit braziers meet his vision as he stands by the window. The lake in Lodhi

Gardens looks as if it has a covering, but as he stares at it, the cover moves and a swarm of bats fly into the air.

Morty Saxena is in Delhi to visit his grandmother. They meet for a drink at Shiv's flat. It is a fine evening. Birdcalls float in through the open windows. The sheer linen curtains shift in the breeze. Shiv tells Morty about Gandhi's ashram, the renewed sense of purpose he discovered there. "I know his thinking but to see it in action is so inspiring. He practices everything he preaches. And he is deeply invested in how this entire bid for independence will turn out not just for us, for India now, but for the world, for future generations."

"I'm glad you're part of it. I thought, for some strange reason, faced with life here, you would run back to England. You've become such an Englishman."

Shiv groans. "Please, my mother can't stop reminding me of that every day. 'What has happened to you?' she asks. But I am thinking of going back there for a month or so."

"What? Now?"

"Yes, it's not really a wild idea. I've been planning to go back to London to hand over the succession of *Forward* to someone else, and clear up the flat in Covent Garden, where I left everything behind, and where the vestiges of my life with my wife and child lie around, waiting to be rescued. I'll rush back—"

"You want to leave now? The first Quit India meeting is going to take place at Gandhi's ashram in August. Of course you'll be invited. How can you miss that?"

"I won't. It's only June. I could be back by August."

Morty rolls his eyes. Seven weeks there, seven weeks back—still wartime routes—and then two months there. And the oceans are getting ever more dangerous, with submarines and patrolling enemy ships everywhere. What is Shiv thinking? "At the earliest, you'll be back here in October."

Shiv closes his eyes. He has to go, he has to respond. He has to see Lucy in person, to tell him that another life has claimed him, that he must fulfil his destiny.

"As the months go by, the pressure here will increase. It's not going to get any easier to leave. Now is the time."

"And how will you manage the fare? Is the government paying you enough?"

He remembers telling Morty that his parents were not doing well financially, that his upkeep was becoming a burden. "I'll find a way."

"Don't fool yourself. It will take six months for you to wrap everything up and be back here. Can they spare you?"

"I'll make a case."

Morty sighs. "You'll come back, eh?"

Surprised, Shiv answers, "Of course. Why would I stay there when there's so much going on here for me?"

Morty nods. "I'll lend you the money for ship's passage. You're a government lad now, you're good for the loan."

It is a solution and Shiv surprises himself by accepting it readily.

There are three hurdles left. Gandhi. His parents. Iris.

BAPU RECEIVES HIM warmly. His embrace is deep and genuine. Shiv explains he's leaving for a quick trip to London, to tie up his affairs there, his home and other business.

"It will not be quick. It will mean six months, nearly two each way and then some weeks there to complete your business. Why are you leaving now?" Gandhi asks.

"Because it will get harder. Everything is heating up here and soon I will not be able to tear myself away."

Gandhi looks at him intently. "You have left so much behind in England? So much that you will undertake a fourteen-week journey in wartime to retrieve what you cannot live without?"

"For my child, Gandhiji; she has little to remind her of her mother. I journeyed straight here after I was shot in Glasgow. All our things are still in London. Also, it's Mrs. Chesley's flat and she should regain use of it." It sounds weak, he knows it. But there's also *Forward*, the charge he's placed on himself to find it a new and effective editor. Gandhi nods. He says, "Georgina is not pressing you. I know her nature. But I remember that ten-year-old boy who brought me my shawl. When I asked you if you could give up desire, you thought it was like eating ice cream, and you answered accordingly. The second time I asked you, at the Polaks' in London, you didn't answer. You looked at the floor. It is possible that something involving desire is taking you back there. But I hope that it is a desire for India that brings you back."

Gandhi hugs him and says, "If we cannot pull you back, then perhaps you were never for us. Safe journey, son, and come back soon."

He decides to tell both his parents at once. It is a soggy morning when he arrives in Hyderabad Sind by train. Deep rain puddles fill the driveway as he walks from the station to his family home. His trousers are soaked when he arrives at the front door. Their servant lets out a cry of alarm seeing Shiv's drenched form. People come rushing, fetch fresh clothes from his closet; he is led up to his room, while the heater is switched on for hot water so he can soak in eucalyptus-scented water, sure to keep colds away. He performs all the actions required of him with a heavy heart.

When finally he is bathed and warmed by hot tea, he asks to meet with his parents. His mother comes down the stairs. "You never told us you were coming! We have a very simple dinner planned. Father has an upset stomach, so we are going to have a light dinner of soup and pear jelly."

"Can Father meet with me?"

"Now?"

"Yes."

"Let me see how he's feeling." She goes back up the stairs. Shiv waits downstairs framing his explanations, but the words are like matchsticks tumbling out of a box onto the floor. He's lost his tongue and his mind is a jumble.

While his mother is gone, he goes up to Iris's bedroom. She's playing intently with an elaborate doll house, another of her uncle Jacob's extravagant gifts, he assumes. Its windows gleam with lights, its little sofas and chairs and needlepoint footstools and thick velvet curtains and bookcases are inviting and homely. Iris has pulled out all the inhabitants—a blond-haired mother, a red-haired father, a baby in a pram, and a young boy. She puts the mother's hands on the bar of the pram, the little boy's hand in his father's. Then she puts the baby in the pram. "Where are you taking them, Iris?"

"To the park," she says. There are no parks outside her house in Hyderabad Sind. What park? He stares at her, then his eyes blur. She's thinking of a park, some park, where her parents used to take her. Or is it from a storybook her grandfather read to her? He says, "Iris, come here."

"No," she says.

"Please." She gauges him, her purple-blue eyes crystalline, fixed on his face—how much does he want it?—then she comes to him.

He is tongue-tied as he looks down at her radiant little face. She mutters and hums and plays with his shirt collar, his face. He can't say a word. He holds her close, breathes her scent in as he listens to the sound of crumbling ramparts within.

———

STILL REELING, HE appears at the dining table and greets his mother again, embraces his father. "What is it, Father?" Shiv asks.

"I don't know—something I must have eaten. Fruits don't always get washed properly in this house now," he says, looking accusingly at his wife. "She's too busy playing with Iris." She rolls her eyes and gazes fondly at her granddaughter. Iris is staring at her father as if he is a stranger. She's never been clear on who he is. She won't know now for a little while.

"How is Delhi treating you, son?" His father looks at him proudly. "Gandhiji says Justice Kania is very happy with your work. He says you consistently offer valuable suggestions, which he employs. Well done!"

Shiv smiles. "Yes, I am happy working for him."

"So what brings you here, so unexpectedly?" His mother knows something is up.

He says, "I have to go to London for a few months."

There is pin-drop silence. "Why now?" she asks.

He doesn't know if it's the ticking of the hall clock or his heart that beats so loudly in his ear. "There is no good time. Now is the best time, as far as I can see. Julia's mother's flat needs to be cleaned out so she can use it again. All our possessions are there, waiting to fill a new home. Which will be in Delhi." His father looks up sharply. "Or here," Shiv adds.

His father appears puzzled.

"Things are clearer now, Father," he says. "And it is also apparent that this is all going to accelerate quickly. There are constant negotiations, and agreements are being discussed and implemented every day. Lord Linlithgow has installed a telephone booth in Gandhiji's ashram so he can speak to him every day. There is no other way of reaching him. Soon Gandhi will be moving to Delhi as things are moving swiftly. If I delay—"

His father nods. "All right, I understand. But do you have the money for passage? We can't."

Shiv nods. "Yes, I have savings."

"Good," his mother says. "But we expect you back here as soon as everything is finished. Safe journey, son."

They are at the door, waving goodbye, as he leaves his home. He will return, he tells himself, and see India free.

Making his way through the puddles in the ruts of the driveway, he walks back to the station, where, mindful of the sacrifices to come, he purchases a third-class ticket to Karachi and sits in a boisterous compartment with farmers, their gunnysacks of buckwheat and rice and their small cages of crying birds, chickens and roosters, and the train lulls them to sleep all the way back to the city.

Back in his flat, he makes arrangements to take the next ship back to London from Bombay. His colleagues at the Bombay Presidency intercede to get him a cabin on a packed ship sailing for Glasgow in ten days, on 2nd July. He writes a letter to Iris, gives it to his valet to mail to her, care of his parents. *Dear Iris, I have gone away for a little while now but I will be back soon. I love you, my child, and will bring back something very special for you from London. Be good! Your loving Uncle Bubbles.*

When his valet comes in to say, "Mister Jacob is here," Shiv considers why his brother-in-law might have left a hectic schedule in Karachi at a time of celebrations of holy days (Eid was in June) and intense negotiations between their governments to make a sudden trip to Delhi. Jacob walks in, an anxious smile on his face. "Hello, brother," Shiv says. "What a surprise!"

Jacob nods grimly. "You didn't tell me you were going back to London." He sits down on the sofa and leans forward. His hands are clasped together and pressed against his chin. His brow is knitted, he's absolutely furious.

"I did say I might—"

"*Might* is a word indicating possibility, not certainty."

Shiv stares at Jacob. Of course he is right. What is he thinking? Going off to London without telling his brother-in-law, a trusted emissary of the British in India, that he was leaving? "I'm sorry—"

"Shiv, I don't know what is going on with you." Jacob's full-beam look is both an alarm sounding off and an inquisition. "You're going back to trouble."

"What do you mean? What sort of trouble? I'm planning to hand over the magazine to an able successor. I'll bring back some of our possessions and clear out the flat. What's the problem?"

They both fall silent, aware of something much larger than them both in that room. Jacob knows something that he can't reveal without harming himself and his trusted position. Suddenly it becomes imperative to Shiv that he should know what it is. In the uncomfortable silence that grows between them, Shiv thinks: he suspects that it's not about the flat, that it's something else. They stare at each other. Then, judging by Jacob's pained expression, it occurs to him that it probably has something to do with the government, and it is costing him a great deal to break his sworn allegiance to his employers.

When Jacob speaks, it's in a flat voice, devoid of emotion. He says, "I see there is no choice but to share with you what I know. In fact, at this point, I'd rather get it off my chest. While you were living in Lancaster Gate, Julia confided in me that she was being followed. She didn't know by whom. She began fearing for both your lives. The move to Covent Garden, she thought, and I did, too, was providential. Perhaps the stalkers would be put off the scent. She was right.

After Iris's birth, the trailing stopped." He moves about restlessly on the sofa.

"Did they have something to do with me, with the shooting in Glasgow? Or worse, with Julia's death?" Shiv's head is spinning, his hands turn into fists, as if aiming to punch someone. "What are you telling me, Jacob? I had a hunch it was the British government, known for following most Indian students around. Those of us in unions were most certainly under their watch, but it's guaranteed that someone like me, running an anti-fascist magazine, one with a solid anti-colonial bent, would have been trailed. I suspected it, and you're here, presumably, to tell me that I was right. That they shot me on behalf of the British government. . . ."

"No!" Jacob gets up and paces the room. "Don't apportion blame where there is none."

Stunned, Shiv looks back at Jacob. "What?"

"It wasn't the government. You might have been watched by them, in fact, you most certainly were, but those ridiculous gum-shoes outside the building were definitely not government hires."

"Who, then? I know you know, it's on your face, Jacob, so you might as well tell me."

Jacob throws himself down again on a chair. "He hated you," he says, with a long sigh. "The day you met him at White's was a terrible one in our family. He spends the night at Mother's when he's in town. He came back from lunch shouting uncontrollably and told Georgina she was terrible mother material. If you had supervised Julia better, this would not have happened, he told her. Mother left and went to a friend's. When she met you and Julia at Fortnum's for lunch, she hadn't come from her flat in Holland Park, she'd come from a friend's house in London. She couldn't bear to be in his presence."

Shiv takes in his words, wondering where this was all leading. Jacob's determined face tells Shiv he's decided to tell him the whole story. "It's the children—he didn't want half-castes in the family. My father is a furious man by nature. Alcohol, cigars, horses, golf, and money calm him down. His house in Castle Combe is his palace—he lords it over everyone there. He never cared much for me. I couldn't hold a gun straight on my first shoot and cried when birds came falling down from the skies into the heather. I called him a murderer back then for killing them and loathed him for gloating in his haul every day. Julia was the apple of his eye—she was what made life worth living. Horsy, sharp, very pretty—she had all his attention. I had Mother's, which I far preferred. Then you came along and stole her affections—or at least, that's how he saw it. He was determined to get even with you. He hired those buffoons—in hindsight, it's a good thing they were so obvious and inept at their jobs. You became aware of them and that they were shadowing you both, and it kept you alive. Had they been saber-toothed Rottweilers determined to accomplish their mission. . . ."

"So the men who shot me were his hired guns?"

"Yes." Jacob shifts uncomfortably in his chair. "You can see this gives me no great pleasure. That he should have considered this . . . and then seen it to fruition . . . well, not quite, you're still here, thank god. But that's what I've come here to warn you about. If he gets wind of the fact that you're back. . . ."

"He might try again? And perhaps succeed this time?"

Jacob shakes his head and looks away, as if he can't bear acknowledging that his father has such a wild, vengeful streak in him. "I'd imagine only a psychopath bent on self-destruction would try again. But you never know. He managed to convince the authorities that the men were extortionists, blackmailers out for the money. He was under investigation, of course, as is routine, but you know how it is when you have friends in high places . . . and the toll of war on all the services. . . . I imagine they dropped it since no one had actually been killed in the process."

Shiv rolls his eyes, contemplates the bizarre turn of events. William Chesley had seemed unreasonable, a bully, a white supremacist coddled by society and determined to have things his way. Angry, thoroughly distasteful. But a murderer? History had shown us the fate of disobedient daughters, nieces, sisters; of women who spurned men: Antigone, Juliet, Dido, Cordelia, Daphne, Desdemona . . . a long line of women punished for crossing the line, for perceived disloyalty. Perhaps it was true then—a father incensed by a beloved daughter turned traitor birthed a rage like no other. He was William's Othello; Julia, his Desdemona. "Did he have anything to do with Julia's death?"

"No. No, let me relieve you of that burden. He wouldn't have hurt a hair on her head."

Shiv takes a gulp of whiskey. "Let's face it, Jacob. I am an Indian who wasn't killed as intended, and he is a well-known type of English gentleman—landed gentry, doing what landed gentry do best—shoot, ride, and manage their estates. There's a war on—corpses strewn about on the streets. Who, and why, should anyone care about an attempt on a brown man's life that didn't succeed? Of course they're going to let it go. But—that he should get away with it. . . . How did you find out about all of this?"

"Mother. American resourcefulness came to her rescue. A few weeks after you were shot in Glasgow—when was that, spring or summer, I think, of 1941—the men came to the flat, demanding money, talking about not having been paid for months. They said they had been hired to kill a Mr. Shiv Advani by Mr. William Chesley. Mother was nonplussed, didn't understand a thing, not why they were there or what they were demanding. She asked Sophie to make tea and crumpets for the men, went away and rang the police from her bedroom. 'I have two murderers in my drawing room,' she told them. Mother came back and calmly sat with them. 'I've never seen such hungry men,' she told me. While Sophie brought out plateful after plateful of crumpets, Mother told them about Gandhi and non-violence and her time in his ashram in India. By the time the police arrived, Mother was quite deflated. She has an evangelical streak in her, as you might have noticed, and told me, 'I think they were getting really interested in Gandhi,' as if the police had been an interruption."

Shiv shakes his head, and laughs. "That's Georgina. Such a strong woman."

"Yes, she's quite spectacular, really. American resourcefulness and Jewish mettle. It's invincible. Perhaps that's where Iris gets it from."

"The mettle?"

"Yes, she's the most determined child I've ever known." He knows, Shiv thinks, Jacob knows in a way he, the father, doesn't. He has nothing to add, no qualifiers. He's grateful for the insight yet disturbed, even impoverished by it.

"What happened to the men?"

"In the clink. They surrendered without protest. Father was under investigation but in the end, they bought his story that the men were blackmailers. So he's out in the country ravaging our bird population even as we speak."

They sit quietly. His valet, Suresh, brings in a tray of tea and biscuits. "No, thanks," Jacob turns down the proffered cup.

"Bring the scotch, Suresh," Shiv says. He turns to Jacob. "I'm not changing a thing."

Nursing their single malts, Shiv thinks Jacob is the brother he never had. Jacob, watching Shiv quietly solidify his plans to return to England, says, "Mother won't know you're coming back unless I tell her."

"I have to see her; she is as beloved to me as my own mother. I'll go to Holland Park as soon as I'm back. The bigger question here for me"—he gives Jacob a quick glance and forges ahead—"is Georgina— why a splendid person like her has stayed with him. They don't seem to have a thing in common."

"Fair question." Jacob considers it. "He hasn't aged well. But he was once a keen, loving, charming young man who swept her off her feet, made her give up America and make England her home, and their beginnings were strongly rooted in hope. And humour. Georgina loved his sense of humour. 'You can melt ice with it,' she used to tell him. He lost it along the way. Now"—he shakes his head and sighs—"she's forbidden him to ever cross her path. They've widened the separation they were living with earlier. He will stay in the country, shoot grouse, smoke cigars, and get drunk and rowdy every evening with the neighbours; she'll stay in London, surrounded by caring friends, like Millie Polak, who has been a godsend. She says she hopes to never see his face again."

"But why not make a clean break of it, if it's already deteriorated so much?"

"Mother. I think he'd be quite happy to push off if she filled his bank account and left him to his own devices. But tolerance is her religion. It isn't tolerance if it's not tested. He's her test. Her hair shirt. Our home-grown Gandhi! And she likes to control what he does with her money. She pays all the bills, as you know."

"I'm terrified at one level of going back. It feels like there's nothing there for me now. And yet, my past life, all those years of learning, growing, loving, becoming—they're all there, waiting for me, waiting to take me back in their fold."

Jacob shakes his head. "Don't tarry. Get what you need to done and come back here to claim your place in the front lines. Iris and India need you. Ask Muriel to arrange your meetings with Mother at Kingsley Hall. Don't meet in a public place. Good luck, brother! Here's to your safe return. When we next meet, you'll be India's new justice minister, and I'll be in a semi-detached in Putney, with a dog at my feet, stoking logs in the fireplace and regaling neighbours with stories about my glory days in Injah!"

They both laugh.

"You'll be as dashing as ever, Jacob, and your audience, wherever you are, will be fortunate to have an entertaining host like you. Take care, brother. I'm reading the leaves—no Putney for you, I'm afraid. You'll be here as one of us, the natives."

On 2 July, Shiv boards the SS *Ariadne* from Bombay to Glasgow. He is going back to a war zone, a treasured city tottering under the on-slaught of constant bombardment. Gazing at the water as his ship pulls away from the Gateway of India at the harbour in Bombay, he considers his own situation, which seems as murky as ever. The planets of the heart were desire, obstruction, and reason; its watery terrain the emotions. On this battlefield, the soul fought with the heart, the heart with the mind, the mind with the will. This war for self-realization would never cease; it would only be fought at differ-ent levels of intensity throughout one's life. There were lulls in every battle. And then there was the field where combat took place. It was the only true battle one had to fight in life. Entelechy, Aristotle called it, potential made actual, self-expression realized. Where was he going? He senses the inner compulsion, but his compass is shattered.

As he catches his last glimpse of Bombay harbour, he thinks, I left these shores a would-be hero, I returned an invalid, I leave as a soldier battling unknown forces. Home-leaving, homecoming, home-losing. The only word they shared in common was *home*.

# London, 1 September, 1944

The streets of London are unrecognizable. While Paris has just been liberated, with its squares, buildings, and monuments largely intact, in London the impact of the war is horrifying and its scars are everywhere. Sorrow fills me as I see well-loved places—a café, a bookshop—burned away. Charred buildings stand like the ramparts of castle ruins; dusty craters, like open graves, show where a church or a building had once been. The ground is littered with shattered glass. The dust in the air clings to your face like a mask, it is in your hair, an ash taste in your mouth. It is often difficult to breathe. Crews of men in hats and helmets are cleaning the city. Stained sandbags line the streets. This city has been hit hard and it has suffered. It is worn out, exhausted, and still being punished cruelly for being at war; neglect shows in the growing water stains on the sides of buildings, a yellow fog makes seeing difficult, and there are hospital smells of disinfectant everywhere.

As I make my way by foot to East London, I wonder what will be left? How will this city reclaim its soul? "Gemme of all joy . . . ," Dunbar's paean to the city comes to me. Even as glass crunches under my feet, and smoke fills my lungs, I feel the city's inner shining, its small strong glimmers of strength.

Muriel is waiting for me at Kingsley Hall. As I enter, she embraces me warmly. I feel as if I have come home. She uses a flashlight and beams it ahead as we go up the stairs. It is an overcast day but we sit on the low swing bed in the balcony and talk. Sitting there without Iris by my side, I feel the full weight of what I lack. In the near dark, it is easier to speak from the heart. I tell her how hard it has been to live as an uncle, not as a father, to Iris. She says, it is wise that you did not disclose your identity. You don't know where you're going at the moment, do you? No, I admit. I thought I knew when I left India but it's already very confusing being back in London, and I've only been here a few hours. She says it has been difficult for her, living with what she had to do—she says she feared that her letter would force me to break with my family, my child. She asks me, what did you tell them?

Looking into Muriel's eyes is an experience in itself. They are lion yellow eyes that understand and see everything. I don't see them now, but I imagine her intensity as she listens, her deep concentration. I tell her everything is going well in India, that my future there seems certain. I'm beginning to consider Delhi my home finally. I tell her about my visit to Gandhi's ashram, where she had spent some time. "He is the leader of a spiritual army, where vows are repeated every day like battle cries." She laughs. Yes, she says. But religion is the Indian's command centre. He knows this, and he's taken over the reins from the priests so the movement can be efficient, can be employed to fight a war. He doesn't have actual weapons but he does have faith, which, as we well know, is the strongest weapon of all. She's right, of course. So why did you come back? Muriel asks. I know why I've come back—to clear out the flat, to find another editor for *Forward*. And to see Lucy. I tell her this. She sighs, says, "Yes." It is laden with anxiety, filled with unease the way she says it. I hear it again. "Yes." A few minutes pass before I dare to ask, "How is he, Muriel?"

"Not well," she says, looking into the distance, clearly still uncomfortable with the thought that I am here. "He was admitted to a convalescent home, suffering from mental exhaustion and a badly scarred body. You know the rest, how the French farmers rescued him and nursed him back to life and health."

"When did he get in touch with you?"

"A few weeks after he was better. His mother and I are in different worlds now. Ne'er did Belgravia and the East End meet! But we have remained friends. After Lucy came to see me, his mother telephoned to say that his one wish was to see you again, that the desire to see you, he told her, was what kept him alive. He felt sure that you would be there awaiting his return." She shakes her head. "This hasn't been easy for me. I often know when I've done or said something wrong immediately. Now I don't know. I had to write to you. I didn't know what you would do. But you had to know his condition."

She gives me his address. With a shock, I realize it is our flat, our cold Bayswater flat. With so much of London bombed, it was still standing, improbably, and was a place he could move into immediately. I remember exactly where it is—the scene of my desertion of him, of our rejection of each other. I thank Muriel and prepare to leave. She says, "He is very fragile. He will need care." And then she says what she always says, "May God be with you." I never heard these words properly before. This time I do.

I have my small suitcase with me. Muriel again offers Kingsley Hall for the night but I cannot stand being in Gandhi's presence. It is still there on that terrace, in the room where he had slept all those months. Already, the fullness of loss is threatening to cripple me.

She says it is dangerous to walk about on the streets at night. The V-1 Flying Bombs, or Doodlebugs as they're commonly known, are small vessels that fly in at dawn and dusk, splitting the air with their whirring buzzing sounds. When they dive down, there is an explosion killing everything in sight. "Nearly a hundred we've seen in a single day flying like locusts through the sky," Muriel explains. "Stay here for the night, Shiv." I insist on leaving. I feel as if I'm drowning and must be saved before I'm under. This time Kingsley Hall cannot save me. She says, "The buses are running but their destinations aren't lit up—too much light—so here's a flashlight. Shine it to see where the bus is going and to alert the driver to your presence there. It's not something I usually recommend but then no one is foolish enough to voluntarily trudge through the streets of a wartorn city at night."

"It isn't voluntary," I say. "I don't have a choice."

She gives me a quick appraising look. "Yes, I see that," she says.

She suggests I leave my suitcase there for the night and come back for it tomorrow. Take what you need and put it in here—she gives me a canvas bag. You may have to walk a long way, she warns me, so travel light.

Night blackness is always deep in London, the low lights of street lamps ringed by halos of damp air creating double shadows and an atmosphere of ghostliness, but this darkness is so total you can actually see quite well. Sounds are sharp: tumbling bricks, crunching glass, the terrified shrieks of owls. Shadows and outlines are clear, visible, people's footsteps some distance away thud across pavements, and only the blue lights permitted by the authorities to mark establishments like restaurants, pubs, and dance halls gleam spectrally at night.

When the bus stops in Bayswater, I stand in the street for a moment. The evidence of violence all around me is chilling. Someone yells out, "Turn off that torch!" I realize I will have to walk in darkness. Luckily, it's not too far but was any road longer, more winding, more filled with debris, more circuitous than the one I'm on now?

I go up the stairs very quietly, not wanting to wake him should he be sleeping. The ruts on those stairs, so well-known once, come back to me as my feet step into the grooves. I begin carefully, assessing the sturdiness of each step as I ascend. When I reach the top, I see the door is slightly ajar, as if he is expecting me. I stand there for a moment, taking stock of my beating heart. Always before that door, my heart raced. I push it open and stand there, looking in. How well this place had held us, protected us. I put my canvas bag down by the door and walk into the living room. He is sitting on the sofa in a blue robe. His face in the half-light of the flat looks gaunt, his curls are flatter, his hair is shorter, he is so lean. I walk towards him. His eyes are pinned to my face. I sit down on the sofa beside him. On the table next to the sofa there is a battered-looking book. Homer's *Odyssey*. I recognize it from the large H impressed on its cloth front. The new translation I was reviewing for *Forward* when I saw him bound for war. In the smoky light of Victoria Station, his eyes had held mine while another war was slowly forming the bridge between us. His supervisor handed the book to him, with my message inside it: "If you ever need me, contact Muriel Lester at Kingsley Hall." He had brought it back from the battlefield and come home, to me.

Moments pass. I reach for his hand. He lets me take it. I close my eyes and a long sigh rises to my lips. I can't look at his face. When I exhale, my breath catches the candle's flame and as it flickers and rises high again, I turn to look at him. How soft, like fresh grass, his eyes are. He says, "Close the door." I look at him; there are so many questions in that one command. I hesitate. Then he leans forward and takes my face in his hands. I look at him again, at the familiar beauty of him, but I am not prepared for the way he kisses my lips. Hard, strong, he is in my mouth, I, in his, and the years slip away silently as we embrace each other. How I had dreamt of this. We reach for the familiar places we had known—he for the tender spot in my neck where my heart beats loudest; I for the scar by his right shoulder blade, where his skin always jumps when touched. There would be new scars now. We have so much to learn.

"Close the door, Shiv," he says again. I shut my eyes; despairing, elated, my body thrilling to his touch, I hear the turmoil within, the wild churning. I feel myself shaking. Entire worlds are suspended before me, their jangling cries fill my ears. What am I doing? What am I doing? STOP. HALT. VERBOTEN. Those old dreaded words come to me again now, each one a bar. Then the shaking stops. The storm clears, and its quiet aftermath calms me. I rise and go to the door. Quietly, deliberately, I press it shut.

WHEN I GET back to the sofa, I hear the music playing in the background. Ella singing, singing softly, so softly, I hadn't heard it when I first entered the room. *"Into each life some rain must fall, but too much is falling in mine. . . ."*

Healing rain, we need so much of it.

# Acknowledgments

India won its independence from the British in 1947, three years after this story ends. But the end of colonialism in India was in sight, in no small part, due to the courage, the intelligence, and the eloquence of these soulful, hopeful young men in England, who left India between the 1880s and 1930s and returned home like saplings caught in a fire. It is a novelist's response to a period that had been sending out haunting vapors for a long time. I was struck by the fact that these men had not been accorded their place in India's struggle for independence. I wanted to know more about how that struggle shaped them and affected their lives in a foreign land, and what they did to survive.

I would like to offer deep thanks to the "dream team"—my agent, Marly Rusoff, and my publisher, Amy Einhorn—for their faith in the book from the start. Their suggestions and contributions have strengthened it and sharpened its central focus. Marly is a treasure— a person who truly cares about the written word and does everything to support it. Amy was a superb editor, homing in on all the obscure, fuzzy bits, and her insightful questions helped me sharpen and deepen what was on the page. Several new scenes were written as a result of her keen prodding, and the novel is richer for it. Lori Kusatzky has always been so responsive, warm, and helpful. Thank you! And to the Crown team, thank you for the cordial welcome. I look forward to our work together.

My friend Sarah Dimont Sorkin, comrade since our early years in London, heard so much of this novel on the phone. Her finely attuned ear, so sensitive to dissonance, was invaluable. To my endless gratitude, she was and is always there. Her support has counted for so much.

Marjorie ("Marje") Horvitz, superb copy editor to so many luminaries of our time, was a light in the dark years and a beloved friend. Her last words to me before she died were "Finish that novel!"

Trent Duffy copyedited this novel beautifully. Copy editors do not get the thanks they deserve. Thank you, Trent, for doing such a wonderful job. Anna South was a keen and perceptive first reader for the manuscript. Thanks, too, to the production team at Crown: Patricia Shaw, Andrea Lau, Heather Williamson, and Anna Kochman for their work on the book.

Blanche Wiesen Cook, dear friend and unfailingly enthusiastic supporter of my work, thank you for your marvellous readings of the work in progress. Sally C. B. Lee, who has read everything I ever wrote, is one of the smartest readers I know. I'm thankful for her welcoming home, her humor, her insights, and her deep belief in my work.

For the time to brood, plot, read, and write, I give heartfelt thanks to: Yaddo, the MacDowell Colony, Ledig House/Writers Omi, Hedgebrook, Jentel Arts, and Hawthornden Castle for residencies there. *The English Problem* was begun at Yaddo and nurtured and finished there over the course of several years.

Libraries have always been beloved sanctuaries in my life. To the London Library, "gemme of joy," which gave me intellectual refuge under their Scholar program when I was a student, and to the incomparable Douglas Matthews, Librarian, I will always be indebted. To the New York Public Library, with its extraordinary staff, its welcoming spaces, its vast research resources and collections, I offer boundless thanks.

To my family, who indulged a hopeless book addict's passions by paying for built-in bookshelves; the complete OED; the Historical Thesaurus of the OED; and special reading lamps for the book obsessed—there are no words, strangely enough, for that kind of support. And to a mother who said "I now have an author daughter!" before she died in 2023, and laughed proudly at the joy of it, thank you.

Thanks to the many authors whom I edited, and who brought their richness to me; and the students I taught for nearly two decades, who thrilled me when they asked for additional reading lists at the end of each semester.

Miron Grindea, editor of *Adam International Review*, was a mentor to me as I navigated literary London. A true cosmopolite, he led this twenty-year-old deep into his marvellous world of books and artists and introduced me to his "Finchleystrasse," where we drank the best coffee to be had in London and bit into cinnamon-scented biscuits, and discussed Rimbaud and Verlaine and Madame D'Arblay while it rained English rain out in the streets.

Barnaby Bryan, librarian at the Middle Temple in London, found critical records for my uncle, who inspired this story, sending shock waves through my system as I sat in a London pub with friends while my iPhone pinged and pinged like an emissary from the gods. He existed! He lived! Thank you so much for all you did to find the records, especially his signature when he was called to the bar.

Robert Fagles welcomed me into his world of classical literature and deepened my love for the classics as we worked together on his translations of Homer and Virgil. I particularly cherished all I learnt from him when we were working on the *Odyssey* together, glimmers of which are in this novel; whatever strength they may have is due to his inspiring influence.

For a grant in fiction from the Connecticut Commission on the Arts, and for the Yeovil Literary Award for a novel in progress, I remain deeply grateful. Thanks to the de Csilléry family—Tricia, Michael, and to my godchildren, Ella and Tom, for amazing hospitality. Thanks, too, to the following individuals who have helped me on my journey: A. M. Homes, Amrita Bhandari, Andrew Solomon, Anisa Kamlani, Barbara Epler, Bilal Qureshi, Bill Henderson, Caitlin O'Shaughnessy, Candace Wait, Charles Dimont, Chris Wait, Christin Williams, Dr. Clive Wake, Dan Blank, Daniel Simon, David Gough, Deborah Hrbek, Deepak Kamlani, Deirdre Kamlani, Don Lee,

D. W. Gibson, Elaina Richardson, Fiona McCrae, Grace Mary Linnell, Hanya Yanagihara, Jamila Singh, Jane Campbell, Jayshree Bhusan, Jeanne-Marie Musto, Jeremy Moakes, John Seilern, John Siciliano, Joseph O'Neill, Julia Strayer, Konstantin Troussevitch, Lauren Groff, Liz Pike, Lynne Fagles, Manjari Mehta, Margot Livesey, Maria Gillan, Mary Gannon, Mary-Jane Edwards, Mitchell Kaplan, Nancy Nordhoff, Neltje, Peter Blackstock, Quiteria de Mello, Reena Kashyap, Robert Kanigel, Ruth Ozeki, Serena Kamlani, Shaila Bhandari, Sherry Kamlani, Suneel Kamlani, Suneeta and Nanik Vaswani, Tom O'Neill, Tory Klose—so many allies and supporters along the way, I could not hope to name them all here. Thanks to all, named and unnamed, for their kindness and their generosity.

—B.K.

New York, 2024

The letter from Gandhi to Ramdas Advani on *pages 413–414* exists in its original form as a letter from Gandhi to my grandfather about his son Atma. Only the name has been changed to Shiv Advani. Otherwise, the letter remains as it was in the original. Citation: Letter 468, vol. 64 of Gandhi's Collected Works (20 May 1934–15 September 1934). The letter is dated 5 September, 1934, and is on pages 399–400. (Courtesy: Pyarelal Papers.)

*pages 211–214:* The letter from Shiv Advani to *The Guardian* exists in its original form as letters to the editor from Atma Kamlani in *The Free Press & Post* (Saturday, 28 May, 1932, and Saturday, 2 July, 1932).

*pages 415–416:* The newspaper article reproduced here was published when Atma Kamlani returned to Hyderabad Sind from Britain by ship. All attempts to confirm the source of the cutting (*The Sind Observer*, most likely) have been unsuccessful.

Among all the books and papers and monographs I read as research for this story, the following were particularly helpful:

*Mahatma Gandhi* by H.S.L. Polak, H. N. Brailsford, Lord Pethick-Lawrence; *The Raj Syndrome* by Suhash Chakravarty; Gandhi's letters, as collected and published online by Sabarmati Ashram, India; Virginia Woolf's body of work—the novels, essays, diaries, and letters, especially the diaries for 1931–1935 and 1936–1941 and vols. 4, 5, and 6 of the Letters; Leonard Woolf's autobiographies, especially *Downhill All the Way* and *Growing*; John Lehmann's *Thrown to the Woolfs* and *A Marriage of True Minds* by George Spater and Ian Parsons; *Virginia Woolf* by Gillian Gill; *Leonard and Virginia Woolf: The Hogarth Press and the Networks of Modernism*, ed. Helen Southworth; *Conversations in Bloomsbury* and *Untouchable* by Mulk Raj Anand; *Empires of the Indus* by Alice Albinia; *Thames* by Peter Ackroyd; *White Mughals* by William Dalrymple; *Noblesse Oblige* by Nancy Mitford; *The Dangers of Being a Gentleman* by Harold Laski; "The 'Sticky Sediment' of Daily Life," on Kingsley Hall by Seth Koven in *Representations*, vol. 120, no. 1 (2012); *Nights Out: Life in Cosmo-*

*politan London* by Judith R. Walkowitz; *The Intellectual and Cultural World of the Early Modern Inns of Court*, eds. Jayne Elisabeth Archer, Elizabeth Goldring, and Sarah Knight; *Ayahs, Lascars and Princes*, Rozina Visram; *Ambassadress of Reconciliation* by Muriel Lester; *The Periplus of the Erythraean Sea* by Anonymous; *Gazetteer of the Province of Sind* by A. W. Hughes (1876); *The East India Trade: A Most Profitable Trade to the Kingdom and Best Secured and Improved in a Company and Joint Stock*, London (1677).

Quotations and song snatches not accompanied by sources are:

*pages 43–44*: Macaulay quote: Minute, 2 Febuary, 1835, Thomas Babington Macaulay.

*page 108*: Pablo Neruda, *One Hundred Love Sonnets*, XVII, tr. Stephen Tapscott.

*pages 120–121*: "Savoir-Faire," *The Sunday Times*, 13 February, 1881.

*page 197*: "The Empire is perishing . . . ," "Thunder at Wembley," Virginia Woolf, *Nation & Athenaeum* (28 June, 1924).

*page 253*: "Love Walked In," George Gershwin/Ira Gershwin.

*page 273*: "For ever alone, alone . . ." Virginia Woolf, *The Waves*, p. 151.

*page 335*: Ovid, *Tristia*, tr. Peter Green, Bk II, lines 93–96.

*page 341*: Albert Camus, "The Almond Trees" from *Lyrical and Critical Essays*, tr. Philip Thody (1940).

*pages 341–342*: David Jones, *Anathemata*, p. 130.

*page 386*: Virgil, *The Aeneid*, tr. Robert Fagles, Bk. 2, lines 984–86.

*page 443*: "Everything Stops for Tea," by Al Hoffmann, Maurice Sigler, Al Goodhart (1935).

*page 466*: "Into Each Life Some Rain . . ." by Allan Roberts and Doris Fisher (1944).

# ABOUT THE AUTHOR

Beena Kamlani is a Pushcart Prize–winning fiction writer whose work has appeared in *Virginia Quarterly Review; Ploughshares; Identity Lessons: Learning to Be American,* eds. Gillan (1999); *Growing Up Ethnic in America,* eds. Gillan (2000); *The Lifted Brow* (2008); *World Literature Today;* and other publications. She has been awarded fellowships at Yaddo, MacDowell, Ledig House/Art Omi: Writers, Hawthornden Castle, Jentel Arts, and Hedgebrook. A former senior editor for the Penguin Group, she taught book editing at New York University for nearly two decades and received an award for teaching excellence there. *The English Problem* is her first novel.